Other books by Anne Britting Oleson

The Book of the Mandolin Player
Dovecote
Tapiser

COW PALACE

Cow Palace

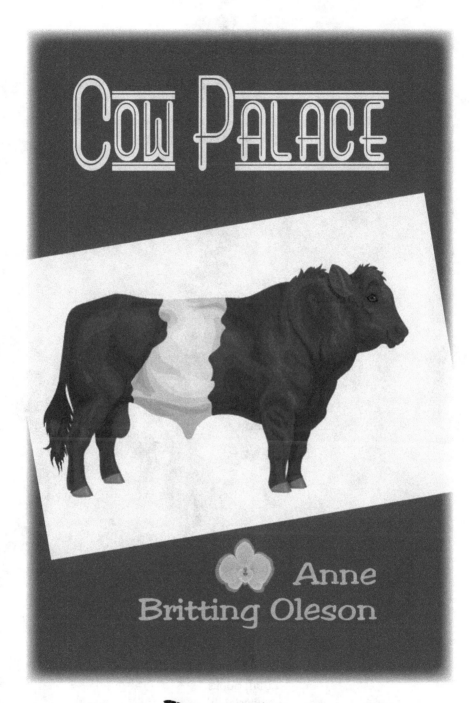

Anne
Britting Oleson

BInk *Bink Books*
Bedazzled Ink Publishing Company • Fairfield, California

978-1-949290-41-7 paperback

Cover Design
by

Bink Books
a division of
Bedazzled Ink Publishing, LLC
Fairfield, California
http://www.bedazzledink.com

For Stephen Benatar, the novelist,
who asked me once,
in James Smith & Sons on New Oxford Street in London,
whether I was a novelist;
And who asked me that same question again, twenty-two years later,
in front of a Japanese restaurant on Warwick Street.
Thank you for having faith.

PART I

Hors d'oeuvres

One

THE NOISES FROM below stairs did not at first sink into Dinah's consciousness, because she was on the telephone. Mirelle, as had become her custom of late, was giving a new spin to the concept of hysterical depression. Chain smoking, Dinah figured, probably lighting one cigarette from the lipsticked butt of another. She had been after Mirelle to quit, with sporadic success, for she didn't know how many years; but even now she could almost smell the smoke over the wire. Unless the smoke was from Mirelle's blazing fury.

"Calm down and tell me about it," Dinah suggested, throwing herself back on the sofa. "As if I had any other choice but to listen."

A crash resounded from the restaurant kitchen below, followed by a barely audible tinkling of broken glassware.

"Dinah!" Perry's panicked voice rushed up the stairs toward her.

In her other ear Mirelle sniffed, hurt. "If you don't have time for your oldest and best friend—"

"Just tell me," Dinah repeated. She pulled the elastic from her ponytail, and her hair cascaded down around her neck. "Just shut up and tell me, okay?"

"It's Wallace."

It was always Wallace. Since they had married, seven or eight years ago. Before Dinah and Ross had moved back to town. Mirelle's second marriage.

"Oh, Di, you don't know what he's done this time." Mirelle's voice shimmied up the register. "It's simply beyond words."

"Not for you, Holstein." Making a gun of her thumb and forefinger, Dinah wrapped the elastic around it, then shot it across the room with a twang. It landed on the piano, just beyond Ross's photograph.

High female cursing screeched up from the restaurant.

"Dinah!" Perry called again, frantic. "Dinah, where are you, for God's sake?"

"He brought her to the faculty picnic. Can you believe the absolute gall of the man?"

Dinah shook her head. "Brought who?"

"His . . . *woman*, damn it. His . . . his *floozy!*"

"He doesn't have to *bring* her, does he? I thought she was on the faculty."

Footsteps pounded up the flight of stairs.

"Jesus Christ!" A furious male voice shouted below. "The idiot's gone running to her again!"

"Jesus," the high female voice echoed.

Dinah closed her eyes tightly, trying to sort out the voices, the sounds. As though she had to. Grimacing, she stood. She'd have to go downstairs. Not for the first time did she wish Ross was here to run interference.

"Di, are you listening? What the hell's going on? I need a little sympathy here, okay?" Mirelle's voice had morphed into a squawk from the receiver. "Are you there?"

Perry burst into the room from the landing, his pale face flushed and blotchy, his fine yellow hair swinging over his eyes. "You've got to do something," he gasped, waving back over his shoulder. "They're going to kill each other this time."

"Let them do it and be damned," Dinah groaned. Still, she tossed Perry what she hoped was a reassuring look and turned her attention back to the phone. "Listen, Mirelle, I've got to go. You aren't the only one with marital difficulties around here. The Addams Family is at it again."

"Ooh." Immediately Mirelle's attention was diverted. "Can I come watch?"

"Suit yourself. I've got to go protect my investment." Dropping the receiver into the cradle, Dinah turned back to Perry. "Let's go, Uncle Festus."

"Uncle Festus is bald," he replied peevishly.

"Never mind." Dinah pushed past him and peered down the back steps. "What the hell are they doing down there this time?" She had to get rid of them, she knew; this time, she really had to do it.

She hated herself for not having the nerve to fire them sooner. She took a deep breath and pounded down the steps, attempting to sound masterful and in control. Out of cowardice. She wanted them to hear her coming, wanted them to clean up their act before she got there. Avoidance. They all could continue pretending nothing was happening, and she could put off the confrontation once again. The ploy had worked up to this point. The chef and the front-of-house manager would smile, and she would pretend that she believed the explanation of the ruckus.

"I don't know what it was," Perry panted after her. "I was prepping sauces, so I missed most of it. Something about her not pulling her weight, something about his drinking like a fish, and if he had any balls they'd have their own restaurant instead of always working for somebody else—"

Dinah cursed. Her own fault; she would be the first to admit it, should anyone ask. If only she hadn't been so desperate to keep the dream of the restaurant afloat after Ross's death. If only she hadn't been willing to overlook

Rob's pomposity in favor of his unquestionable cooking skills. *If only.* She took a deep breath, let the air fill up her lungs and head and bloodstream, then burst her way through the door at the foot of the stairs.

"Hey, Dinah," Rob greeted her, laughing a bit awkwardly. He was in his whites, though without his hat. On the counter before him lay the side of shark, which he should have, by her calculations, have carved into steaks by now.

"What's going on here?" she demanded, framing herself in the doorway, trying to make herself taller.

Perry skidded up behind her, his warm breath crawling on the back of her neck, and she reached up to wipe the moist sensation away.

"I heard a crash, and yelling."

"Oh—" Kelly giggled. She spun away from the sink, her fine yellow hair swinging. A large damp spot on the front of her green dress grew larger as she swabbed at it with a kitchen sponge. "Oh, that was just me. I spilled something." She smiled, but her expression was curiously lopsided: her lipstick was smeared, and the mascara trailed weakly away from her left eye.

"I heard pots and pans," Dina insisted grimly, glancing between the two, trying to catch them up, hoping she didn't. "A crash."

"I tripped," Rob supplied hurriedly. "On some pans."

"The pans," Dinah reminded him slowly, watching the color creep up toward his receding hairline, "are all hanging up." She let her eyes flicker pointedly to the cast iron frame suspended above the work counter; the copper bottomed cookware, suspended from it, swung gently, as if blown by a cool breeze.

"Hit his head," Kelly corrected quickly. "He doesn't know what he's saying. He hit his head, and he feels a bit groggy, don't you, Robert? We were wondering if he'd qualify for worker's comp for that. He tripped, and hit his head, and it scared me so I spilled—*something.*" She turned her innocent wide eyes to her husband for support. "Isn't that right?"

Rob flashed her a look, and she snapped her mouth shut. Behind Kelly, the kitchen curtain fluttered, and this time an obvious warm breeze swayed the pot rack, against its own creaking protests.

Dinah shook her head, but let herself be distracted. She took a step toward the window. "Feeling a little warm, are we? And not even serving time yet."

"No, really, Dinah," Kelly squeaked, blocking her path and laying a tiny white hand on her arm. "We were feeling the heat a little bit, and it'll only get worse later on—"

Setting Kelly aside was, even to Dinah, like swatting a fly. She pushed the curtain to one side to close the window, but the pane was broken, not open.

Jagged pieces of glass reached out menacingly from both the inside and outside windows. Kelly's torrent of protest stopped suddenly as though dammed.

"Oh, for crying out loud," Perry said. "Did you hit that with your head, too, Rob?"

"Perry, shut up." Dinah let the curtain fall, then turned, arms crossed. "Would anyone care to explain this to me? I'm all ears here."

Again Kelly flashed a desperate look toward her husband. He did not look up, concentrating on the whisper of his knife as he sharpened it. She opened her mouth, closed it, opened it again, like a fish. "I told you. I spilled something."

"I usually open the window first, myself." Turning away from them, Dinah looked out onto the rear lawn, where a still-freezer-wrapped Cornish game hen rested in the neatly trimmed grass. A five-inch sliver of glass stuck neatly out of its breast, glittering in the afternoon sun. "From the looks of this window and that hen, you must have spilled it from halfway across the kitchen."

"I swear, Dinah, I have no idea—" Kelly stood on her toes to peer through the broken window. "I just don't know—"

"Hello?"

They all froze at the call from the dining room.

"Is anyone here?"

The kitchen door swung open at the hands of a tall thin stranger looking uncomfortable in suit and tie. "Hello?"

Dinah felt rather than saw Perry shift slightly. "Why, hello." His voice was nearly a purr.

Rob rolled his eyes and smacked the knife down on the block.

Dinah cleared her throat, discomfort like catarrh. "Hi. Can I help you? We don't open until five." She stepped away from the window, trying not to be too obvious. When she smiled, it felt like a rictus.

"I'm looking for the owner?" He looked at each in turn. Perry's expression had fallen. "Mrs. Galloway?"

"I'm Dinah." She offered her hand. "And you are—"

The visitor blushed slightly under his tan. Yet when he shook her hand, his grip was confident. "Mark Burdette. From the *Gazette*?"

Perry's laugh was high, affected. "Oh, that rhymes."

Dinah wished she could tell him to shut up again. Instead she indicated the dining room door. "You'll have to pardon Perry. He's a line cook." The smile still hurt her face. "We were just having a conference about the menu. Quite frankly, I'd forgotten you were coming." *Damn Rob and Kelly. Damn Perry. Damn Mirelle.*

The swinging doors flapped closed behind them. In the dining room, the air was cooler. Without the lights on, the east-facing room was dim, the tables with their settings white ghosts. Dinah took a deep breath, feeling slightly less anxious away from the others.

"I hope it's not inconvenient. My editor was hoping to run the story of Galloway's on Sunday."

Dinah was not fooled. *Inconvenient my eye.* She would not be doing them a favor; it was the other way around—good publicity meant good business. *Save me, Ross,* she prayed.

"It's not a problem at all," she reassured him quickly. "Unless you wanted to order the Cornish game hen."

"Pardon?" Mark had the tall person's habit of leaning slightly forward when he spoke, to minimize his height; however, it made the conversation feel more intimate. At such close range, age fell away from him. Mid-twenties was Dinah's guess, now that she'd had a good look at the brown eyes, the sandy hair. About the right age for Perry, though the persuasion was difficult to guess on such short acquaintance.

"The game hen. We're unexpectedly out this evening." The joke had gone flat. Dinah waved a hand toward the club chairs before the fireplace. "Would you like to have a seat? Can I get you a drink?"

In the winter, the fireplace would be the focal point of the double dining room. This afternoon one of Gillian's floral arrangements filled the space behind the brass dogs. The club chairs were inviting, but Mark pulled a notebook from his jacket pocket and pointed to a table in one of the bow windows instead. "Could we sit there instead? More light."

Of course. He needed to take some notes, and it could only benefit her and the restaurant that they be legible. Mark held her chair for her before taking his own across the table. Outside the window, the late spring garden was bursting into pink and white bloom. Dinah glanced over her shoulder. She found herself wishing he had chosen a table beyond the great front bay windows, further from the kitchen door. No noise now from that quarter, for which she was grateful. One never knew what to expect with Rob and Kelly, Vesuvius and Aetna. Or with Perry, come to think of it.

"I'll wait for that drink until my editor arrives, thanks."

His voice, far too deep for his appearance, drew her back sharply.

"I'm sorry," she said, trying to clear the cobwebs. She shoved her hair away from her face, wishing for her elastic. "I'm sorry. I'm afraid you've taken me by surprise. You're far too young to be the restaurant writer for the paper."

Not what she meant to say. Feeling herself flush, Dinah tugged at the sleeves of her cotton sweater. She wished she had changed her clothes. She wished she had put on lipstick. *She wished she hadn't forgotten, damn it.*

To her discomfiture, he laughed, leaning back slightly to hook his elbow over the rungs of the chair back. "I'm not sure what to make of that. How old, exactly, is a restaurant writer supposed to be?"

Old enough to be allowed to have a knife at the table. Dinah grimaced. "At least twenty years older than you are. Portly. With gray hair. A goatee." She was flailing, her skin hot. "At least as old as I am."

"And why's that?"

"Good God. So I can flirt with him, of course. So that if the meal or the service is not to his liking, he'll at least remember the proprietor fondly."

Mark Burdette raised his eyebrows. They were fine, slightly darker than his curling hair, the same deep brown as his eyes. "You expect I'll be disappointed with Galloway's?"

His question gave Dinah pause, and she looked at him with new interest. "That certainly sounded like a restaurant writer's question."

"Ah. Still you doubt my qualifications."

"I'm wary of your sharp tongue. Do you wield a laser printer so sharp?"

"Sharper. I grind it on a whetstone every evening before I go out to eat."

"That must be boring for your date."

He shrugged. "The unlimited expense account makes up for it all, I'm sure."

"Your editor is your date? Of course you'd need one, the better to sample a variety of our kitchen's concoctions." An image of the speared game hen passed before her mind's eye, and she quickly bit her lip. *Not that concoction.*

"You assume correctly. My date will be joining me around five. This interview was what I expected would bore her."

Wow. Zing. Dinah felt her eyes widen. "Thank you very much, I'm sure."

He winked.

Mark glanced around the dining room. Dinah took a deep breath, content to let him look: she was pleased with the appearance of both public rooms. The hardwood floors gleamed darkly; the marbled fireplace, with its dragon fan behind the flowers, and the lapis lazuli inlay, contrasted against the Oriental-patterned wallpaper. From the high tin ceilings, the crystal pendants of the chandeliers would drip prisms of color over the white tablecloths when the lights were turned on.

"It's very nice," he murmured. "Elegant, and soothing. It will be interesting to see in action."

"People have seemed to like it," Dinah agreed, cupping her hands under her chin, allowing her eyes to roam over the features of this dining room, all chosen by herself—Ross had given her free reign with the decor. Try as she might, she simply could not see it with the eyes of a stranger. "We've already established some strong relationships with return customers in the time we've been open."

She felt a rush of air.

"Di?"

A squeal from the wide porch. Dinah squeezed her eyes shut. *Hang up on the devil and she will appear.* And in her usual manner. Mirelle thrust both of the double doors open before her. Mark spun in his chair. It was an entrance: Mirelle stood framed in the light, which added an unnecessary fire to her brilliant red hair. She flashed her even white teeth in a smile as she sailed into the dining room. The surprise she showed at finding the two *tete-a-tete* was obviously feigned. How long had she been outside?

"Why, Dinah," she exclaimed, shaking her hair back, a long-fingered hand to her white throat. "I didn't know you had company." She fluttered her long eyelashes: they were natural, she claimed.

"Why, Mirelle," Dinah returned. "I didn't know you had bad eyesight."

Mark had clambered to his feet. One had to grant him his impeccable manners.

"I'd like you to meet Mark Burdette. He's the food writer from the *Gazette*. Mr. Burdette—"

"Mark," he interrupted, holding out a hand.

"—this is Mirelle Holstein." It might have been a slip. It might not have been.

Mirelle's azure eyes flashed. "Holbein Mirelle Holbein. Like the artist." She took the hand Mark proffered and clasped it between her own. "It's so nice to meet you. I've enjoyed your reviews in the paper The write-up you did on Christie's a while back was *so* good. So accurate! I couldn't have agreed with you more."

"Thank you. I'm glad you found it interesting."

To his credit, Dinah observed, Mark did not quite seem to be taking Mirelle at face value; there was a slight glint in his eyes as he leaned toward her.

"I expect you'll be able to write up some glowing things about the Cow Palace here," Mirelle continued breathlessly. She had not let go of his hand.

Petty revenge. Dinah curled her fists tightly at her sides, resisting the impulse to strangle Mirelle.

"Cow Palace?" Mark laughed. Puzzled. "I'm sorry. I don't think—"

Mirelle's trilling laugh swooped up toward the high tin ceiling. "Oh, that's just our inside joke. Here at Dinah's." She made it sound as though the restaurant were a grimy diner on the wrong side of the tracks. "Galloway, you see. Her last name. It's a breed of cow, you know. The belted Galloway? They have black heads and black butts, and their middles are white. Oreo cookie cows."

"Ah." Mark's smile was slightly less enthusiastic. "Of course."

"Mirelle, dearheart," Dinah broke in, coming to her feet. "Mr. Burdette and I have some business to discuss that I'm sure couldn't interest you in the least bit."

Mirelle tossed back her hair and batted her eyelashes. "Don't be silly. I'm very interested." She took a tiny dance step closer to lay a hand on Mark's sleeve; her long nails were painted fire engine red.

Dinah sighed. She should have figured that Mirelle would turn up, considering her near-hysteria on the phone earlier. She should have figured. As much as she loved Mirelle, she had known her for years—since childhood—and knew just how solipsistic she could be; one *didn't* cut her off in mid-hysteria. She cleared her throat. "No, you're not interested at all. I think you should wait upstairs, and I'll join you as soon as I can."

The standoff was familiar, but Mirelle's glare fell first, as it always did. With a sniff, she dropped Mark's arm and walked toward the door at the foot of the stairs. She turned and managed a reasonably winning smile.

"Perhaps another time, then," she cooed before the door swung shut again behind her.

Dinah slid back down into her chair, rubbing her brow lightly. All composure gone.

"Is she—?"

"No," Dinah whispered, holding up a hand. "Wait." She held his eyes, trying to compel him, until Mirelle apparently decided to head upstairs. When the footsteps receded, she let out a long breath.

"She eavesdrops?" Mark let out a laugh. He looked windblown—the usual effect Mirelle elicited from strangers. Especially men.

"You *were* going to say something about her, after all."

"Who *is* she?" His glance roved to the ceiling. They could hear her movements on the floor above. "And more to the point, *what* is she? Is she for real? She looks as though she belongs next door, in your theater."

Dinah shrugged. "Yes and no. She's my friend. She's a music teacher at the private school in Elmwood. And she's terrifically melodramatic, though no, she's not been cast in a role at our theater." She sighed. "You know, it's a pity you couldn't have put off your visit for a few more weeks, when the summer season opens—you could have taken in a show, too."

"Did I imagine that, or was she coming on to me right then?"

Was he blushing? He suddenly seemed, again, very young. Too young to be doing this job. Dinah sighed louder. "And here I thought we were going to talk about the restaurant. I should have known better just as soon as Mirelle sailed through that door. Next to her, I'm mud."

"Well, *was* she?"

"Again, yes, and no. She was just trying you out, for your reaction. She does that to everyone. I doubt she even thinks about it anymore."

"Everyone?"

"Correction: every male." She smiled at him, wondering whether that constituted an ego blow. "She means no harm. She's really a lot of fun, though she can try your patience sometimes." *Like this time.* "But what about the restaurant? What do you need to know?"

Slowly he came back to earth, the smile still pulling at the corners of his mouth. He shuffled through his notebook. "Let me check my notes." He let out a half-laugh, a relieved sound. "We've certainly gotten off to an auspicious start."

"You could call it that." Dinah dropped her gaze, fingering the fern playing second fiddle to the full-blown peony in the bud vase on the table between them.

"What I'd really like to do right now, as I told you when we spoke over the phone Tuesday, is to get some background. The usual stuff—how long you've been open, what drew you to the area, your background as a restaurateur." He took a pen from his breast pocket, made some quick marks on a blank page in the notebook.

Dinah held up a hand. "I have to tell you that I have no idea what the usual stuff entails, because I've never been written up before. This is my first, and hopefully my only, foray into the restaurant field. Galloway's was my husband's dream. My late husband's. He's been gone for nearly a year now." She lifted her shoulders, then let them fall. The pang was familiar, but no less painful. "I hope that doesn't disqualify me in your eyes."

"Gotta start somewhere," he answered noncommittally, his gaze speculative, and sympathetic. "I wrote my first review once."

Probably when he was eight. "Comforting thought," Dinah returned tartly. "My chef, Robert Carvey, on the other hand—that would have been Rob in the kitchen with his wife Kelly, along with Perry and Lindsay, two of our other cooks—he's been in the business for years. He went to school in Providence, and did a turn in Paris and New York before Ross hired him on. We meant to open last year, but Ross's death delayed that." She blinked at the sudden tears. "When I first opened, I would have been lost without him. He finished organizing the kitchen, and we worked on the menus together."

"A real partnership?"

For some reason the word conjured up the image of the brutally skewered game hen, lying in state in the clipped grass. She shivered. "*Not* exactly. But he's been a great help." She wondered if Kelly considered him a real partner. Or vice versa.

"And you've been open here for some time now?"

He probably knew exactly how long they'd been open.

"Five months. It was slow at first, of course, but we've been serving full houses for quite some time now." Dinah tried to sound confident, but somehow the words seemed defensive. She took a deep breath, attempted to relax, to answer Mark's questions honestly and thoroughly. *He really does know what he's doing,* she surprised herself by thinking, watching his pen trail across page after page of the notebook. His handwriting was small, and he'd covered several pages before the grandfather clock in the foyer bonged the half hour. She'd lost track of time.

"Good God. Is that three-thirty?"

Mark slipped back his French cuff to look at his watch. The band, of black leather, was cracked and worn. "That's right."

An hour and a half until opening. Gill and Dirk would be in soon. And Dinah not even dressed. She started back from the table so quickly her chair fell over with a crash. Mark stood, too, and stretched out a long arm to retrieve the chair.

"Go on ahead," he suggested, his eyes flickering to the ceiling, the upstairs, Mirelle. There was no sound from up there; Mirelle was probably reposing to greatest advantage on the chaise, just in case someone should come along to gaze upon her perfection. "I'll just write up my notes, then wander about the gardens, if that's all right." He glanced at the big face of his watch again. "My dinner guest ought to be along eventually."

"Thank you." Dinah's smile felt constrained. Hesitant. It was so difficult to be sure about people like this: reporters who might invite or repel customers. "Please. Make yourself comfortable. Are you sure I can't get you a drink of something while you wait?" She felt herself flush immediately. Buying a good review, a positive article? *Stupid move.*

Mark's smile in return seemed ironic, as though he sensed her discomfort. "Water?"

That was an easy one. Harmless. Dinah slipped behind the bar and pulled a pint glass, filled it with ice and ran it under the tap. She left it before him on the tablecloth, then inched her way through the kitchen door. Only then did she dash out to the rear lawn to retrieve the impaled Cornish game hen.

Two

MIRELLE HAD HELPED herself to a stiff drink—vodka tonic, Dinah guessed, noting the little bit of lime swimming among the ice cubes—and was indeed draped over the chaise. In her other hand she held the photograph, in its silver frame, which usually reposed on the piano. With one finger she was twanging the elastic she'd wrapped around the frame's corner.

"It's about time," she said, sipping at her drink. "Ross and I were just having a bit of a natter. We'd about decided you'd seduced young Mr. Burdette, you were taking so long downstairs."

Dinah glared, snatching the picture frame from Mirelle's long fingers. "It's all about sex with you, isn't it?" She wiped at the glass with the hem of her sweater as though disinfecting it. "Besides. Ross knows I'm not that kind of girl."

Mirelle snorted in a particularly unattractive way.

Dinah ignored her, kicking off her sandals before crossing the sun-dappled rug to the piano. The lid was down; someone had written *dust me* across the mahogany. The place where the photograph belonged was clearly marked, an oasis in a sea of dust. Carefully Dinah replaced the frame in its accustomed position.

Struck anew by the momentary flash of grief, she did not immediately release the photograph. Rather, she stood looking down into the wide grin of her late husband. She smiled back at him, unable to help herself, as she had never been able to help herself. With a finger, she touched the dimple in his chin, traced the unruly fall of gray hair across his forehead.

"You're looking sad again," Mirelle said. There was the slightest of creaks from the chaise.

Dinah sighed. "Did Ross have anything more to say to you about me, then?"

Mirelle was the only person she knew who could hold conversations with photographs of people who had been dead for nearly a year. Quickly Dinah blinked and turned away from those all-knowing gray eyes.

There was a clink of glass on glass, and Mirelle was suddenly at her side, pressing a drink into her hand. Without looking, Dinah took a gulp. Single malt.

She swallowed, gasped, and wiped her mouth with the back of her hand. "God. That's like drinking a wood stove straight up."

"You looked like you needed a good shock."

"Thanks. That sure was one." Dinah looked around for a coaster.

Mirelle circled the room like an exotic bird looking for a place to light. Her silky caftan, in whorls of green and blue, swirled about her as she flitted from window to sofa to bookshelf.

"All of Ross's conversation is about you. We all know that."

Dinah took the sadness in her voice for sympathy and was grateful. Mirelle wafted beyond the breakfast bar which separated the kitchenette from the rest of the front room and deposited her now empty glass in the sink. Abruptly she laughed, a glittering fake sound which grated slightly.

"He says you're undersexed."

Dinah closed her eyes. "He doesn't."

She thought about another smaller sip from her own glass, one less likely to combust her innards, but that first was enough for the time being. She felt a sudden surge of resentment that Mirelle even should imagine such a thing from Ross. What had been between her and her husband was just that: between her and her husband.

"He doesn't."

"Oh, come on," Mirelle scoffed, leaning on the bar, tossing her fiery head. "Almost a year, Dinah. Without stud service. If that's not undersexed, what is?"

"Stud service?" Dinah choked. Wracked by the onset of a coughing fit, she went to the sink for a glass of water. Her eyes watered. "Stud service? You make me sound like some sort of a broodmare." She drank. The water did not help.

Mirelle waved this off. "Semantics. You know what I mean."

"I'd rather pretend I didn't, thanks." Dinah wiped her eyes with her sleeve. "I'd rather retain my innocence. And take a shower."

"Innocence my eye," Mirelle retorted. "After circling around that beautiful man down there, you'd better make it a cold shower and you know it."

"Jesus, Mirelle." With a sudden peevish tip of her hand, Dinah dumped the rest of her water down the drain. "As someone I knew long ago always said, 'Your low class is showing.'"

She heard a car door slam and looked down through the side window into the yard below. It was not followed, as she half-expected it might be, by the squealing of tires as Kelly made a fast getaway. Thank God for that, anyway. In fact, the Carveys' elderly BMW still reposed in the far corner of the lot. Rather, Dinah saw the sleek chignon of Gillian, the head waitress, disappear beneath the porch overhang below.

"Ross said that?"

Dinah's smile was wry. "Ross's first wife said that."

THERE WAS STILL residual guilt there, after all these years. Which was why she usually shoved the thought of Ross's first wife back into the dark closet when it appeared.

Her name was Sherry, and she was the mother of Ross's daughter, who had long ago decamped to Arizona. Sherry had reacted very badly, if her cool, cultured sarcasm could have been construed as *bad,* to what she perceived as Dinah's encroachment into their lives.

"You could have at least had the grace to wait until the divorce papers were signed," Sherry had said at their first meeting.

Dinah, even now, could remember every detail of that auspicious occasion. She could picture her twenty-two-year-old self: her worn jeans and tee shirt, her wind-ruffled hair, her bare feet, and her hands dirty from working in the garden. All this in stark contrast to Sherry Galloway's cream linen suit with its razor-sharp creases, and her razor-cut hair, black as a raven's wing. Sherry carried herself with a demeanor Dinah could never have hoped to emulate, and which now, some twenty years later, still escaped her. That afternoon, Ross's first wife might have wandered out of the pages of *Vogue,* while Dinah had escaped from *Mother Jones.*

They had stood awkwardly in the front door of the duplex apartment Dinah had rented then, her first year out of college. *Do you invite the wife of your lover into your home?* The etiquette of such a situation was beyond her. Dinah had shifted uncertainly, one hand on the door, as Sherry's eyes traveled over the scant furnishing, the uncurtained windows.

"I just came by to have a look at you," Sherry said then, coldly. Her black glance raked over Dinah like talons. "I'd always wondered what the other woman looked like. I'd never imagined I'd really be in a position to find out firsthand."

Useless to protest that she had not been the cause of the marital breakup. Dinah had remained silent, flushing hotly, allowing the language of resentment to wash over her like a storm tide. Useless to say that Ross and Sherry had been separated for eleven months, that he was only waiting for the judge's gavel to pound that marriage into oblivion. All Dinah was able to think of, looking into Sherry Galloway's icy gaze, was the moment when she had first touched Ross's hand reaching for the same pair of secateurs on the rack at the greenhouse shop. That touch had had the power then to make her shiver. The memory of it had the power *still* to make her shiver.

Useless to tell Sherry Galloway that she had not truly been the other woman. But had she met Ross when he had still been living under the same roof with his wife, would it have made any difference in her feelings? Would it have made a difference in whether she would have acted upon them?

From the first touch, the merest brushing of hands and the laughing apologies which followed, Ross had rushed Dinah as though his life were one long football play. And she had fallen for it. Hard. Hard enough not to have cared for a moment about the difference in their ages. Because always there had been between them that incredible insatiable hunger. Something, over the nearly seventeen years of their own marriage which had never lessened.

Until the spring day, pruning the apple trees. They'd just moved back to town from Northampton, sinking their savings into the restoration of this house, in which they'd planned to open a restaurant. Out in the orchard, beneath the new blue sky, his heart had given out.

Undersexed? Dinah slammed back into the present, into the bathroom of the upstairs apartment she had thought to share with her husband for much longer than she had. She shook her head under the fall of water from the shower she'd leapt into to avoid Mirelle. *Oh, no my friend. I'm fine.* She was fine. She didn't need any more sex, in this short time into this widowhood. Or perhaps it was that she didn't need any *other* sex. For even now she still felt that keen longing for the touch of Ross's hand, that same hand which had grown cold in her own, on that interminable ambulance ride to the hospital.

"SO, IS HE married?" Mirelle demanded. "He's rather good looking, in a beanpole sort of way. An attractive face, and the voice is really quite sexy." She examined her nails. "And he can write."

"I should hope so, or he'd need to get another job." Her shower done, Dinah picked through her wardrobe, trying to find something that would—she had to admit it—influence the review. Something elegant, perhaps understated, but something that would not merely cause her to blend into the woodwork. Something, at the same time, that would not jar with the setting, either. Something Ross would approve of.

"That's not the important part, though." When Mirelle grew impatient, her voice became strident. "*Is* Mark Burdette married?"

"Why the hell do you care?" Dinah responded over her shoulder, replacing a green dress on the closet rail. "*You're* married."

"Yes and no," Mirelle replied pettishly. "*I* am, but my *husband* apparently isn't."

There was a rustle as she slid from the bed, where she had thrown herself in seeming abandon. She slipped behind Dinah and peered over her shoulder into the closet. "Do tell me what it is you're looking for. I can be your fashion consultant."

Dinah turned. She had to tilt her chin—this close, the difference in their heights was obvious, and she felt Mirelle towering over her.

"I am looking," she said slowly, "for something that says the same thing as the restaurant."

"So he's not married."

"Screw you, too. We've already been through this, Holstein. I don't want his body. I want his good word in the *Gazette*."

Mirelle lifted an artfully shaped eyebrows. "If you get the one, dearheart, you'll probably get the other." She struck a suggestive pose, hand on hip, full breasts thrust forward, and batted those eyelashes.

"Holstein, you are so lascivious." Dinah drew forth a black dress of clingy velvet, with a shaped bodice, sleeveless. Paired with black pumps and gold jewelry, it would be both simple and elegant.

"I'm not kidding. You remember when the Albion in Elmwood got its new artistic director three years ago? And you remember how we hated all the plays that season, but Jackie Lehrer absolutely slobbered over them in the Sunday *Gazette*?"

The dress whispered softly down over her camisole. "But, Mirelle," Dinah protested, her voice muffled. "He was gay. You also remember how he got caught in *flagrante delicto* on the set of *Noises Off* after a show one night."

"Yes, darling, but when seducing Jackie Lehrer, it was simply a matter of putting his art before everything else. You had to notice that after that first rumor seeped out, her reviews really started blasting his shows."

"Mirelle, your husband is getting to you." Dinah selected a pair of chunky gold earrings. "Not only do you think he's screwing everything that moves, but you're beginning to see that tendency in everyone else."

"Just check if he's married, why don't you? I didn't see a ring, but that doesn't necessarily mean anything."

"He's invited a date. Now, if I don't get down there to make sure all the waitresses that are supposed to be here *are* here, I'll probably live to regret it. After the Big Bang Theory was proven this afternoon in the kitchen, I don't think Kelly will remember to do foolish things like her *job*." Dinah held out a chunky gold chain, the match of the earrings, then turned to the mirror, and lifted her hair away from her neck as Mirelle hooked the clasp.

"Mind if I stick around?" Mirelle's voice was still playful, but suddenly the expression behind her eyes was bleak, lonely. "There's nothing much going on at my house tonight, I'm afraid." She turned away quickly, but not before Dinah saw the color creeping up into her cheeks. Her shoulders were slumped, and her flitting movements seemed now a listless inability to settle. The life had gone out of her, like air out of a balloon.

Sometimes it was easy to forget just how human Mirelle really was, beneath the melodramatic show. It wasn't that the familiarity bred contempt, but blindness. How long had they known one another? Since elementary school, and even then Mirelle had been turning heads. Dinah sighed and patted her arm on the way by. Maybe the big personality was only a disguise sometimes.

Her hand on the knob, Dinah turned. "Make yourself comfortable. Fix yourself another drink. Come down later for dinner, if you want."

Mirelle nodded.

Three

BUSINESS WAS BRISK for a weekday night. The main dining room, nearly filled, hummed with the quiet contented sound of conversation, punctuated by the clink of silver against plates; a few parties lingered over their meals in the west room. The shark steak special was proving to be more popular than Dinah had hoped; by her quick calculations, watching the platters fly out of the kitchen from her post at the bar, they'd be out of mako by eight.

Holding down the bar while Dirk changed out a keg, Dinah swabbed down the blonde wood, then set about replenishing the orange slices in the tray. As she worked, she kept a wary eye on Kelly, who had dabbed the wayward mascara from her eyes, and who had smiled at every new party in that high brittle way they all loved and Dinah abhorred. Ah, well. It worked, didn't it? She had to admit, albeit grudgingly, that Kelly had not yet hurled a Cornish game hen at a guest, and wasn't that what counted, after all?

From her position in the west room, she was able to keep a cautious eye on Mark Burdette's table as well. He and his editor were seated in the alcove created by one of the front bow windows; having arrived around ten past five, that woman was far from the svelte pseudo-socialite Dinah had expected. Turning her attention to the maraschino cherries, Dinah watched the couple surreptitiously. The woman was easily in her early fifties, with graying hair and slight rolls of extra flesh her loose dress did not disguise. Dinah had witnessed their greeting when the woman had first entered the dining room, saw the two laugh as Mark leaned in to kiss her cheek. His editor, he had said? But the bar orders were moving quickly, and she had little time to wonder.

Several other visitors she knew—or at least recognized—and she lifted a hand to them. A few of the teachers she had met through Mirelle shared the wraparound booth in the corner; they appeared inclined to continue the festive atmosphere of the faculty picnic as long as possible, sharing several appetizers between them over drinks. Every so often a raucous burst of laughter erupted from the general area. More than once Dinah considered calling upstairs, to see if Mirelle wanted to join them, but then was distracted by drink orders. It would be good for Mirelle to come down and join in the fun in the corner; it would be something to get the poor woman's mind off of Wally and his *contretemps* with the gym teacher. The unguarded moment, when Mirelle had seemed so lost, so unlike her usual self, haunted her.

Poor Mirelle.

In spite of herself, Dinah caught her wry expression in the mirrored back bar. Mirelle wouldn't be poor for long, if she truly was poor at all to begin with. One had to admire that drama, that fire. Enough to make a person wonder about the sanity of such a man as Wallace Holbein, taking his wife for granted, and more, shoving her aside for—what? Dinah wasn't certain, having never yet come across this gym teacher, but surely she couldn't measure up to Mirelle in the excitement department. No one could.

"Ta, Dinah." Sailing past on the way through to the kitchen, Gillian dropped off a wine order. Mark Burdette's table. Dinah pulled the bottle from the rack beneath the bar. Impressive. By the bottle, no less. A nice chardonnay. Those unlimited expense accounts he had mentioned earlier must really be something. She set the bottle, the corkscrew, and two glasses on the cork-bottomed tray.

Unless that wasn't really his editor.

God, Mirelle was a bad influence.

She had attempted to listen for their order—curious—as Gillian had pointed first to Mark's menu, then to his companion's. The Herculean feat had been beyond her, the bar too far from the bay window alcove, the buzz of surrounding conversation just a smidgen too loud. Still, Gillian was the best waitress in the house, with just enough glint in her eye and British clip to her voice to win over any customer. Dinah sighed, trying to relax. There would be no problem with the service, at least. If only—she uttered a little prayer and knocked her knuckles on the bar to cover the bases—if only she could be sure that Kelly wouldn't choose this evening to slip a foreign substance into the food writer's meal, just to spite Rob. A wily and unpredictable pair, those two. Dinah prayed harder.

"What'd they order?" she pressed Gillian, as she collected the wine and glasses.

Gill cocked her head slightly, balancing the tray on her left hand. "They're having a go at the Queen Victoria soup and the oysters for starters—"

"And the main course?"

Gillian laughed at Dinah's urgency. "Stop fussing. Everything's fine over there."

"I can't help it. What did they order for dinner?"

"Hold on, and I'll tell you. He wants to try the duck in strawberry sauce, and she's interested in the sole gratinée. No afters yet." She quirked a fine eyebrow. "He did say something odd about a Cornish game hen, though. I didn't think we had any on tonight, but when I told him I'd check, he just laughed and said not to bother." With a shrug, she whirled away.

Dinah felt her face grow hot, and was grateful for the relative dimness of the bar. She ducked down again as Gillian swished off with the wine. Nothing needed restocking below the bar just yet, though it looked as though bottled beer was going to be more popular than the brews on tap this evening. The low buzz in the restaurant was growing more intense as the evening light, patterning the floor, lengthened and began to fade. She had to keep her mind on her business. She straightened, turned to the back bar to check the optics, a fresh bottle of bourbon in hand.

Mark Burdette was watching her in the mirror.

When she caught the glance, he lifted his eyebrows and his wineglass in a salute.

Dinah dropped the bottle of Johnny Walker, which smashed into a million sparkling pieces at her feet.

DIRK REAPPEARED WHILE she was mopping up the last of the glass and the whisky. The floor was going to be sticky for the rest of the night, until they had a chance to give it a thorough wash.

"Nice work, Grace," he said, patting her head on the way by.

She hurled the bar rag at him. Missed.

Gillian brought another bottle of Johnnie Walker from the stores, which she passed to Dirk with a grin. "Our Dinah's worried about the restaurant fellow—over there at the window table. You can just see him through the door. Suddenly she's all thumbs."

Dumping the last dustpan full of shards into the trash can, Dinah straightened. "I suppose," she murmured warily, "I should go on over and ask them how things are. Do the owner thing."

Gill waved the suggestion away. "Don't be in such a hurry. Let them eat something first. Or at the very least, let them get rather nicely-thank-you."

"You're as bad as Mirelle." Dinah jabbed a finger. "*She* wanted me to seduce him for the article. Now you want me to get him drunk."

"Ta for that." Gill collected a round of martinis for one of her tables and balanced them on her tray. "It's ever so much easier to do the one if you've done the other first."

The broom and dustpan belonged on a hook behind the kitchen door. Hurriedly Dinah flitted to the back passage, but when she slipped through the swinging door, she found Rob wielding his knife with such hostility that she drew back, surprised. Kelly was nowhere to be seen, thank God, which meant she must be out on the dining room floor. There seemed to be a lull in the orders.

"What is that?" She hung up the broom, then peered more closely. "Rob, is that an onion? Where's the sous chef?"

Rob glared, swishing the knife through layers of vegetables. "Too busy to do his job, I suppose." His teeth were clenched.

There was a clank and a roar as the dishwasher went into action at the rear of the kitchen.

"Not true," Perry retorted, emerging from the walk-in with a brick of butter in each hand. "He never asked. Never said he needed more sliced onion."

"You should have known," Rob muttered and added something under his breath which Dinah thought best to ignore. The kitchen was hot, the tempers high, the atmosphere ugly.

"Get it together, all right?" she said. "Remember: the newspaper guy's here."

"Oh, for Chrissake," Rob snarled. He turned back to the cooktop where various pans sizzled and steamed. Lindsay glanced up from the grill, and then quickly back again. "I know what I'm doing. And it's only one newspaper guy. He probably doesn't know his ass from a teakettle."

"Just save it, the bunch of you. That's all I'm asking."

Pushing her way back out into the main dining room, it occurred to Dinah, not for the first time, just how much she had come to dislike Rob over the last several months. Still, Ross had hired him; Ross thought Rob knew what he was doing. She, quite frankly, was only just getting her feet under the table. She sighed. And Kelly—add her to the list, she thought, as the hostess smiled her greasiest smile at some newcomers, checked her list, and led the two into the west room.

Dinah skidded to a halt. She clutched at the back of a chair.

Holy Mary, Mother of God.

The woman was unfamiliar: Dinah had never seen the long-term substitute phys-ed teacher before, and Mirelle's descriptions were far too biased to be taken as accurate. But Wallace Holbein, slightly portly, with his receding hairline, was recognizable anywhere. She felt the revulsion rising from her gullet. That he would bring that woman here, to her restaurant, knowing of her friendship with Mirelle. She looked around quickly, panicked. Mirelle, upstairs, watching the news, or *Wheel of Fortune*, oblivious. Mirelle. If she came down, if she saw them, the world would end.

Mirelle would tear the place apart.

Dinah followed them into the dining room. Her hands were clenched. She bit down hard on her lip as she willed Kelly to seat them at each empty table they passed. The fates were against her tonight, and she cursed them. Kelly showed the pair through to the far end of the main dining room, to a table just two over from Mark Burdette and his companion.

Could she lock Mirelle upstairs?

Could she throw Wallace out, without attracting Mark's attention?

Wallace hadn't seen her. She slipped back into the shadow of the bar, busying herself with the clipboard, watching in the mirror. Wallace Holbein waved to the teachers at the corner table, but made no move to join them. The woman had already seated herself—maybe you didn't have to hold chairs for mistresses, Dinah mused—and was perusing the menu Kelly had handed her. She hoped, meanly, that they wanted Cornish game hen.

Mistress.

An odd word. Dinah shuddered, pressed her eyes closed for a moment, rubbed the crease between her brows. She supposed, when she thought about it—and she usually chose not to think about it—that for a while there, she had been one of those. She had been a mistress. Ross's mistress, in those first few months of their relationship, in those last two months of his marriage to Sherry. An uncomfortable thought. But at least Ross had no longer been living with Sherry, while sleeping with Dinah. Right? *Right?* Dinah stared long and hard in the mirror, at the reflection of the woman with Wallace, over the sheaf of papers on the clipboard she held as camouflage.

She wondered if Sherry—or Sherry's friends—had felt the same outrage with Ross and her, as she felt now, looking at the couple across the dining room. Maybe they did. Right now she wanted to leap across the bar and wring their necks. Had Sherry's friends wished to do the same to her? She rubbed her own neck.

Her situation had been entirely different.

Of course it had.

And as far as she knew, in all her meetings with Ross, way back then, Sherry had not once been right upstairs.

SHE THREW THE clipboard down on the bar and dropped her head into her hands.

The stool beyond her emptied, and Dirk appeared to collect the empty pilsner glass left behind.

"What d'ya need, gorgeous?" he asked.

"A lobotomy," she ground, skewing her glance toward the two hot tables and away again. Then back. It was no use. She couldn't keep her eyes away from them. Dirk lifted a knife from beneath the bar and brandished it with a quirk of his fair eyebrows, an offer; but she shook her head. "Thanks, but I prefer scissors. Maybe you could practice on those two at the far table."

Wallace was now examining the menu; the two did not appear to speak to one another. Perhaps the attraction wasn't conversational.

"That's the principal, isn't it?" Dirk asked. He replaced the knife, at the same time clinking the beer glass into the bus pan. He brought out a cloth and quickly wiped off the ring the pilsner had left on the bar. "Your friend Mirelle's husband. Who's that he's got with him?" He tossed the cloth into the sink, then drew a half pint of Guinness, which he placed at Dinah's elbow.

Why did everyone assume she needed to drink?

She stepped aside from the computer to let Gillian tot up a check. Slipping around to the vacant barstool, she wiped her face with her hands, which felt cold. "Dirk, what the hell am I supposed to do? How could he bring her here?"

"That's the other woman, then, is it?" Dirk inspected his garnish tray.

"You know?"

From the basket under the bar he produced a lemon and went for his knife again. "Everybody knows. It's a small town."

"They must. If they didn't know before, they do now, especially if he's taking her out to dinner in highly public restaurants. Poor Mirelle." She rubbed her eyes, then looked to the mirror again, to watch Wallace. "I mean, look at him. He doesn't even care where his wife is right now."

"And where precisely *is* his wife right now?" Dirk asked, slicing the lemon into precisely equal crescents.

He must know; her car would have been around back. How had Wallace not seen it? Unless, of course, he had, and simply didn't care.

"Oh, just upstairs. Having her nightly rendezvous with the *Newshour*. And of course, I invited her to come on down and dig in when she starts feeling hungry."

"Smooth move."

Suddenly, as though realizing he was under surveillance, Wallace looked up from his menu to catch her eye in the mirror. His smile was slow and lazy in the intimate lighting, his even capped teeth gleaming like those of a shark.

How *dare* he?

She straightened her shoulders, turning toward his table, stepping down from the barstool. She knocked the half-pint, and Guinness sloshed onto the bar.

"Dinah, don't," Dirk said quickly, throwing out a hand.

She ignored him.

Wallace had the grace to stand as she approached. His smile mocked her.

"Dinah," he said genially. "How are you? Have you met Alix? This is Alix Mailloux. She's taking the gym classes for us for the rest of the year. She's come out with me to talk school business." If anything, his smile grew wider. "Alix, this is Dinah Galloway. She owns the restaurant."

He was talking too damned much.

Alix's smile was less certain than Wallace's. Her pink-lipsticked mouth seemed pinched.

"I feel as though we've met," Dinah replied, her voice full of sharp edges.

She turned herself slightly, back to the table seating Mark and his companion. She was aware of the group in the corner having gone quiet, the bunch of teachers eyeing the situation expectantly.

"My friend Mirelle—Wally's wife?—she's told me so much about you already." She turned her gaze back to Wallace. "Oh, please. Don't stand on my account. I wouldn't want you to be uncomfortable. You've probably had an—exhausting—day." Oh, but she wanted him—them—uncomfortable: walking on proverbial coals, or more appropriately, lying on the proverbial bed of nails. Her smile was hard, her eyes narrowed. Wallace fell back into his chair as though pushed.

Even in the intimate lighting—the daylight outside was failing—she could see that Alix Mailloux's cheeks had flushed; her face, lit from below by the candle on the table, looked uneven, blotchy. Her entire body was plump, hardly what Dinah would have expected from a physical education teacher. Surely running about with students would have this woman exercised to a fierce leanness? *Wally must not be giving her enough of a workout.* Dinah's smile turned vicious. In about ten years, all that cuddly plumpness would be aging to fat; already there was a hint of a second chin, left undisguised by the cling of her blonde pageboy to her jawline. Again Dinah felt the wave of revulsion and resentment.

"You know my friend Mirelle, don't you?" she nearly cooed, looking into Alix's deep-set hazel eyes. "But of course you do. You work in neighboring school districts. And besides, she's hard to miss, isn't she? So dramatic."

"Dinah—" Was Wallace reaching across the table for Alix's hand? If he was, she quickly shook him off.

Dinah grinned.

"Yes," Alix said quietly, dropping her eyes. "I know Mirelle."

"And she knows you. She was so excited about seeing you at the faculty picnic. She told me all about it." Now Dinah frowned. "Come to think of it, I wonder where Mirelle is tonight, while you two are parading your—relationship—through my restaurant."

The pause stretched.

"Dinah, I think that's enough." Wallace was scowling, but, still seated, he was at a disadvantage.

"Not hardly," Dinah replied dryly. "And do me the favor of not speaking to me as though I were one of your adolescent charges. As you've already pointed out, I own the place, and I'll decide when it's enough." A quick glance over her shoulder told her the restaurant writer and his date were deep into their meal and their conversation. She leaned forward, to speak into Wallace's ear. She kept her voice low. "I came over here to tell you just how repulsed I am by your behavior. You, Wally. You can't be serious, thinking you'd come here and humiliate my friend and make me a party to it."

"Dinah." Wallace awkwardly pulled himself away from the table to regain his feet. Alix, across from him, looked as though she might burst into tears; her round face had paled, her expression crumpled. Wallace put out a hand, which Dinah dodged. "Control yourself. Or I'm afraid we'll have to leave."

Pompous ass. As though that would hurt anyone's feelings.

"Suit yourself," Dinah said coolly. "After all, I reserve the right to refuse service to anyone in my restaurant, and I refuse to serve you."

"But I don't."

Mirelle was a blur of fiery hair and temper as she brushed past Dinah, waitress tray on her left arm. With a thrust of her free hand, Mirelle grabbed the bar bottle of Dos Equiis and turned it upside down, forcing it into her husband's belt; then she dumped the martini down Alix Mailloux's cleavage.

"Your drink order," she announced, slamming the tray down on the table before spinning on her heel and sailing away. The three women teachers at the corner table raised a cheer, standing and clapping; the one man looked at the table.

Dinah, turning away, met the eyes of Mark Burdette.

"Just the floor show," she said. "Nothing serious."

Four

JUST BECAUSE YOU'RE slow to boil, doesn't mean your temper isn't hot.

Ross used to tell Dinah that, shaking his head each time he witnessed the aftermath of her wrath. But then, until they'd returned to Harrisburg, he'd not known Mirelle well—Mirelle, whose temper could be more accurately described as a flash fire: quick to ignite, fierce to burn, and taking forever to extinguish. Even now, after her excruciatingly public triumph over her husband and his *hussy*, she was not able to lean back and enjoy it. Her hair a wild swirl, her painted fingernails clawing at the air, she stormed around the confines of Dinah's living room like an animal in a cage.

"What are you smiling about? What the hell is there to smile about?" she shrieked. "I can't believe you let that man and his whore into your restaurant."

Dinah sank onto the chaise, stripping her black shoes away from her pinched toes; despite the low heels, they had the same effect on her feet as a night in four-inch spikes. She found herself wondering how sneakers would look with the black dress.

"My husband. I'm thinking about my husband." She extended her legs, examining her feet for signs of swelling.

"Oh, for God's sake. Not all men are as brilliantly—*wonderful*—as your Ross." Mirelle's voice was bitter. She plucked a glass paperweight from the bookshelf and passed it hand to hand as if measuring its worth as a weapon; finding it wanting, she returned it to its place. "Your husband didn't go whoring about in public like mine. Anyway, we're not talking about your husband. We're talking about Wallace."

Dinah winced. "Remember—you're talking to a second wife here."

Mirelle waved this objection away as she would a mosquito. "Nearly twenty years you had him. That's close enough for you to be considered monogamous to me."

Dinah rubbed her eyes.

"Anyway, I don't want to be monogamous like you," Mirelle complained. She paused in her pacing at the drinks table, poured herself a jot of whisky, then apparently thought better of it and walked off, leaving the glass behind. "Not when my husband gets to be polygamous. It's hardly fair. How *could* you have let him in here tonight?"

Clasping the throw pillow to her breast, Dinah sank further back into the comfort of the chaise. She closed her eyes wearily. "As you may recall, I was in the process of throwing him out when you shoved the beer down his shorts." She yawned. "I ought to kill Gillian for letting you take her tray like that."

"She didn't let me. I just did it." From the foyer below came the ringing of the grandfather clock. With each ring, Mirelle clenched and unclenched her fingers. "Besides. Kill Gillian and you lose a perfectly good bar manager into the bargain." She threw herself onto the couch, then got to her feet again, unable to remain still.

"Dirk?"

"That's right. Dirk and Gill. Look out the window. They're getting better acquainted down in the parking lot even as we speak." At the window, Mirelle eased the curtain aside. "And guess who's playing peeping Tom from the back apartment."

"Someone besides you? They're pretty popular, then, aren't they, Dirk and Gill? Maybe they should sell tickets." With her eyes closed, Dinah could almost convince herself that she was asleep. That this was all a bad, bad dream. Almost.

"The other apartment, you idiot. Your cook and hostess. Gomez and Morticia." Mirelle snorted, whirling away and letting the curtain fall again. "That's just peachy. They're all pairing up out there. I'm a single in a world of doubles."

"Or you're a triple," Dinah suggested with another yawn. "Depending on how you look at it."

"Great. Sleeping triple in a double bed. Just doesn't quite have that hit country song ring to it, does it?" For a moment Mirelle's animated face wore that same expression Alix Mailloux's had, when she looked as though she would crumple. Dinah held her breath. Mirelle held on.

"There's nothing wrong with being single, anyway. I'm single." All Dinah wanted to do now was go to bed. To end this day. Her neck and shoulders ached.

Unexpectedly, Mirelle dropped to her knees on the rug beside the sofa. Her expression had faded to the bleak one she had tried to hide this afternoon. "Not by choice. You'd still be married now, if you had a choice."

This was true. The familiar longing was surging to the fore again. *Ross.* "I would," she said, her laugh short and sad.

"And that's just it." Mirelle leaned forward, put a hand on Dinah's knee. "Don't you see? I'm going to have to get divorced again, and I don't want to be alone." She looked terrified of the thought.

Slowly Dinah got to her feet. Perhaps she should invite Mirelle to stay the night on the fold-out couch. "It doesn't necessarily follow that just because you get a divorce, you have to be alone. You ought to know that. You've married twice. You're a beautiful and vibrant woman. Guys'll be lining up. And the great thing is—you don't really even have to marry the bastards."

Mirelle stayed where she was, on her knees, like some mourning statue. Her brilliant hair hung down to hide her face. She did not answer.

"For God's sake, woman, you had that restaurant writer overheating there this afternoon—and he's at least ten years younger than you are. He rather thought you were coming on to him. You don't have to be alone. You can have anyone you want." Dinah crossed to the drinks table and lifted the abandoned glass to her lips. The whisky tasted as wrong now as it had in the afternoon.

"But I don't know if I want anyone."

Dinah's groan was deep. "You can't live with 'em and you can't live without 'em. I guess that's why some genius invented the vibrator." She decided against the whisky and set the glass down with a decided click. "Look, darling heart. I hate to sound callous, but I'm beat. I've had too much excitement for one day, and I need to go to bed. You are more than welcome here if you want to stay. Just make sure you turn off the light, whatever you decide."

DESPITE HER BONE-WEARINESS, Dinah had a hard time settling into a restful sleep. With each wholehearted dive into unconsciousness, the scene in the west room—and what a scene!—unfolded in her dreams: variations on a theme. Alix Mailloux's surprised little shriek: what in the name of God had she been expecting, after all? Wallace's wide-eyed, shell-shocked look as the inverted bottle of beer gurgled merrily into his crotch. Then always the camera flashed about to Mark Burdette, and the curiously amused dark eyes he raised to meet hers. Sometimes in her dreams he was laughing, sometimes sympathetically, sometimes sarcastically: difficult to read. But each time Dinah clawed her way back to consciousness in horror.

What a review this was going to be. There had been nothing to say to him, really, nor to his companion, to close out the evening. *You aren't going to write this, are you?* Of course she could not have said that to him. Mark Burdette was a professional, she reasoned forlornly, not to be influenced by pleas for mercy, offers of chocolate amaretto cheesecake, propositions of sexual favors. She could see it now, as clearly as though she was holding the newspaper in her shaking hands: food great, service lousy. No, service downright dangerous. Negative stars for that one, surely.

The rest of the evening had tormented her in its endlessness. Mirelle, flying the flag of victory, had fled back upstairs. Wallace Holbein had marched out with as much dignity as a man who looked as though he needed Depends could muster; Alix Mailloux had followed a few steps behind, head down. Dinah hoped they'd been suitably mortified—how could they not be, soaked as they were? Something good had to come out of this fiasco, after all. The rest of the guests began to trickle away—the food writer and his date had disappeared around seven-thirty—and the kitchen closed at nine. Dinah, by that time, was exhausted, and Kelly and Rob, for some reason, were not speaking to one another. All in all, the evening had not been what one could call an unqualified success. After the afternoon, Dinah had fully expected Kelly and Rob to kill one another with the filleting knives, to lunge for heart's blood over the restaurant critic's table. She had been on her guard against that. But she had not had the time nor the foresight to prevent Mirelle from drowning her husband—or at least his offending parts—in Mexican beer. That had been an attack from an unexpected quarter.

"Cheer up," Mirelle had spat when first confronted with her transgression. "It could have been a butt of Malmsey."

"By God, I wish it had been. At least then there would have been some literary precedent to back up my stupid excuse. Floor show my eye."

Maybe this was one of those instances they were supposed to be able to laugh about together when they were old and gray. Dinah turned over onto her back and stared up through the darkness at the ceiling. After all, the evening did have that ludicrous possibility. But first, as with all tragicomedy, it had to hurt or embarrass. Or mortify. Or ruin the business you had dreamed of starting up, all that time ago with your husband. Her head was pounding.

I've made a mess of it, Ross. Between my friends and my employees, I'm running this dream into the ground.

Of course, there was Mirelle to think of, always. She was right: there would have to be a divorce. Never mind any feeling Mirelle might have left for Wallace; that was a moot point. Now the relationship had boiled down to issues of respect, of power, of will to dominate and humiliate. Dinah winced. She knew how she would feel in Mirelle's place. Yes, there would have to be a divorce. It was imperative. If Mirelle did not file, Dinah was more than a little inclined to march down to that courthouse and do it for her.

She pushed all thoughts of Sherry Galloway from her mind.

Five

DINAH SLEPT THROUGH the alarm clock, as well as the sounds of the destruction of an entire tray of water glasses, from the dining room below—though she would not discover that until later. The morning sun was blazing through the curtains at her; in her haste to get to bed, she had neglected to pull the shades in the high windows. Yet once again it was the frantic pounding of Perry's feet on the back stairs that brought her to the surface, her head still aching, and her mouth dry.

"Dinah," he called through the door. She had not forgotten to lock that, thank God, or he would have burst through it. Or had Mirelle locked it? "Dinah." He pounded a few times with what sounded like a battering ram. "Are you still asleep?"

She waited a few moments to see if Mirelle would answer the door, if in fact she were still here. The last person she wanted to see this morning was Perry, God love him. The last thing she needed to hear was another tale of woe at the havoc Rob and Kelly were wreaking this time. She rolled over, pulling the covers over her head, but the light and sound were not shut out.

"Dinah?"

"Could you keep it down, Perry?" Mirelle, finally, her voice rife with impatience. "I'm on the phone." There was a sound like a kick against the bedroom door. "Dinah, will you get the hell up and deal with this kid?"

The clock read 9:41. Definitely overslept, though her body in no way felt ready to face this new day. When she groped her way out of bed, most of the blankets came with her, and she left them in a heap on the floor. *To hell with it.* She couldn't find her robe in all the mess, but that hardly mattered, with her flannel old lady nightgown. Nothing exposed there. She stumbled into the living room, waving her hands to clear the air before her. Mirelle knew enough not to smoke in the apartment, but the smell lingered, indicating she'd put in a fair few outside. A miasma swirled about Mirelle where she lounged on the couch, as though she was chain-smoking where she sat. She had the telephone cradled against her should, and was writing busily, grunting into the mouthpiece.

"It's your little friend," she growled out of the side of her mouth.

"Don't be a bitch." She crossed to the door, leaned against it instead of opening it. "What is it, Perry?"

"Dinah, you've got to come down."

What a way to start the day.

"Can't you stand up to the idiots for once?" she demanded peevishly, shoving her hair out of her face. "What are they doing now?"

"No, no, it's not that at all, Dinah." His voice was far more excited than upset. "It's Gahan. Gahan Godfrey. He's here."

Oh, hell. Her eyes strayed quickly to the desk calendar, too far away to read anyway. Was this the day he was supposed to be here? Another appointment forgotten. Too many things were happening, one on top of another. On the couch, Mirelle had paused in her monosyllabic conversation, arching her finely drawn eyebrows inquiringly.

"Tell him I'll be right there. Give him some coffee—whatever you can find for breakfast." She tugged at her tangled hair. A shower. That was first on the agenda. Listening to Perry's excited footsteps receding, she hoped he could be counted on to take care of Gahan without interruption from Rob.

"It's today?" Mirelle asked. Her voice was pitched slightly higher than normal. "Your beloved director is here today?"

"Why aren't you at school?" Dinah demanded, whirling back toward the bathroom. "It's not the weekend yet."

"I took the day off. Called in sick. They can do without me for a day." Abruptly Mirelle turned back to her phone conversation. "Yeah, that's the one. The twenty-four footer. Probably the dolly, too. Can you do it? And what's the price going to be on that?" She quickly jotted down a few more notes. The calculating look in her eye gave Dinah the shivers. Those eyes were not azure this morning: they were ice cold blue.

"What are you doing?"

Mirelle picked up a coffee mug, took a sip, then set it back down on the side table. "Renting a truck. Hurry up with that shower. I want to go down and meet this Gahan God guy with you."

"He's not a god," Dinah protested. Still, she hadn't seen him in months, not since he'd agreed to take the project on; she felt her own excitement rising. She quickened her steps to the bathroom and her shower.

"IF I'D KNOWN I was going to be staying, I would have brought some other clothes." Mirelle fluffed her brilliant hair in front of the mirror.

Dinah had slipped into some jeans and a white shirt. "You could borrow something of mine," she offered, peering under the couch for her other sandal.

Mirelle adjusted her caftan and looked at Dinah critically. "If I'd known your new artistic director was making his entrance today, I *really* would have brought some other clothes."

There it was. Dinah shoved her foot into the offending shoe. At the door she slid back the lock and stepped onto the landing. "You are still a married woman."

"Not for long," Mirelle shot back, and there was a decided hardness to her voice. "And since we've already come to the conclusion that I can't live without 'em, I might as well line one up for the next dance, wouldn't you say?"

Dinah could have told her—perhaps already had, it was so hard to remember—that Gahan Godfrey was probably not Mirelle's next waltz partner. He was waiting for them in the dining room, seated at the table by the front window, tucking away a light egg concoction under Perry's watchful eye. He had a napkin stuck into his collar, and there were toast crumbs cascading the length of his white beard. The morning sunlight glistened along the top of his balding head. He smiled brightly at their entrance.

"Dinah, sweetheart," he greeted, squinting slightly. He made a half-hearted move to get to his feet, but she stopped him with a hand on his shoulder.

"I made him an omelet," Perry said. Today he was wearing his pale hair pulled back into a ponytail. "With ham and cheese and leeks."

"Leeks?" Mirelle looked skeptical.

Gahan spread his great hands wide and gestured over the top of his plate, as though performing some sort of magic trick. "Oh, and it's so good. I've not had anything quite this fine for breakfast since the last time I was in Paris. This is quite a chef you've got here, Dinah, my girl."

"You were in Paris?" Mirelle slid easily into the chair beside him. "When?"

"1972, wasn't it, Gahan?" Dinah asked, raising her eyebrows. He frowned at her before turning a beatific smile on Mirelle.

"I'm not the chef," Perry broke in. "I'm just a line cook, Mr. Godfrey."

"And a damned good one, I'm sure," Gahan returned, scraping up a large bit of omelet between his fork and a slice of toast. "This is almost as delectable as the dish I'm sitting beside. Dinah, you didn't tell me you had such a gorgeous woman working for you."

Mirelle's smile was equally beatific.

Dinah coughed. "She doesn't work here," she growled, thinking to grab a chair for support. "Thank God." Waitresses of Mirelle's ilk would have had her out of business within the first week of opening.

"I'm such a terrible waitress." Mirelle batted her eyelashes. "I drop orders in people's laps, all that kind of thing. That just doesn't go over well at a classy kind of joint like the Cow Palace."

Perry snorted, even though he'd heard it all before.

"Gahan," Dinah snarled, "this is my former best friend, Mirelle Holstein."

"Holbein," Mirelle cut in. "Like the artist."

Gahan's smile grew wider in the wilderness of his beard. He held out a hand to Mirelle, and when she placed her white fingers in it, covered them with his other hand. "I am very excited to meet you, my dear. I'm sure I've heard all kinds of wonderful things about you."

"I'm not sure you have," Mirelle said, shifting her narrowed glance to Dinah and back. "Not if your only source of information was Chicky, here."

"Chicky?" Perry's snorting was now full-blown laughter. His round face grew bright red.

Gahan ignored him. "And will you be working with us this season?" His voice was smooth.

"Your omelet," Perry interrupted now. "It's going to get cold."

"Screw the omelet," Mirelle returned ungenerously. She placed her other hand over Gahan's. They were now, as far as Dinah could see, inextricably entwined. It was a good thing the theater season didn't start for another few weeks. "Working with you? I don't understand." She was, however, working those eyelashes for all they were worth.

"On the stage, my dear Mirelle—a sweet name. Are you French? Dinah and I have planned a wonderful lineup of shows this season, just wonderful. And oh, how wonderful it would be if you could play some parts for us."

Dinah cut in quickly. "Mirelle has a job. A wonderful job."

But Dinah, it would seem, as well as the omelet, had been forgotten. Mirelle slid her chair closer to Gahan's. "I really hadn't thought about it, you know. I'm free all summer—once the school year ends in a few more days. Of course, I haven't been in a show for years. I daresay I'm a little rusty."

"Well, listen. Why don't we try this?" Already Gahan was nodding in agreement with his own idea in the way that always filled Dinah with trepidation. "The company has a meeting tonight in the theater. Why don't you come? Maybe you could get a feel for it."

"Be careful. I think he wants to get a feel for you." Dinah narrowed her eyes.

"Don't be a bitch, Dinah," they both said.

She looked at Perry and sighed. "How well they know me."

"I still like you," Perry comforted. He draped an arm over her shoulders, leaned his head into hers.

"Thanks."

A crash from the kitchen.

"Oh, hell. Here we go again."

Gahan started from his chair. He made a half-hearted move to follow Dinah toward the kitchen door. Only half-hearted. She knew him too well to believe he'd show courage under fire anyway.

"What's going on?" he called.

She didn't answer. Perry came close at her heels; at least when she led, he had the courage to follow, and for this, she was grateful. She heard Mirelle's explanation behind them. "It's the Addams Family. Dinah runs a house of horrors on the side, you know."

"I'm not surprised," Gahan replied.

Six

THEY DENIED EVERYTHING, of course.

Dinah saw Gahan ensconced in the theater, and then, still inwardly cursing Kelly and Rob, she slipped out into the yard. The late spring morning was ripe and green, the birds and crickets competing for some prize in joyful noisemaking. She scowled, trudging to the roadside and the paper box. Might as well cap this morning off with a good kick in the gut. She cursed, too, at a fat red-breasted robin prancing across the lawn, a worm dangling from its beak, great advertisement for a restaurant. It paid no heed whatsoever.

The wide front porch was still in shade. Ignoring the wicker furniture and the swing which moved slightly back and forth in a nearly nonexistent breeze, Dinah settled on the bottom step and shook out the newspaper. She stared stupidly at the front page and its headlines, which made no sense at all to her. Rather like looking up the announcement of your own execution, she thought. It really made no difference whether she read the entire paper slowly, or rushed straight to the review—which must be in the lifestyle and entertainment section. Either way, the bad news would still be there: in her hands, and in the hands of everyone else in the catchment area of the *Gazette*. By lunchtime everyone would know how hazardous to one's health it would be to have dinner at Galloway's. Custom would fall off precipitously. The restaurant would go belly-up. The bank would foreclose on the mortgage. Soon enough, Dinah would find herself living in a cardboard box on the side of the road. All because of Mirelle.

Oh, hell.

Gritting her teeth, Dinah tossed aside the first section of the paper, then the sports. There it was, finally. She scanned the first page of the lifestyle section for the review. The metallic taste of doom was in her mouth. She wished for a cup of coffee, black, bitter, and thick. That would get the taste out.

> In the mood for an unusual dining experience? I have yet to find any more interesting place to satisfy that urge than Galloway's.

Sarcasm. Cleverly aimed. Dinah could picture Mark, that ridiculous dimple becoming more pronounced as he typed away on his computer with tongue in cheek. She let the breath out through her mouth, slowly. She needed that cup of coffee. No, she needed a stiff drink, even if it was only ten-thirty in the morning. It was five o'clock somewhere, right?

> Tastefully decorated, the dining rooms feature tall windows and high ceilings which mute the conversations of surrounding tables; this is an ideal setting for enjoyable dining and pleasant company. The service, too, is prompt yet unobtrusive—though I can't promise that each waitperson will speak with the pleasing British accent of our waitress.

Points for Gillian. Dinah reminded herself to give that woman a raise. She read on, quickly, chewing on her lower lip. The bomb had to be planted here somewhere.

> And then we come to the food. Oh, the food. Though I searched the menu for some mention of Cornish game hen, I found none, which is just as well, for the owner, Dinah Galloway, assured me that they were out the evening I was there.

Dinah groaned. That hen. That damned hen. It would haunt her forever.

> Instead I ordered a Queen Victoria soup for starters, while my friend opted for a plate of oysters on the half-shell. The soup was rich, with a cream base providing a background for a delightful mixture of chicken, ham, mushrooms, and onion, with a few slices of hard-boiled egg floating on top. The oysters were fresh, attractively presented on a bed of greens with a garnish of red onion, with a choice of horseradish sauce, or a milder cocktail sauce, both of which are made fresh daily in the restaurant's kitchen.
>
> The raspberry duck entree was cooked superbly, with the skin a succulent crackling brown beneath the fruit sauce. My dining partner found her sole gratinee a bit on the bland side, but we both agreed that the mixed garden vegetables and red potatoes with rosemary as side dishes were more than adequate

to take up any slack. A magnificent chocolate amaretto mousse, garnished with homemade whipped cream and chocolate shavings, rounded off the meal, and indeed came close to being the most memorable part of the evening.

Dinah skimmed the rest of Mark Burdette's column hurriedly. Damn his eyes. If not the mousse, then what *had* been the most memorable part of the evening? He made no mention of the scene he'd witnessed, being in the absolute wrong place at the absolute wrong time. She sighed, thinking she ought to drop him a note to thank him for his forbearance. But when she at last reached the bottom of the page, where the restaurant's rating was given in stars, she found his dig in the notation.

Food: ***
Service: ****
Entertainment: ****

Damn his sarcastic dark eyes. She hurled the newspaper at the fat robin, who didn't even bother to fly away.

Seven

Dear Mark,

Dear Mr. Burdette,
I would like to thank you

Dear Mr. Burdette,
I would like to apologize for

Dear Mark,
Sorry about

UPSTAIRS, DINAH TORE off each successive sheet and hurled it disgustedly into the empty fireplace grate. She threw herself onto the sofa, then grabbed a pillow and hurled that across the room, too. It sailed over the breakfast bar to knock some magnets off the refrigerator; those weren't called throw pillows for nothing. She suddenly wished she had a cat, a big, fluffy, overweight, bad-tempered one, so she could throw it as well.

Jesus. Look what she was becoming.

What would Ross write?

The question came to her unbidden, and despite everything she found herself smiling. Because, of course, she knew the answer. Her late husband—as always, the blade of longing pierced her—would laugh it off and send along a brief note of tongue-in-cheek thanks for the review. And then go about his business with a further full laugh. If she squeezed her eyes closed right now, she could hear that sound.

His face, though. It struck her painfully that it was growing more difficult to imagine his face and make out his features as the months piled up. She was angry about that. The man to whom she'd been married for nearly twenty years, and she couldn't clearly remember what he looked like. Abruptly she stood, tossing the pad of paper aside, and went to the piano to take his picture into her hands. It was a relief to stare into those eyes, to track those brows with a finger.

She returned to the couch, clutching the photograph tightly. She set the frame on the side table, facing her late husband fully as she plucked the pen from behind her ear. With the flat of her hand, she smoothed a fresh sheet of paper.

"Come on, Ross," she whispered to his smiling face. "Dictate."

Dear Mark,

Thank you so much for the review in this morning's Gazette. Your kind words, with any luck, will bring in some new business to our establishment.

Please feel free to stop in again anytime.

With a tiny flourish, she signed her full name, then sealed the note up inside its envelope. With any luck, she repeated wryly. With any luck, she had achieved just the right level of nonchalance.

She dug a book of stamps out of the drawer in the roll-top desk and slapped one onto the envelope. Then she headed downstairs for a quick jog down the length of the driveway to the mailbox, holding the envelope between the tips of two fingers as though it were in some way contagious.

PART II

Appetizers

Eight

DINAH HAD MET Gahan in college, when she had taken her first theater class. All these years later, she had no idea what had possessed her to enroll; she had never even acted in a high school production. As she was daily blown over and overpowered by Professor Godfrey's tirades, she came to realize that she was not cut out for the thespian life, either. Too many other people in the class were huge personalities, raging over the smallest insults, becoming euphoric at the slightest hint of a smile. Rather like Mirelle—an enormous roomful of Mirelles—the childhood friend she had escaped from by choosing this college, far away from home.

She had approached him hesitantly after the first week of class, seeking permission to drop, permission he had adamantly refused.

"But I'm no good at this," she protested. "I can't stand up against these people."

Gahan Godfrey made a face that involved pursing his lips, lowering his impressive brows, and narrowing his eyes. Bearded chin in hand, he glared at Dinah for a moment, then stood and did a slow circuit about her, inspecting her from all sides, rather like a judge at a livestock show.

"Lift your chin," he ordered after a moment. "A bit more."

She did as she was bidden, too overawed not to.

The silence stretched as he considered. Then suddenly he shook his head and resumed his seat, the elderly desk chair creaking backward in a way that made Dinah cringe. "No. You're all wrong for the tragic heroine type."

Dinah felt the blood rush into her cheeks. "I just want to take something practical. Like accounting. I don't know why I ever thought I could get by in a theater class."

"You aren't ruthless enough for a Lady Macbeth," he said, and it sounded like some form of agreement. "You aren't a killer."

"Some of the people in this class are."

He ignored her. Leaning back further in the protesting chair, he stuck a cowboy boot up on his desk, displacing a flutter of papers and a script or two. His eyes studied her face intently, as though his lines had been inscribed there.

"But you aren't weak, either. Definitely not an Ophelia."

"Besides. I know how to swim." She couldn't help herself. She felt out of place in this conversation.

A few more scripts and a magazine followed the newspaper to the floor when he stuck his other foot up and crossed his legs. "See? That's just it. You're too damned practical. You need to be a Portia: you need to take on the world and outsmart everyone. Or perhaps you need to be a Beatrice."

"I need to get out of this class." She glanced toward the open door, beyond which the occasional student wandered. She needed to get out of this office.

"A comedic heroine." He seemed totally uninterested in her protestations.

"This is a farce."

The generous eyebrows lifted once again. "Then go with it, Dinah, my dear." It was the first time he had used her name, and the first time she felt that he had actually addressed *her* in the course of the conversation. When she met his eyes now, the expression in them was kind, but with an edge of calculation. Despite her resolve, she began to wonder if perhaps there wasn't something in what he said. Perhaps she should give it another try. "You'll stay in the class. You'll study this script"—he dug around and pulled out a dog-eared copy of *Twelfth Night*, which he tossed into her lap—"and you'll speak Viola to me first thing on Monday."

Speak Viola?

His smile, as he showed her to the door of his office, was kind, but again there was an edginess to it. He patted her shoulder reassuringly. "You're not an accountant, Dinah. Don't undersell yourself. You've got stuff going on under there that you simply haven't let people know about yet."

She looked at him askance.

"I'm not kidding you, my dear. I know about that of which I speak." He tapped the script she held in her hand. "It's women like you who scare the living hell out of me."

It wasn't until she was halfway across the quad that she realized she had allowed herself to be bowled over by Gahan Godfrey. She couldn't begin to comprehend how. She vowed, though, to let that be the last time she would allow him to change her mind. She had never quite figured out, however, what kind of woman *a woman like her* was. Nor how she could scare him, or anyone else for that matter.

MIRELLE SEEMED TO have fallen under Gahan Godfrey's persuasive spell.

"He says," Mirelle laughed gleefully, running her tongue along her teeth and widening her azure eyes, "that he admires my fire."

"Yup." Dinah peered up over the rims of her reading glasses before dropping her eyes again to the newspaper. She had brought it upstairs to read the review more closely, hoping the glasses would somehow magically transform the piece into—something else. She didn't know what. There was no magic. Mark's sly digs dug just as slyly up here as they had done on the porch. She wished she had the sports section to take her mind off his words, but that had blown into the street to be run over by a tractor-trailer truck. "Fire's good. Unless you're firing on my customers."

Dinah also wished she'd put an elastic in her hair, so she could take it out and fire it at her friend. Mirelle, in her fluttering mode, made a moving target. With her long nails, cinnamon colored now—where'd she find nail polish around here?—she picked at the window latch, before moving on to pick up a blue transferware vase from the cherry lowboy. After a second or two, she set that down to move on to the piano, where she tapped an A-flat several times in succession.

"Come on," she urged. "Just go along with me on this one, Di. Gahan says I have star potential."

"Only potential?" This time Dinah didn't even bother to look up. She shoved the newspaper aside and tugged absently at her hair. "Have you fired at him, yet?"

"Ha, ha." Mirelle twirled about until she reached the chervil mirror. "Why do you have to be such a bitch, Di?" She bundled up her wild hair and piled it in a red nest atop her head, then tilted her chin to examine her cheekbones. "You're just moaning about that restaurant review. This isn't about you. It's about me."

"It always is," Dinah mumbled. The glasses were pinching the bridge of her nose. Wearily she took them off and put them aside on the coffee table. How in the name of God was she going to get through tonight?

Probably after this review, there wouldn't be any custom tonight anyway.

"What?"

"You heard me. It always *is* about you."

Mirelle turned her head to study her other cheek critically, and, apparently finding it to her satisfaction, let her hair tumble back down about her shoulders. These she shrugged elegantly. "Your point?"

Frustrated, Dinah kicked the notebook out of her way with her toes. There was a streak of black newsprint across her palm. For a moment she considered wiping it down her face, a kind of camouflage. "My point is that in your pathetic rage against your pathetic husband, you damn near dumped dinner on a restaurant writer who has the power to make or break my means of support. Because it's always about you, *my* life gets screwed up, thank you very much."

"Oh, come off it. It was drinks, not dinner, and I only gave your boy a show, not a scare. Besides—he gave the Cow Palace four stars for entertainment. Four! And that was me. I should take the review down to show Gahan. Not even on stage, and my show is earning four stars." Tired of pirouetting before the mirror, Mirelle lighted gracefully on the chaise longue and plucked a pack of cigarettes from her purse. The cover of her gold lighter flashed as she lit up.

Wordlessly, Dinah leaned over and plucked the cigarette, its end now solidly lipsticked, from Mirelle's mouth. She went to the window, slid up the sash, and flipped the cigarette out into the morning light.

Mirelle's hand still hung in the air. Her wide eyes turned on Dinah. "What the hell are you doing? That was my butt."

Dinah wished it were.

"And this, as you recall, is my house. It's a no-smoking zone."

Their eyes locked. Mirelle's long fingers drew out another cigarette. She slid it between her lips, but before she could get the lighter out a second time, Dinah snatched the cigarette away and sent it sailing out the window after the first. Hands on hips, she glared at Mirelle.

"Self-righteous bitch," Mirelle snarled.

"Self-centered bitch," Dinah shot back.

"You wanna go?"

The challenge was only half-joking. Mirelle might be taller, but Dinah was more solidly built, and knew she could take her. But the all-too-familiar pounding on the stairs stopped her as she took a step toward the chaise.

"Come on, then," Mirelle challenged mockingly, her face nearly as red as her hair. "What are you waiting for?"

"Listen—"

The pounding on the stairs transformed into pounding on the door.

"Dinah!"

Perry's voice, high and wild and panicked.

"Not now, you idiot. We're in the middle of something important." Mirelle's eyes were still locked on Dinah's.

"Dinah!" Perry shouted again, pounding on the door as though he'd come right through it. "Hurry up! They're at it again!"

"Oh, for Chrissake," Dinah spat.

She spun toward the door. *Not again.* They were growing worse and worse— she remembered almost fondly a time when they had limited themselves to explosions only every month or so. She remembered a time when Ross took care of unpleasantness.

"Who's he talking about?"

Dinah shook her head, sliding back the latch. "You know damn well who. Kelly and Rob. Your Addams Family. You want to see how to do this dust-up right? Come watch the experts."

"WHY ARE WE sneaking?"

For once Dinah had not attempted to announce her imminent arrival at the kitchen. Now she put a finger to her lips at the same time Perry clapped a hand over Mirelle's brilliant red mouth; after a fraction of a second, he let out a little shriek and jerked his hand away.

"Hush, already," Dinah urged.

From the other side of the swinging door came a scream, the clank of metal against metal, and then once again the sparkling shatter of glass.

Dinah winced.

"She bit me," Perry protested in a hoarse whisper.

"I'll bite you in a minute if you don't shut up," Dinah whispered.

"It's always you, isn't it?" Rob's voice was muffled by the door. "You, you, you—"

"See?" Mirelle demanded, elbowing Dinah in the ribs. "Not me. *Her.*"

"Shut up, will you?"

Another crash.

Dinah took a deep breath and thrust open the swinging door. She had to duck to avoid the spatula, whistling past, ricocheting off Perry, clattering into the dining room.

Perry let out another shriek and clutched his arm.

Mirelle pushed past Dinah and stopped short. "Oh, my God."

Rob and Kelly, suddenly no longer fighting, were on the butcher block, she straddling him, his hands splayed across the back of her filmy blouse. If their tongues had been any deeper into each other's mouths, they would have choked each other to death. Or eaten each other whole. Like boa constrictors, almost. Or piranhas.

"Yuck," Dinah said loudly.

"You know," Mirelle mused, "I think I've seen this scene in a movie somewhere. It had Jack Nicholson in it."

"Yes," Perry exclaimed gleefully. "And Jessica Lange. I've always liked Jessica Lange."

Dinah took a step into the kitchen, and broken crockery ground beneath her feet. She cleared her throat without looking down; she did not want to know what of hers they had broken this time. Not yet. Maybe later.

Count two. No reaction.

Kelly moaned. Dinah tasted bile.

She cleared her throat again, more loudly, drawing the rasp out to its ridiculous end.

Suddenly Rob let himself fall all the way back onto the butcher's block. Kelly pressed herself down upon him, her hair cascading along the sides of her face. Was that panting?

"Yuck," she repeated.

Perry giggled.

A shadowy figure loomed up in the back doorway, blocking the sunlight.

"Oh, ho!" a voice boomed in delight. Gahan's voice.

Dinah grimaced. In another minute he'd whip out a camera and start filming.

"What's all this, then, eh?"

With a shrill cry, Kelly struggled up from her husband's groping form. Her plaid skirt caught on the edge of the butcher's block, treating all to a view of her black satin bikini.

A whistle from Gahan. "Very nice. Victoria's Secret, is it?"

"You would know, Gahan, wouldn't you?" Dinah beckoned him into the kitchen. "Come on into the firing range." She glared at Rob and Kelly, but the look had no effect. It never did.

Rob rolled to his feet, a bit dazed. Kelly tugged desperately at her skirt in an attempt to free herself. Her face was red, her lipstick smeared, and she looked near tears.

Rob opened his mouth, his hand at his half-mast fly. "We were just—"

"Performing a taste-test?" Perry was still giggling.

"Shut up," Rob snarled.

The screen door slammed behind Gahan. He sailed in and dropped an arm around Dinah's shoulders. "You know, darling, I think it would make a wonderful name for a new dish. Sex in the Kitchen. Maybe it would work for a dessert."

"Shut up," Rob repeated, whipping his head around.

"Oh, ho!" Gahan laughed. "All this hostility, and you don't even know who I am, my good man."

"Shut up anyway." Rob's face was nearly as red as his wife's. His eyes had a glassy look. But then, his eyes always had a glassy look, so that meant nothing. "Who the hell *are* you, anyway?"

"No sex in the kitchen," Dinah broke in impatiently. "With or without dessert. Why don't the pair of you just go take a cold shower or something."

Perry chortled again. "And I'll disinfect the butcher's block."

"I should think so," Mirelle concurred. She winked slyly at Gahan, who in turn waggled playful fingers at her.

With yet another cry, Kelly wrenched her skirt free and yanked it savagely into place. She fled from the kitchen, banging the screen door behind her. Rob, for his part, glanced around as though searching for something to say—the proverbial last word—before rushing outside after his wife.

"Oh, my," Mirelle breathed. She slumped back against the wall and shook her head. "Oh. My."

Gahan gave Dinah's shoulders a quick squeeze. "I assume, my dear, that you keep that delightful couple around for their entertainment value. Otherwise, I assume they're basically useless."

Her shoulders could have used far more than a mere squeeze; a full massage work-up would have been better at this point. Her jaw was tense, too, she discovered, when she wiped her face with her cold hands. She sighed, let her hands fall away, and looked helplessly around the sunny kitchen. It suddenly seemed so huge. Too huge. "Perry, I hope you weren't kidding about disinfecting. Just the thought of them—where we prepare food—I feel like throwing up."

"Poor Dinah." Perry petted her shoulder on the way by. "Is it too early for a drink? You look as though you need one." He opened the cupboard beside the great stainless steel sink, where he surveyed the cleaners in their neat row before selecting one.

"Good idea," Gahan agreed heartily.

Not for the first time did Dinah find herself wishing he wasn't such a loud guy. Drinks, to him, were always a good idea. She allowed him to propel her toward the dining room.

"Drinks on the house," he announced.

"Yeah, right." Dinah snorted. But weakly. "It's my house."

Mirelle linked her arm through Dinah's free one, all hostilities forgotten. "Look on the bright side, kiddo."

"There's a bright side?"

"Sure," Gahan said. "I could have been the restaurant critic at the door."

"Or the health inspector," Perry called cheerily.

Nine

"HE'S HERE," GILLIAN murmured in Dinah's ear as she eased by, tray balanced on her shoulder.

"Who?"

Gill didn't stop to elaborate. At this point, *he* could have been any one of a number of men, none of whom Dinah thought she'd like to see. Gahan—no, he was still out in the theater; Dinah had just come from there, where they had been discussing the progress of the ongoing renovations. Way behind, there, too; the first production of the Repertory was due to go up in just a few weeks' time, and the painting still wasn't complete. Rob was out in the kitchen, or at least he had better be; Gillian had cruised on by with an overflowing tray, and someone had to have cooked up those entrees. Maybe she meant Wallace, and if he was here, she'd have to take strong measures: kill him, maybe, just to save face at this point. The final possibility was Mark Burdette, and sure enough, when she turned to the doorway of the main dining room, there he was, alone, at the same table he'd occupied the other night, examining the menu intently, a frown between his brows.

"The food critic fellow," Gillian replied, now unnecessarily, as she sped past in the opposite direction, tray emptied. "Over there."

"I see him already."

With a hurried glance around for Mirelle, Dinah eased into the shadow of the entry. He had not seen her yet. What on earth was he doing here, back again already? Of course, she had invited him to return, in that damned note, but surely he had the intelligence to recognize a social nicety for the lie it was? Clenching her teeth, she studied him studying the menu. He couldn't have forgotten what was on it so soon. He did not wear a suit this evening, but rather slacks and a gray sweater; the color, Dinah noticed—or maybe it was the way the light fell—gave his hair a reddish cast she didn't recall its having before. Beautiful hair, a color she wouldn't mind having, and indeed had a few times attempted to give herself, straight out of a bottle. With that hair and her own not-half-bad green eyes, she could give Mirelle a run for the money, as it were. She straightened, envious of things she couldn't quite identify. As she did, Mark Burdette lifted his own eyes from the menu to look straight at her. His broad smile made her flush guiltily. He must see her. He *had* to. He probably knew exactly how long she'd been lurking, too. Feeling extremely stupid, she smoothed her skirt, lifted her chin, and made for his table.

Mark stood as she approached, still smiling. The grin, she noted, was lopsided, and made his sandy eyebrows arch up in a way she could only read as ironic. She held out a hand, and he grasped it confidently.

"Mr. Burdette," she said, meeting his smile and raising the ante just the slightest bit. "So good to see you again. You got my note?"

"Mark. Please. And I did get the card." His voice was deeper than she remembered. In the intimate lighting, she could not read his brown eyes. Perhaps that was best. "Thank you."

"Thank you for the thank you?"

He was still holding her hand. Dinah waited a moment, then pulled hers away, immediately worrying that she'd been too obvious.

"Join me?" Mark drew out the chair opposite his own. "That is, if you have a moment."

Again Dinah glanced hurriedly around the dining room. Mirelle was nowhere to be seen, so they were safe there. She recognized some of the regular customers, but none of them appeared to be any sort of threat. Gillian and the other waitresses moved briskly and quietly among the tables; Dirk, polishing some glassware at the bar, winked at her. No sudden noises erupted through the swinging doors to the kitchen.

"Thank you. I think I might just have a moment or two." She slipped into the chair he held, and he seated himself across from her.

"I'm having a gin and tonic," he said. "Will you have something?"

Gillian was hovering. She wore the pressed-lip look which always meant a smile would appear as soon as she left the table.

"I'll have a Perrier with lime."

Gillian scurried off.

Mark made a face. "I hate Perrier."

So did Dinah, but she wasn't about to admit it. "I don't drink and drive, as it were."

Perrier with lime was all she could think of that sounded halfway sophisticated and non-alcoholic. She needed to keep a clear head. Only partly because of Mark. Mostly because of all the volatile possibilities inherent in the crazy people who surrounded her.

"You're here for dinner?" she asked after an awkward moment. "What are you thinking of trying this evening?"

Mark rippled his fingers over the maroon cover of the menu. "I hadn't quite decided. What would you recommend?"

One of the waitresses slipped out of the kitchen, her face pale; immediately there was a crash. Dinah started. She felt Mark's eyes upon her. The sound was not repeated. Not even a shout came from beyond the swinging door. She took a deep breath, trying to calm her heart palpitations. When she looked up, Mark was still watching her with some interest. No, with amusement. His lips quirked to the side, and there was a gleam in his eye.

"Is there a problem?" he asked with deceptive gentleness. "You seem awfully nervous, Dinah."

She wished she hadn't invited him to use her given name. A bit of formality would have come in handy at this point, a weapon of defense. His eyes were still gleaming. She straightened her back. "No problem. I'm fine."

"Your waitress—Mirelle, isn't it?—isn't out in the kitchen, is she?"

He had to be laughing at her.

"She's not my waitress."

Gillian materialized with the drinks. She set them on maroon serviettes on the table. Dinah's was suspiciously amber colored. There was no lime. Without another word, Gillian slipped away again.

"*This* is your waitress, then? And this is your Perrier with lime?" Now that laughter in his voice was unmistakable.

Dinah threw a glance to the bar, where Dirk, polishing the optics, carefully did not look at her. He was watching the reflection in the mirror, she knew fully well. Still, he made no acknowledgment.

"Gillian is a fine waitress," she said haughtily. "As you no doubt know from the service the other night. At least, you praised the service in your review."

Mark looked gratified. "It's always so nice to know your work is being read by a discriminating audience."

"Mirelle, you know, is a friend."

"Yes. And one, apparently, with an explosive temper."

"Only where her husband is concerned."

She hadn't meant to speak the thought aloud. His laugh had her cursing herself. *Open mouth, insert foot.* She grabbed her tumbler and took a hurried mouthful. Big mistake. Whisky, no water, no ice. Without the adequate preparation, it was like swallowing an atomic bomb. The heat ran down her throat and up into her ears.

"Your eyes are watering," Mark said.

"I know." Coughing, she set the glass down and scrambled for the napkin. She held it to her face with both hands and closed her eyes. "I know."

He seemed to be having a whale of a time; his voice was rich with amusement. "Look. Would you like me to go out and come in again, so we can start this all over?"

She shook her head. "No. Not unless you take care of your bar tab first."

"Ah. A suspicious mind. I like that in a woman."

"I'm just protecting my investment."

Dinah looked at him through laced fingers, wondering where all her conversational thrusts and parries had gone wrong. He was making her tired. She couldn't think of anything sparkling and witty to say next, so she remained silent and waited.

Mark sipped his drink, his eyes on the menu. "From the sounds of things, part of your investment seems to have just crashed to the floor in the kitchen. Is that what's making you jumpy?"

"If I jumped every time a glass gets broken, I would have had to retire from the restaurant business the moment I started. Don't be ridiculous."

"Okay, then, what?" Mark lifted the menu to look at an entry a bit more closely. "Surely it's not me. I mean, I'm not here on official business this time. I'm not taking notes. I didn't bring my editor."

"So why are you here?" Dinah lifted her head, tried to summon a challenge into her voice.

"You invited me."

She took another, more controlled drink. "Okay, let's try this again. Why are you here, really?"

Gillian reappeared at the table. "Would you like to order now, sir, or do you need a few more moments?"

"I'm quite ready, I think," Mark said, shifting his glance and smiling. "You, Dinah?"

"I won't be dining, thank you."

His look was almost imploring; she met it obdurately, her lips pressed together. She wondered inanely whether any of her lipstick remained.

"Very well." He glanced at the menu once more. "I'd like to start with the blackened taster, and I'll follow that with the hanger steak with shallots."

They conferred on the starch and the salad dressing. Gill wrote swiftly, then disappeared.

Mark took a drink, then cleared his throat. "You know, that doesn't make me feel very confident."

"What?"

"The owner won't dine at her own restaurant."

Dinah took a breath and blew it out her nose, her best imitation of a mythical fire-breathing dragon. "Okay, look. You say you're not here on official business. No reviews this time?"

He cocked his head. "Yes. That's precisely what I said. Why?"

"Because I'm about to hurl this drink at your head."

Mark clicked his tongue. "I'm getting to you."

"Yes. The question is—why the hell would you want to?"

Mark Burdette'ssmile was wide and genuine, and somehow magically disarming. He looked, Dinah reminded herself swiftly, very, very young.

"I don't know. I really don't. And I'm sorry. I just get so full of myself sometimes. And you seem like a good sport."

She wouldn't let herself get sucked in by his boyish charm. Charmers, she knew quite well, were a dime a dozen, and she had lost her fair share of calm to them over the years. "I'm a damn good sport, and one with a handful of whisky. Now, why don't you tell me why you came back?"

He hung his head in mock apology. "I'm sorry. I had such an interesting time here the other night, I just had to come back to see if that was the regular fare. I was curious."

There was another sudden crash from the kitchen. Dinah sucked in a breath. Mark looked from the kitchen doors to her face and back.

"I have to tell you," she said, through teeth clenched so tightly that her jaw ached, "that what they say about curiosity killing the cat just might be true. Especially around here. So you'd best be careful."

Perry's head appeared at the door, his eyes wide with that look Dinah had grown to know all too well, the look which she had come to fear. He glanced around. Dinah saw Dirk gesture in her direction; as soon as Perry's eyes found her, he beckoned desperately.

"Look, Mark," she said, taking a last frantic mouthful of the whisky—she was going to need it, that was certain, "I gotta run. It's been nice—"

"Dinah," Perry called, his voice unsteady. Then he was shoved roughly out of the way, and Kelly rushed past him, through the dining room and out the front door.

"Can I help?" she heard Mark call after her. She shook her head, realizing somewhat sadly as she made her way between tables of curious diners, that his brown eyes were flecked with green.

Gorgeous eyes.

"WHY WAS SHE crying?"

Rob didn't look up at her, but continued flipping a tuna steak in a sizzling pan. "Beats me. Look. I've got a kitchen to run here, all right?"

"She's your wife," Dinah protested.

Rob tossed the steak expertly again and caught it. The pan sizzled some more, and suddenly flamed up. *Ninja chef.*

Rob swore. He plated the fish, and passed the dish off to the line cook to his right. Then he tossed a second steak into the pan.

There was no other answer. Leaving the pan, Rob turned to the worktop, picked up a knife, and addressed some mushrooms.

"And since when do you slice vegetables? Since when are you a prep cook?"

"Get me a halfway decent prep cook instead of some whiny mama's boy, and maybe I wouldn't have to."

Perry didn't even turn from the grill. "Screw you, Rob."

"You wish."

"You're not exactly my type, darling."

Dinah whistled sharply through her teeth. "Look, do I have to send you both to your rooms? What the hell are you doing? I've got a full house, people who all need to be fed and fed well, and all I've got to do it with is a bunch of cooks too busy sniping at one another to notice that they're burning up the entrees."

"I've never burnt an entree in my life," Rob snorted.

A shrill beeping cut him off.

"What the hell—?"

"Smoke alarm." Mark Burdette slipped past Dinah to grab the smoking pan from the range. His swearing cut across the noise; he shoved the pan aside and shook his hand. "You've burned something now, buddy."

"Who are you? What are you doing in my kitchen?" Rob faced him, knife still in hand.

Mark leapt out of arm's reach, still shaking his hand. "Where's that alarm?"

"Correction," Dinah snarled. "My kitchen. My restaurant. You burn it down, Rob, and you're out on your ass. Clear?"

Rob glared through the dispersing smoke.

The alarm continued. The acrid smoke made Dinah's eyes sting. The kitchen smelled of charred fish. She thought she heard shouting from the dining room, and hoped to God Gillian could keep things under control there. Maybe Dirk would pour some quick and reassuring refills.

"The alarm?" Mark demanded again. He coughed. After a second, he saw it and lunged.

From somewhere behind her, in the sudden deafening silence, Perry giggled.

She spun. "Perry, get your rear in gear and get something going to replace this—" She waved toward the smoking pan. "This is somebody's dinner. Somebody's waiting for it."

"All right, Di," Perry said soothingly. He reached overhead for another pan and thunked it onto a burner. With glares all around, Rob reached into the small refrigerator under the counter and pulled out a slab of fish, which he slapped unceremoniously into the pan.

The smoke alarm reset, Mark opened the screen door. The sudden rush of cool evening air smelled of freshly cut grass and lilacs. Wordlessly, Dinah passed through the door and into the yard.

HIS RIGHT HAND was wrapped in a wet cloth, and his left was wrapped around an old-fashioned glass. He leaned his red-gold head against the back of the wicker chair. Overhead a pair of moths circled the porch light. Through the door behind them, the murmurs of the last diners, reassured that the place wasn't about to burn down around their ears, rose and fell irregularly.

"Do they do that often? Rob and Kelly?"

Dinah closed her eyes and shook her head. "Every day. Every single God-damned day."

"So why do you keep them on?"

She couldn't answer. The acrid smell of charred tuna lingered in her nose, despite her attempts to clear her head. She was haunted by the image of the entire kitchen going up in flames.

Mark set his glass down on the wicker table between them and adjusted his makeshift cold pack. "I'm sorry. It's really none of my business. Forget I asked."

"No, no. It's all right."

Dinah felt the exhaustion deep in her joints, as though she had spent the day lifting heavy weights with no purpose. She knew she should open her eyes and look at him, converse with him as one reasonable adult to another. But it was too hard to do. It was even too hard to think about.

They had come around to the porch to sit in the cooling night air. Mark's burn was now a deep hard red across his fingers and palm. So far no blistering, though.

"What about your dinner?" she had asked him.

He had laughed. "I find I'm not all that hungry anymore."

She had found some salve in the kitchen first aid kit, but no bandage large enough. Mark had shrugged it off. "I just need another drink."

The salving and wrapping of his hand had been awkward, but the drinking was easy. Dinah had switched to water. She had to keep a clear head.

"So they always carry on like this, do they? Don't you find it kind of—?"

"Kind of like living in a Three Stooges movie? Or with the Addams Family? That's what Mirelle calls them. Yes. Between Perry, Rob, and Kelly, not to mention Mirelle, I think I'm going to lose my mind. If I don't lose the restaurant first." She shook her head, trying to rid herself of the sound of the smoke alarm. Even in memory it gave her a headache. The water, though—that might help. Unless it didn't. She took a mouthful, willing to give it a try.

"But you keep them on."

"Ross hired them." As if that explained everything. Except that it did. She sighed. She couldn't remember how much she'd told him for the write-up. "Ross knew about restaurants. Kitchens. Mirelle put us on to this place when we were looking to move back to the area. Ross refurbished it, hired back of house staff. And then—" She took another drink. "And then he died."

They sat in silence for a few moments.

"But now you're in charge," Mark said. "And doing well. Well enough to make some changes, if you need to." In the angled light, he glanced over at her and shrugged. "If you want to. But again, not my place."

Slowly Dinah rocked on the swing, listening to the creak of the chains. The moths had disappeared, moved on to some more attractive flame. Mark was right, of course. Had Ross seen the degeneration of the staff he'd hired, he'd have thrown them out long ago. *He* hadn't been afraid to do that sort of thing.

The side door opened, closed. After a moment, a couple of cars left the parking lot and eased out into the thin traffic.

"Then there's Mirelle. Your friend, not your staff." Mark swirled the liquid in his glass. His ice cubes had long since melted away. "She certainly adds an element of excitement."

His voice held a trace of awe.

"Especially when she's shoving drinks down people's pants."

Mark shivered and drank.

Ten

THERE WAS NOTHING for it, really. She was going to have to fire them. Both.

Dinah was sitting on the sofa with her chin in her hands when Mirelle burst into the apartment the next morning.

"Look," she ordered without preamble. "You've got to come with me. I need your help."

"Get your new boyfriend to help," Dinah replied dully. She snatched up *The New Yorker* magazine from the coffee table, opened it randomly, and held it up before her face. A shield. "I'm busy."

The whole place shook as Mirelle slammed the door. She strode across the room, grabbed the magazine, and tossed it away. "I don't have a boyfriend. I don't want a boyfriend. And if you mean Gahan, he's busy checking on some props or scenery or some such crap."

"That crap, as you so classily put it, will be supporting me so that I'm able to provide you with all this material comfort in your time of misery." Without her magazine, Dinah picked up the mug of tea on the coffee table. "Go get yourself your own cup from the kitchen."

"Screw the tea—I just came up from your perennially open bar." Mirelle lunged for the mug, but Dinah held it out of reach. "Put that down. I mean it. I've rented the truck and I'm supposed to have it back by four." Her unruly hair was fluffing about her face, and her eyes blazed with a glint Dinah found unhealthy. Mirelle rubbed her hands together impatiently.

"If I were to come with you—"

"Good. Let's go."

"Hold your horses." Dinah drained the tea, set the mug down, then crossed her arms defensively. "I said *if. If* I were to come with you. Where would we be going with this truck?"

"Suit yourself, then." Mirelle was off, through the door and down the stairs, leaving Dinah to wallow in her curiosity. Which, of course, had been the plan.

Reluctantly, Dinah followed Mirelle down and out into the yard. There, gleaming in the sun, a twenty-four-foot U-Haul graced the parking lot. Mirelle was already behind the wheel, revving the engine, which roared like some caged beast.

"Get in!" she shouted over the noise, leaning to open the passenger side door. "And hurry up!"

Nothing good could come of this.

The glint in Mirelle's eye had grown dangerous. Dinah glanced around for aid, which was not forthcoming.

"Jesus, Mary, and Joseph," she breathed.

She leaped into the already-rolling truck, then slammed the door, locking it, and scrabbling for the safety belt. The truck was a standard, and it bucked and jerked as Mirelle let out the clutch unevenly.

"Do you even know how to drive this thing?" Dinah demanded, gripping the door handle, the dash—anything—to steady herself. At this rate she'd be suffering from whiplash before they hit the roadway.

With one hand Mirelle shoved back her fiery hair; the truck pulled sharply to the left. "I intend to learn through practical hands-on experience."

"Hold onto the wheel!" Dinah hissed. "Or we'll die trying to gain your experience. Where the hell are we going?"

"To my house." The squeal of brakes followed them as they pulled out onto the street; behind them a car horn blared furiously, and someone screamed curses. "Perry should be there by now. I said we'd meet him."

"You gave my line cook the day off?"

The truck lurched as Mirelle changed gears. "I knew you wouldn't mind, not for this. And besides, there's plenty of time before things really get cooking over at the Palace, as you well know."

"Yeah. Thanks. Thanks a whole hell of a lot. Take over the whole operation, why don't you."

"Boy, you really are vile-tempered today." Mirelle released the wheel for a moment, to dig through her purse for her cigarettes. The truck veered left again, straddling the yellow line.

"You're going to get a ticket, and you'll deserve it. And I'm vile tempered because I've been kidnapped and I don't know where we're going and nothing will be ready for dinner at the restaurant this evening because my chef and his wife are axe-murderers and my prep cook has taken the day off, but it doesn't matter anyway, because since the restaurant reviews came out, no one will ever want to go there again anyway. So yeah. I'm vile tempered."

"Calm yourself. You'll give yourself ulcers."

"Not if you give them to me first."

Perry's car, a prehistoric Toyota Camry painted a putrid shade of green, was idling on the side of the road in front of the house as Mirelle wheeled the U-Haul into the driveway, coming dangerously close in the course of her inexpert turn. The truck stopped with a jolt, and Dinah found she had been sucking in her breath, her hands clenched. Mirelle, however, leaped out almost before she had cut the engine. Perry unfolded his lanky frame from his car, and slowly Dinah joined them, leaving the truck door open behind her.

"Got a key?" Perry asked, looking about. "The door's locked. I checked already."

Mirelle plucked a key from the close confines of her hip pocket to hold up triumphantly. As she approached the door, however, her expression darkened.

"What is it?" Dinah hurriedly checked the distance back to the relative safety of the U-Haul.

"That bastard," Mirelle breathed. She held the key out now like some sort of weapon. "That bastard." Her voice ran up the register. "I can't believe he did this."

Their footsteps crunched, and Dinah glanced down at the wood shavings scattered lightly over the walk. The paint about the shiny brass door handle was scarred.

"He's had the lock changed," Mirelle shouted, shaking her head in a frenzy. "He's changed the lock on me in my own house."

"So what do we do now?" Perry left the stoop to peer in through one of the front windows, his hand cupped to the glass.

"We go home." Dinah, with something akin to relief, took a tentative step toward the truck. "Back to my place. Back to work."

Mirelle threw the useless key down, as though throwing down the proverbial gauntlet. "No, damn it, we don't. This is *my* house. He can't do this to me. He can't keep me out of my own God-damned house, and he's an idiot if he thinks a locked door is going to stop me."

"Holstein—" Dinah held out a hand, but Mirelle rushed past, a hurricane. "Mirelle. Wait."

"Give me a rock." Brushing her hair away from her furious cheeks, Mirelle held out an imperious hand. The rock Perry gave her from the border was not to her liking. "A rock, damn you. Not a pebble."

"What are you going to do?" Dinah couldn't keep the trepidation from her voice. She hated to ask, sure she did not want to hear the answer.

"I'll break a window. I'm going in through a window." Mirelle hefted a new rock speculatively before winding up .

Dinah caught her arm. "No. Not yet."

"I'm going in, I tell you." Mirelle tried to wrest her way from Dinah's grasp.

"For Christ's sake, at least see if there's a window open before you start smashing them."

For a long moment Mirelle did not answer. Then, tearing herself away, she dashed around the side of the house. She did not, however, abandon the rock.

"I don't like this," Dinah moaned, looking again, longingly, at the U-Haul. "Perry, I don't like this."

Perry had started after Mirelle. "It's an adventure," he called back over his shoulder. His face was flushed with excitement. Reluctantly Dinah followed.

Mirelle was at the rear of the house, gazing up over the porch roof at the bathroom window. She tossed the stone from palm to palm. The window sash was cracked a few inches. She threw a quick glance at the other two as they drew up beside her, then returned her attention to the window. A flutter of curtain showed at the open sash.

"I told you," Dinah said breathlessly. "It's your house, like you said. There's no point in breaking your own windows if you don't have to."

"One of us has to get up there, then," Perry said. He tilted his head back, running a hand through his thin sandy hair.

"Right." Abruptly Mirelle handed off the stone to Dinah, who dropped it and kicked it aside. Mirelle had rid herself of her shoes. "I'm on my way."

"No," Perry interrupted, catching her by the shoulder before she could shinny up onto the roof. "Look at the window."

"It's open." Mirelle glared at him. "Hands off, Perry. I'm not your type. And I've got to get in to open the doors for you guys."

"It's a half-window. Even opened all the way it's going to be a squeeze for the smallest of us." His pale eyes were on Dinah.

"Oh, no," Dinah protested, holding up her hands. "No."

"Yes." Mirelle dropped her own gaze to Dinah, who stood about five inches shorter than either of them. "Yes, Per, I think you're right there."

"Oh, no," Dinah repeated, backing away. "No, no, no. No way. I'm not going up there, and I'm not breaking into your house." She crossed her arms and squared her chin determinedly. "I won't do it."

"Don't think of it as breaking into the house," Mirelle coaxed. "Think of it as you would if I'd lost my keys. It's just about the same thing."

Again Dinah shook her head. "It's not. If Wally's ugly enough to change the locks on the doors, he's ugly enough to shoot anybody who's idiot enough to come in through the bathroom window. Which I am not going to do, by the way."

"Wally isn't here, Dinah, darling," Mirelle reminded her. "His car's not in the drive."

"Don't be a spoilsport, Di," Perry urged. "Do it for the adventure."

"I don't like heights." Wheeling away from Mirelle's beseeching hands, Dinah took a determined seat on the porch step. "I'm not going up there."

"Please?"

"No."

"Not even for me?"

"Especially not for you. Not for nobody, nowhere, nohow."

They glared at each other. Perry grinned.

"This is a matter of life and death," Mirelle said at last.

Dinah looked up and the sun burned into her eyes; she could not make out the faces of the other two—only their silhouettes, blazing. But she could have sworn there was a certain element of craft, of calculation in the words.

"If you don't go up there through that window—"

"What?" Dinah shot back. "You'll never forgive me? And how long will *never* be this time? Two days? A week? I tell you, I'm not going up there. I don't want to get shot by your husband, and I don't want to fall off that porch roof and break my neck."

Mirelle continued on, unfazed. "Not for me so much as for yourself. Because, you see, if you don't go up there and get into that house, I shall have to move in with you permanently."

Mirelle's voice held an unmistakable note of triumph.

Dinah gazed up along Mirelle's silhouette; she tried to make out any trace of a smirk. She squinted, her temples pounding. "Are you serious?" Her head was filled with an image of her own big apartment above the restaurant, squeezed, constricted by an overflow of Mirelle, her noise, her color, her clothes strewn about, the bathroom sink grimed with dabs of foundation and toothpaste and smears of mascara.

"Because, Dinah—" Mirelle stepped closer, out of the glare of the sun, and batted her eyelashes. "Where will I go? What will I do?"

"You're serious."

"See? You *do* give a damn after all."

"Here." Perry wove his fingers into a basket and held them out before him. "Let me give you a boost up."

Dinah looked dubiously at Perry's hands, then stood to look up at the roof where the sun glinted off the asphalt shingles. The alternative, when she considered it, was far too frightening to bear: to have to spend the rest of her life, however short that might be, cooped up in her apartment with Mirelle. A life, more than likely, dramatically shortened from the strain of it. Shuddering, she scraped off her sneakers and put her foot in Perry's hand. With a grin, he lifted until she could gain purchase on the overhang. She scrabbled, swinging a knee up, throwing her weight forward.

"If I get arrested for breaking and entering," she ground between her teeth, trying not to look down, trying to keep her head from whirling, "I'll kill you all."

"A perfectly good reason why we should not bail you out." Perry laughed. He shaded his eyes with his hands to look up at her, the idiotic grin still playing about his mouth.

"Just go on through the window, will you?" Mirelle waved toward the bathroom with an impatient hand. "Hurry up. We haven't got all day. We're on a schedule."

The black shingles were unpleasantly warm through the denim of Dinah's jeans; and the sun, unhindered by shade trees, blazed down on her. With her eyes closed, she could almost picture herself at the beach, tanning. Of course, with her luck, and her skin, that tan would actually end up being lobster red— until it all peeled off. She kept her eyes closed, too, for the most part, in a desperate effort to keep her head. She did not like heights. She had not been kidding about that. Slowly she inched across the shingles, the rough asphalt scraping against her feet and palms. Thank God it was not a steep pitch—far less steep than the roof on the main house.

"Come on, will you?" Mirelle shouted over a growing background noise.

A wail.

"The cops!" Perry sounded weirdly delighted. "Better hurry in, Di, or they'll bag you for sure."

"Don't be stupid, Perry," Mirelle ordered quickly. "They're not coming here. And it's probably not the cops anyway. A fire truck, probably."

Dinah froze, one hand on the window sash. "You mean, I'm up here on your roof and your house is burning down?"

"They're not coming here," Mirelle insisted. "Hurry up and get in."

"Dive in, Dinah," Perry urged, laughing. "It's the only way to save yourself."

"I hate you all." But having forced the sash up several inches further, Dinah clambered through, head and shoulders first, and fell rather clumsily into the bathtub.

Eleven

THE POLICEMAN WAS kind, though formal. He looked a little bit like Officer Jim Reed from *Adam-12* reruns, Dinah thought, watching him speak into the radio clipped to his shoulder. He had not yet arrested her on suspicion of breaking and entering; the police were still trying to find Wallace Holbein, to determine whether he wished to press charges.

It was probably a good thing she was here, secure in the back seat of the police cruiser; if they let her go, she'd probably have to be arrested almost immediately. This time on murder charges, because if she caught up with Mirelle, that Holstein was as good as dead. Dinah clenched and unclenched her fingers in her lap, imagining wrapping them around Mirelle's elegant white throat and throttling her.

It *had* been the cops, damn it, and they *had* been coming to the house.

When they arrived, Dinah had been the only person they'd found. Perry and Mirelle had vanished.

Dinah had been the only person Officer Jim Reed had detained. For questioning. For suspicion.

Now she sat in the back of the idling squad car, refusing to look out at the small gathering of curious people across the street. It could be worse, she told herself. She could have been summarily arrested, brought to a station for booking and processing. Instead of the relative comfort and privacy of the back of the cruiser, she could be sitting in a line of hard chairs in the squad room, being processed along with all the other people arrested for petty criminal activity, watching her cohorts change in the hours of her wait time. It had only been twenty minutes here in the car, she realized, glancing at her watch; but it felt like years.

She sighed angrily, staring straight ahead at the officers conversing in the driveway, occasionally speaking on their mics, presumably to dispatch. No sign of Wallace yet. Absolutely no sign of Mirelle. Perry's Toyota was long gone.

Perry had better have gotten back to the restaurant to prep, that was all she could say.

No, it wasn't. Rob and Kelly had better not have torn the place apart, either, before she could fire them.

She dropped her head into her hands.

There was a squawk and some static from the car radio. She saw lights blinking from the onboard computer. Dinah glanced away, and saw Mark Burdette, in bike shirt and helmet, pushing a bicycle up the driveway. She hid her face in her hands again.

There was a quick light knock on her window, which she ignored. After a moment, though, she looked up to see Mark in close conversation with Officer Jim Reed and his partner. She wished she could hear, but had to satisfy herself with watching the gestures and pointing.

This was all she needed. Not just her name in the police blotter for the *Gazette*, but now a full story. Maybe on the front page. She'd be famous, but not the way she wanted to be. Notorious. Like Al Capone or someone. All the more reason to kill Mirelle, she thought darkly.

Mark held the bike with one hand, leaning against the crossbar. He'd unbuckled his helmet as he talked with the officers. They seemed to be having a jolly old good time. She added Mark to her hit list.

Then suddenly Jim Reed appeared at the cruiser door and opened it. "Mrs. Galloway? Dispatch hasn't found Mr. Holbein yet—he appears to have gone to a conference and won't be back until evening, his secretary says. But Mrs. Holbein says she's not interested in pressing charges."

Stiffly Dinah slid out of the car and stood. Her jaw was tight. "Oh, that's kind of her."

"She says she would have been here to straighten this misunderstanding out, but that she has an important meeting."

Beyond the officer's shoulder, Mark Burdette broke into laughter.

"You're free to go," Jim Reed said.

"Got your shoes?" Mark wheeled his bike over. "I'll walk you home. Unless you want me to carry you piggy-back?"

She glared, leaning against the squad car to pull her sneakers on.

IT WAS DIFFICULT to know what to say. So she said nothing.

Mark filled the gap.

"B and E. You were looking at B and E." He shook his head. "A one-woman crime ring, you."

She looked away. It was only a mile to the restaurant, to the apartment, to home. She was mortified to have to walk it with Mark Burdette, but she would be damned before she called anyone at Galloway's to come get her.

Mark laughed. "We always manage to meet under such unusual circumstances."

"Always? We've met twice before. Three times, now, total."

"Is that all?" He glanced down at her, then returned his gaze to the Main Street traffic. "But breaking and entering. With your crew, I might have expected assault—but of course, I'd forgotten. That's your friend who attacks people, not you."

Dinah grimaced, kept her eyes on the road ahead. They'd reached the point where the sidewalk through town ended; Mark and his bike took the outside, between her and oncoming traffic.

"And in bare feet, too," he continued. "I never thought you had it in you."

"Yeah, well, it's hard to be a cat burglar with your shoes on, you know?" A suddenly wave of weariness washed over her, and she wished she could just return to the apartment and take a nap. For a very long time.

"And that was the principal's house, wasn't it? Holbein?" He skewed another glance her way. "Your friend's house. Mirelle."

She nodded.

"This is obviously a complicated story. And I came in late." It was an invitation. With a hand he pushed his helmet back on his forehead. "You broke into your friend's house, the friend who shoved a beer down her husband's pants."

"I'm not feeling too friendly toward her right now."

"Come on. I'd love for you to tell me this story."

"I refuse to say anything which might incriminate me." A car whizzed by, apparently unaware that a police car or two lurked just a little bit along the road. "And besides, you work for the newspaper. I'd rather you didn't contribute to my notoriety."

"Okay. I'll think this through out loud, and you just nod when I'm close."

Dinah looked away.

"If you were breaking into Principal Holbein's house, your friend Mirelle would not have been far behind. But where was she?" A pause, which Dinah did not fill. "Was she there? Did she take off? Leave you holding the proverbial bag?"

She sniffed.

"I'll take that as a yes. And if I were you, I'd kill her."

"Oh, believe me, I will. Just as soon as I see her. Just as soon as I can get my hands on her."

Despite her exhaustion and anger, she had to admit that his laugh, deep and full-throated—was attractive. This admission added to her resentment: she had no inclination to join in on the laughter, attractive or otherwise. She bit her lip, grateful that they need only round that last corner, and they'd be at the restaurant.

Where, sadly, there'd be a whole new set of problems.

Twelve

DINAH REMEMBERED VIVIDLY the last time she had been held by a man.

It had been Ross, the morning of his death. If she closed her eyes, Dinah could remember the scent of his skin so clearly she ached; it was a smell beyond the soap he used, the spicy smell which she always breathed in deeply when he pressed her to his chest. She could feel the gentle rasp of his chest hair against her cheek, the strength in his arm and his legs.

Then nothing.

She still woke sometimes in the night and groped for him on the other side of the bed. How he had always been quick to respond when she had done that . . . Dinah hadn't cried herself back to sleep for quite a while, but the feeling of longing had not lessened at all. It was that seventeen years, she supposed, that damned seventeen years they had shared. That feeling of connection. That whatever had happened during the course of her day, Ross would be interested in hearing about it, just as she wanted to know what he thought about who he had seen and what he had done since they'd parted in the morning. Just being able to sit down at the dinner table—or on a hike up Borestone—or at the beach—and talk.

As wonderful as that had been, there had always been the touches. A hand on his shoulder in passing. His fingers in her hair. A companionable bump of hips at the stove. So many things said without a word—but always, that *frisson* of excitement beneath it, that later, later, there would be the lovemaking.

Seventeen years of it.

Then nothing.

And now, on the walk home, despite her anger and exhaustion and relief at the escape, and trepidation about what was to come from the kitchen this evening, she was surprised, and maybe a bit embarrassed, but certainly *very* guilt-ridden, by her physical reaction to Mark. She wished, stupidly, that she had allowed him to carry her home.

Maybe, just maybe, Mirelle had been right.

Thirteen

DINAH SNUCK IN and up the stairs, Mark following closely behind. The dining room was still empty; the only sounds were muted by the kitchen door. No one seemed to notice their entrance; things appeared to be moving along as usual.

She wondered what excuse Perry had made for her absence.

Dinah also wondered if Mirelle were out in the theater with Gahan and his troupe. *She had better not be up in the apartment.*

But the apartment was empty and still. Dinah headed straight toward the bathroom, leaving Mark to shut the door behind them. The dull murmur from the kitchen below was instantly cut off.

"Fix yourself a drink or something," she said over her shoulder. "I'll be right out. Ice in the freezer, if your hand still hurts."

Mark shook his head. "I'm fine. Go ahead."

The shower took five minutes. Dinah dressed hurriedly, fluffing her damp hair with her fingers. When she returned to the living room, Mark was shuffling through her abandoned *New Yorker* magazine, his brow furrowed, a glass in his free hand. He stood as she entered the room, a formality she noted appreciatively, especially from a guy in bike shorts. The look he gave her dress suit, dark and conservative, was appraising.

"You're not going down there, are you?" He looked surprised. "You're not going to work? Not after nearly being arrested and all."

"Of course I'm going to work." She frowned. A stupid question.

He set the glass down on the coffee table. "You're too dedicated to be true. You've just been sprung from police custody. Can't you even take the night off?"

The look she cast him was pitying. He couldn't possibly understand, though he ought to have had a hint after the performance he had witnessed the previous night.

"No," she said. "Look. I really appreciate your walking me home—"

"But mind my own business, right?" He shook his head, then indicated the couch. "Don't get all stuffy on me now. At least sit down for a minute. Come on."

His look was kind, sympathetic, suggesting an understanding of the bone-weariness she had felt creeping up on her all day. How she wanted to sit down.

How she wanted to just say to hell with it for this one night. Why did it always depend upon her to save the restaurant, and the world, after all? Why was she supposed to sacrifice her own comfort and well-being for the sake of her friends, her coworkers, everyone else? *It's so unfair.* Yet she fought against the feeling of malaise, which just added to the general confusion and weariness. *Stop whining,* the other voice inside her ordered. *Ross would go down there.*

"Really, I can't." Despite her protestation, though, she allowed herself to sink into the cushions, shoving aside all thought of Ross. She put her bare feet up on the coffee table, sliding down her spine. A compromise. "Just a minute, mind you. That's all I can spare."

"Can you spare enough time for a drink?"

Suddenly Dinah laughed. "I don't know why, these past couple of days, everyone I know has been trying to give me a drink. Do I look like I'm that bad off? Or, barring that, do I look like I'm a raging alcoholic?"

Mark smiled. He had a nice smile, which did not stop at his mouth, but which involved his entire face, including those brown eyes. "No. To both. You just look stressed out, that's all." He handed her his glass, which contained two fingers of scotch. "I promise I haven't drunk from this yet. You take it. I'll get another. With more ice, for my hand."

She made a move to stand, frowning, but he waved her back down.

"I'll get it." He returned in a moment and sat next to her. He moved to put his feet up beside hers on the coffee table, then paused, reconsidered, and kicked off his bike shoes. Then he leaned back, making himself comfortable. "That's better, isn't it?"

"Make yourself right at home." Though her voice was wry, she didn't mind him. That surprised her.

"It *is* a nice place," he said after a sip of his whisky. He looked up at the high ceiling, its pressed tin fleur-de-lis in shadows. "Have you lived here since you moved back?"

Dinah nodded, then pressed her head against the back of the couch. "Yes. We sold the house in Northampton to buy this house and put the restaurant in."

"You and Ross."

"He died. I told you that, didn't I? A while ago. A heart attack."

Mark's response was on an intake of breath. "Yes. You did. I'm sorry."

Dinah ducked her head. "Thanks." She too took a sip from her glass. She didn't mind the burning in her throat tonight, either. "We wanted something new after seventeen years. But—he never got to enjoy it, really. The restaurant, the apartment, any of it."

"But you keep on."

"It keeps me occupied."

Mark leaned against the arm of the couch, his head on his hand. "How occupied does it keep you? Do you *ever* take a day off?"

"We *are* closed on Mondays." But she lowered her eyes to stare into the amber depths of her drink.

He was watching her intently, and she had the uncomfortable feeling that he was reading her as easily as he'd been reading *The New Yorker* earlier. "So you do nothing then. Nothing having to do with the restaurant. No ordering, no planning the menu, no having things repaired."

When had she last taken a day when she'd done nothing for the business? She quashed the thought. She was keeping it running. For Ross.

"No wonder you're wiped out."

"I'm not wiped out."

Mark continued on as though she hadn't spoken. "It's obvious that you've put a lot of work into this place. It's obvious that you work hard at it. You've got a nice restaurant downstairs, good food, some good help—"

Dinah snorted.

Mark threw her a glance. "Did I say something funny? I was trying to give you a compliment, here." He turned his glass in his long fingers. He had a Band-Aid at the side of his palm.

She looked at him archly. "Like the ones you put in the review?"

If she had expected him to look abashed at having been caught out, she was disappointed. He merely winked at her. "Picked up what I was laying down, did you? I was kind of hoping you would." He looked, in fact, quite pleased with himself.

Dinah drained her Scotch, looking at him over the rim of her glass. "Four stars for entertainment? What the hell was that all about?"

"It *was* entertaining, you have to admit that much." He took her glass. "Another one?"

She turned her wrist over to look at her watch, which she discovered she had forgotten to put on. "No. No, really, I can't. I've got to get downstairs."

Mark stood. "Just a few minutes more, Dinah. The place isn't going to go to hell without you."

She shot him a look as sharp as a razor. "So you say. Last night you saw Rob and Kelly in action—the Addams Family. That was on a good night. My chef and his wife. And where the hell is Mirelle right now? She's prepared to take the whole place down if she has to, if her husband shows up—you've seen her try.

I have to go protect my investment." She stood up slowly and stretched. Her back and shoulders ached.

"Here." Mark set his glass down and stood as well. "Let me." With a hand on her shoulder, he turned her back to him, and kneaded her muscles. Slowly.

"No, really," she protested, but the resistance was token only. She tried to gather her will together, but it was nowhere to be found. "I barely know you. You made fun of my restaurant in a review."

"Teasing," he reassured her, working the muscles at the base of her neck. "Teasing only. And you know me well enough. For God's sake, I just walked you home from your near-arrest."

She dropped her head forward, putty in his hands. Those hands worked down to her shoulder blades. She sighed deeply. He was good. His hands were magic.

What the hell was she doing?

She refused to heed that warning voice in her head. The responsible voice. Its counterpoint, which sounded suspiciously like Mirelle, was far more enticing.

Her knees felt like they could no longer support her weight. She didn't want them to. She felt herself sagging against his hands.

He chuckled. "Come on, then. Sit down."

She did.

Fourteen

THE SIRENS WOKE her.

At first Dinah thought she was dreaming, reliving in her sleep the adventures of the afternoon. Without opening her eyes, she did a mental inventory. She was not on a roof, or in a bathtub, but on the couch, still. Leaning against a chest that rose and fell with calm regularity.

Her eyes shot open and she sat bolt upright.

"Jesus," she exclaimed.

"No. Mark." He smiled, that teasing grin. He had not moved from his place on the couch.

"What in the name of God am I doing?" Dinah ran her hands up into her hair, digging her fingertips into her scalp. "What am I doing?"

Ross, tell me what I'm doing.

"Last I knew, you were sleeping," Mark offered genially.

Sleeping. Against the chest of a man she barely knew. A man who was at least ten years younger than she was, if not more. A man not Ross.

He had not noticed the sirens; perhaps she was being too sensitive? The noise was drawing closer. They were obviously not part of her dreams, either. She glanced around the dim room. "What time is it?"

Mark looked at his watch, strapped around his right wrist. She had not noticed he was left-handed. "Quarter to nine. Relax."

Blue lights strobed across the ceiling. The sirens were now just outside.

There was a police car in the yard of the restaurant.

Dinah dashed for the door and down the stairs.

No one was in the kitchen. She leapt over a puddle of what might have been cream soup, or vomit—no time to check. Shoving her way through the swinging doors into the main dining room, she found that empty as well. A small knot of people was clustered in the doorway to the west room; a policeman—oh, God, Officer Jim Reed—held them back.

She couldn't see past them.

"Let me through," she said sharply. "I'm the owner, damn it. Let me through."

Somehow she managed to weave her way past bodies and under arms, dodging the grasp of the policeman when he tried to stop her.

Perry, one eye nearly swollen shut and a trickle of blood running away from his lower lip, was planted firmly on Rob's prone but still struggling form. Next to the fireplace, Kelly leaned against the wall, her arms wrapped around her. She was whimpering. In front of her, Mirelle towered, holding the cast iron fireplace poker.

"Put the poker down, Miss," the second officer instructed sternly. He held both hands out before him, ostensibly a calming gesture.

"Get him out of here first," Mirelle ordered, gesturing toward Rob, who made a sudden move that nearly unseated Perry.

"Let me up, damn it," Rob snarled.

"Take a chill pill, Big Man." Perry elbowed him in the back of the head.

"What the hell—?" Dinah couldn't finish.

Kelly let out a long wail, tightening her arms around her chest. She made herself smaller against the wall.

"Dinah!" Perry's bruised face lightened at the sight of her. Other than the blood, it might just have been another adventure for him.

There was general hubbub as everyone spoke at once. Dinah felt a hand on her shoulder: Mark. When she turned back, Mirelle was wrestling with the policeman over possession of the fireplace poker. Jim Reed pulled Perry off Rob, who scrambled to his feet and lunged toward his wife; the officer pinned him to the bar with a firm hand to the chest.

"Don't move, buddy," the officer ordered. "Don't you even move."

Over it all, Kelly's voice rose in a pitch, forming barely distinguishable words. All Dinah made out was "damn you," and "bastard."

"Coming through," someone shouted from the door. An ambulance attendant pushed past, two others following with a stretcher. Only when they surrounded Kelly did Mirelle surrender the poker to the policeman, bestowing upon him her most beatific smile.

"Time to move out, folks," the second policeman shouted. The clump of gaping people broke up slowly, reluctantly. Out of the corner of her eye, Dinah saw Gillian, the ever-efficient, slipping dinner checks into unsuspecting hands.

After a few moments, the attendants had Kelly strapped onto the stretcher, her small form mummified with blankets. As they wheeled her past, Dinah gestured toward her. "Mark, this is Kelly." Then she took a step nearer to Rob, still pinned against the bar by the policeman's hand. "And you remember Rob. Rob, you're fired."

PART III

Main Course

Fifteen

"SO WHAT HAPPENED?"

The place cleared of customers, the remaining staff huddled at the bar. Everyone looked pale and pinched; most grasped the drinks Dirk had doled out, at Dinah's suggestion, like lifelines. Another open bar. This, if nothing else, would bankrupt her. Dirk, she noted, had taken special care over Gillian's drink, and now stood beside her, a protective giant.

Dinah swung herself up onto a bar stool.

"It was after she came back—"

"I didn't see a thing until they came charging out of the kitchen—"

"What a flaming bastard—"

Dinah held up her hands. "One at a time. What happened? She came back? Kelly? Where had she gone?"

The other three waitresses had taken themselves off to a booth nearby, where they put their dark heads together to comment in an undertone on the proceedings. Dirk looked to Perry, who flushed and took over the story.

"Well, the reason I called the police—"

"You called the police, Perry. You." It was all too difficult to take in. "You, who have to come to me with everything, every question, every concern. You were the one who called the police."

Mirelle sucked in an impatient breath, then sucked down a large proportion of her campari with lime. "He just said that, Dinah. Listen. Do you want to hear the story or not? If you do, then just shut up."

All gazes on her now, with various stages of impatience, accusation, and curiosity.

"All right, all right." Dinah subsided onto her stool, crossing her arms before her; but then she shot out a hand to grab the drink nearest her. Eying them all challengingly over the rim, she took a long slurpy sip before setting the glass down again with a splash. "Just tell me the entire sordid story. Do not leave out a single detail. Only do me the favor of starting at the beginning this time, instead of at the end."

Perry cleared his throat. "They were sniping at each other when I got in this afternoon." He paused, glancing at Dinah nervously.

After he ran off and left me to be arrested. Dinah said nothing, merely grasped her elbows to keep from lunging at him.

"They kept it up. He'd say something, she'd say something. Finally she broke into tears and locked herself in the bathroom. When she came back, she told him she only did it to be a conscientious employee—that if it wasn't for her job, she'd have walked out then and that would be the end. A few minutes later she went into the walk-in for something for the waitress station, and Rob followed her in." Perry lowered his head. "I didn't realize what was going on until Kelly staggered back out, screaming."

She had been crying, leaning against the wall.

Perry licked his lips. "As soon as she said the word *hit*, I dialed 911. I didn't know where you were, Dinah, and I was scared. Really scared. Rob came out after her, and he was smiling, carrying on like nothing had happened inside the walk-in. He walked right past Kelly like he owned her or something. Never even acknowledged that she was crying. He just picked up a knife, still smiling, and started boning a duck. Just like that. So I called the cops on my cell phone." Perry recited his story flatly, without emotion, as though he had rehearsed it many times in his mind. His eyes were still on Dinah. "When I did that, Rob grabbed it away from me and threw it into the sink. Then he slammed my head against the wall." That explained the bloody lip and the black eye, anyway. "My cell phone's ruined."

Dinah felt sick.

"I didn't know where you'd gone," Perry continued. "I didn't know if you'd even got back. I figured you couldn't be around anywhere, since you didn't come out to see what the noise was all about."

Dinah pressed her hands to her eyes. She felt tears well up, and she tried to hold them off. All the noise. Oh, God. To think she'd been up there all the time, upstairs, dozing away against the bicycle-shirted chest of Mark Burdette, instead of minding the restaurant like she was supposed to do. Instead of protecting Kelly, as she should have done. Ross would have been down here. Ross would have been minding their business. He would not have failed in his duty—to everyone.

"I'm sorry," she whispered.

She didn't think anyone heard.

"And that's where you came in. After he'd chased her into the dining room, and I'd chased him, and the police showed up."

"I'm sorry," she whispered again. No one else said anything.

Sixteen

MIRELLE WAS PROWLING the living room when Dinah returned from a series of early meetings with Perry, the accountant, and the theater's business manager.

"No," Dinah said, crossing to the couch and throwing herself down. "I've just put out ads for a new chef, and I don't have any idea how we're going to manage tonight or tomorrow or the next day. I've called the hospital, and Kelly's fine, and she'll be released later, and she doesn't want to press charges against Rob, and I don't know what to do about her, either. I'm worn out already and this day has barely begun for me. So no."

Mirelle whirled. Having, apparently, gained access at last to her own closet, today she was wearing a skintight pair of orange leather pants and a matching orange paisley top of some flowing material that crisscrossed between her breasts. A wide orange band held her hair away from her face. She tossed aside the script she had been examining.

"No?"

"No. Whatever it is you want from me right now, the answer is no."

"I haven't asked you for anything." A hand splayed across her chest, tipped with blaze orange nails, Mirelle wore a monumentally innocent expression.

"Yet."

Dinah picked up the much abused issue of *The New Yorker*, opened it to a random page, and held it before her face. A clear dismissal. Or so she thought. But Mirelle was never dismissed that easily. Dinah stared at an advertisement along the side of the page, the picture showing a sculpture that might have be Michelangelo's *Pieta*. Or someone's Pieta. She could never tell one from the other of them. *Philistine.* She bet Mark Burdette could. She didn't want to think about him right now. There was too much to worry about, and she had discovered last night what a distraction he was, a distraction when she so obviously could least afford it.

"What do you mean, *yet?*" Mirelle demanded, her voice sulky. "Why do you think I always want something from you? Perhaps I've just stopped by to see how you are. You did have rather an eventful day yesterday." She raised her fine eyebrows. "And an eventful evening, as well."

"I'm fine. Thanks for your concern." Suddenly she tossed the magazine aside on the couch. "I notice you didn't feel all that much concern yesterday afternoon when the police were nearly cuffing me for breaking and entering your house, and tossing me into the back of the paddy wagon."

"Panic, that's all. Just panic. I saw the police, and I thought Wallace must have called them on me." Mirelle clasped her hands together before her, widening her beautiful blue eyes. "Oh, Dinah, you don't know how he would have *loved* to watch me be manhandled by a bunch of pigs into a squad car."

"But Wally wasn't home. Wally was at a conference."

"I didn't know about the conference then, did I?" Mirelle fluttered the eyelashes, the ingénue in a drama of her own devising. An ingénue in blaze orange. "I'm sorry, Dinah. I'm so sorry for putting you through that. I—never even thought."

You never do.

Then Mirelle straightened, twirling out as in a ballet, her apologetic mien flying away as quickly as it had come. "But you have to admit that I more than made up for my cowardice with that courageous defense of Kelly last night, when Rob came after her." She held her long-fingered hands in the air before her, as though once again brandishing the fireplace poker. "I saved her life, I'm willing to bet. That Rob wouldn't have dared touch her with me standing guard."

"*That Rob,*" Dinah countered, "couldn't touch her again anyway, since Perry had him tackled and pinned to the ground."

"Well, there was that," Mirelle conceded. "But *that Rob* was on a tear, Dinah. You should have seen him! They came flying out of the kitchen, absolutely screaming at each other. Perry was trying to break it up—I'd just come in from the theater meeting with Gahan—I don't know where he got to—"

"He heard the commotion and ran for cover," Dinah suggested wryly. "He has a low tolerance for potential danger."

Mirelle was not to be stopped in her recitation. "Anyway, they charged straight into the west room, all yelling, and he lunged at her—that's when I stepped in."

"And when Perry jumped him."

"And when Perry jumped him," Mirelle agreed, without breaking stride. "Leaped right on him, did our Perry. I never would have thought him capable of such a thing. I never thought Rob was his type. Then, of course, the police showed up."

"Right when I did."

"They seemed to be quite prompt about things yesterday, all told. I feel quite secure in our level of police protection here in town." Mirelle nodded approvingly. "Well, you know the rest, because you were there." After a moment's hesitation, her expression grew crafty. "You were there. Along with that handsome restaurant critic boy." Again, she raised the eyebrows expectantly. "He looked quite good in those bicycle shorts."

Dinah pressed her lips together tightly.

"So. I take it he isn't married. Or otherwise taken. The field is wide open for you."

Dinah crossed her arms and glared.

Mirelle plumped herself down on the couch and grabbed a pillow. "Come on. Tell me. I'm your best and most beloved friend. Ever since we were tiny tots in school. And I've only got your best interests at heart. Where'd you pick him up yesterday?"

"I didn't. He picked me up." *Picked me up and walked me right through town with his bike.* "Outside your house. Where your antics so unkindly left me in a cruiser, I might add."

"Oh, are we back to this again?" Mirelle looked hurt. "I've apologized already. Do I have to apologize for the rest of my natural life?"

"Yes."

Mirelle pouted, throwing herself back against the couch cushions. She smote her breast theatrically. "*Mea culpa*, then, all right? *Mea culpa, mea culpa, mea culpa.*" She cast her eyes heavenward. "Forgive me, Dinah, for I have sinned."

"Oh, go to hell." Despite herself, Dinah felt a wry grin tug at the corner of her mouth. It was so difficult to remain angry with Mirelle for long, no matter how hard she tried to hold a grudge. She pictured her friend again, standing guard over Kelly with a fireplace poker. Mirelle would have used it, too.

Mirelle sprang to her feet. "Can't. Not today, anyway. I've got another errand to run, and I've got to get it done by two-thirty—that's when I promised I'd pick Kelly up at Midland. She called me this morning. Anyway, you want to come with me on my errand? It'll take your mind off things."

The bells and sirens went off in Dinah's head, the enormous red warning signals popping up everywhere. *Don't do it don't do it don't do it.*

Mirelle, as though sensing her hesitation, turned a brilliant smile, no doubt meant to be reassuring, on her. It was like a heat lamp. "I promise. There will be no police involved. I will not abandon you. You will be perfectly safe."

"This doesn't sound like a mere errand to me," Dinah said warily. "It doesn't sound like we're just going to the post office for a book of stamps."

Mirelle frowned. "The post office." She tapped an orange nail against her lower lip. "Now, that might not be a bad idea at all."

THE HOLBEIN HOUSE smelled of unpleasantly sweet furniture polish, with undernotes of stale perfume. *Eau de* fruit salad.

A disgusted look on her face, Mirelle moved from room to room, throwing open the windows.

"It smells of her, doesn't it?" she said, her mouth in a *moue* of distaste. "He had her here night before last, I know he did."

It did, now that Dinah thought back, smell rather like the perfume Alix Mailloux had been wearing the other night in the restaurant. Still, it was beyond the realm of her imagining that Wallace would have brought that woman back to this house after the sideshow with his wife at Galloway's. Then again, he'd had a locksmith change all the locks before he took off for his principals' conference. The same confused locksmith, apparently, that Mirelle had hired yesterday afternoon to come back and change all the locks once again.

Mirelle now breezed through the sun room toward the kitchen. "Shut the door," she instructed Perry. "Anything we take can go right out the front door."

Dinah pulled up. "We're taking stuff out?"

Mirelle looked pityingly upon her obvious stupidity. "Of course. That's why we still have the truck. I'm glad the U-Haul people let me keep it for one more day. I put it on Wallace's charge card."

Somewhere down the hall Perry was bumping and banging about.

"Do you mean to tell me that all this was a trick? That I climbed up onto that roof yesterday, and got myself arrested, so you wouldn't have to live with me forever—only so we could move *you out*?"

This time Mirelle did not even deign to look at her. "Really. Sometimes I think you must be braindead. *I'm* not moving out. *Wallace* is. Only he doesn't know it yet." She paused and sniffed at the sickly sweetish air, her face assuming a dangerous look. "And, I gather, old Alix doesn't, either." She spun about and hurried down the hall after Perry. "I'll start upstairs with his clothes and stuff. By God, if that woman thinks for a minute she's going to move into my house—it's bad enough that she's sleeping with my husband, but I draw the line at my house."

Dinah looked around the kitchen, with its zany faux-fifties decor, then shrugged and turned to follow. A tap at the door stopped her. *Deja vu.* Something told her it was the police even before Mirelle sailed by to do her hostess duties. Officer Jim Reed and his partner stood on the porch. A nightmare relived. Dinah dropped onto the bottom stair, the first available seat, and held out her wrists for the cuffs. She wondered if she could find Mark's number in her phone.

"Mrs. Holbein?" The second policeman shuffled his feet, his hands curled at his sides. "We saw the truck. We thought we'd check to make sure everything was all right." He leaned back, pointed toward the foundation. "You've got a broken cellar window there, by the way—an invitation to housebreakers."

Dinah shrank back against the wall, but in the face of Mirelle's brilliance, it was doubtful the officers could see her anyway. Mirelle was laughing up into the face of the senior officer, her orange-tipped fingers touching her fiery hair lightly.

"Oh, everything is fine," she cooed, a fluttery sound like doves. "I'm truly grateful, too, that we have policeman like yourselves to watch out for our property when we're not able to." She peered down at the foundation, where the officer was pointing, then shrugged. "I'll have my young friend Perry fix that later." She stood back away from the door, beckoning them inside. "Can I give you a cup of coffee, or anything?"

Dinah wondered about that slight pause before the word *anything*. Officer Jim Reed was pretty good looking, in a seventies kind of way.

They shook their heads, neither of them able to find words. With Mirelle cranked up to full volume like this, it was no wonder that Perry and Dinah had the same effect on the officers as so much raw hamburger. Dinah still made herself as small as possible at the foot of the hall staircase, watching the policemen's faces as they backed out into the dooryard. Mirelle was a vampire, bleeding those poor guys out of every reaction they had.

Later, Dinah would curse her friend and wonder why, instead of a cup of coffee, Mirelle had not offered the officers this one-of-a-kind opportunity to help strip the house of every trace of Wallace: why Mirelle had not suggested that the policemen help them hoist the desk and file cabinets out of Wallace's study and into the back of the U-Haul, why she had not let them trundle his clothing out of the bedroom closet. Or maybe Dinah was just feeling old, reeling from the crack of furniture against her shins one time too many, the pinch of her fingers between the reclining chair and a doorframe. The trips up and down the stairs winded her, until she finally took Mirelle's advice and threw Wallace's stuff over the banister into a huge pile in the hallway below.

"Don't forget his bureau," Mirelle called over her shoulder as she disappeared into the study once again.

"I'm not touching his underwear," Dinah retorted. "You're still the wife here, don't forget."

THE MOST INTERESTING part of all was pulling up in front of the school in the big orange U-Haul—a truck which was as much a part of Mirelle's fashion statement as the orange leather pants. For her part, Mirelle still drove the truck wildly, wielding the U-Haul as if it were a club to beat away all other comers. By the time she braked to a stop at the top of the circular driveway, it was closing on twelve-fifteen; half-day, Mirelle had said, and most of the students had already left. There were only a few straggling teachers, doing a post-mortem of the day at the front door, when Mirelle, Perry, and Dinah burst out to unload the truck.

"It's going to be tough getting some of this through those doors," Dinah said warily. "The easy chair, and maybe that desk."

"We're not going in." With an evil grin, Mirelle slid her Ray-bans up along the bridge of her nose. Going incognito. "We'll just be leaving it here, on the grass. He can decide on his own decorating plan." She nodded to the teachers, some of whom now stood agape in the doorway; a few more had come to join them and watch the sideshow.

Perry seemed to be enjoying himself a great deal; and Mirelle's vengeful cheerfulness was beyond measure. Still, as Dinah bent to hand down one of the file cabinet drawers, she could not help but feel nervous. None of the teachers had moved. She recognized a couple of them from the restaurant the other night, but whether they were some of the ones who had applauded Mirelle's use of the bottle of Dos Equis, she couldn't tell.

"Just throw it in a pile," Mirelle sang out, dropping a lamp haphazardly into the seat of the reclining chair. "He can sort it all out when he has a minute."

"What if he comes?" Dinah asked nervously. "You said he was back from the conference today." She tossed Perry a pair of black dress shoes, one at a time; he in turn flung them onto the pile. "Hurry up. We've got to get back to work."

Mirelle's laugh was pure spite. "Let him come. What's he going to do, cause a scene?" She threw an armload of books onto the grass. "You forget. I cause the scenes around here. He only gets to be the butt of them."

"Couldn't we just drop a match?" Perry was breathing heavily as he and Dinah edged the desk off the truck. "I still think a bonfire would be far more dramatic. Not to mention effective."

Mirelle smiled at him patiently. "Oh, no, my charming young person. That might frighten him. Or worse yet, it might somehow give him the preposterous idea that he had angered me enough to make me lose control of my temper." Her smile flattened into a snarl, her lips pulling away to bare her teeth.

"And besides," Dinah panted, lowering her end of the desk onto the grass. "We don't have a fire permit."

"Damn," Perry whined. "I knew we should have asked those policemen for one more thing."

"Organization," Dinah murmured. "That's the key."

The knot of teachers standing at the door had grown into a full-fledged crowd; she could hear their constant undertone, but none made a move to lend a hand.

"Surely it must be obvious to them what you're up to," she suggested to Mirelle.

Mirelle only shrugged, dumping the contents of her husband's underwear drawer onto the growing mound. "You can't blame them, really. In a way, we are littering. Defacing school property. They could get into trouble."

As no doubt Mirelle would.

"They're afraid of Wally, you mean," Dinah said. She didn't doubt for a moment that Mirelle knew exactly what she was getting into. "Wonderful Wally." Her own voice dripped with scorn.

"That's the guy." The malicious grin still curled Mirelle's lips as she pulled the rolling door closed on the now-empty belly of the truck. "He's going to be some ticked off about this, and anyone who's within firing range is going to get blown up." With a casual wave of the hand, she indicated the doorway where the crowd of onlookers had suddenly dispersed, though not too far. "You see?"

Dinah did see. Wallace Holbein's stubby figure was stumbling up the hallway; his silhouette was unmistakable behind the wall of windows. His fists were flailing at the air, and with every other step, his head swiveled to look out into the yard. The scene reminded Dinah of an overacted silent movie. She dashed for the cab of the truck. The teachers had fled from the doorway.

Now even Perry's nerve failed him. He scrambled up onto the high seat of the U-Haul, his long blonde ponytail swinging. "Come on, Mirelle, let's get the hell out of Dodge."

Mirelle's answering laughter was tinged with hysteria. "As much as I want to see his face, up close and personal, I think you've probably got a good idea going there, Per." She pirouetted lightly at the bumper, waving to anyone left to see, before hefting herself up behind the wheel. "Goodbye," she called to her husband as she slammed the door. "I'll see you in court."

The revving engine drowned out Wallace's shouted reply. As the U-Haul jerked away from the curb, Dinah could make out his receding figure in the passenger side mirror, fists waving, eyes bulging in shock and disbelief.

Seventeen

"NOW," MIRELLE SAID, dropping Dinah and Perry off in the driveway of Galloway's, where the sign out front creaked in the breeze, "I must go to the hospital."

Dinah jerked her head up. "Whatever for?" To her, all hospitals still meant the ER, and death.

"To pick up Kelly, of course. I already told you. You know they kept her overnight for observation." Mirelle fluttered her fingers at them, then bucked the truck out into the road.

Dinah turned to Perry, frowning. "In a U-Haul?"

Perry shrugged. "What can you do? Probably all the limousines were taken." He shaded his eyes with his hands and looked back at the restaurant. "Well, come on, then. You and I have to get ready for tonight. Since we're down one in the kitchen. Since you fired Rob."

"Crap." She kicked at the gravel with the toe of her shoe. "But it's not just us. There's Alan and Lindsay and Paul and the dishwasher."

Perry trotted toward the kitchen door. "Yes, but one or the other of us—that's you or me, Dinah—is going to have to be the head chef tonight. And for as long as it takes to get us another." He skidded to a stop, drawing a quarter from his pocket. "You want to flip for it?"

She shoved past him. "Let's make it a labor-cooperative kitchen. Nobody's in charge. We're all equal."

"Sounds like chaos to me," Perry answered cheerfully. "Let's do it."

Inside, however, there was already a bustle of activity. Alan, Paul, Lindsay, and Kevin the dishwasher were already hard at it, under the hoarse direction of Rob Carvey. Wearing whites which looked as though he'd slept in them, his eyes bloodshot and red-rimmed, he was slicing again. Every time Dinah had spoken to him in the past several days, he had been cutting something up. Meat, fish, potatoes, tomatoes. Whatever. He was a regular Mac the Knife.

Dinah halted, staring at the gleaming blade sliding through the veal on the butcher block before him. She wasn't sure if the hiss she heard with each pass was the knife, or her own shocked breath escaping her throat. Perry screeched to a halt behind her, his own breath hot on the back of her neck.

"Dinah," Rob drawled, straightening. He did not set the knife down.

The others in the kitchen looked nervous.

A thin smile playing over Rob's lips. "We need to talk about tonight's veal special. We need to discuss saucing it."

For one appalled moment she could not speak. Then she rasped out, in a voice that couldn't possibly have been her own, "What the hell are you doing here?"

"Working. What do you think I'm doing?" There was a hardness in him, a defiance which was ugly and frightening.

Dinah could not swallow her revulsion. She took a step backward. Recoiling. A mistake, she realized immediately; Rob's smile grew slimier. He read her reaction as fear; she saw satisfaction in his flat eyes.

"I fired you, Rob," she reminded him grimly. "Last night. So get out."

No one moved. The kitchen help carefully did not look at either of them. The industrial dishwasher hummed in the background.

Rob cut off a hunk of veal and slapped it aside. "Dinah, I can't deal with last night right now. I have dinner to get on here, or don't you remember?" He brought the knife back down on the meat before him. There was blood smeared across the front of his tunic. "Or maybe you've been too concerned with *other* things to worry about the restaurant lately."

Evade and deflect. She knew this through experience, especially with him. When people talked like this, it was a diversion, a stall tactic. She wouldn't fall for it, no matter how badly she wanted to get into a screaming match with him. No matter how much she wanted to point out that last night had been the first night since they'd opened that she hadn't been in the restaurant from open to close, until the last meal had been served, and beyond. No matter. Rob was trying to get to her, gaslight her, make her out to be the unreasonable one. She wouldn't let him.

She had to stick to her guns. She looked at the flashing knife blade again and wished she actually had a gun. If nothing else, it would give her more confidence to do what had to be done.

"I want you out. Now." She squared her shoulders and raised her chin. "Out of my restaurant. Off my property. You're fired."

Rob looked at her for a long moment. His dark eyes were shadowed and his brow glistened beneath his thinning hair, with the sweat of exertion and the warm afternoon. At first he did not speak. Slowly he set the knife down, then went to the sink to sluice the blood from his hands. At last he turned to face her.

"Dinah, can we talk about this?" He threw a meaningful glance toward the others. "Without an audience?"

"There's nothing to talk about," she said. Her lips felt stiff. She balled her hands into fists to prevent their shaking.

Now Rob held open the swinging pass door into the dining room. "Please, Dinah. Just for a moment."

Against her better judgment, she took a step forward, determined not to let him intimidate her. Perry laid a hand on her arm.

"Don't," he breathed. Concern stamped his round face. "Dinah, *don't*."

She steeled her spine, throwing Perry a reassuring smile. "Take care of the kitchen for me, will you, Perry? I'll be right back. After I throw this asshole out."

She was careful to hold herself away from Rob as she passed by him and into the dining room. In the early afternoon, the wood gleamed, the place settings sparkled dimly. It was a nice room, a nice restaurant, she reminded herself, drawing strength from it; she had done a good job in the time since Ross's death. She moved through the main dining room to the door of the west room to look inside. It would remain a nice restaurant, which meant that Rob would go. The light over the bar glittered off the optics, casting shattered diamonds over the floor and tables. She was doing the right thing.

"You're fired, Rob," she repeated, taking a deep breath.

"Why?"

Her shoulder blades ached with the strain of holding her back straight and her head high. Dinah turned, and he was right there. She had not heard his footsteps. He was so close she could see the amber flecks in his eyes. She could smell his breath, hot and sour. She took a step back. He smiled, and took a step toward her.

"You know why." She had to keep her voice steady. She had to avoid babbling. "I don't care if she is your wife. I won't tolerate your abusiveness. You can't hit her and think I'd just let it pass."

His smile was slow, too, his lips widening before opening slightly to reveal teeth much like a predator's. "That's what they told you."

Dinah nodded grimly.

"And if I told you I didn't hit her?"

"Get out."

"Dinah, Dinah, Dinah." Her name in his mouth was unpleasant. "You're making a big mistake."

"No mistake." She licked her lips.

"You don't want to do this, Dinah," he said slowly, his voice nearly a purr. He was still smiling; he had to know how hard it was for her to deal with him while he grinned like that. "What would you do without me, Dinah, dearest? Who would run your kitchen?"

She didn't know, and wouldn't, until someone answered the ads. At this point, she didn't care, either. She had to get him out of the restaurant. It was imperative. The back of her neck was prickling, and she felt sweat break out on her forehead. She had to get him out of here.

"I've made this place for you, and you know it." He was watching her, waiting for his words to sink in, waiting for her to come to the realization that without him she was lost, without him she was nothing. She certainly couldn't do the cooking, not all of it; she was untrained, she didn't know the first thing about running a kitchen like Galloway's—

Hold your ground. He's trying to frighten you.

"You've been a great help over the past year." She swallowed. "But that doesn't make your behavior any more acceptable."

His face took on a supplicating look, though his eyes remained hard. "It was a one-time thing, Dinah." He must have registered her tiny shake of disbelief, for he laughed, a little self-deprecating sound. He took another step closer. "Oh, I know Kelly and I have had some difficulties lately, but every marriage goes through this sort of thing every once in a while. Ours were just little spats."

"A little spat that put your wife in the hospital," Dinah reminded him.

He shrugged, almost helplessly. "It just got a little out of control last night, that's all. It's never happened before. And I promise you, Dinah—it will never happen again." He put a hand out to her. "I promise you that."

She looked down at his hand, and instinctively thrust hers behind her back. The idea of touching him was repulsive.

"No, Rob," she said. She fell back another step. "No. Last night—that was too much. You behaving like that to Kelly. In my restaurant. In my dining room."

Just like that, the supplicating look was gone, wiped clean from his face as though with a washcloth. In its place appeared an expression of anger and contempt. "Oh, that's it, then isn't it? It's all about how things look. Here. In *your restaurant*. In *your dining room*. Everything has to be smooth, under your control. We all have to make nice for you, isn't that what it's all about?" He sneered. "And for that punk of a *restaurant critic*, the one you're upstairs dropping your panties for while we're all down here slaving for you."

Dinah took a step away from his inexorable approach and found her back pressed to the bar. Rob stepped closer, one hand gripping the wood on either side of her. He was taller by several inches, and he leaned his face in to hers, his voice low.

"Or maybe it's just that I treated *Kelly* that way that's got you all upset, eh, Dinah?"

She shouldn't have come in here with him alone. She should have listened to Perry. The blood was pounding in her ears.

His flat eyes were darkening. Dinah turned her head to the side to avoid his breath; he brought up a hand to take her chin between his thumb and forefinger, tightly, painfully. "Maybe you want me to treat *you* that way. Maybe that's it. Maybe you're like Kelly, and you like things a little rough."

He had her pinned to the bar, his face close to hers.

Dinah kicked upward as hard as she could, ramming her knee into Rob's groin.

He let out a curse and stumbled backward, doubling up and clutching himself. "You bitch," he shouted, but that was all he could get out before she kneed him again, this time in the face. His arms flew up as he fell, crashing into a table, taking the tablecloth and place settings down with him. The tinkling of breaking glass seemed to go on and on.

"Dinah!"

Mark burst through the porch door.

Nice timing.

"Are you all right?" he demanded.

She stepped over the tangle that was Rob and the tablecloth. "We'll have to get someone to clean up the mess." Then she sighed, concentrating on walking a straight line, with her suddenly weak knees. "I hope to God next time I fire someone, he stays fired."

Behind her, Rob was struggling to his knees. "You *bitch*," he shouted again, but more weakly this time. Blood ran down his face, to mingle with the stains already on his tunic.

Mark brushed past her to grab Rob by his collar and drag him to his feet. Rob scuffled weakly as Mark hauled him to the porch door and shoved him outside, where he tumbled down the steps and into the gravel drive.

"You have twenty minutes," Mark ground out, "to get your stuff out of that apartment and get the hell out of here."

"Or what?" Rob demanded from his knees, wiping a hand across his bloody face.

"Or I'll let Dinah beat the crap out of you some more."

Eighteen

IMMEDIATELY AFTER MARK had sent her toward the stairs for a wash and change ("I'll keep an eye on things here—you go ahead"), the shrill peal of the landline demanded her attention. Dinah pelted up the steps to catch it before the caller hung up. Or before the answering machine could kick in. She hated the sound of her own recorded voice, nasal and unfamiliar. The thought of someone else listening to the recorded message and grimacing was more than she could bear right now.

Why the hell was she even worrying about this?

So she wouldn't have to worry about those other things.

Breathless, and with a pain shooting down her legs, she stumbled to the table and grabbed up the receiver. The adrenaline was making her jittery.

"Took your own sweet time," Mirelle complained.

"If I'd known it was you, I would have taken forever."

"Don't kid yourself. You know you love me."

"Ours is the original love-hate relationship." Letting out a little cough from her tight chest, Dinah slumped into her usual corner of the couch to rub her thighs with her free hand. A bruise was starting on her knee. She was still shaky. She had to calm down. "Did you get Kelly from the hospital all right?"

"Oh, yes, and she's going to stay here at the house for a day or two."

A frightening concept, the two of them together.

"But that's not why I called." Mirelle giggled. *Giggled?*

"So what do you want?"

"I want you to give up smoking and get some exercise," Mirelle said. "No, wait. That's me."

"Yeah right." *Had she been drinking already?* "I repeat. What do you want?" Maybe a drink was just the thing.

"Unfriendly this evening, aren't we? Too much excitement for you in one day?"

If you call being terrorized by Rob Carvey too much excitement.

Dinah didn't say it. Her discomfort was slowly subsiding, and, distracted, she found herself considering the benefits of more exercise. Kickboxing, maybe. Or running downtown and shouting at Mirelle a few times. Wow, but she was feeling violent all of a sudden. She blamed the Carveys.

"I was downstairs. Getting things straight for tonight."

"And you ran for the phone. I'm touched."

"In the words of George Bernard Shaw, more or less, I'd like to touch you with a broomstick."

"And that's what I'm calling about." Mirelle's voice suddenly rose by what seemed a few thousand decibels.

"George Bernard Shaw?"

"No, you idiot. Your best buddy. Gahan."

A new set of nightmares arose behind Dinah's closed eyes. Mirelle and Gahan going at it now. Finally they must have reached the outer limits of their tolerance of one another, and were preparing for war.

"He's not my best buddy."

Mirelle laughed gleefully. "Well, he's about to be mine."

Far worse than she thought. Far worse. "Oh, God, Mirelle. No. Don't sleep with him. Please don't do it. Just the thought is too much for me to bear."

"Jealous?"

"Nauseated."

Again Mirelle laughed. "Not to worry. I'm not sleeping with him." She paused for a fraction of a moment, just long enough for Dinah to fill in the word *yet*. It was always *yet* with Mirelle. "It's even better than that."

Better than sleeping with Gahan Godfrey. Hmm. Let's see. Dinah began counting up the things she knew were better than sleeping with Gahan Godfrey, but ran out of fingers and toes. "Okay. I give up."

"I got a part."

A part.

Mirelle wasn't finished. Her voice continued to rise. "I got a part. I got a part. I got a part!"

Dinah held the receiver away from her ear. "I'm sorry. I didn't quite make that out. Did you say you got a part?"

"Screw you. I did. Gahan Godfrey cast me in one of the shows." Again the laughter. When Dinah closed her eyes this time, she could picture Mirelle doing a jig of sheer glee over in her own living room.

"Riverdance?"

"Better. *Blithe Spirit.* Isn't this great?"

Blithe Spirit. Just one of Dinah's favorite plays. The one she had been overjoyed to convince Gahan to do. Now with Mirelle in it. She covered her eyes with her free hand. Dinah knew the answer to her question before she even bothered to ask. "Which part?"

"Elvira, of course."

Of course. "The bad-tempered first wife, I see."

Mirelle snorted. "I prefer to think of her as the mischievous, slighted first wife, thank you."

"Ah." Dinah knew now, with all her heart, that hiring Gahan had been a mistake. Possibly right up there with hiring Rob and Kelly, and then keeping them on. She shuddered. Things would be so much easier if only she had a brain. She just hoped Mark Burdette wasn't the theater critic, too.

THE SECOND TIME the phone rang, Dinah was just emerging from the shower. She was slowly returning to feeling vaguely human, though her knee was beginning to hurt where the bruise was blooming. Struggling into her robe, she took her time getting out to the living room to answer. Probably Mirelle had forgotten some other juicy tidbit she could use to ruin the rest of the evening— such as having also been cast as Eliza Doolittle and Lady Macbeth. Toweling her hair, Dinah hoped Mirelle would give up and bother someone else. Except there never was anyone else for Mirelle to bother, it seemed. Therein lay the problem.

Her hand hovered, and the phone pealed again. Making a face, Dinah picked up. "What the hell do you want this time?"

"Dinah?"

At first she didn't recognized the voice.

"Dinah? It's Wallace. Wallace Holbein."

Great. Even worse than Mirelle calling back.

"Wally, I'm pretty disgusted with the male species right now, and with you in particular. This had better be damned good, or I'm hanging up."

"I thought you were bigger than that, Dinah."

"You have no idea how big I am, Wally. And so far, you haven't convinced me to listen." With a last swipe at her hair, she hurled the towel in the general direction of the laundry closet.

"It's about the other night."

"Yeah?" She hoped she sounded as belligerent as she felt. Where the hell did these guys get off? If Mirelle deserved a slap, Wallace deserved a big old knee to the groin, and she'd already got in her practice kicks for the day. They were all out of control. She was out of control. She hadn't felt this violent in ages. Maybe never. She felt vaguely ashamed, but dismissed the feeling hurriedly. "You'd better be calling to apologize."

She heard the sound of a deep breath. Wallace, she knew from experience, was sliding into his strained-patience-school-principal mode.

"I think there was fault on all sides, Dinah."

"You mean you and your gym teacher both were to blame for the idiotic decision to flaunt your affair in my restaurant? Maybe she should call to apologize, too." Dinah shifted the phone to her other ear. "Do you know what they call gym teachers in England, Wally? Games mistresses. What kind of games does your mistress play?"

"Don't be crude, Dinah."

"Look. Let's get to your point, shall we?" The repetition of her name was beginning to wear thin. "What is it exactly that you want from me?"

Getting to the point, however, appeared not to be something Wallace was good at. For a moment there was an awkward silence, as though he was flailing for something to say. "What I want—"

"Yes?"

"What I want is to know when Mirelle intends to let me back into the house."

The sheer gall made Dinah shudder. "Never, I hope. But you'd be better off asking her, not me."

This answer was not to his liking. Wallace's patience snapped with a nearly audible sound. "No need to be so nasty, Dinah. Just because you were married to someone old enough to be your father—"

"Bastard," she replied, and slammed the receiver down.

Blindly she reached out a hand for the chair and sat.

For what seemed like the millionth time, Dinah wished she could trade the restaurant for her husband. She wished she could go back or forward or someplace entirely different. But she couldn't believe that Wallace Holbein could have been so cruel.

"Bastard," she said again, fighting back tears. "You bastard, Wally."

The third time the phone rang, she ignored it.

Nineteen

A GAME PLAN had been hatched in the kitchen, which was already redolent with the smells of wine and garlic, while she was upstairs. Dinah found Mark and Perry sorting through recipes for veal; Mark was wearing a chef's white tunic over his jeans. He grinned happily at her as she came through the swinging doors.

"I haven't had a chance to do this since right after I graduated from culinary arts school," he said. "Perry and I've decided I should start off with something simple, so we think a veal cutlet with lemon mustard sauce would make a nice special. Okay with you?"

She stared at him. "You went to cooking school?"

"Well, yeah." Mark winked. "How do you think I earned the right to tell people whether their restaurants are any good or not?" He blew on his fingernails and polished them lightly against his chest. "In Rhode Island. A very nice school, I might add. But I haven't been a practicing professional for about a century. Still, Perry can get me back into the swing of things, can't you, Perry?"

Perry appeared out of the black maw of the walk-in, arms fully loaded, and kicked the door shut behind him. "Sure. Just be sure you tell my boss how much I deserve a promotion."

Mark took a bowl from Perry. "He deserves a promotion."

Perry deposited the rest of his load on the counter. "And a raise. Have you started the water for the pasta?"

Mark nodded. "Just tell me what you want next."

"The sauce," Perry instructed, nodding to the jars of chicken broth and Dijon mustard. "We can get that made up ahead and ready."

Dinah watched in appreciation as Mark measured out the ingredients into a large stainless steel bowl and whisked them to within an inch of their lives.

"But you're cooking in my kitchen," she protested at last. Weakly.

He didn't look up. A slight frown of concentration wrinkled his forehead. "Better than in your bathroom, you have to admit."

"I think there's something in the health regulations against that, actually," Perry said, opening the door to the cavernous oven to peer inside.

"You're the restaurant critic." That sounded stupid to her own ears.

"One way to ensure a good review." Mark sifted some flour over his liquid, then whisked away the lumps. "Anyway, not tonight, I'm not. I'm the under-chef-in-training at Galloway's." He glanced up, with a small smile. "I'm a friend of the owner. She's in a bind. I'm offering my services."

Dinah felt her face flush, but maybe it was the heat from the oven. "Thank you," she said, wondering whether she would choke up. The tears weren't all that far away today, that was for certain. "This—this is really kind of you. I don't know what to say."

He turned away to Perry, tipping the stainless bowl. "Look at this, will you? Do you think it'll be enough?"

Perry made a face, then nodded. "Pour it into one of those small containers with the spouts and put it in the cooler by the cooktop until we need it."

She watched Mark do as he was bidden; then he handed his utensils off to the dishwasher with a quick pat on the shoulder. On his way back to Perry, he paused to give Dinah the smallest of pecks on the cheek. "Don't say anything. I'm glad to be of use."

When he had turned his back, she lifted a slow hand to her cheek. Her skin felt hot. Out of the corner of her eye, she saw Perry watching her, a mischievous glint in his eye. She glared at him and snatched her hand away.

"But you aren't volunteering," she corrected. "Nobody works for me for free. You'll take the same wage Perry gets."

"Then I want the same wage Rob got," Perry interjected.

"Be careful what you say around this woman," Mark advised. "Rob earned himself a kick in the balls, that's what he got."

"Damn skippy," Dinah growled. She turned on her heel and left the kitchen, preparing to pull a full shift as hostess in place of Kelly.

Twenty

THEIR HANDS HAD touched in the garden shop, reaching for the same pair of secateurs, but it wasn't until they met again in the One-Stop a half hour later that they actually spoke. Then it was only because he dropped a cup of coffee at her feet at the self-serve counter.

She leapt back, just barely holding on to her own cup.

"I'm sorry," he exclaimed, reaching out a quick hand to steady her. This time his touch on her elbow intensified the effect he'd had on her earlier. "Did I get any on you? Let me mop this up, will you?"

Dinah instinctively grabbed some napkins on the counter, setting her tea down before dropping to the floor to help him wipe up the mess. In a moment or two, all was in order again, save the sodden pile of napkins between them. He scooped them up awkwardly and dumped them in the trash.

"Here, I've got some on your shoes." Before she realized what he was doing, he had bent to wipe the toe of her gardening boots. Pink wellies. He grinned up at her. "Nice boots."

"I always wear waterproof boots when I plan to have strange men spill coffee on me," she retorted wryly.

"Works for me." He poured another cup of coffee for himself; she watched as he dropped in two creamers, one sugar. "Thanks. I'm Ross, by the way. Ross Galloway."

"Dinah Sullivan."

Even then there was an undercurrent of expectation, of something on the verge of happening. Her stomach quivering slightly, Dinah walked with him up to the counter, where he paid for both their coffees.

"You can't—" she said.

He cut her off, smiling. "You can pay next time."

She had met his eyes then, understanding what he had meant her to understand, and flushing with the pleasure of it. "Thanks. I will."

Out in the parking lot they leaned against the side of her little green Ranger, drinking slowly. The spring sunlight was warm, the ground at the edge of the parking lot muddy, smelling of worms. She studied Ross, the sun lightening his brown hair and nearly disguising his greying temples, picking out the hair of his arms, revealed by his rolled-up shirt sleeves. The cuffs of his jeans were worn where he walked on them.

What did they talk about? The weather led to spring and planting, gardening, pruning, not enough time because of their respective jobs: his as a member of the history department at the university, her various positions selling advertising for theater programs, hostessing at a nearby restaurant. When he mentioned his pending divorce, she felt a tiny shiver run up her backbone, but only a tiny one. Because she knew. She had known from the moment he had touched her hand in the garden shop. This conversation was only a sort of foreplay, building excitement for what would naturally follow.

"You probably figured out," he said finally, gazing into the empty coffee cup he held in his broad hands, "that I followed you. From Allard's"—he nodded in the direction of the shop next door with its outside displays of rakes, hoes, wheelbarrows—"into the One-Stop."

Somehow Dinah had known that, too. But she said nothing.

"And when you didn't seem to notice me—" Ross's mouth turned up at one corner for a moment, a lopsided half-smile she'd later come to know so well but even now she found endearing. He raised his eyes to look into her face, and she had to bite her lower lip at his expression. "I dropped that coffee intentionally."

He followed her back to the duplex, ostensibly to have a look at the shrubs Dinah had been pruning up until the bolt of the ancient pair of secateurs had given up the ghost. Somewhere between the front door and the back, however, something had happened, and the next thing Dinah knew, she was in his arms, her own fingers twined in his hair. Kissing a man she had only known for a few hours. Kissing him more deeply than she had ever kissed anyone. When his fingers fumbled at the buttons of her shirt, she reached up to help him.

"I've never picked up a man at the garden shop before," she murmured against his mouth. "This is not like me."

"I've never picked up a woman in the garden shop before, either," he said. "This is not like me, either."

After their fevered love-making, lying next to his lean long body, Dinah knew that she wanted this—the feeling of being turned inside out at Ross's hands, of having every nerve ending in her body open to the air—*to be like her* for the rest of her life.

And for the rest of his.

Twenty-one

"DINAH, THERE'S SOMEONE in your shower."

Dinah rolled over, pulling the comforter more closely around her head. The mattress cradled her, and the room enveloped her in darkness. She did not open her eyes, for then she would have to check the clock to find out by how much she had overslept. Again.

"Dinah, wake up. Don't be an idiot. There's someone in your shower."

Mirelle's voice, of course, could only be part of a bad dream. Groggily, Dinah concentrated on changing the dream channel to something else, something more pleasant and less demanding. Back, perhaps, to dreams of Ross.

The scrape and swish of the opening draperies was followed immediately by a blinding light, brilliant mottled red through Dinah's eyelids.

"You are a nightmare," she moaned. Her tongue felt wide and fuzzy in her mouth.

"You sound hung over." Mirelle approached the bed, hands on hips. She sniffed, lifting her patrician nose in distaste. "You smell hung over, too."

"Thanks. I only had one drink last night. Go away."

Mirelle whipped the covers back. "Come on, then. Get up and tend to your responsibilities, woman. I've told you already, there's someone in your shower."

"At least he's not singing." Now Dinah could hear the splash of water from the other side of the wall. The Tylenol was in the cabinet in the bathroom. Damn.

"He?" Mirelle's eyebrows arched. "He who? And you're wearing those pajamas?"

Wearily Dinah swung her legs over the edge of the bed and poked around with her feet for her slippers. Her toes only encountered one. She grimaced and gave up.

"Why don't you go make some coffee, Holstein?" she suggested. "You do know how to make coffee, don't you?"

"Ooh, you're avoiding the issue."

"Ooh. I wish I could avoid you. At least this early in the morning."

"It's nearly nine."

The waterfall noises from the shower ceased.

"And the coffee's already on."

"Thanks." Suddenly it wasn't so bad having Mirelle around after all. "I think I love you."

Mirelle's smile was fleeting as she shook her head. "Don't thank me. It must have been your shower mate." She raised an eyebrow.

"He just stayed because we don't know where Rob is." The night, though, had been quiet. Rob apparently was lying low.

Dinah stumbled out into the living room at the same time Mark emerged from the bathroom, toweling his hair, which gleamed with darker red lights in this wet state. He wore his clothes from the previous evening, save the jacket; his feet were bare and his shirt untucked.

"Your turn."

Mirelle threw him an appraising glance and whistled.

He grinned at her, lifting a cup of coffee Dinah had noticed he'd left poured for himself on the counter. "How are you, Mirelle? I missed you last night."

"If you're meaning that to sound kinky," Mirelle replied tartly, tossing her head, "it won't work. Not as long as Dinah's wearing those God-awful pajamas."

"Hey, lay off the duds, will you?" Dinah pulled her mug from the cupboard and poured herself a cup of coffee. The smell filled her nose and she welcomed it. A caffeine rush right about now would save the world, she was sure. "I've had these pajamas forever."

"They look it." Mirelle grabbed Mark's towel and threw it casually toward the door of the laundry closet. She then drew her purse toward herself across the countertop and looked into it longingly.

A red nightshirt and blue sweatpants. Dinah patted her own shoulder as she slid onto a stool at the breakfast bar. "There isn't anything at all wrong with these."

"Come on, now. They just aren't sexy." Mirelle raised her eyes from the depths of her purse to appeal to Mark. "Are they sexy?"

He looked at Dinah and sadly shook his head. "They are not sexy." He sipped at his coffee, then set it down to go to the couch. There he plucked up a rumpled blanket and shook it out.

"Great." Dinah too set her mug down. "Write a review. And no, Holstein, you can't smoke in my house."

Mirelle hastily closed her purse. "I wasn't even thinking about it."

"WHAT HAPPENED TO Mark?" He'd been gone by the time she'd finished her shower.

The question had been lurking in the back of Dinah's thoughts since they'd climbed into the car. Now, as they slid into Mirelle's driveway, Dinah hoped she'd found a casual enough tone to use when she asked it.

Not that preparation mattered. Mirelle's expression had grown more and more stony as they'd approached the house, as hard as Dinah had ever seen it, maybe more so. "He went home to change before he went to his office. He said he'd be back by one."

"He didn't want to come with us?" Dinah wasn't sure why this should disappoint her. Surely Mark's curiosity would have been sparked by something like this: going to Mirelle's to check on Kelly.

The look Mirelle cast her as they clambered out of the car was not pleasant. "I told him this was a girl thing."

So he *had* wanted to come.

Dinah slammed the door. "You told my house guest to take a hike. After you've spent however long trying to shove us together. I can't believe you."

Mirelle glared over the car roof, and then whirled, with an inferno of hair, to do a quick march to the front door. She threw her words over her shoulder like so many live hand grenades. "Never mind about your boyfriend. You didn't even sleep with him, which would solve so many of your problems. Anyway, Kelly's one of us. She needs us."

Dinah grabbed Mirelle's freckled arm at the door. "Look. I feel badly for her, and don't get me wrong—I'll do what I can to help her. But Kelly has been jerking me around for a long time. She is not *one of us*. The only thing that woman and I have in common is a female body."

Mirelle's arched brows climbed even higher. Her expression was clear: gender was enough. She said nothing further, did not even attempt to shake Dinah's grip on her arm. She merely inserted her key into the lock and shoved her way forward into the house, pulling Dinah along with her.

"Oh, thank God!" Kelly was seated on the maroon leather couch beneath the big front window, her petite form sunk into and almost swallowed by the upholstery. Dinah recognized the cranberry trousers and matching silk shirt as the clothes she had been wearing the last time she'd seen her, though they were now creased and a bit askew. Kelly struggled up out of the seat and threw herself at Mirelle, who gathered her up much like a baby, or a puppy. "Thank God you're here."

With a part of her mind, Dinah noticed Kelly's wince in Mirelle's embrace. Mirelle, however, seemed to swell into it, assuming the part of the beneficent Earth Mother.

Now Kelly drew away slightly, peering around behind them toward the still-open door. "Are you sure you're alone? He didn't follow you, did he?"

Mirelle gave Kelly a last reassuring pat as she maneuvered them down the hall toward the kitchen. "No. He didn't. I watched for him, but I never saw him anywhere around Dinah's when we left. Let's go out on the back deck, shall we?" She glanced over her shoulder. "Coming, Dinah? Close that door, will you?"

They settled, well out of view of the street, after Mirelle produced a pitcher from the refrigerator. "Mimosas, industrial size and strength. Perfect for early morning."

"No, no," Kelly said from the chair where she sat huddled, her knees drawn up against her chest, her arms wrapped around them protectively. "The doctor said I can't have anything alcoholic with this pain medication he prescribed for me."

"I'll have a drink," Dinah said.

"Help yourself." All of Mirelle's attention was on her guest, none left over for Dinah. "Can I get you something else, Kelly? Some water? Juice? Soda?"

"Anything. Whatever's the least trouble." Kelly's thin voice, which fit so perfectly with her little-girl figure, was tragic.

Mirelle disappeared, back inside the house.

Now Kelly sighed hugely. "I told her no alcohol. You'd think she'd remember that about my condition."

Dinah opened her mouth, but no words came out.

Mirelle reappeared just as Perry rounded the corner of the house from the drive. "I saw your car out front, Dinah—"

"Come join us," Dinah interrupted him.

She breathed a deep sigh, ignoring the icy looks from both the other women. She didn't care what problems they had with her invitation; she suddenly felt as though she needed someone there for herself, too, to even things out. Perry would do. He was a relief. Dinah did not feel so alone with him there.

Mirelle's whisper hardly counted as such. "I told you this was a female thing. We don't need any males."

Dinah grimaced. "Perry's okay. Leave him alone." She pointed to the pitcher of mimosas. "Get yourself a drink, Per, and join us."

With a glare at Dinah, Mirelle drew up a chair beside Kelly. Protective. But from what? Dinah took a chair on the other side of the umbrella table and leaned back, resting her feet on one of the iron table legs. From there she examined Kelly's white face, with its pale wings of brow, and paler lashes, with its Cupid's bow of a mouth, its delicate cheekbones. No artist could have drawn tragedy more clearly.

Judgmental bitch. She felt immediately guilty. Dinah ran a hand into her hair and tried to smooth it, along with her thoughts. Kelly had just returned from the hospital, for God's sake. She was a victim, she had every right to look like a victim. She didn't need snide backhand remarks—or thoughts. She didn't deserve them. Yet there was some nagging thing which impeded Dinah's unconditional sympathy. Dinah stared down into her mimosa for a moment, considering the floating orange pulp. She took a sip. It wasn't really that bad. She took another.

Perry sailed out from the kitchen with a champagne flute of his own. "Where's your coffee maker?" he demanded of Mirelle. "What I really wanted was a cup of coffee." Resigning himself to his fate, however, he poured himself a drink from the mimosa pitcher before slipping into the chair beside Dinah.

"I don't know. It's disappeared." Suddenly Mirelle glared at him. "Don't you break that glass," she warned, her eyes slitted.

He made a face. "*I'm* not the one who's always breaking glasses," he said, with a pointed look at Kelly.

She flushed. "It wasn't me. It wasn't ever me. It was always Rob."

"Does Rob know where you are?" Dinah asked over the rim of her glass.

"No!" Kelly's reply was quick, breathless, a gut reaction. "No, and I don't want him to. You've got to promise me you won't tell him where I am. *Please.* You've got to promise me."

Dinah held up her free hand. "Fine, if that's what you want. I don't even know where Rob is now. I threw him out."

A complicated expression flickered over Kelly's pinched face—a smidgeon of apprehension leavened with a healthy dollop of gratification. She almost looked as though she could lick her lips.

Perry hadn't noticed. "You know I told you the other night I'd do what I could for you." He might have preened.

"The other night?" Dinah scoffed. "When you were busy playing the manly man and hurling yourself on Rob?"

Perry sniffed. "No need to get petty, Dinah. Just because you weren't there to help when it counted. Just because you copped out on us."

Dinah glared at him fiercely. "Copped out—now there's a totally appropriate turn of phrase for it." She rubbed her wrists, imagining handcuffs there.

"Ah, yes." It seemed Mirelle had to get in her jabs as well. "After you got back. With the restaurant critic guy. Mark. The one who was in your shower this morning." She turned her fine head slowly to give Dinah the benefit of her long blue stare.

"Oh, my God!" Perry exclaimed in high horror. "You're not sleeping with that restaurant critic guy, are you? I've heard of trying to influence critics for a good review, but this—this—from you, Dinah! It's just too awful to bear."

Even Kelly, momentarily out of the spotlight, had abandoned her pout to look at her with something akin to interest.

"No. For the millionth time, no," Dinah cried out in exasperation. "I'm not sleeping with Mark Burdette."

Perry deflated, his chin dropping to his chest in disappointment. "Well, then, you're a hell of a lot stupider than I gave you credit for being."

"For God's sake, I don't need to be in a relationship." Dinah emptied her glass. "Let's quit talking about me. This conversation is asinine. And, I assume, not what we're here for."

"Yes," Kelly added; the pout was back, more pronounced than before. "This is hardly a laughing matter." Dinah shifted uneasily in her chair, and Kelly lifted her head now to look straight into her eyes. The younger woman's expression held an unknown variable, a creepy kind of knowledge. But she continued, her voice still tragic. "We're talking about the end of my marriage. Because I can never go back to him. Not after he hit me." She drew her arms up around her protectively. "In—in the chest."

The chest?

Dinah frowned, puzzled.

"It never shows there," Mirelle said, with an unexpected bitterness. "At least, not when you're wearing clothes. So no one ever knows unless you tell them."

Dinah had no time to consider what Mirelle knew about these things before Kelly burst into tears.

"That's what he said," she sobbed out. "That it wouldn't show." She covered her pale face with her hands, her body shaking in her seat.

Dinah looked on helplessly, while Mirelle dropped to her knees at Kelly's side and put her arms around the smaller woman.

"It's all right," Mirelle murmured soothingly.

"But it's not!" Kelly cried out. "Don't you see? He's always told me I'm too skinny, and he wished I had a bigger chest. It's just part of the way he's always treated me."

Kelly was wracked with sobs. Mirelle rocked her gently in the chair, the red head and the blonde pressed together.

"Damn," Dinah whispered, glancing at Perry, her uneasiness about Kelly receding, far away.

Twenty-two

ROB WAS GONE, anyway.

At least his car was gone, Dinah had to concede. The ancient dusty blue BMW was not in the yard. She had grown, over the past months, so used to seeing it there that its absence was jarring when she looked to the rear of the building.

In the kitchen, Mark and Perry once again divided up tasks. As they began preparations for the evening, they moved around one another so gracefully they might have been choreographed. Dancers. The other line cooks, the *corps de ballet*, wove their way in and out as needed. No wasted movement. No snarling at one another. No hurling glassware.

Another thing jarring in its absence.

Not that she missed it, of course. Even now she could calculate the small fortune she was saving in glassware by no longer employing Rob and Kelly.

Wait. Was she still employing Kelly? It was hard to tell. When she and Perry had left Mirelle's to return to work, the other women remained out on the back deck in the sunshine; Kelly had made no move at all to get up. She gave no hint whatsoever that she intended to come in to the restaurant for the evening.

Dinah sighed. She fished the key ring from the rear pocket of her jeans and inserted the key into the Yale lock of the rear apartment door. She hoped Rob had left Kelly's things, at least. The poor woman needed something else to wear other than that one outfit; and nothing of Mirelle's would fit, as Mirelle was so much taller.

"I need you to get some of my clothes," Kelly had instructed before Dinah had left in with Perry in the Toyota. "Bring them back before the restaurant opens." She'd looked up from her seat on Mirelle's deck, her eyes hidden behind wide sunglasses. "Be sure to get the pearl gray skirt suit."

Remember her situation, Dinah had had to remind herself sternly, and had only nodded. Kelly had had a difficult time, and manners were the first to go. Again, Dinah felt guilty.

The apartment door was stuck and required a healthy dose of persuasion on her part.

"Need some help with that?"

Gahan lumbered up behind her, looking like a beach bum on crack, in a violent orange Hawaiian shirt over a pair of cargo shorts, along with purple flip-flops. His hair stuck up in silvery licks. As he approached, he lifted his wraparound sunglasses from his nose and perched them precariously atop his head.

She stepped aside and let him have a go at the key and lock.

"So he's gone for good, is he? That ruffian?" Gahan leaned close and peered at the recalcitrant Yale. He grunted, and grasped the key again. "Bastard."

"Rob? Or the lock?" Dinah crossed her arms and looked up at the copper weathervane.

"Both." With another highly unattractive grunt, he popped the lock and shoved open the door with a foot. "Got it."

The open door let in a slant of sun which sliced across the carpet. And everything strewn across it.

Dinah gasped, her stomach dropping. The entire front room of what had formerly been Rob and Kelly's apartment had been trashed. The heavy floral couch and matching easy chair had been overturned. The coffee table was leaning against one wall at an impossible angle, one leg broken clear off. This leg had been thrust unceremoniously through the screen of the flat-screen TV. Magazines and clothing were strewn over everything. The venetian blinds on one of the rear windows hung precariously from the side of the sash.

Gahan took a step into the room. A crunching sound came from beneath his feet; he ignored it. Hands on hips, thrusting back the tails of his orange shirt, he turned in a circle, gazing about appreciatively.

"This is a mess," he announced, nodding. It was all a stage set to him. Fodder for his director's mind.

"Thanks for telling me," Dinah said wryly. She felt sick. "I never would have known otherwise."

She bent down to retrieve a torn skirt from the carpet. Pearl gray. She wondered where the jacket was. She wondered what Kelly's reaction would be when she was unable to bring the suit along as ordered.

Cautiously Dinah made her way through the living room, squeezing between the upended sofa and the wall to get to the bedroom door. This she could only push open part way, as the mattress, pulled from the box spring, was shoved up against it. The dresser was denuded of its drawers, she could see from where she stood; more clothing, all Kelly's, was tossed every which way. Holding her breath, she slid into the bedroom to grab up a few pairs of panties. She took a pair of jeans, a black skirt, and two shirts as well. Her sick feeling had progressed to dizziness. Kelly would have to make do with these, she decided, balling the clothes up against her chest and maneuvering her way back out again to the living room.

Gahan had found a scrap of paper and the nub of a pencil; he stood in the same place, in the middle of the ransacked living room, sketching gleefully. The tip of his tongue protruded between his teeth.

He looked up at the sound of disgust she made. "It's wonderful!" he exclaimed. "No stage designer could ever construct anything as realistic as this."

"That's because it *is* real, you idiot," Dinah hissed. "Contrary to popular belief, life is *not* a stage."

Gahan shot out his arm and pointed a demanding finger at her. "Provenance?"

"Screw provenance." Dinah hurled the wad of clothing in his general direction and spun toward the kitchen. She was reluctant to look at what havoc had been wrought there; yet at the same time a sick fascination dragged her forward.

Talk about broken glassware. Rob had to have known Kelly had blamed all that on him, and had set out to prove her right. The cupboards gaped like open mouths, spitting their contents out onto the floor, which glittered brightly with shards of glass and dishware. Interspersed among the pieces were knives and forks and spoons, tossed randomly out of their drawer. Dinah could not bring herself to move from the doorway. Everything, as far as she could tell, which could be broken—had been broken. The place could not have been more devastated had a hurricane blown through.

Gahan moved behind her to look over her shoulder, his sketching for some future stage design apparently completed. The pencil stub was jammed behind his ear.

"Wowza," he breathed in wonder. "That guy must really hate you."

"Not as much," Dinah whispered, "as I hate him."

"Are we going to call the cops?"

The cops.

Not again. Dinah didn't think she could bear Officer Jim Reed showing up in her life one more time. She squeezed her eyes shut until they watered. "No. No cops."

Twenty-three

AFTER THE DOOR had been locked behind the last guest, and the last dish washed up and put away, Dinah drew up a barstool in the west room across from Mark. Only the light over the back bar was left on, casting an intimate circle around them. He had mixed them both mudslides, which seemed rather more festive than the occasion called for. The half-full blender stood guard on the counter between their glasses. Now he leaned back on his stool, peering under the bar.

"What do you need?" she asked.

"I'm trying to figure out what your guy Dirk has under here for tunes."

She shrugged. "He probably plugs in his phone. Pandora. You know."

Mark scowled, held up his own iPhone. "Dead." He tossed it on the bar, then pulled out one CD case, then another. "We'll have to go old school." Finding one at last to his satisfaction, he slid the disk into the player beneath the counter. After a moment, a muted trumpet swelled into the room. He nodded approvingly. "This is a good one. You can tell Dirk he has good taste."

Dinah licked the mudslide from her upper lip. "You never know. I could be the one with the good taste. This could be my CD."

"Is it?"

"No."

Mark laughed. She held out her hand for the jewel case, and he slipped it to her, his fingers light in her palm. Dinah turned the CD over and looked at the photo on the front. Nice trumpet, she decided. The guy holding it wasn't really her type, his hair way too spiky. *A Thousand Kisses Deep.* Chris Botti. Nice title, that, she decided. She handed back the case and took another sip of her drink.

"What was it you wanted to tell me?" she asked.

Mark slid the case under the counter and brought out a deck of battered playing cards. He shuffled them briskly in his long-fingered hands. "I actually wanted to show you something. I snitched a copy of your ad as it will appear in tomorrow's paper. Those get printed earlier." He slapped the deck of cards onto the bar before her. "Cut."

While she did so, he drew a rolled-up sheet of newspaper from his rear pocket. The roll had been flattened and creased. Mark opened it out on the counter, running his hands over it carefully, so as not to smear the newsprint.

"Here," he said, tapping the ad.

There was the Galloway's logo, an orchid in full flower. Dinah leaned forward, squinting at the print. *Seeking experienced chef.* Yep. It was all there. She hoped the ad would spark some interest, generate some phone calls. Then she saw the cow in the lower right hand corner of the advertisement.

A black and white cow. Black head, black hindquarters, white stripe running around its midsection.

An Oreo cookie cow.

Dinah lifted her eyes slowly and dangerously to Mark's.

"What the hell have you done to my ad?" she demanded.

He grinned wickedly. "I knew you'd get a kick out of it."

She narrowed her eyes to slits. "I'd kick you if there wasn't a solid wood bar between us."

"Such expressions of violence from a woman of such a kindly appearance." Mark widened his eyes in mock horror.

"And we all know how deceptive appearances can be," she warned.

"True. I've seen that kick in action."

She slumped back on her stool and slapped her hands on the bar. "Damn it all, you've put a God-damned cow in my help wanted ad. A god-damned cow! You're as bad as Mirelle any day."

"Worse on some," he agreed cheerfully. "Want another drink?" He lifted the blender jug invitingly.

"No, I don't want another drink. I don't even want this one." With a sweep of the hand, she shoved the crumpled page of newsprint aside. "I can't believe every household in half the state is going to find that in their papers tomorrow morning. Whyever would you do such a thing?"

Mark shrugged. "For fun. Why else would you do anything?" He raised his eyebrows at her, a challenge. "Why'd you open the Cow Palace, anyway? For fun, wasn't it?" He retrieved the cut deck of cards and fanned them out on the bar. "Pick a card."

Dinah subsided. She'd opened the restaurant because Ross had wanted it, and then Ross was dead. She dropped her eyes to look into her glass, as though for the secrets of the universe. If the mudslide knew what those were, it wasn't letting on. She sighed. With a finger, she slid a card from the fan and flicked the edge.

He was right. Mark was right. She and Ross had thought to open the restaurant together, because it seemed like a fun idea, something to do that they both enjoyed, something that they both knew something about and wanted to try as Ross's retirement approached. She had kept on with it, partly in his honor, his memory. Somehow, though, with Ross's death, and then Rob and Kelly's idiocy, the fun had bled away from the adventure. Rob and Kelly were gone now, though, she reminded herself, shaking her head quickly. She could hire someone else, someone competent and less pathological, and maybe the fun would come back.

"The fun *will* come back," Mark said softly after a moment, reading her mind. He put a hand over hers on the bar. His grasp was warm, comforting. Then he let go and flipped over the card. Two of clubs. "It will be fun again. Your card says so."

She nodded, silently.

A few more moments passed. A siren went by out on the main road, and she stiffened, then relaxed once it had passed. Mark cleared his throat.

"About the paper—"

Dinah looked up.

With his free hand he pulled it back. "You didn't notice this, on the opposite page, did you?"

He pointed to a half-page advertisement for Waldemann's. On one side, the picture: the owner, Jake Waldemann, devilish hair and eyes more pronounced in the newsprint than in person, shaking hands with Rob Carvey, resplendent in a tall chef's hat. Jake was smiling; Rob's expression resembled more of the grimace of a person who's just swallowed something really unpleasant. Cyanide, Dinah could only hope. Opposite the photograph, the text.

Waldemann's by the Lake Welcomes New Executive Chef Robert Carvey IV.

Dinah's jaw dropped. That certainly hadn't taken long. Rob must have gone straight to Jake Waldemann the moment he'd been fired. As soon as he'd picked himself up off the gravel driveway and washed the blood from his face.

Then she read the smaller print.

Formerly of Galloway's.

"That bastard," Dinah whispered. She looked up at Mark, stricken. "Both of them. Both those bastards."

Mark's rueful smile was somehow sympathetic at the same time. "Look on the bright side, Dinah."

"There's a bright side?"

He nodded. "Now you don't have to worry about picking up his unemployment insurance."

She lifted her glass and drained the remainder of her mudslide. She felt as though she were caught in a mudslide, stuck, buried, even. "That's a real comfort. Thanks a lot."

"Pick another card?"

"Thanks, but I'm having too much fun already."

Twenty-four

"LISTEN," MIRELLE'S VOICE squawked over the receiver, which Dinah cradled between her ear and the pillow. "You didn't take my hair dryer, did you?"

Not exactly the question Dinah had expected. But then, she hadn't expected the telephone to ring so early, with the insistence of a siren.

No sirens. There had been sirens enough already.

"Your what?"

"Hair dryer." There was a sigh of impatient disgust. "Hair. Dryer. It looks like a fat black gun. You use it to dry your hair. You know."

"Why would I take your hair dryer?" Dinah yawned. The light was slicing across the far wall and down to the floor. She closed her eyes against it. "I have one of my own. I hardly ever use it, but I have one of my own."

"You might have taken it to just annoy the hell out of me." Mirelle sounded peeved.

"I don't need your hair dryer to do that," Dinah responded.

"You're right there, anyway."

A sudden thought. "Ask your houseguest. Ask Kelly."

"She's the one who was looking for it. I just figured she didn't know where to look, but it's not in the vanity drawer where it's supposed to be. I swear I tore that bathroom apart. No hairdryer."

Kelly. "Holstein," Dinah said, rolling onto her back amongst the pillows. "Did Kelly get those clothes? I sent them over last night with Gahan?"

"Gahan." Suddenly Mirelle's voice was a purr. "Yes. He was here. We had a lovely chat."

That didn't really sound all that healthy. "Oh, really?" Quite frankly, it sounded rather euphemistic, and Dinah was immediately sorry she'd probed further.

"About the play, you idiot. The play." Mirelle's high laugh tinkled along the phone wire. "About Elvira, and what my reading of her is."

Phew, anyway. "But what about the clothes?"

"Oh, that." Mirelle came back to earth from the other plane with a decided thump. "Kelly wanted you to know that she was unhappy that you didn't send on the gray suit. She wants that for job interviews."

"*She has job interviews?*" The entire idea of Kelly getting out of her own way seemed ludicrous. Again, immediately, Dinah cursed herself for not being more supportive.

"Well, not yet. She's looking in the want ads right now." There was a murmur in the background, then Mirelle added, "She wants you to get that suit and bring it over this morning."

A bit demanding, isn't she?

"Tell her I need the magic word," Dinah countered dryly. There was supportive, and there was supportive.

Mirelle sucked in a breath. "Really. Don't be such a bitch. She's been through a lot these past couple of days. You need to cut her some slack."

Dinah could almost imagine Mirelle's wagging finger; but she could wag her own finger with the best of them. "Doesn't mean she gets to forget common courtesy. Besides. I got what I could for her out of the apartment. Or what used to be the apartment, before Rob trashed the place."

"He did what?" The telephone line reverberated with Mirelle's shock.

"Absolutely demolished that apartment. Threw my furniture around. Busted up some stuff. Hurled Kelly's things everywhere, after he tore them up."

"And did you call the police?"

"Look, Holstein." Dinah sighed. "All my life I've been a law-abiding citizen. Harmless in the eyes of the law. I never even got a traffic ticket—do you hear what I'm saying? In the past couple of days I've had more close encounters with the police than I can count. I've been nearly *arrested*, Holstein. Do I want another encounter? No. No, I do not."

"Now, now," Mirelle said quickly. "No need to get all wound up about this. But you know if you want to collect insurance or anything, you'd have to call the cops."

With a grunt Dinah sat up and swung her legs over the edge of the bed. "No. It's not that big a deal. Not enough to worry about insurance. Even the television I can replace for less than my deductible. It's just the annoyance of the thing, you know? I'm going to have to go in there and clean it all up. Probably Kelly should come and have a look and see what she can salvage of her stuff."

Another murmur from the other end of the line, then Mirelle was back. "She says you can take care of it. She doesn't feel quite up to it yet. And she wants to know—since she was injured on the job, isn't she entitled to worker's compensation?"

Twenty-five

"YOU KNOW WHAT?" Mark asked, slicing a honeydew melon in half on the work table. He scooped the seeds into a stainless steel bowl, scraped down the inside of the melon lightly, then picked up the melon baller, examining it to decide which end was better for attacking the pale green flesh.

"I know a lot of things." Dinah ducked into the walk-in for a moment, rooting in the dimness for coffee creamer. "Many, many things."

"She does know many things," Perry confirmed. He too was busy, pounding chicken breasts to near-transparency with the meat mallet. "More than Alex Trebek, even, and he knows some very bright people."

In another bowl, a mountain of honeydew melon balls began to form. Mark finished with the first half of the melon, then began on the second. A few more honeydews, some cantaloupe, and a whole watermelon still awaited his ministrations. "You haven't had a day off in a century or two, Dinah. I think you should take Monday off."

"Don't be foolish," Dinah said.

She was only listening with half her attention; the other half was formulating interview questions for prospective kitchen hires. She'd been up late fielding online applications the night before. She held a carton of creamer in either hand. Still another six cartons in there; on the way out she made a note on the pad beside the door. When she closed the walk-in, she immediately missed the brush of the cool air on her skin.

The kitchen extension rang. Lindsay called her name.

Another returned call. She jotted down the name, giving a time and instructions.

"That's why I can't take Monday off," she informed Mark. "That's the third callback already about the position. I have someone coming in at eight-thirty, someone at nine-thirty, and now someone at ten-thirty. Interviews."

"You *are* going to have them cook something," Perry said. He lay another flattened chicken breast in the prep pan, as gently as he would lay a baby to bed.

Dinah sighed. "Can you help me with this, Per? Can you put them through their paces with something easy after I talk to them? You can spot a kitchen poser better than I can, even if he—or she—talks a good line."

Perry shrugged. "Sure." The pan was nearly full of chicken. "How about it?" he asked Mark. "You want to give me a hand?"

Mark paused in his slicing up of a cantaloupe. He held up the knife. "I will—*if* Dinah will promise to come out to lunch with me afterward. Just lunch."

"Oh, she will." The last flat chicken breast laid aside, Perry began scrubbing down the work surface.

Gillian appeared at the swinging doors. "Got that cream, have you, Dinah?"

Dinah handed off the cartons. She glared at Perry. "Stop speaking for me. Stop arranging my life for me. I haven't abdicated total responsibility yet."

"Tell her, Gill," Perry said quickly as the head waitress, tactfully, attempted to slip away. "Tell her to take a couple hours off. Here she's got a lunch invitation, well after tomorrow's interviews, and she won't agree to take it."

Gillian considered for a moment, tilting her head to look at Dinah appraisingly. "Free lunch, someone else footing the bill—take it, Di. You'd be foolish not to. Who's it with?"

Mark popped a ball of cantaloupe into Gill's mouth as he passed with the huge bowl on the way to the walk-in. "Me."

"All the more reason to accept the invite," Gill said. She smiled, bumping open the pass door with her hip and disappearing through it.

"The oracle speaks," Mark said, passing the other way with a pound of butter in each hand. "So far, the opinion polls seem to be running in my favor. I think you'd better come out to lunch with me. I can't see how, in good conscience, you can say no."

"All those in favor of Dinah going out to lunch with Mark tomorrow, raise your hands," Perry instructed. Having finished pummeling chicken breasts, he now began to layer ham, cheese, and broccoli on each one, before rolling the entire construction into a ball.

Perry, Mark, Brian, Lindsay, and the dishwasher all raised their hands.

Mark laughed. "Be ready at one."

EXCEPT IT WOULDN'T be a date. Just lunch with a friend. The last time she had been on a date with anyone other than Ross had been twenty years ago, give or take a few. Dinah frowned, pondering the contents of her closet. What did one wear to lunch at some unknown location with a man who was just a friend?

"It is too a date, and it's about time, too. Get out of those proverbial mourning weeds and get on with your life. You know every time you go down into the blasted restaurant, you wear black? Anyway, what were you wearing the first day you met the guy?" Mirelle examined herself in the full-length mirror, leaning close to peer at her eyes, turning her face to one side and then the other. "Do you think I'm getting wrinkles?"

"No. I've already got your share." Dinah swept hangers aside impatiently. Nothing screamed out *wear me*. Everything hung limply, unattractive, making her wonder how she could ever have spent money on any of it. "When I met him, I was wearing blue jeans and a sweater. Nothing fancy. A pair of sandals."

Now Mirelle had turned her attention to her hair, which seemed, this morning, to lie flatter than usual. Almost lifeless, as though some of the fire had gone out of it. She ran her fingers up into it and fluffed it a bit, then wound it into a loose bun on the back of her neck. Dissatisfied, she let it tumble down again around her shoulders. "So go for the casual look again. He seemed to like it well enough then."

But this was not a date.

Dinah hadn't ever really gone on a date with Ross, unless one counted drinking coffee before falling into bed together counted.

"Casual. I'm good at that." She ran her hands into her own hair, but instead of fluffing it, she grabbed great handfuls and pulled.

"So you *do* want to impress our boy Mark." This delighted Mirelle. For a moment she took her eyes off her own reflections to appraise Dinah. Only for a moment. Then it was back to her hair. "I wish I knew what happened to my hair dryer."

"No, I don't want to impress him," Dinah gritted. "And I don't want him to think I want to impress him. I wish I could make you understand that I don't want a relationship."

Mirelle's sigh was mighty and impatient. "Now you aren't making any sense at all." She gave up on her reflection, threw herself across the bed, and turned her critical eye on Dinah. "Why on earth are you so self-conscious all of a sudden? Could it be—*could it be?*—that our Dinah is protesting too much?"

Dinah tossed one of the sandals she had been considering at Mirelle. "No. Just stop that now. I am not looking for a relationship with Mark—or with anyone else, either. I like him. He's a friend. We're just going out to lunch, because he claims I never relax. That's all."

Mirelle, amazingly, had caught the sandal with one hand. She looked it over, grimacing, and threw it back down at Dinah's feet. "Don't wear those. Not attractive at all."

"Thanks. And I guess the short skirt's out, what with the bruises I'm about to develop from your hurling shoes at me."

"You started it." Mirelle yawned, leaning her head back. "Besides. Think of it as an opportunity. If our boy Mark is so concerned about your health and well-being, he might welcome the opportunity to tend to your injury." She winked. "He might think a deep-tissue massage is in order."

"On my legs?"

"Or somewhere near there."

Dinah shot Mirelle a quick glare before turning back to her highly unsatisfactory wardrobe. "Do you have a one-track mind or what? Does everything have to be about sex with you?"

"What else is there?" Mirelle laughed. "Honestly, Galloway, what can you be thinking? Absolutely nothing, is what I'm afraid of. Here you have a hot guy—a superb example of manhood, if I may say so, complete with handsome face, gorgeous eyes, really nice hair, a terrific bike-rider's butt—and he's a good guy, into the bargain. What an opportunity, Dinah. You're unattached, he's unattached, you haven't slept with a man since Ross. I can't see any downside to this at all."

Dinah whirled, a white dress with a pattern of grey ferns in her hand. "Jesus Christ, Holstein! Do I look that desperate?"

"Yes."

"Well, I'm not. I've told you this before." She took a step closer to the bed, hand on hip, chin high. "There's no shame in being a single woman. There's nothing that says we all have to be the ants marching two by two. I'm doing just fine on my own. I don't need a husband, a boyfriend, a lover. Mark's a friend, and I'm fine with that."

"All right, if you say so." Mirelle threw up her hands, clambering to her feet. "I know what you've told me. That's why God invented vibrators. But"—and she leaned forward to whisper on the way by—"a real man vibrates a hell of a lot better."

SHE WAS GLAD she'd chosen jeans and comfortable shoes when Mark pulled his Volvo into a rutted turnoff along the side of the road.

"Rotten timing," he said ruefully, turning off the ignition. The sound of John Hiatt and his perfectly good guitar was swallowed up into silence.

"Why?"

Mark grinned. "My favorite song was coming up. 'Loving a Hurricane.'"

Dinah laughed. "Are you kidding?"

"No, but probably John Hiatt was. You've really got to love a guy who's in it for fun." Mark reached for the backpack on the rear seat. "Come on." He shoved open the door with his knee and climbed out of the car.

Dinah, too, got out. She stretched her arms high over her head, feeling her back crack. They'd been driving for a while. A path wove away from the turnoff, uphill into the trees. "Lunch is up there?"

"Lunch is in here." Mark slung the pack over his shoulder, then came around the car. "The dining room is up there." He nodded approvingly at her shoes. "I love a woman who dresses for any occasion."

Ha.

She followed him up the hill. He walked easily, fitting the stride of his long legs to her shorter one. Dinah was grateful as the hill grew gradually steeper; her legs ached almost immediately, and she was ashamed of just how out of shape she was.

"Just a bit more," Mark reassured her. "It levels out in a bit."

"For all this work," she said, "lunch had better be worth it."

He laughed. "Oh, it will be."

The path did level off shortly. They traced their way through mostly hardwood, though an occasional small stand of evergreen appeared off to the side. At one point Mark pointed to a clump of three yellow lady's slippers.

"Endangered," he said. "I'd pick you one, but then *you'd* be bailing *me* out of jail."

They continued on, the branches whispering above them in the barely perceptible breeze. They left the main path and skirted a giant stone outcrop. Mark took a sharp left through a cleft, then clambered up until the rock flattened and the trees opened up. The view before them was undulating land, varicolored trees, and far to the west, a shimmering pond. Some eighty miles further but appearing deceptively close, Mt. Washington, still tipped with white.

Dinah stepped forward, placing her palms on the rail fashioned out of rough cedar poles which marked the end of the path. The breeze whispered, the new leaves barely fluttering. She breathed in the loamy forest smell, sucking it deep into her lungs.

"Well?" he asked, at her side at the rail. "Worth taking the afternoon off for?"

"It's beautiful."

"I thought you might like it."

He was so close she could feel him, though they did not quite touch. She made no move. After a moment, he stepped away. "Come on."

The disappointment was sudden and sharp. She looked out on the pond longingly. "We're not eating here?"

His smile was mischievous. "I have a better place. Come on."

He edged his way around the cedar railing and began scrambling downhill. After a doubtful moment, Dinah followed. The path to the overlook had ended, but a far less worn track wound down into the trees, tucking back on itself along the hillside. A few scrabbling steps downward, and she could no longer see the rail she had held just moments before. Below her, Mark rounded a corner; when she caught up to him, he stood on a scrap of level ground, just large enough for the blanket he was spreading out. She craned her neck, but could not see the railing above.

"Have a seat," he invited.

He settled himself on the blanket, then delved into his backpack to withdraw a collection of insulated cooler bags. From the bottom of his sack came a pair of paper plates and some silverware, which he handed to her as she sat, folding her legs beneath her. One by one he unwrapped his treasures, naming them as he went.

"Salmon pate and crackers. Cherry fruit salad with honey-yogurt dressing. And the *piece de resistance:* smoked turkey breast, mozzarella, and sliced tomatoes on rosemary focaccia with fresh basil and garlic mayonnaise."

Dinah was stunned. When she had regained her voice, she still sounded breathless to her own ears. "You're only missing something to drink."

"Ah, but you don't think I'd forget that?" Mark produced a bottle opener and two plastic wine glasses, which he passed to her, then brought out a bottle with a narrow neck and gold labeling. "Dragonfly Sabrevois. You approve?"

She frowned. "Shouldn't we have a white with this sandwich?"

"Wine snob." Gently Mark uncorked the bottle, and poured into the glasses. "Smell that. Seriously. Isn't it wonderful?"

Again she nodded, holding the glass under her nose. She took a small sip, watching him construct sandwiches for them both, then spoon out the fruit salad and dressing. The crackers were pale, irregularly shaped things she recognized from the co-op; Mark jabbed a knife into the container of paté and invited her to help herself as he made up their plates.

"Did you make all this?" she asked at last, still breathless at the feast spread before her.

Mark pressed a dramatic hand to his breast. "I, madam, am a chef. Cordon bleu trained. And I press wine grapes with my bare feet in my spare time."

"Yes, but did you make all this?"

He shrugged, passing her a plate. "Well, no." He winked. "I made the focaccia. I will admit to that. As for the rest—what do you think Perry and I had those interviewees do all morning? You wanted us to give them a test drive. What better way to do that than to make them fix our lunch?"

Dinah laughed. "What a great idea. Sneaky and underhanded and extremely useful." She dipped her spoon into the cherry fruit salad. "Which of the three made what?"

Mark shook his head. "I'm not going to tell. You need to decide what of this you like, and then we can compare notes on our respective cooks."

The salad was cool on her tongue, the dressing sweet and tangy at the same time. Dinah rinsed her palate with the wine, then took a bite of the sandwich. The mayonnaise, she decided, perfectly melded the flavors of cheese, turkey, and tomato. She ate slowly, savoring the tastes. When she took another bite, tomato juice and seeds spurted down her chin. She didn't mind; she didn't even mind when Mark tossed her a napkin. He was grinning. It was infectious. She smiled back.

Slowly they enjoyed their lunch, sipping the wine until the bottle was empty. The breeze provided a soothing accompaniment, whispering through the trees and cooling the air around them. The sun filtered through the canopy of branches above, speckling the blanket. The breeze itself barely touched them, tucked into the steep side of the hill as they were.

"Karl Jung always lived near the water, you know." Mark licked the tines of his fork clean. "He said the negative ions moving water gave off energized his brain."

"I don't know about energizing." Her sandwich and salad gone, Dinah nibbled on a cracker. The salmon pate was to die for. "But it's sure clearing my brain, anyway." She sighed, leaning back on the blanket and gazing up into the green canopy overhead. "This is a gorgeous place, Mark. However did you find it?"

He slewed his eyes sideways. "I have my sources. Which I refuse to reveal."

Dinah closed her eyes and let the quiet fill her ears. Let those negative ions penetrate her body. "Ah. That means you must bring all the ladies here."

"Every last one of them," he agreed. He slipped a few of the now-empty wrappers into the backpack. "But they all have to stay in the car, because they don't wear sensible shoes."

He was still grinning at her.

"What if I kick my shoes off?" she asked.

"I wish you would."

She did. Nimbly she peeled her socks off, using the toes of the opposite foot. The air felt good on her bare skin. She wiggled her toes.

"Better?"

"Better."

Mark, too, lay back on the blanket. They did not touch; the container of pate and the paper bag of crackers separated them. "Good. I'd like to think you're comfortable. Comfortable with me."

"I am." She said the words without thinking. Once they were out, though, she felt the heat flush her cheeks. "We're friends."

"And I want you to know how glad I am that you agreed to come out with me," he continued slowly. "On this. Our first date." She couldn't tell whether his voice was teasing.

"This—" she stuttered. "This is not a date."

"No?" Mark sounded surprised, and a bit disappointed. "What is it, then?"

"Lunch. Just lunch. Because we're friends. So we're having lunch." She was babbling now and she knew it and she couldn't stop herself. "Because this can't be a date. Because I'm way too old for you."

She felt rather than saw him roll over onto his side, his elbow down, his head propped on his hand. She barely dared to look at him.

"How old is way too old, Dinah?" he asked. "I'm thirty. I'll be thirty-one in August. How old are you, a hundred?"

"Forty-two," she said. "I'm forty-two."

"Woo-hoo." He snorted. "You're old enough to be my mother, if you'd started when you were twelve."

Still she refused to turn her head, to meet those eyes. "Very funny."

"It is," he agreed. "It's utterly silly. Because it doesn't matter. Even if you were a hundred."

"Of course it does."

Mark snorted again, more impatiently. "Listen to me. How often do you think about your age? When you're wandering through your days? How often do you stop and think about how old you are?"

"That's not a fair question. I don't know." Roughly she massaged her head with her fingers. "I don't go around all day chanting 'I'm forty-two, I'm forty-two,' if that's what you're asking."

"And tell me." Mark paused dramatically, as though preparing to drop a major bombshell. "How much older than you was Ross?"

She fell silent, wondering at her husband's name on Mark's lips. It seemed odd, wrong. There was a part of her that shrank away at the touch of the word from him, a wound that had not yet completely skinned over. But the question hung between them, words strung across the air.

"Eighteen years," she answered at last. "Ross was eighteen years older than me."

"And you dated him." Mark reached out a finger and tipped her chin toward him. "And you loved him, and you married him."

Sudden tears sprang up behind her eyelids. She nodded. "Yes. Yes, to all three."

"Was that wrong?"

"No." She shook her head. "No."

"So this *date*"—and Mark smiled at her, gently tapping her chin with his finger—"is not wrong, either. In fact, as far as I'm concerned, it's pretty damned right."

But the conversation died, much as if Ross had come to sit with them on the blanket.

Truthfully, Dinah wished he had.

Twenty-six

MARK DROPPED HER off just as the sun was beginning to paint long shadows across the yard. For a moment she thought he might lean across the console between the seats and kiss her, but he didn't. As she made her way upstairs to the apartment, an odd fluttery feeling the in the pit of her stomach told her she was relieved. Almost.

She looked across at the photograph of Ross on the piano and felt guilty.

She had wanted him to kiss her. She had wanted him to be Ross.

Dinah leaned her back against the closed door, staring dumbly at the empty room. Yes, that was exactly what she had wanted, after that conversation. What a mess her life was.

So when she heard the car door slam from the yard below, half of her wanted to lock the door against him. Indecision held her where she stood until the footsteps coming up the stairs told her two things: she had neglected to lock the outside door behind her; and there was no way in hell Mark could sound so light on the steps anyway. She heaved herself away from the door just as the first tap sounded.

It was Kelly Carvey.

"Dinah," she said, in her high voice. "Thank God you're home. We tried calling you earlier, but no one answered. I need your help."

Dinah held the door open reluctantly. "What do you need, Kelly?" Her voice held more disappointment than she meant it to. She wanted to add *this time*, but Mirelle's warning of the other day still lingered in her head. She had to be supportive. She had to stop being so damned judgmental.

"I need to get to Waldemann's," Kelly said, spinning so that her fine silver-blond hair fanned out, and then settled like a cloud around her shoulders. "Mirelle can't take me, because she has rehearsal, and anyway, afterward, she has to go to Walmart to buy a toaster."

"A toaster?" Information overload. This did not compute.

"She doesn't have one." Kelly waved this away with her delicate white hand, a small bird in flight. "Or at least she can't find it."

"Right. Has she looked in her kitchen?"

Kelly shifted impatiently. "So can you take me? To Waldemann's?"

Dinah still held the door open. "To Waldemann's? That's where Rob is working, you know."

"I know." Kelly looked at Dinah as though doubting her mental capacity.

"I thought the idea was to stay away from Rob."

Kelly's lipsticked mouth thinned. "Look. If you don't want to help me, just say so. Here I am, trying to get back on my feet, and I've got a job interview tomorrow, but I need the car. All I need from you is a ride over to Waldemann's, that's all. If it's too much for you—"

"Hold on already." Dinah threw up a hand against the onslaught. "I didn't say I wouldn't give you a ride over there. A job interview?" This sounded promising. It could get Kelly, as she said, back on her feet. It could make Dinah feel somehow less responsible for her. "Where?"

Kelly's eyes slewed sideways. "Oh, a computer place in Portland. It's what I used to do before I married Rob. I was in computer sales and support." She lifted her hand again, moving back toward the door. "So you'll do it? Just a ride over there. That's all I need."

"Let me get my keys."

Against her better judgment, Dinah followed Kelly down the stairs and out to the yard. They climbed into the Mazda; Dinah started the car and headed out, taking a left at the road.

"Rob knows you're coming for the car?" she asked.

"Rob knows nothing." Kelly stared straight ahead.

Dinah nearly slammed on the brakes. "What do you mean, he knows nothing?"

A tiny smile played around Kelly's lips. "He's working. I've got my keys, so you can just drop me off, and I'll take the car."

"You're going to steal the car." Dinah drove blindly now, taking a left onto a cross street. "You're going to *steal* the car."

"Of course not." Kelly's voice dripped with impatience. "The title's in both our names. It's my car, too. You can't steal something that belongs to you."

Dinah fell silent. What Kelly said made sense, but that didn't ease the nerves balling at the pit of her stomach. Kelly was going to steal that BMW. She, Dinah, was driving her over to Waldemann's to do it. Dinah was aiding and abetting. Rob wasn't going to like this when he got out of work, whenever Waldemann's kitchen closed down. And Dinah had already seen too much of Rob's unpleasantness to be looking forward to having any more of it directed at her.

"I don't know if I want to be a part of this." She spoke the thought aloud. Waldemann's appeared atop the hill ahead, its enormous sign already alight, though it was still early, sun still in the sky. Jake Waldemann did not take Mondays off. Dinah stepped on the brake.

"Are you afraid, then?" Now Kelly's voice was scathing. "I need this one thing from you, this one bit of help. And you're too afraid to help me?"

"Oh, for God's sake. Stop playing the victim card with me, all right?" Dinah gritted her teeth. "I'm driving you to the damned place, aren't I?"

Still, she couldn't help but wonder where the BMW would be parked, whether Rob would have a view of it from the restaurant's kitchen. She couldn't help wondering what his reaction would be. Would he call the police? Come after them?

"Here," Kelly instructed, pointing. "Turn here. Keep to the edge of the lot. Keep some cars between us and the building."

Carefully Dinah did as she was bidden, turning into the back of the parking lot. Though not full, the lot held a respectable number of cars for an early Monday evening. She maneuvered slowly down one row, Kelly peering out the window as they passed car after car.

"There," Kelly hissed finally. "It's over there." She opened her purse and fumbled for her keys. Her hands, Dinah noted, were shaking. Almost as much as Dinah's own. "Stop just down here."

An enormous super cab Chevy truck straddled two spaces at the end of the row. Dinah slid to a halt behind it, hoping again that they could not be seen from the kitchen. In the farthest corner of the lot, as close to the rear door as possible, the blue BMW squatted in the dying sunlight. Dinah's breathing was shallow; she could hear her heart thumping against her ribcage.

Don'tcomeout don'tcomeout don'tcomeout.

The words ran themselves together in her head, a mantra.

Kelly's hand was on the door handle. "Wait for me," she said, despite her earlier directive. "Make sure I can get into the car. Don't leave until I'm in."

She opened the door, the narrowest of cracks, and slid out. She pressed it closed, listening for the telltale click. Then she crouched low, easing around the back of the super cab; as Dinah watched her nervously, she darted from car to car, hugging their shadows as much as possible. The kitchen door remained closed so far. What would they do if Rob burst through it? She prayed fervently that he wouldn't.

Kelly had reached the door of the BMW now, and she crouched, slotting the key into the door handle. Then she had the door open; she leapt in and had the engine started even before she slammed the door closed again. The car ripped into reverse, then kicked up gravel as Kelly tore out of the lot and to the road. Dinah jerked her steering wheel around and followed as fast as the Mazda would go. Her tires squealed as she took the sharp right turn onto the tar.

In the rearview mirror, she saw Rob charge through the kitchen door. He was shouting, his mouth moving, his arms flailing, but she could hear nothing above the whine of her engine. He hurled a cloth to the ground, then gave them the finger.

Yep. They were in trouble now.

Twenty-seven

"SO," MIRELLE DEMANDED, floating into the apartment the next morning, "did you sleep with him?"

Mirelle played only one note. Dinah looked up frostily from her desk, where she was paying the water bill online. She yawned. She had not slept well.

"So," she said, "how'd you lose your toaster?"

Mirellenarrowed her eyes. She was momentarily diverted. "What do you know about my toaster?"

"The same thing you know about my love life. Zip, zero, zilch, nada, nothing."

"I'm not asking about your love life," Mirelle countered. "Who gives a damn about your love life? I'm asking about your sex life."

"About which you know nothing, either." Dinah signed out of her water district account and moved on to the electric company website. Wrong password. She pushed away from the desk. It was delicate, a lady's writing desk, in walnut, with finely turned legs and a breakfront. She could still remember the day Ross brought it home and set it proudly before her. "And if I can help it, you will remain in total ignorance about my sex life. It will remain my own private business."

"Oh, be that way." Mirelle threw herself into the wing chair in disgust, draping her long legs, bare below a pair of yellow pedal-pushers, over the arm. With the fingers of one hand, she twirled a strand of her hair. She looked up. "What *do* you know about my toaster, anyway? Did you borrow my toaster?" She flitted her eyes suspiciously to the kitchen counter.

"No, I did not borrow your toaster." Dinah picked up her empty coffee mug and carried it to the sink. "Just like I didn't borrow your hair dryer the other day, either."

Mirelle's fine features puckered into a frown. "What about my coffee maker?"

"For God's sake." The mug rinsed, she set it in the strainer. "I didn't borrow your coffee maker, either. I have small appliances enough of my own. I don't need any of yours."

"Well, it's weird and I don't like it." Mirelle's frown deepened into a full-fledged scowl.

It *was* weird. But then, much in Mirelle's life was weird. Dinah returned to the couch, tucking her bare feet between the cushions. "When did you last see this alleged toaster?" she asked in her most Joe Friday-ish voice.

Mirelle's scowl did not lighten. "I don't know. What kind of a question is that? Who notices things like toasters? They're just there. It's not as though I walk into my house every day after work and make an inventory of small appliances."

"Maybe you should," Dinah suggested dryly. "What with all of them going missing like this."

"Screw that," Mirelle snarled inelegantly.

Dinah sighed. "All right, then. Take all the fun out of this investigation. When did you last use the damned toaster? Could Wally have taken it with him before you changed the locks?"

"Why would he have? He didn't know I was going to change them. He thought he was coming back to his home to contentedly toast things with his mistress." Mirelle rubbed her eyes, then stood quickly to examine herself in the mirror. "I had a bagel for breakfast on Thursday, if that's what you mean."

"Aha." Dinah jabbed a finger in the air. "So it was there after you recaptured the house."

"Yes."

"And the other things?" When Dinah thought about it, this was indeed a puzzle. It was, in fact, exacerbating her exhaustion. "Perry noticed the coffee maker was missing, the other morning, when we were all there."

"I don't know," Mirelle repeated. "I'm telling you, it's weird and I don't like it at all. Not one bit." Satisfied with touching up her eyeliner, she paced the room.

Dinah watched for a moment, then closed her eyes against the constant back and forth. "There's got to be a logical explanation for it all. Maybe Kelly is a closet kleptomaniac." She shook her head. "But I'd never really noticed that tendency in her—just a tendency to bust things up. And cry a lot."

"Don't be catty." The retort was almost automatic. Dinah watched Mirelle pause near the piano, where she lifted the lid and fluttered her fingers along a B major chord. Then she moved them down a step: A major. This time she added the seventh. Aside from her fingers, she was perfectly still. "Tell me something," she said slowly, without turning around. She might have been reading sheet music suspended before her, so still was she.

"What?"

"Why won't you sleep with Mark?"

So much for keeping away from that subject. Dinah flushed. "I thought I told you my love life, or my sex life, or whatever it is—"

"Or isn't," Mirelle interrupted pointedly.

"—is my business."

Still Mirelle did not turn. "You had the perfect opportunity yesterday. Oh, maybe not to sleep with him, maybe I'm being euphemistic here." She played another chord: G. "What I mean is that you had the perfect opportunity to enter into a relationship of some sort with him. Any sort. Dinah, for God's sake, the man asked you out. He asked you out on a date."

"It wasn't a date," Dinah contradicted. "And we have a relationship. We're friends. That's a pretty good relationship, I should think."

"That's crap and you know it. Why wasn't it a date, then?"

Dinah tugged at her hair in frustration. Must she have this conversation every day for the rest of her natural life? "Because. I'm too old for him. I'm twelve years older than he is, Mirelle. Twelve."

"That is also crap. If it doesn't matter to Mark, why should it matter to you?"

"How do you know it doesn't matter to Mark?"

"*Because he asked you out, damn it!*" Mirelle spun to face her at last. Her pale cheeks were flushed. "He's showing interest here, in the most obvious way. Why don't you return it?"

"I—" But Dinah found no words.

"It's Ross, isn't it?" Mirelle jerked up her arm and held out the photograph in its frame, the one from atop the piano. "You've got some weird hang-up still about your husband. Your late husband, Dinah. *Late* being the operative word here."

Dinah shook her head, her eyes fixed on the photograph in Mirelle's hands. She licked her lips. "No, I'm not. That's not it."

"It *is* it," Mirelle insisted, as though she had discovered the great secret of the universe. "Even after all this time, you aren't letting go of Ross. That's what it's all about." Frowning, she turned the picture around in her hands to stare into Ross's face. "I know you think he was a great guy, Dinah, but he's gone now. You're here. So you have to do something about it. And as far as I can figure, you've got a great chance here with Mark."

"No." Dinah wasn't sure what she was vetoing. Perhaps all of it. "It's too soon."

"Well, you and I both know Ross wouldn't want you wasting the rest of your life on the memory of him—"

"How do you know?" Her vehemence surprised Dinah, as did her words. "How do you know what he would want? Because you really only knew him a short time, remember?"

"Oh, but I do," Mirelle corrected, then paused and took a deep breath. "I've listened to you talk about him for years. Met him on your fleeting visits back here. And I *did* know him for a short time, once you two moved back. So I know him. And I know I'm right. You know I'm right. So you need to let Ross go now, Dinah."

She'd turned on her heel before Dinah had a clue to her intentions. One hand on the sash, she threw the window open.

"Don't!"

It was too late. Mirelle sent the photograph of Ross flying out the window.

DINAH COULD REMEMBER their very first argument, though at times she was unclear about what had precipitated it.

Ross was not confrontational, and neither was she. He withdrew to his computer and his books and papers, while Dinah threw herself into cleaning and gardening and bringing order to things which were already orderly. First she would do dishes, then she would wash down all the countertops. When the cupboards were organized to her liking, she got down on her hands and knees to scrub the tile floor. First the kitchen straightened, then bathroom, living room, bedroom, and finally the yard.

They were not yet married, though they had been living together for three months. It had taken Dinah a while to get used to turning around and finding another person in the duplex—it was really too small; they'd already begun to look for a larger house. She'd find herself looking for things—the coffee, the toothpaste—which Ross would have left somewhere other than where she was used to, and she'd have to take a deep breath to keep from speaking. This day, it might have been the dustpan. Or something else equally unimportant.

Now she scrubbed, shoving the cloth back and forth until her upper arms ached from the work of it. The smell of sudsy water was up her nose and she welcomed it. She sloshed the cloth around in the pail, then started again. Somewhere out in the living room, she heard the opening and closing of a door, but she refused to look up.

Ross paused in the kitchen doorway, pulling on his jacket. "I'm going out."

"Don't step on the floor," she answered, leaning back on her heels and scrubbing the same spot over and over again. "It's wet."

Perversely, he stepped onto the tiles, his boat shoes appearing just beneath her nose.

"What the hell are you doing? I just washed there," Dinah complained.

Ross said nothing, but did not move.

"This is not the way out," she said.

She shoved at his feet with the hands holding her wet scrub cloth. When that did not work, she pushed at his legs.

Slowly Ross bent down, then lowered himself to his knees, his face on level with hers. He took the cloth from her, though she resisted at first.

"What do you want?" she demanded. She fixed her eyes on his hands. "You said you were going out. What do you want?"

"I want you to look at me."

She stubbornly did not lift her eyes.

"I want you to look at me, Dinah."

She did.

He had such beautiful eyes. She felt her own tearing up.

"I don't want us to fight," Ross said.

"No," she agreed after a moment, her voice thicker than she intended.

Ross leaned forward to kiss her. He knocked over the pail, sending a wave of dirty water over their legs. In leaping away, he instead tangled his feet and tumbled onto the wet floor, Dinah falling atop him.

"Because I will lose," he said. "Because you can take me down."

She laughed.

They kissed.

"I think you'd better marry me," Ross suggested. "To keep me safe."

"I think I'd better," she agreed.

That had been the first fight. What had begun it didn't matter anymore now than it had then. How it had ended—that was what was important. With a laugh, and a kiss, and a proposal. Somehow, over the next seventeen years, they had managed to keep ending arguments that way. Sometimes, instead of a proposal, one or the other had managed to end an argument with a proposition. Which had had an equally pleasurable effect.

Almost worth fighting for.

DINAH SHOVED MIRELLE out of the way and wrenched aside the curtain so hard the rail fell down.

The photograph lay balanced precariously on the edge of the porch roof, where a breath of wind would send it tumbling into the yard. Panicked, Dinah pushed the window up as far as it would go, then ducked through it, pulling herself out onto the warm shingles.

"What the hell are you doing?" Mirelle grabbed at her legs, but Dinah kicked her hands off.

She had never been out on this roof before, but now she was out here, it occurred to her just how much higher up this was than Mirelle's roof. And just how much steeper a pitch this roof had. She found herself falling forward onto her chest, scraping her chin on the asphalt shingles. Slowly she pulled herself to her hands and knees. The frame was perhaps eight feet away; her faculties for estimation, she suddenly discovered, suffered from her fear of heights. She closed her eyes for a moment to steady herself. It didn't work: when she opened them again, the roof—the yard—everything—swirled.

"Come in off there," Mirelle shouted, her red head poking out the window. The rest of her, however, stayed safely inside. "You're going to fall off and kill yourself."

"Thanks for your encouragement." The first order of business, obviously, was to turn herself around, so she could back down the roof. The thought of crawling down the incline with her head lower than her backside did not agree with her at all. "You're the one who threw Ross out here."

"It's not Ross," Mirelle shot back. "It's a picture. That's all. A God-damned picture. Get yourself back in here where it's safe."

Holding her breath, Dinah inched around. Maybe she could slide down on her butt? She felt dizzy. There wasn't enough oxygen at this height.

"You come out and get it, then," she demanded.

"Screw that. And kill myself? Maybe break a nail? No, thank you. Besides. I have to be to rehearsal in a few minutes."

Dinah sighed and turned over onto her seat, her legs stuck out in front of her, her hands behind. A slow crab walk would do it. The movement of traffic below caught her eye, cars going by on the main road. One or two slowed down, passing, and more than one finger pointed out a window at her. A mourning dove flew past, to perch on the telephone line and coo at her. Another one joined it. She hoped they weren't mourning her, before the fact.

She inched down slowly, her eyes on the picture frame where it lay precariously at the edge. When was the last time she'd had this roof checked? She hoped it was in good shape. She hoped it would hold her weight. She envisioned herself caught up in a collapsed roof, half above the shingle, half below. That would really slow traffic now, wouldn't it? She grimaced.

"Dinah!" Mirelle's shout now seemed halfhearted, as though she knew what the response would be, but felt compelled to make the attempt anyway.

"Dinah!" This time the shout came from below. Was there an echo here?

The window behind her slammed closed. The vibration was just enough to tip the picture and send it sliding toward the edge. Dinah made a quick lunge downward, awkward in her position, and got a hand on the frame. Her momentum sent her rolling toward the roof edge. She scrabbled with her free hand at the shingles, for a grip, anything to stop the roll.

No use.

There was no roof beneath her. In the fraction of a second available to her, she steeled herself for her meeting with planet Earth—

—which turned out to be harder, a lot lumpier than she remembered her yard beneath the porch being. And prickly. And which swore a lot more.

"What in the name of God—?" She couldn't catch a breath.

"Jesus, but you're a hell of a lot heavier than I expected," Mark grunted from beneath her in the hedge.

Dinah rolled to the side, further into the greenery. A pain shot up from her ankle into her leg.

"I think I've cracked a rib trying to catch you," he gasped, wrapping his arms across his chest. A trickle of blood wound its way out of his left nostril. "I wonder if this counts as a worker's comp injury."

"You two all right?" Perry, in the yard, looked them up and down and began to laugh.

"Perry, shut up, or I'm going to come over there and kill you." It hurt to speak.

"You can't," he gasped through his laughter. "The way you keep beating the crap out of the kitchen help, I'm just about the only one you have left."

Ignoring the pain in her ankle, Dinah rolled over to look at Mark. He still held his ribs, but was, she noted, breathing. She decided to take this as a good sign. He managed a small half-smile, green needles clinging to his hair.

"Way to go, Grace," he said. His gaze moved to her hands, clasped before her.

She still held Ross's picture.

Twenty-eight

"WHY IS IT," Dinah asked morosely, limping up onto the stage to lower herself awkwardly onto the settee before the mockup of a fireplace, "that all the good threesomes are always made up of two women and one man?"

Gahan was hunched over a small desk in the first row of seats beyond the proscenium, scribbling furious hieroglyphics in a notebook. The lamp on his desk cast a circle of light over his hands and the lower part of his beard. The rehearsal was over for the morning; it would resume after the break for lunch.

"Because, my darling imbecile, it's a male-dominated world. The *menage-a-trois* was in invention of some insecure sot trying to make himself feel more studly." Gahan flipped to a new page in his notebook and scratched some more. "Anyway, what good threesomes might you be thinking of?"

Dinah sighed. She lifted her strapped ankle up onto the arm of the sofa, eying it with disgust. She had never really liked ace bandages, all pinky-beige flesh-tone, like they were trying to kid someone. "All the ones around here. Mirelle, for example, with her husband Wally and his charming girlfriend Alix."

"Ah, the absolutely enchanting Mirelle." For a moment Gahan said nothing, a moment of appreciative silence, during which he lay down his pen thoughtfully. "And then there's the unfortunate Alix."

"Unfortunate?" Dinah echoed, surprised. "Unfortunate *Alix?*"

Gahan chuckled. "Don't be so silly, Dinah, darling." He stood and stretched, giving vent to a yawn which bore a slight resemblance to a foghorn. Then he came around to mount the makeshift steps at the proscenium. "I don't know the woman myself, but I daresay anyone who's been gulled into running afoul of our Mirelle would not have a comfortable time of it at her hands."

Again Dinah looked at her ankle and sighed.

A sigh which was not lost on Gahan. "As you well know. You, a friend of hers of very long standing." He crossed the stage to take the chair across from Dinah's settee. His sandaled feet sounded heavy on the bare boards, and he frowned. "We'll need to find a carpet here." He settled into the chair and the seat sagged dangerously.

"And a different chair," Dinah suggested dryly.

"And a different chair." He folded his hands behind his head. "Anyway, I say 'poor Alix' for a particular reason. Not because she isn't at fault here—she most certainly is. She wouldn't have half the trouble she's having with Mirelle, if she'd just had the sense to play Anne Boleyn on Wally."

"What on earth do you mean?" Dinah asked. "Who's Anne Boleyn when she's at home, aside from Henry VIII's second wife?"

In answer, Gahan fluttered his eyelashes and threw up his hands in mock horror. "No, no," he protested in falsetto, "not until we're married." He dropped his voice. "*That* Anne Boleyn."

Dinah winced, a sudden pang having nothing to do with her sprained ankle.

If Gahan noticed, he did not let on. "But some people simply don't know enough to hold out when a man offers his irresistible self to them."

Wally. Irresistible.

Dinah nearly choked. She would not have put those two words in the same sentence. Or in the same dictionary.

"Funny, that," Gahan mused. "Or ironic, that, I should say. That with all that going on in her personal life, I've cast our Mirelle in another *menage a trois* in this play."

"Very ironic, that," Dinah agreed.

He tossed her an impatient look. "Of course. You're being imbecilic again. It's just that in this particular play, one of the women is dead."

"Until two of them are," Dinah said. "But there it is again. Two women, one man. How come the man has all the fun?"

Gahan's look was positively pitying. "In this case, my darling, it's because a man wrote the play."

"A gay man."

Gahan waved that small point away. "And who says ol' Charles Condomine is having fun? Both the women plague him, and one of them tries to kill him."

"Oh, don't give me that." Dinah made a face. "He's having fun. He's the center of attention, no matter how much of a pain he pretends it is." She smoothed her bandage absently, adjusted her seat.

They sat in silence.

"You know, I've been thinking." Gahan's lips pursed in his beard.

"Always dangerous."

"Catty, darling. But listen. Imagine how therapeutic this play will be for our Mirelle. She'll get to attempt to kill her husband in it. Without any legal or moral repercussions at all. That ought to help her work through some of her deep-seated anger."

Dinah shook her head. "Doesn't Elvira try to kill what's-his-face—Charles—because she wants him to herself? That's not the way it is for Mirelle. She'd try to kill Wally because she wants him *dead.*"

Gahan's smile, suddenly broadening his face beneath that beard, was annoyingly superior. "You think?"

She glared at him. "Oh, what do you know about it, anyway? As you pointed out just a moment ago, she's my friend. My friend of *very long standing.* You've known her now for what? A week? Two?"

"Ohh, let's get all possessive and territorial, shall we?" Gahan stretched his arms over his head, his Sex Pistols tee shirt climbing upwards to reveal a very round hairy belly. He yawned once more, sliding down in the chair, his legs thrust out before him. "It might be *because* you are Mirelle's friend that you don't see what a relative stranger might. A relative stranger like myself."

While she pondered this, she watched Gahan's narrowed eyes travel over the sparsely furnished stage and up into the flies. He pursed his lips again in a silent whistle. She thought she could see the wheels spinning inside his head as he constructed his stage set up there and attempted to live in it.

"You know, these threesomes of yours—" he remarked, shattering any illusions she might have had about what he was really constructing.

"Not mine," she countered quickly.

"I was just thinking of their curious permutations in our little world." He might not have heard her protest. "Take our lad Perry, for instance. His requisite threesome, you have to admit, would not be two women and a man. It would be him and a couple of other guys."

"True," Dinah conceded. She could not get comfortable on the settee; when she shifted, her ankle let her know about it. "Or two guys and a girl, maybe, if the other guy was wishy-washy."

"And then there's me."

Permutations indeed.

Dinah caught his mischievous look and laughed.

"My threesome might be transgender, crossgender, multigender," he mused, each possibility seeming to delight him more than the last. "It just depends on my mood. Or the day of the week."

"Always the egalitarian."

"Equal opportunity, *c'est moi.*"

"I hope we're talking about an emotional triangle here, and not a physical one," Dinah said. "I'm not sure I need to know the details of your sex life at this point."

"Now, now," Gahan admonished, his large hands falling limply over the arms of the chair. "No need to be catty—I've already told you that." He winked. "And what about you, oh, my lovely Dinah? If I recall correctly, shortly after you and I met, you had your own peculiar threesome going on."

He had noticed her wince, then. But like the Gahan she knew and loved, he had held his ammunition until he could figure out how best to put it to use.

"What was her name, then?" he prodded. For all the world as though he didn't remember. For all the world as though he wasn't the one to whom Dinah had gone, shaking, after the visit from Ross's estranged wife.

Dinah bit her lip, turning awkwardly to face him. He still sprawled over— on—across the chair. How could he lay such a trap, drop such a bomb, and then simply laze there as though he'd made some perfectly innocuous remark about the weather? "Her name," she reminded him, speaking distinctly, "was Sherry. As well you know."

His smile was slow, mocking. Dinah resented it.

"You sound a bit touchy this afternoon on the subject of Ross's wife."

"Ex-wife."

"Of course. I apologize." Gahan didn't sound sorry at all. "You were her successor."

"For seventeen years," she reminded him. "Look. What's your point? Why are you bringing this all up?"

He shrugged, pressing his fingers together to form a tent, over which he gazed at her. "It just seemed *apropos* to our discussion. And I've seemed to have touched a nerve. I'm very interested in this."

"Well, you can be interested in hell," Dinah returned sharply. "I'm not touchy about Ross and Sherry. And me. Our situation was completely different from Mirelle's. I'm not the Alix here. Even if I was, that was nearly twenty years ago. It's way too late to worry about it now."

So why was she?

She glared at Gahan. He smiled genially back.

"This is why I love you so dearly, Dinah," he said. "Because under that practical exterior, you're so self-delusional. It's good to know I'm not alone in the world in that respect."

"You're a bastard, Gahan."

"And that's why *you* love *me.*" Again he yawned, then stood, flexing his back. "But I'm getting old, and old men need sustenance to continue working through the afternoon and into the evening. Let me walk you back to the house." He held out his arm.

For a long moment she remained seated, still glaring, refusing to touch him. The smile had stretched into the beatific, but with a glint behind the eyes. He knew she'd cave. Because despite herself, she did love him, and all his annoying ways.

"All right." Grudging. She grabbed his elbow and pulled herself up, wincing when she put weight on her ankle. "I'll let you walk me home. Just this once."

He matched his steps to hers, let her lean heavily on his arm as they navigated across the stage and down the steps. "And on the way, you can tell me all about your new and exciting threesome."

The center aisle was dim, and she could not see his expression now, for which she was grateful. "What the hell are you talking about?"

Was he still grinning?

"The one with you, and that delightful young Mark—such a handsome boy—"

"And the third player?"

"Why, Ross, of course. He's your Elvira. Don't be an imbecile, darling."

Twenty-nine

SHE WATCHED THE taillights of first Dirk's car, then Gillian's car, disappear down the road, the restaurant buttoned up for the night. Restless, Dinah could not bring herself to re-enter the house, to head upstairs. The night air was cool on her warm face, and felt better than the air-conditioning in the dining room; the breeze smelled of roses, and the floribunda growing by the theater door glowed. The sky was clear, spangled with constellations she couldn't recognize if she tried.

Abruptly she turned her back on the restaurant and stepped out onto the lawn, damp now with dew. Her ankle twinged, but she ignored it. A few crickets chirped and fell silent as she passed.

She slid into the driver's seat of the Mazda and dug the extra key from under the seat. It didn't take long to follow Dirk and Gill out onto the deserted road; it took only a few minutes more before she turned into the driveway beside Mirelle's house, pulling up behind the hulk of Kelly's BMW.

There was a light on upstairs, and when she mounted the porch steps, Dinah saw that the light over Mirelle's kitchen sink was still burning as well. She tapped lightly on the screen door, and after a moment, Mirelle appeared, brushing aside the curtain to peer out suspiciously.

Mirelle jerked the door open and walked away. "Oh, it's just you."

"Thanks for the enthusiastic welcome." Dinah let herself in and closed the door behind her.

"Lock it."

Dinah did.

Mirelle had slipped into a ladderbacked chair at the kitchen table. A cigarette burned in an ashtray next to her script, which lay face-down.

"A bit dark in here for reading, isn't it?" Dinah slid into the chair opposite.

"Memorizing. I'm memorizing. I don't need light for that." Mirelle picked up the cigarette and took a long drag. She blew the smoke out, and her eyes glinted through the haze. "What are you doing out so late?"

"You never used to complain when we were teenagers."

"I used to let you in through the window when we were teenagers."

"And look how far we've come." Dinah watched the tendrils of smoke curl upward toward the ceiling. She tried identifying shapes, animals. Was that a dragon? "Where's your house guest?"

Mirelle tossed her head toward the hallway and the stairs. "Gone up to bed. She's had a hard day of it. Interviewing."

"Any luck yet?"

Mirelle gave a shrug of her elegant shoulders under the silk shirt. "Not that I know of." With a sudden impatient gesture, Mirelle jammed the cigarette into the ashtray, crushing it out. "Look. Dinah. I'm sorry about this afternoon. I honestly didn't know you'd go out onto the roof like that. And I honestly didn't expect you to fall off and break your neck."

"Ha," Dinah scoffed. "You'd probably just discovered the provisions of my will. Where you inherit the entire fortune."

Mirelle picked up her pack of cigarettes, but threw it down again almost immediately. "Damn it all, Di, this is an apology. From me. Probably the only one you've ever gotten. Certainly the only one you'll ever hear from here on in."

This was true, anyway. Dinah nodded. "I know. I know you didn't mean to kill me. If you had, you would have been more efficient. And it's only a slight sprain. I'll live."

"Thanks to our young Mark, playing the hero and catching you on the way down."

Dinah pointed an accusing finger. "This is where we draw the line. Our young Mark wouldn't have had to play the hero if you hadn't been so intent upon having me sleep with him to begin with. So maybe you and I ought not talk about our young Mark, if you don't mind."

Before Mirelle could answer, they both hear the thunk of a car door outside. She threw a quick glance to the door, then back.

"You didn't invite Perry to join us this evening, did you?" she demanded, her voice low.

Dinah shook her head.

A little shriek rolled down to them from upstairs.

Mirelle was at the door swiftly, checking the lock. She leaned back against the wall, peering sideways through the window to the drive, looking for all the world like one of Charlie's Angels.

"Go up and see what she needs," she ordered through clenched teeth. "And for God's sake, keep her quiet."

Dinah dodged around her. "Who's out there?"

"Go *on*," Mirelle repeated.

The urgency in her voice propelled Dinah to the foot of the stairs. Above her in the dimness, she could make out Kelly's form, crouching behind the newel post.

"Who is that?" Kelly squealed, and Dinah started up the stairs.

"Just me."

Kelly did not rise from her crouch. She peered beyond Dinah, fearfully. "Did you see him? Is he out there? Does he have a gun?"

Dinah's stomach lurched. She grabbed Kelly by her thin arm, urging her toward the back bedroom. "Who? Does who have a gun?" She shoved the door open and dashed toward the window overlooking the driveway.

Kelly hung back, her breathing shallow. "He's going to kill me this time. I know he's going to kill me this time."

Don't panic don't panic don't panic.

The streetlight at the end of the driveway cast grotesque shadows across the yard toward the porch. Immediately below her was the roof of Mirelle's car; behind that, the BMW hulked with its driver's side door open. Her own Mazda brought up the rear of the line. She could see no one; perhaps someone was on the porch.

"Kelly," she whispered harshly, "is that Rob down there?"

Still Kelly hung back.

The porch door was locked. Did Rob know anyone in the house was awake? What was he doing down there? Obviously, he was after the car, but jammed between the two others, it was immovable.

"Kelly," Dinah ordered. "Get the phone. Call the police."

Kelly didn't move.

"Oh, for Christ's sake." With one hand Dinah twisted the latch atop the window and slid the sash up as quietly as she could manage. With the other she groped blindly behind her on the bedside table for the landline extension. When she put the receiver to her ear, she found Mirelle already on the line.

"—509 Main Street. Yellow house. Number's on the front." Mirelle's voice was hushed.

"An officer will be there shortly, Mrs. Holbein," a flat female voice replied.

"Mirelle," Dinah cut in. "Kelly thinks he's got a gun."

A pounding began, a fist on wood. Dinah heard it simultaneously through the window and the telephone line.

"Answer the door!" Rob's voice.

The pounding intensified. The door was hidden by the porch roof; Dinah could see nothing.

"Please hurry," Mirelle urged into the phone. Then the line went dead.

Dinah tossed the extension aside and pressed her forehead to the screen in the window, listening.

"Open up," Rob demanded.

"What do you want?" Mirelle shouted.

Kelly shrieked, sinking to the floor. "I don't want to die."

"Hush. Listen," Dinah ordered.

"Could you move that car, so I can get mine out?"

"He's going to kill me," Kelly wailed.

"No, he's not. He wants the car," Dinah said.

Immediately Kelly sat up. "Tell him he can't have it. Damn it, I won't let him have it. That's my car."

Dinah sucked in a breath.

"I'm not moving anything. Go home, Rob. It's the middle of the night." Mirelle's voice was filled with contempt.

"I'm not going anywhere without my car," Rob shouted.

Dinah wished he would move out from under the porch roof. She wished she could see him.

In the distance a siren wailed.

"I've called the cops, Rob," Mirelle yelled.

Kelly crept closer.

"I'm not going without the car," he repeated.

Then the yard was strobed in blue, a surreal look which was becoming all too familiar. There was a squawk from a radio, a shout, a slam from a door.

"Would you step away from the door, sir?" an authoritative voice asked. Somehow it didn't sound like a request. Two shadowy officers stood in the driveway, each holding a flashlight aimed toward the porch, each with his spare hand at his gun belt. "And keep your hands where we can see them."

A shuffling sorted itself into footsteps, then Rob's foreshortened figure appeared, stepping gingerly down the steps into the driveway. Even from the unflattering angle, he looked unkempt—hair a mess, shirt untucked at the back. He held his hands out from his sides.

One of the policemen quickly stepped forward and ran expert hands over Rob. "Are you armed, sir? The caller said you were armed."

"I'm not. I just want my car."

Satisfied with the pat-down, the policeman stepped back. In his hand, Rob's wallet. "Is your identification in here, sir? Can we see it?" Again, not quite a request.

The second officer disappeared under the porch roof.

"Come on," Dinah hissed at Kelly. She dodged for the door and the stairs. When she reached the end of the dark hallway, Mirelle had the door open for the second policeman. Officer Jim Reed. Of course. He made no sign that he recognized Dinah.

"His wife is here—upstairs." Mirelle's expression was hard, harder than Dinah had ever seen it. "She's been here since she was released from the hospital after he hit her." She flicked a sideways glance at Dinah. "When he showed up tonight, we were afraid of what he might do."

"He says he wants to take the car. Is it his?" The officer glanced back at his partner and Rob.

"It's mine." Kelly had appeared soundlessly. Bathed from the overhead light, which Mirelle had flicked on with the advent of the police, her high cheekbones looked pinched and pointy. Her unmade-up face seemed entirely taken up by the dark circles under her eyes. "I'm Kelly Carvey. The car is mine."

The policeman's face remained impassive. "It's registered to you?"

Kelly swallowed. "To both of us. The registration is in the glove compartment, if you want to check. But"—and she sounded desperate—"he's taken everything else from me. I need the car."

"Well, ma'am," Jim Reed said, clearing his throat lightly, "we're in no position to settle property disputes—that's a court issue. But as long as your name is on the registration as well as his, he can't make the claim that you've stolen the car."

Kelly's tiny smile was triumphant.

Through the window Dinah could see Rob and the other policeman in discussion. As she watched, Rob's expression became more animated. His voice rose. She heard him repeat, "I'm not leaving until I have the car."

"I want him out of here," Mirelle said through clenched teeth. "You know he's here to intimidate his wife. Did you check to see if he's got a gun?"

"We patted him down. No gun on him."

"He owns one," Kelly said, clenching her hands. "I don't think it's registered," she added spitefully. "And he's a felon."

The officer made no move, yet somehow now seemed more poised to spring into emergency action. He caught his partner's eye, jerked his head in Rob's direction, and tapped his gun belt. The other policeman nodded, said something into his shoulder mic.

"No gun on him," Jim Reed repeated.

"Can't you make him go?" Mirelle demanded.

"If Mr. Carvey refuses to leave, when you, the property owner, tell him to, in front of us as witnesses, we can arrest him for criminal trespass."

Mirelle lifted her chin. "Let's do it, then." She brushed past the policeman and out onto the porch. "Rob," she called.

Rob turned. His face was contorted with anger.

Dinah flinched, even though she knew he couldn't see her. Behind her, Kelly was clenching and unclenching her fists. Her expression was calculating. And somehow satisfied.

"Rob," Mirelle repeated. "I want you off my property."

"I told you already," he replied. "I told you all. I'm not leaving without the car. Move this other one."

"Mr. Carvey," the deep-voiced officer said. "Mrs. Holbein has told you to leave her private property. Are you refusing?"

For a moment Rob hesitated. The glance he flashed Mirelle was full of loathing, as was the glance he shot toward the upper windows, behind which, presumably, his wife cowered. Then he looked squarely at the policemen.

"Yes," he said. "I'm refusing."

"Then you give me no choice but to have to place you under arrest."

Dinah watched as Rob was instructed to lean against the car with his arms and legs spread. Officer Reed patted him down again—still no gun, Kelly's words notwithstanding—before drawing first one hand, then the other, down behind his back to slip the cuffs on. The other policeman read the Miranda warning in his stentorian voice.

When they led Rob away down the driveway, where the blue lights were still strobing the neighborhood, Dinah glanced sideways at Kelly. Her eyes were gleaming, and she was grinning.

Thirty

"YOU'VE GOT TO go with her," Mirelle had said. "You can't expect her to go apply for a protection order at the courthouse all alone. What if he shows up? I have to be at rehearsal—we're blocking act two, and Elvira is absolutely vital there. So it has to be you."

That was how Dinah now found herself sitting in a hard-backed chair in an empty conference room in the district courthouse while Kelly filled out a long form at the table. Kelly leaned over the paper, her lower lip caught between her teeth, as she wrote in her answers to the questions. She wrote painfully slowly, forming each letter separately, with curlicues reminiscent of those of an adolescent girl. When she finally flipped the paper over to the other side, chewing on the end of her pen, Dinah could see the great white space at the middle, and could read the question upside down. Kelly had to describe the incident, or series of incidents, which led to her applying for this temporary protection order.

This could take years.

And possibly several other sheets of paper

Again, the nagging feeling of guilt. For the life of her, Dinah could not imagine why she could not warm up to Kelly. She knew she ought to say something intelligent here, something wise and comforting. For God's sake, she could be helping to fill this damned form. She had been there last night, after all, when the policeman had informed Kelly of her best bet, applying for this order against Rob. Dinah sighed, dissatisfied with her own gut response and unable to figure out why. Sure, she felt sympathy for the poor woman—who wouldn't? Yet it seemed vague, general, a weird detached sort of sympathy. For the situation, not the victim. Dinah loathed herself for this.

Kelly looked up sharply. "I'm filling this out just as fast as I can," she said defensively.

"No, no." Dinah waved a hand quickly. "Take your time."

"I'm just getting to the part where the police came and arrested Rob." Kelly's voice had softened; her face had taken on that odd expression of satisfaction it had worn last night. Kelly chewed the end of the pen for a moment, then bent again to write some more. "I wonder if he's still in jail." She looked around swiftly. "I wonder where the jail is." She said this as though she thought Rob might leap out of the woodwork at any minute.

Dinah stood. Her ankle twinged; she had wrapped it again this morning. Still, walking about the room had to be better than just sitting in that hard-backed chair. The exercise had to be good for her. She went to the closed door to peer out into the hallway, through a crisscrossing of wire sandwiched between layers of safety glass. At the desk in the lobby, a skinny man in a baseball cap was opening his wallet and peering inside: paying some sort of fine or fee. A pair of police officers strolled past, hats in hand. Near the desk stood an enormous palm-like plant, its fronds shiny like plastic. Dinah turned away.

The window on the far side of the room overlooked the parking lot, which sloped away downhill from the street, so that this window was on a level high above the cars. Dinah leaned against the side and looked down at the blue BMW.

"No, he's not still in jail," she said.

"*What?*"

Rob was looking furtively over his shoulder as he edged toward the BMW; he kept his head low as he made his way between the rows of cars, as though trying to avoid detection.

"He's going for the car."

Kelly's chair fell as she leapt away from the table and rushed to join her at the window. Rob was on his knees next to the car. He slipped a key into the lock, and opened the door.

"I need a policeman," Kelly hissed, and disappeared out into the lobby.

Dinah watched. Whatever policeman Kelly could find to come to her rescue, it would be too late. Rob was in the car, one foot still on the pavement. Was he turning the key in the ignition? Would he be squealing out in a spray of gravel momentarily? He'd have to be off soon. Or would he? It seemed to be taking an inordinate amount of time for him to start the engine; she wished the window opened, so she could at least hear what was going on. The car wasn't starting. Dinah wondered why; it had started just fine for Kelly when they'd left Mirelle's.

A tall policeman, his glasses hiding his eyes, approached the BMW warily, hand at his belt. In a moment Kelly reappeared at Dinah's side, peering around her with a look of excited expectation.

"Has he arrested Rob again yet?" she demanded.

"Give them a minute. Your police guy just got there."

Rob emerged from the car, and the conversation between the two men became more animated—at least on Rob's side. The policeman's expression, from this distance, and disguised by those wraparound sunglasses, was impossible to read.

"He couldn't get the car started anyway," Dinah said.

Kelly clapped her hands together, laughing. "I know. It has an ignition security code. I changed it. If Rob doesn't know what it is, he can't start the car. No matter how many keys he has." She laughed again. An unpleasant sound.

Outside, Rob slammed the car door. The policeman spoke, and Rob's expression turned surly as he fell into step beside the officer. His short legs had to work overtime to keep up with the other man's long strides.

"Looks like they're coming in." Dinah couldn't keep the dismay from her voice. She hadn't signed up for this. She had no desire whatsoever to see her former employee, to speak to him, to even be in the same room with him. Were those butterflies in her stomach, or was she just going to throw up?

Kelly's laugh died away, and she looked grim. "That's not what I asked for. I told that policeman Rob was stealing the car. I didn't ask him to bring Rob in here."

They waited.

The door opened to admit the officer, who held it for Rob. Still wearing the surly expression, Rob flicked his eyes from his wife to Dinah and back.

"Mrs. Carvey?" The policeman had a deep voice. From her place near the window, Dinah looked up. He had not removed his sunglasses. "You didn't tell me the person attempting to steal your car was your husband." The tone was bland, but the words were accusation enough.

Kelly's glance slewed away, and under her expertly madeup face, her skin pinkened. "I—I didn't see who it was."

Rob snorted.

The policeman turned to Rob for the shortest of moments. Rob shut up. Dinah wished she had that kind of power.

Now Kelly's words rushed out, as though she were fearful that the officer would force her to shut up as well, and she had to get everything out before he did so. "I'm applying for a protection order, officer." She fluttered a hand toward the paperwork on the table. "Rob is dangerous. I've just been released from the hospital—and he's the one who put me there. I have the car, and now he wants to take it from me. Can't you help me?" She turned her wide eyes, now filmy with tears, on him.

The officer remained unmoved. "I don't have the power to make decisions about your marital property, Mrs. Carvey."

He could have been quoting out of the same script as Officer Jim Reed the previous evening. He had the key to the BMW in his hand. He now set it on the table between Rob and Kelly. Both stared at it hungrily, two wild animals slavering after the same bit of prey.

"Are you a friend of these two people, ma'am?" he asked Dinah.

Dinah licked her lips nervously. "I know them both, yes," she answered warily. Unwilling to commit further than that.

"I'll leave it to you, then, to decide which of them should take the car for the time being. Until the question goes before a judge. You know them better than I."

The officer turned on his shiny black heel and went quickly out the door. He was obviously glad to be free of the lot of them.

"But—"

"Please—"

Kelly and Rob called after him at the same time. He did not return.

Don't leave me here with this, Dinah wanted to call after him, but it would be of no use. She turned back to the pair, still with the key between them.

"It doesn't matter which of you takes that," she said after a tense moment. "Kelly's already got a key, and she's the only one who knows the ignition code."

Rob swore.

That slow mean smile spread over Kelly's small face.

Again Rob swore and stomped from the room.

Dinah wished that she too could wash her hands of them as quickly as the policeman had. "I'll be outside, Kelly, when you get that thing filed."

Thirty-one

IT WAS STILL early when they returned to the restaurant. Dinah climbed out of the BMW and slammed the door without saying goodbye. Kelly, for her part, pulled out of the driveway with more spinning of tires than was strictly necessary. In the roadway, a squeal of brakes and a honking of horns. Hearing no crash, Dinah didn't bother to turn. Let them settle it in the way of all ornery drivers, flipping each other off in the rearview, a bizarre tribal dance in sign language.

She limped into the kitchen and paused in the double doorway to catch her breath. The morning sun gleamed off the copper, and she forced herself to fall back on the one thing that had made her feel better over the past several months: admiring the restaurant she and Ross had dreamed up. It almost looked like something out of a film: perfection, the way a kitchen was supposed to look. She breathed out, turning slowly. Everything in its place. The counters were all scrubbed and gleaming, the floor swept and washed from the previous evening. She crossed her arms and leaned against the doorframe, missing Ross desperately. Never mind that in an hour and a half the place would be overrun by Mark, and Perry, and all the others whose work would quickly dispel any patina of perfection.

It could be worse, though, she had to admit.

It *had* been worse. She smiled wryly.

She would make cookies, she decided. She went to the great refrigeration unit and hauled open the door. The rubber sealing gasket gave way with a rude sucking noise. The blast of cool air which washed over her skin was welcome; the morning had warmed up considerably. She resisted the urge to remain in the walk-in, inviting though it was—inviting though the idea of leaping out at Perry and causing him heart failure was. She giggled.

The recipe, she was grateful to realize, was still filed away in her memory, despite not having been consulted for some time. How often had she baked cookies for Ross? She felt a childish sort of pleasure in the act, the same kind he took in scooping a finger full of cookie dough from the bowl on his way through the kitchen. She'd always slapped his hand away, but it was a game: she was baking for her husband. Now she brought forth the hand mixer that no one ever used in the restaurant kitchen; with this she beat the sugars into the butter, scraping down the sides of the bowl with a spatula and singing gently to herself.

The phone rang while she was cracking eggs into the mix; she lined the shells up in a neat row on the worktop, ignoring the peals. *If it's important,* Ross whispered in her ear, *they'll call back.* She felt her face warm. The first time he had whispered those words into her ear, he had been busily unbuttoning her shirt.

Vanilla. Baking soda. Salt. Flour. Chocolate chips. Dinah paused in her mixing to feed herself a handful of chocolate bits. Bittersweet, but in a chocolate pinch, that would do. She paused to draw herself a glass of water, still singing softly.

Dinah turned the dial to preheat the oven.

She used the giant baking sheets, and the medium dough scoop, turning the dough out onto the parchment in neat mounds, tan studded with dark brown. When the thermometer read 350 degrees, she slid first one pan and then the other inside. A glance at the clock. Eight minutes for chewy cookies, a bit more for a harder bake.

Dinah was swishing hot soapy water around in the deep sink when the screen door slapped open.

"What the hell's going on in here?"

Perry's high voice rose in concern until he caught sight of Dinah leaning over her dirty dishes.

"Oh." He sighed in relief. "It's only you."

"Thanks for the enthusiasm?" She rinsed the suds from the big bowl and upended it over the strainer. "It's nice to know I'm loved."

"Don't be silly." Perry picked up her water glass and drained it. "I must love you. I share your germs."

"Gross." Dinah clanked the measuring spoons into the strainer.

He brought the glass to her and held it out. Hands immersed in the hot water, Dinah looked down at the glass as though at some particularly horrendous scientific specimen. Grinning, Perry put it into the sink.

"Really, though," he said, shrugging off the plaid button-down he wore over his white tee shirt. "I had this flashback—"

"I told you to stay off that acid."

"—of coming into the kitchen and finding Rob. Maybe Rob *and* Kelly."

"Fighting." Dinah closed her eyes momentarily and sighed.

"Or worse yet, having sex."

"Gross," Dinah repeated.

"Talk about a bad acid trip." Perry covered his face with his hands, shuddering in a most exaggerated way. "Enough to make anyone decide against going straight, let me tell you." He hung the shirt up behind the back door, which he then opened again to let in the early summer air. "Thank God it was only you, Di, or I would have had to commit ritual suicide."

"Then who would have done dinner?" The dishes washed up, Dinah pushed past Perry to the ovens. When she opened the door, a rush of hot air enveloped her. The cookies were nearly done. "You can't kill yourself, Perry. You're under contract."

"So sue a dead person." He had pulled on his white jacket and now sluiced his hands in the sink.

Mitts on, Dinah drew first one pan out of the oven, then the other. She turned and saw that Perry had set out the wire cooling racks for her. He handed her a spatula, then watched as she slid cookie after cookie onto the racks. She carried the pans and spatula to the sink, knowing full well that as soon as her back was turned, Perry would be into the cookies like some juvenile delinquent. She smiled to herself, reaching for the nylon scrubber. At least she was baking for somebody.

As she finished the pans, Perry paired his phone with the speaker on the windowsill—a new addition to the kitchen, one which had been impossible to contemplate with Rob and Kelly, but which Dinah heartily approved. The music was dreamy, a cross between techno and Gregorian chants.

"You like it?" Perry asked, emerging from the walk-in with a tray of beef. "Delirium. They're Canadian. They kind of grow on you. Get in your head."

The woman's voice swooped upward.

The kitchen phone rang.

"Damn," Dinah said.

Perry slid his pan onto the butcher's block, then picked up the receiver. "Galloway's." His pale glance slewed toward Dinah. "Yeah, she is," he said, ignoring her frantic waving. "Right here. Yes, she wants me to tell you she isn't." He held the receiver out. "It's Mirelle."

Dinah slitted her eyes at his as she took the receiver from his hand. "Consider your contract null and void. Do what you have to do."

Perry blew her a kiss and moved away to concoct.

"I've been calling and calling," Mirelle shrilled into her ear. "Why haven't you answered the phone?"

"Because I've been ignoring and ignoring." If Dinah stretched, she could nearly reach the cooling cookies. She waved her fingers, trying to get Perry's attention. He was busily measuring out cream and pointedly did not look up.

"I knew you were there. I called home and Kelly's already there, so I knew you were back from the courthouse. Ignoring me, then." Mirelle sniffed. "Well, for that, I have half a mind not to tell you about this really weird bit of news I got this morning."

Dinah refused to rise to the bait. Mirelle could no more hold onto a weird bit of news than she could restrain herself from flirting with anything in trousers. Dinah waited. If only she could reach one of those cookies while she waited, though. Perry still did not look in the direction of her flailing hand.

"So? Aren't you sorry you ignored me now? Aren't you going to apologize?"

"No."

At last Perry turned. He looked at Dinah's hand, then pointed silently at the cookies, then to her, his face contorting into mock puzzlement.

She pointed more vigorously.

He still pretended ignorance.

"You're such a bitch, Galloway."

Dinah did not argue. After a moment of waiting, Mirelle sighed, a long, drawn-out, put-upon sound.

"Anyway," she began, as though she had not just threatened to withhold this enormously important tidbit. "I ran into Wally's secretary, Alice Peavey—you know her?—when she apparently was doing the mail run to the post office. She asked me if I'd seen Wally."

"Seen him? You've been married to him for how many years? Eight? Nine? Of course you've seen him." Despite her flipness, Dinah paused, giving up on her futile reaching for a cookie, hand in the air before her.

"Lately, Dinah." Mirelle's sigh was now full of exasperation. "Lately. She wanted to know whether I'd seen him any time in the last few days."

"Why? What's wrong with him?"

"That's just it, Dinah." The laugh was hard to read. "No one's seen him. No one has seen him in a couple of days."

Perversely, Perry chose this moment to shove a cookie into Dinah's open mouth. On her intake of breath, crumbs filled her airway. She spat the cookie out, coughing.

Perry thumped her soundly between the shoulder blades on his way to the walk-in.

"What are you doing?" Mirelle demanded shrilly. "Are you laughing?"

It took a few moments for Dinah to catch her breath. "I'm choking to death," she rasped out at last. "Perry's trying to kill me."

"All right." This information did not seem to particularly interest Mirelle, as she breezed on with her story. "So I'm buying some stamps, and along comes the superintendent. He's got the same question. Have I seen Wally? No one has seen him in days, Dinah." She imparted this bit with a note of wonder in her voice, as though describing a miracle. "Several days."

"He hasn't been in to work at all?"

"Not unless he's invisible."

"Where's his car?"

"What?"

"*Where's his car?*" Sometimes the woman was just plain obtuse.

"It's in his parking space behind the building. Everyone's interested in his dumb car. What does it matter where his car is?"

"Because," Dinah pointed out patiently, "that would give you an idea as to where he might have been last."

The pause indicated that Mirelle was considering this idea. "Nice bit of deduction, Sherlock," she admitted at last. "But what does that tell us?"

"Not a damn thing. Look, are you done with rehearsal this morning? What time do you have to be there this afternoon? Why don't you stop by?" The cookie she had spat out was a sad and broken lump on the tile at her feet. She prodded it gingerly with a toe.

"Yeah, all right. We'll have lunch and see if we can solve this thing before I have my afternoon date with Gahan." The note of wonder seeped back into Mirelle's voice. "Do you suppose he's run away from home, Dinah?"

"He didn't have to run away from home. You already threw him out, remember?"

Thirty-two

"MISSING!" PERRY SWUNG his cleaver into the side of beef enthusiastically.

"Isn't that a turn-up for the books," Mark added. He tapped the wire whisk several times on the side of a frothing stainless steel bowl. "What's this music, Per?" The techno swelled from the bluetooth speaker. "This woman singing sounds familiar."

"Delirium," Dinah tossed over her shoulder. She slid the remainder of the cookies into a container; they'd work their way onto the menu in some form. "They're Canadian."

"Never heard of them." Mark glared down into his bowl, as though somehow holding the contents responsible for his level of ignorance.

"That's because they're Canadian," Mirelle snapped impatiently. "Now where'd I put that glass?" She looked at the countertops in search of the drink she'd brought in from the bar moments earlier.

"I'm Canadian," Perry retorted, his high voice ripe with insult.

"I've never heard of you, either," Mirelle shot back. Glass recovered, she followed Dinah out of the kitchen, through the big dining room, and out onto the porch. Dinah could almost feel Mirelle's eager breath on the back of her neck.

"Pull up a chair," Dinah said, wiping surreptitiously at her hairline with the back of her hand. She settled on the porch swing, kicking off her shoes and depositing the plate of cookies on the table to the side. A salad would have been a more healthy lunch, but she didn't really care. "Tell me again about Wally. How many days, exactly? He hasn't been in to the office, he hasn't called, his car's still in the lot, his secretary doesn't know where he is, and his boss doesn't know where he is."

"That's the gist of it," Mirelle said. "You sure you want me to tell you about it again?"

"Nah, never mind." The ice cubes tinkles against the sweaty sides of her water glass. "His cell phone?"

"On his desk, Alice said."

"You know what that leaves, don't you?"

Now Mirelle's full lips curved into a smile that was best described as unpleasant. "Oh, I know. I didn't go anywhere near her today, though. Believe me."

"Our girl Alix." Dinah helped herself to a cookie. Mirelle apparently had no plans to dilute her drinking by eating anything quite so mundane.

"Our girl Alix." There was satisfaction in Mirelle's voice. "That's where he's been staying, you know. At her place. Whatever sort of place that is." She made a face, as though her husband might be living in a brothel, for all she knew.

"Now, now." A robin lifted off from the lawn, which badly needed watering, half a worm dangling from its beak. Dinah watched it go. The landscaper would be by tomorrow. "Don't let's be catty."

"Why ever not?" Mirelle demanded. "That's half the fun of life. After all, you know both the secretary and the superintendent called her, looking for him, before they thought to ask me. Or maybe it was the other way around— she called them? Something like that, anyway."

"How sad."

"What's sad?" With a creak of the steps, Gahan loomed up before them on the porch. His bulky form blocked out the sun. Which was quite all right, as this afternoon he was bright enough himself in a yellow Hawaiian shirt covered in parrots. "Not my two favorite ladies. Don't tell me that. I won't allow it."

"It's sad that my husband has no sooner moved in with his mistress," Mirelle said tartly, turning her cheek up to be kissed, "then he's apparently out catting around on her."

Gahan raised his bristly eyebrows. "My attention is riveted."

"Tell him the whole story," Dinah suggested, taking another cookie. Just one more; they really were quite good. She hadn't lost her touch.

Mirelle did so, drawing out every strange morsel.

Suddenly Dinah laughed. "Did you ever stop to think that this might just be a continuation of the other weird disappearances?"

Gahan turned. "There are others? Who else is missing?"

"No, not people. Stuff."

"At my house," Mirelle explained. "Small appliances. My coffee maker. My hair dryer. The toaster. Stuff like that."

"And now the appliance gremlins have gone on to bigger and better prizes," Dinah suggested. The idea was attractive.

"Bigger I'll agree to," Mirelle countered. She drained the last of her mint julep and looked down into her empty glass sadly. "But definitely not better."

"Alrighty, then."

Gahan wasn't laughing. His wide face under the beard was creased in a frown. "Has anyone called the police?"

"Really." Mirelle laughed. "It's annoying being without a hairdryer and a coffee maker, but it hardly seemed like something to go rushing to the police about."

Dinah nodded. "Yes. And we've seen quite enough of the police around here lately, if you don't mind. I was up close and personal with them again this morning at the courthouse with Kelly." The thought of the scene in the conference room dampened her humor a bit.

"No, you two extremely shortsighted women." Gahan cut through their merriment. He had taken a cookie from the plate and was crumbling it, tossing the bits out onto the grass. Then he hurled the remainder toward the road and sat in the swing beside Dinah. Something—the chains, perhaps?—groaned. Dinah held her breath.

"So much for being his favorite women," Mirelle pouted. "How fickle men are. Really."

He ignored her. "What I want to know is whether anyone has called the police yet—about your husband?"

They stopped laughing.

Mirelle turned her huge eyes on him, her lashes fluttering. "I feel more inclined to call the police about my coffee maker."

"But what if he's hurt?" Gahan protested. He seemed genuinely concerned. "What if he's been injured? What if, God forbid, someone has kidnapped him?"

Mirelle was having none of it. She waved off the protests with a finely manicured hand. "Who would kidnap him? Some student with a grudge about administrative detention? Come off it, Gahan."

He shifted on the porch swing, and again Dinah looked up toward the hooks in the bead board ceiling. The chains held. Still, she imagined the links pulling apart in super slow motion. She stood up quickly and leaned against the porch railing.

"I can't believe you're being so callous about this, Mirelle." Gahan's voice held oceans of disappointment. "The man is missing. Several days? Something must have happened to him. I can't believe you aren't more concerned."

She turned her face away. Deliberately she lit up a cigarette, then flicked the still-burning match into the shrubbery. Dinah watched its arc in mild concern, hoping it would go out before it burned the place down.

"It's not my place to be concerned," Mirelle said with surprising bitterness. "You want concern, you go ask Alix Mailloux for some."

GAHAN COULDN'T HAVE directed it any better.

As if on cue, a little yellow VW Bug screeched into the parking lot, spewing up gravel.

"Looks like you're about to get your chance," Dinah said, straightening slowly.

"What—?" Gahan stared wide-eyed.

"Alix," Mirelle hissed, blowing a cloud of smoke upward.

Indeed, Alix Mailloux leapt from the driver's side, leaving the door open as she rushed around her car, her blonde hair streaming behind her: a ship under full, though barely controlled, sail. Her round face was white and strained, though her eyes were full of determination.

She pounded up the porch steps and took up a position directly in front of Mirelle, hands on her hips.

"What have you done with him?" she demanded, her voice cracking.

Mirelle gazed at her as though at a specimen from the zoo. "My dear girl, whatever do you mean?"

"*What have you done with him?*" Alix's voice climbed the register. "You know damn well what I mean, Mirelle, so don't play dumb with me. Wallace. I want to know where he is."

Mirelle looked bored. She lifted a hand and examined a nail for chips. "I don't believe, my dear, that it's my job to keep tabs on him any longer. The pair of you have made that frightfully—and, I might add, vulgarly—clear."

Alix took a step closer. Her voice dropped to a near-hiss. "That's just it, isn't it, Mirelle? You're jealous. Of what Wallace and I have together. That's why you've done this."

Dinah clenched her eyes shut, trying to rid herself of the mental picture of anything Alix and Wallace could have together. It was still a bit early in the day to be so violently ill.

But Mirelle had this covered. She leaned back in her chair, crossing her shapely legs lazily. The toe of her shoe flicked the gauzy layers of Alix's long skirt. "Do tell. What is the *this* I've supposedly done? Whatever it was, I hope it was enjoyable. Otherwise, I'd just be wasting my time. Like you're wasting my time."

"You've done something to him, I know you have," Alix repeated. "You couldn't stand the thought of his being with me, of us being together. You couldn't stand it, so now you've done *something* to him."

Mirelle stretched her arms over her head, her cigarette still between two fingers, then slowly got to her feet. Alix took a step back. Mirelle's eyes were contemptuous. She put the cigarette to her lips and took a long draw, then blew the smoke out again. If some of it happened to cloud into Alix's face, Mirelle didn't seem to notice or care.

"Listen, Alix," she said slowly, in the tone Dinah recognized as dangerous. "I don't know what you imagine I might have done to ol' Wally. Perhaps you think I've killed him in a *crime passionel* and buried him in the flower garden. Or perhaps you, like Gahan here, think Wally's been kidnapped—maybe I'm holding him secretly and intend to turn him into some strange sort of sex slave—"

"Poor Wallace!" Alix's hand flew to her mouth.

Mirelle's expression hardened. "Poor Wallace indeed. You can imagine any of those things if it makes you happy, my sweet. But I'm telling you now: I haven't got enough interest in Wally at this point to waste my time on any of those things. I don't know where he is. I don't care where he is. You want him, you find him. Just leave me out of your little farce, will you?"

Alix's eyes were brilliant with unshed tears in her pale face. She dropped her hands from her hips to her sides, where she clenched them into plump fists. Her shoulders shook with the effort of keeping herself under control.

"I'm not leaving here," she insisted, her voice now that of a little frightened girl's, "until you tell me where Wallace is."

The glance Mirelle threw back to Dinah was nearly despairing. *Was she deaf?*

"Well, that leaves me no choice," Mirelle said lazily, taking another drag at her cigarette before tossing it in the direction the match had gone earlier. "If you won't leave, I'll have to." She brushed her fiery hair back, picked up her empty glass, and swung on her heel. The screen door slapped shut behind her.

Gahan frowned slightly, holding his bearded chin between two fingers. "A bit melodramatic, this entire scene, but the exit was pretty good." He stood and kissed Dinah. "Time for rehearsal in a few minutes anyway. See you later, lovey." At the door, however, he lingered, patting his cargo pockets before pulling out his notebook and the stub of a pencil.

Feeling a bit overwhelmed, Dinah brushed past Alix to search the shrubbery for the smoldering cigarette butt. There were flames, and there were flames; she wasn't sure whether she might prefer the conflagration of the restaurant to the emotional kind. She crouched down and peered beneath the greenery for telltale signs of smoke. Out of the corner of her eye, she saw Alix turn first one way, than another, trying to figure out what to do next.

"All right, then," she said at last, in her nervous, little girl voice.

This might have been addressed to either Gahan or Dinah, perhaps both.

"Yes?" Gahan rumbled, his hand on the door.

Dinah stood, holding up the cigarette butt gingerly but triumphantly.

"All right," Alix repeated, this time with more conviction. "It's obvious what I have to do."

She seemed to be waiting for either of them to ask the obvious question.

Gahan obliged. He'd always been the obliging sort. "Yes?"

"I'm going to have to call the police."

She turned on her gold-sandaled heel and marched away to her VW.

Dinah watched the little car reverse jerkily and pull away.

"I think this is where you came in," she told Gahan.

Thirty-three

THE EVENING CROWD—not all that thick to begin with, early on in the week—was thinning out when the front door opened to admit Officer Jim Reed and his partner. Dinah had taken advantage of a lull to correct the spelling in Gahan's draft of the advertisement for opening night; now she set down her pencil to greet them, wanting to head them off before they frightened the remainder of the diners away.

"We meet again," the policeman said, removing his hat. *At least he has a sense of humor.* It was dark out now; his sunglasses were folded safely away in his uniform pocket.

"Officer." Dinah paused. "You know, I don't think I know your name, and since we keep meeting like this, I think I should. We're practically relatives now." *And I keep calling you Jim Reed.* She wouldn't let him in on that dirty little secret. The other policeman did not look like Officer Malloy in the slightest.

"Corporal Roy Teasdale." He held out his hand, and Dinah shook it. "This is my partner, Officer John Billings." The formalities taken care of, his eyes traveled to the few remaining customers in the big dining room. "Is there someplace we can go to talk, Mrs. Galloway? And would Mrs. Mirelle Holbein happen to be here? Perhaps she could join us."

"Mirelle's not here. She was at rehearsal in the theater, but they broke up about half an hour ago. She's not at her home?"

"No. Our last information was that she was here."

She led the way toward the west dining room, closed now, with the tables set into their alcoves. On the way by the bar, Dirk caught her eye. He might have been semaphoring, his concern that clear. Dinah shook her head gently at him. He winked and returned to polishing the optics.

"Can I offer you anything?" Dinah asked, indicating a table close to the hearth. "A cup of coffee?"

Both men waited for her to be seated before taking their chairs. Other than from Mark, she didn't see that sort of manners much anymore, and wondered if that was a class at the police academy.

"Do you have any doughnuts?" Corporal Teasdale asked, smirking. Then he held up his hands. "Kidding. Just kidding."

His partner grinned. Officer Billings had great even white teeth which nearly glowed in the intimate lighting.

Gillian mysteriously appeared with coffee things, then disappeared again just as quickly.

"So. To what do I owe the honor of your visit this evening?" Dinah tried to match Teasdale's tone.

They glanced at each other. Roy Teasdale took the lead, as he had in each of their encounters; Billings played the strong silent type in the background.

"It's rather a delicate position," he said, "and it would be good if we could rely on your discretion."

"No footage on YouTube, that sort of thing?" Dinah raised her eyebrows.

Which police matter qualified as delicate? Rob and Kelly? Mirelle and Wallace? Since they wanted to speak to Mirelle, perhaps Alix Mailloux had indeed driven straight to the police station from here that afternoon, carrying out her threat. Both matters were domestics, messy and noisy. Nothing delicate there.

"It's about Mr. Wallace Holbein. The principal at the high school?" For some reason, the corporal's voice rose on his last word, making it a question. Why? He'd nearly arrested her in Mr. Wallace Holbein's house, for God's sake. He had to know she knew who the man was.

"Wally. Yes," she said. "What about him?"

Teasdale took a small notebook from his front pocket, flipped it open, and consulted some notes. "We've learned that he hasn't shown up for work for several days. The position is curious in that the matter was brought to our attention by a woman wanting to file a missing persons report. A woman"—he coughed slightly—"not his wife."

"Yes. Alix Mailloux. She was here earlier."

Again Gillian appeared, this time setting a white mug before Dinah with a tea bag string and label wrapped around the handle. Always on that ball, that one. Then she slipped away again.

"She was here this afternoon, and she suggested at that time that she wanted to go to the police about the mysterious disappearance of our Wally." Dinah dunked the teabag a few times.

Teasdale nodded. He took up the tiny mug of creamer and poured a dollop into his coffee. Billings pushed the sugar bowl closer with a finger. The spoon clinked against the mug as Teasdale stirred. "Miss Mailloux was told at the station that it would probably be best for Mr. Holbein's wife to file the report."

"I bet that went over a treat."

The two officers exchanged a quick glance.

"Yes," Teasdale said. In the dim lighting it was difficult to read his expression. "She did not seem happy with that suggestion." He seemed to want to say something further; his jaw worked slightly as if he were chewing over his words.

Dinah spread her hands on the table. "If you've spoken to her at any length, you must know the situation. Wallace has moved out of the house he shared with Mirelle, and apparently is now residing with Alix Mailloux. I guess you might say she sees herself as the *de facto* wife in this situation. At the very least the significant other. Or as the postal service used to call it, the POSSLQ."

"Possle cue?"

"Person of Opposite Sex Sharing Living Quarters."

Officer Billings snorted into his cup of coffee. He was taking it black. Dinah could have guessed that.

"Haven't heard that one." Corporal Teasdale lifted his own mug to his lips, blew the steam across the rim, and took a cautious sip. He was probably way too young to have heard that one. He set his mug down again on the tabletop. Too hot.

Billings had drained his mug and now leaned back in his chair, his face a mask of satisfaction as he examined the notes he had taken one-handed. His coffee had apparently been just right. Dinah looked down into her own steeping tea. Probably hers would be the mug that was too cold.

She sighed. Might as well come right out and say it. "No doubt, also, if you've been talking to Alix, you know that she thinks there's some sort of foul play involved with Wally's disappearance."

Another quick glance between the two. Billings made some more notes on his pad, his pen zipping across the page.

"And what do you think?" Teasdale's voice was expressionless, without even a trace of curiosity.

Dinah looked at his bland handsome face, before she covered her own face with her hands. "I don't know. I'd like to think that he's gone off on his own accord, under his own power—because he got fed up with this ludicrous situation he's created. I'd like to think he suddenly realized he couldn't stand these two women fighting over him anymore, and decided to go join a monastery, or something like that."

"You'd like to think that," Teasdale repeated, "but you don't?"

Quick. Without looking up, Dinah shook her head. "It seems kind of unlikely."

"Mr. Holbein has never—gone off—like this before?"

"Not since I've known him." Again Dinah sighed. When she lifted her head and reached for her tea, she found that it was, in fact, too cold. "But then again, he's never had a fling with a gym teacher since I've known him, either. I guess there has to be a first time for everything."

"And do you believe Mrs. Holbein capable of doing violence to her husband, as Miss Mailloux has suggested?"

What an impossible question. She turned back to Corporal Teasdale, whose expression was still bland. He expected her to answer that about her best friend? She laughed.

"Something funny?" Teasdale's facade might have cracked a bit. He didn't sound as though people usually laughed at his relentless questioning.

"I was just thinking." Dinah laughed. "Wondering what you considered violence." She wiped her eyes with the back of her hand. "Because if to you, violence is shoving a full bottle of Mexican beer down your husband's boxers, Mirelle is certainly capable of that."

Across the table, Officer Billings shivered.

THE POLICE LEFT without incident. The restaurant closed. As she eased the door shut behind the last customer, Dinah, exhausted, could see that the lights were all out in the theater. She had expected rehearsal to run late, with opening night so close. Still, when she paused for a moment, listening to the crickets on the night air, no basso hysterics from Gahan floated out to interrupt; he had indeed gone. She leaned against the door.

From the kitchen, she heard the screen door slap shut on what sounded like Perry's goodnight. A few more scrapes and closures, and then a heavy click as the kitchen lights were shut down. She'd already turned off the dining room lights once Dirk and Gill had left, leaving only the green-shaded desk lamp on the hostess's podium, where she'd totted up the night's business. Not as much as she'd hoped. The accountant would not be pleased.

The swinging doors snicked open behind her. She forced herself to breathe slowly; she did not turn.

Mark's hand brushed her elbow, the softest of touches.

"What are you looking at?"

Dinah made room for him at the door. She resisted the urge to lean against him, wishing again for Ross. Mark must have felt her momentary weakness, the slight sway toward him, for he chuckled, his breath warm beside her ear.

"It's all right," he murmured. "Just do it, Di."

She stiffened involuntarily. "Do what?"

"Relax. I keep telling you this."

Perversely, she tensed. "Just in general, or with you in particular?" Through the window she could make out the shadows dappling the yard, black on black.

Above the peaked roof of the theater, the stars spattered thickly across the velvet of the sky. Dinah flattened her palms against the glass and pressed. The warmth of her hands clouded the window around them.

"Either will do." Mark leaned into her gently, and then away again. "I'm your friend, Dinah. If that's what you want from me, that's what you've got."

She was silent. Waiting for the *but*. Wasn't there always a *but*?

"Just friends."

Dinah still said nothing. Was there something in his tone? Was she just being paranoid? She wished desperately that Mirelle would stop trying to pair them up, so that this friendship could feel free and unencumbered. With a sigh, she pushed the door open to step outside, then tipped her head back to look up at the sky. The stars seemed fixed in their positions, butterflies tacked to their dark backdrop with pins. Maybe they were, and she was slowly revolving around them. She couldn't tell.

Mark slipped outside as well. Now he stood well away from her. Carefully. "Tell me what he was like. Your husband. Ross."

She had looked at the sky with Ross, had lain on the beach, on blankets in the backyard. He had tried to teach her the constellations with little success, so they had remade and renamed them many times with much laughter. So much laughter. How could she explain that?

"He liked the night sky," she whispered, longingly. "Sometimes we pretended the stars were singing."

Dinah had not talked of Ross, seriously, since his death. The flippant conversations with Mirelle did not count. They didn't come close to her feelings. She didn't feel comfortable letting those feelings out into the open.

"That's better," Mark answered. With only the desk lamp behind then, providing an ineffectual light, she could not make out his features, though his eyes glinted darkly. "Tell me more."

"What can I tell you?" Dinah threw out her hands helplessly. Her voice, she realized, sounded angry. So angry, at the entire universe: those damned stars. "He was everything I wanted in the world. He fit me perfectly: my taste in music, my sense of humor, the way I can't dance, everything. We had a life. I loved it. I loved—*him.*" The sob surprised her; she hadn't cried in a long time, either. Now, with that one gulp that ached down into her gut, she found she couldn't stop. It was as though a scabbed over place had been ripped open to the brutal air. "I miss him so much, Mark. *So* much."

There was a handkerchief in her hands. She crumpled it up and pressed it to her eyes. She could feel her shoulders shaking, and her skin was cold, so cold. When Mark took her in his arms, she sobbed helplessly into his chest.

"I'm sorry," he said.

His arms, his chest. The way he smelled. He was so different from Ross. So wrong. And no matter how she strained her ears, those damned stars didn't sing, and probably never would again.

Thirty-four

IN THE MORNING, Dinah found herself armed with assorted scrubbers and soaps, scouring the bathroom. The towels, the bath mats, even the curtains had made their way into the washer, which thumped away genially in the utility closet off the kitchen. Her toothbrush—how long had she been using this one, then?—went into the trash; an unopened one, from her last visit to the dentist, made its debut. Every speck of toothpaste dotting the mirror above the sink was wiped away, and while she was at it, she did the window, too. The sink, the bathtub, the toilet: all got the heavy-duty bleach treatment. She was on hands and knees, scrubbing the tile under the sink, when someone coughed in the doorway. Surprised, she jerked her head up and hit the underside of the sink with a sharp crack.

"What the hell?" Blinking away the stars, Dinah turned.

"I should ask the same of you," Mirelle said. She sounded peeved. "What the hell, Dinah?"

"I'm cleaning my bathroom. I'm allowed." Dinah rubbed the back of her head. A lump was already starting. It would go well with her healing, but still sore, ankle. "Some of us don't hire out stuff like that."

"You're not allowed. Not after last night." Mirelle whirled and sailed a few steps into the living room. Then she spun again, her arms wide. She glared for a moment at Dinah, then dropped her hands to her sides in frustration. "What the hell am I supposed to do with you?"

"I haven't got a clue what you're talking about." *Last night?* Which part of the evening might Mirelle mean? The part with the police? The part with Mark? The bump was going to be huge on the back of her skull. The stars before her eyes were slow to set. Dinah wondered if she might have a concussion. She still felt like crying: a crying hangover from last night.

"You were hugging. Right there at the door. I saw you when I was driving by."

That part.

"It's my door. I'm allowed." But Dinah turned away quickly, feeling the blood creeping up her neck and into her face. *I was bawling my eyes out.* But she had no intention of admitting that.

"You were in his arms. Right there."

"Okay."

"And this morning I show up and I find you scrubbing a bathroom floor? Where is he, Dinah? Just tell me that one thing. Where's Mark?"

"He went home."

"This morning?" For a moment there was a sliver of hope in Mirelle's voice.

Slowly Dinah got to her feet. Her knees cramped from the kneeling. She flexed them, then her ankle, then flexed her shoulders into the bargain. Her head still hurt. Shaking it gingerly, she brushed past Mirelle on the way to the kitchen. "Last night."

Mirelle's lips opened and closed; for once she seemed to have lost the power of speech. She lowered herself onto the sofa, one hand bracing on its arm.

The washer had stopped. Dinah peered inside. No, it was only moving into the next cycle, filling slowly with rinse water. Taking a breather. She closed the closet door, leaving the machine to its business.

Mirelle's blue eyes were wide, her lipsticked mouth open.

"You look like a fish," Dinah said. She lifted a hand to brush the hair out of her face. Her skin smelled of bleach.

Mirelle found her voice and made several awkward noises, as though she had no idea what to do with it now. "You're not saying what I think you're saying. Are you?"

Dinah got a drinking glass and ran some cold water into it.

"Are you?"

Dinah took a drink, looking through the window and down into the parking lot. "Give it up, Holstein. I'm not telling you anything. It's none of your business. We've been through this before."

The look on Mirelle's face was of dawning horror. "You *didn't* sleep with him."

Dinah refused to answer.

"Holy Mary, mother of God, Dinah!" Mirelle exclaimed in frustration as she sprang to her feet.

"She didn't sleep with him, either, as far as I know." The water was good. Dinah ran the faucet again. She suddenly felt beads of perspiration at her neck and forehead, though whether from the exertion of cleaning, or from the exertion of holding her impatience in check, she wasn't sure. She lifted the sash. A slight breeze fluttered the curtains. She breathed in the scent of roses and took another drink from the glass.

It was then that she realized that Mirelle had believed her to have taken a man into her bed, and had come over in the morning to check. *Ew.*

"I can't believe this." Mirelle shook her head wildly. "Another perfect opportunity, and you let it go by."

That had been it. There, in the embrace of a truly desirable man, and she was crying desperately for her husband. Mark had been kind, had let her cry, had said nothing.

"Tell me what happened," Mirelle ordered.

"No."

There was a finality in her tone which caused Mirelle to pause and look up; but as always, she did not know when to stop.

"Did he proposition you last night? He came right out and asked you, didn't he? Tell me."

"No." Dinah's water glass was now empty. At the sink, she felt as though the air had thickened, as though she were breathing cotton batting.

"And you turned him down." Mirelle spun and made for the door. "I can't believe this."

"Where are you going?" Dinah had wanted to end this conversation; but now her suspicions were aroused.

"To find Mark," Mirelle spat. "Damn it all, Dinah, if you won't sleep with him, *I will!*"

The door slammed behind her.

SHE HADN'T GONE far.

When Dinah reached the front porch, Mirelle was draped over the open door of her car, conversing animatedly with Perry. One hand clawed furiously at the air above her head. A tractor-trailer truck roared by on the road, drowning out this new tirade.

"Stop talking about me," Dinah shouted at them.

With a scathing look, Mirelle turned her back.

Knowing she shouldn't, Dinah stomped down the steps and to the car. Overhead the sky looked dark and brooding, as though it mirrored Mirelle's moods. On the electric wires overhead, a row of small gray birds swayed back and forth, holding a conversation as animated as Mirelle's. Was the entire world gossiping about her today, then?

"I said, stop talking about me."

"Darling, this isn't about you," Perry said gently, as though breaking terrible news. He put a consoling hand on her shoulder. "You really should see someone about this paranoia."

Mirelle cleared her throat, pointedly refusing to turn. "In any case, Perry, what I was saying before we were so *rudely* interrupted, was that the phone rang nearly every hour last night. Nearly every hour. That foolish Alix Mailloux. *Nearly every hour.*"

"So why didn't you just take the phone off the hook? Block the number?" Dinah stood next to Perry; now Mirelle would have no choice but to either look at both of them, or neither. "Get rid of your landline?"

Perry nodded. His hair today was pulled back into the usual ponytail; he was wearing shorts and Tevas, and a green Hawaiian shirt which looked like a refugee from Gahan Godfrey's wardrobe.

"That would have been the logical course of action, I think," he agreed. He stuffed his hands in his pockets and rocked back on his heels.

"Because," Mirelle said, drawing herself up, "if you must know, I was curious. I wanted to hear what fresh idiocy she could come up with." She sighed. "It was always the same. 'Where is he? What have you done to him?'"

"Still no word, then." Dinah leaned into Perry, who dropped an arm about her shoulders.

Mirelle shook her head, the sun sparking fire from her hair. "Nothing. But I will tell you—that constantly ringing telephone seems to have driven Kelly to distraction. Nothing from her this morning but heavy breathing and baleful looks." Her own baleful looks notwithstanding: Mirelle's eyes kept slicing toward Dinah and away again. "Look, Dinah, this is what I really wanted to talk to you about this morning. Not that"—she glanced at Perry—"other thing."

Perry's radar picked up the unfamiliar signal. "Other thing? What other thing?"

Dinah shot Mirelle a warning look. "Nothing. Nothing at all."

But Mirelle was not to be held off by mere warning looks; it would take an entire platoon of warning, an army. "Just that—" She paused, dramatically. "Our Dinah did not sleep with Mark Burdette *again.*"

Perry's hand fluttered up as though beseeching the heavens. "Not again. Every time I turn around, Dinah isn't sleeping with Mark Burdette." His tone grew wily, and perhaps a bit hopeful. "Do you think—could she be—switching teams? Or—could he?"

Mirelle's expression became thoughtful.

"In your dreams," Dinah said.

Perry sighed, a heart-rending sound which might have earned him a role in the next production, had Gahan been available to hear it. "I *do* have my dreams," he replied defensively. "You can't take those away."

"I don't think I'd dare," Mirelle said, grimacing. She slid into the front seat of her car, pulling the door closed behind her. The engine started with a roar, and Dinah jumped back. Mirelle wound the window open and leaned out;

she had donned a pair of wraparound sunglasses which lent her the look of a distant—very distant—relative of Corporal Roy Teasdale. "And Dinah? I was supposed to give you a message from Kelly. She hasn't found a job yet. She's coming in to work tonight, and she'd like you to pay her in cash."

With another engine roar and a spit of gravel, she was off.

Thirty-five

THE MORNING WAS spent going over orders and the menu with Perry; the afternoon went by just as quickly, as Dinah went over the books with the gloomy accountant. She had meant to stay away from the kitchen once Mark arrived. She didn't think she could bear his sympathy; she felt too raw.

"What if he doesn't?" Perry had demanded. "Arrive, I mean?"

"I'll cook," Dinah had countered irritably. "Kelly's coming in, so I won't have to hostess."

Staying busy, she hoped now, would keep her from worrying. As long as Perry did not come to her in a panic, she had to have faith the situation was under control. There was nothing else she could do without checking in on the kitchen, and she was not yet ready to make an appearance in that beehive while pretending that everything was fine. That nothing had happened the previous evening.

Nothing had happened, she insisted to herself. She'd only had a total emotional breakdown. Not a big deal.

Soon, anyway, the new head cook would be hired, and Mark would wander off into the sunset, back to his real life. Somehow that thought did not comfort her much; she had grown accustomed, in only a matter of days, to having him around. She liked it. He had been a good friend last night. There was no denying that.

Now she ran her hands through her hair, staring out the window down into the rear parking lot without really seeing it. Ambivalence sucked. Mark's car had appeared; she guessed he hadn't taken her breakdown all that badly. Well, he'd just have to live with her surfacing grief—or not. When she tried to examine her feelings in more detail, hold them up in the light, they skittered away like small nocturnal animals. Just as well. She wanted to trap them, force them back into their cages.

Grief. Dinah had thought she was over the worst of it. That it was softening, becoming a dull ache she'd probably always live with. Then she remembered the shiver she had felt, at the first touch of Ross's hand in the hardware store—the instant attraction, the knowledge that that attraction could lead nowhere else but where it did, over and over for seventeen years—*that* was what made her catch her breath. Hell, maybe she would be able to appreciate—maybe even desire—someone else. Still, the instant electrification, the feeling of meeting her other half and wanting nothing more, all the time, than to be part of him: *that* was what she didn't believe she'd ever find again.

Maybe she was being too demanding.

Maybe Ross had spoiled her for anyone else.

Dinah watched as the blue BMW slid into its accustomed space in the rear lot below her window. Kelly stepped out after a moment, looking around suspiciously, then slammed and locked the car door. Foreshortened, Kelly cast an oddly misshapen shadow as she squared her shoulders and adjusted her purse. Then she smoothed her black skirt and flipped her hair back from her shoulders, before moving across the parking lot.

Dinah sighed, her chin cupped in her hands. She had not had a perfect marriage with Ross. On the balance, though, she thought it had been a good one: loving, friendly, sensuous. For seventeen years. Watching Kelly make her way to the rear door, Dinah considered the alternative presented by the Carveys. Or by Mirelle and Wallace Holbein. She had been lucky, pulling out her plum on the first try. That's what would spoil her. That's what would make her too demanding. Fear of sticking her thumb in again and pulling out something like Rob, or Wally. She shuddered.

Okay, so her expectations were high. Maybe she someday might be able to give someone else a chance. But the odds were against her being so lucky again. She knew that. Slowly she straightened and turned to her closet and her clothes for the evening.

Introspection sucked, too. She vowed not to do anymore of it in the near future.

Thirty-six

DINAH BUSIED HERSELF between the main dining room and the west room, only slipping into the kitchen when there was absolutely no choice, and slipping out again before anyone could raise a head to notice. Both dining rooms had been filled nearly to capacity all evening; all three specials had sold out. One of the best things about the brisk pace had been that Dinah had had no chance to exchange more than the briefest of words with Kelly, for which she was grateful.

Now the dining room had emptied, the waitresses done with their side work and disappeared into the night, including Gillian, who had wandered off with Dirk as soon as he had restocked the bar and shut off the lights. Only Kelly remained, fiddling with papers at the hostess desk. She cleared her throat as Dinah saw to the locks at the front doors.

"Um, Dinah?"

Here it comes, Dinah thought, turning to Kelly. "Yes?" A bit formal, but she felt incapable of dealing with Kelly any other way. "What is it?"

"I was wondering?" Kelly had fallen back into her habit of singsonging, as she did when she was uncomfortable, every statement turning into a question. "About tonight? I'm not really working here anymore, you see—"

Dinah folded her arms and waited.

The stance made Kelly more nervous. "And I thought—since I haven't got another job yet—and money is pretty tight for me right now?"

"You've got another paycheck coming at the end of the week, don't worry." If it was only about money, that was a relief. That was plain black-and-white and could be sorted out easily. There wasn't any money. The accountant had made that abundantly clear this morning.

"But, Dinah? I thought for tonight, since I was doing this as a big favor to you—and I'm not really working here anymore—"

"I fired Rob, Kelly. I didn't fire you. Are you telling me you're quitting?"

Kelly looked more flustered.

"And I didn't ask you to come in. As I recall, you merely sent a message by Mirelle saying you'd be here. I'm not at all sure what big favor that entails, quite frankly." Dinah shook her head. "But if you *are* quitting, let's make it official, and I can hire someone else."

Kelly waved that away. "No, no. I thought you could just pay me for tonight. Right now? In cash?" She had staked out her territory behind the hostess desk, and now she held out her hand.

Dinah looked down into the small palm. Kelly still wore her wedding ring, she noted. For a moment neither moved.

"Cash?" Dinah repeated at last. Her mind flashed back again to the meeting with the accountant, the profit margin, his warnings: *seventy-five percent of restaurants fail in the first year.* "You want me to pay you? Cash? Out of the till? Under the table?" She had to get a grip. She was starting to pick up Kelly's annoying speech habit.

Kelly drew back and tucked her hand into the pocket of her skirt as though Dinah had slapped it. "It's not like that. Not really. It's just that you have it. And I'm—I'm—" There were tears in her eyes, suddenly, sparkling. "I'm in such a helpless position right now. I only thought—you might have it in your heart to help me out. That's all."

Helpless as a barracuda.

Dinah leaned back and examined her. "You seem to be doing all right," she said, sounding more heartless than she intended; attempted guilt trips did that to her. "You've only got a couple of days until your next check, Kelly. Hang in there. You've got your free food over at Mirelle's, your free housing—what more could you need?"

The tears disappeared as quickly as they had come. The expression on Kelly's small face became hard, pinched. She squared her shoulders. "Fine. If that's the way you feel about it." She spun on her heel to slam through the swinging kitchen doors, but then turned, completely ruining the effectiveness of the exit. "But don't you expect I'm going to come back here to help you out again tomorrow. Because I won't. You and your stupid restaurant can just go to hell!"

The swinging doors did their thing. Dinah propped her elbow on the hostess desk, her head in her hand. It had been a long day. From the kitchen she heard a last high-pitched shout and a crash before the screen door to the back slammed. Dinah closed her eyes.

When the swinging doors opened again, it was with a far more gentle sound. "Here." A cold bottle was pressed into her palm. Without opening her eyes, she lifted it to her lips and took a drink. Stout.

"You've been avoiding me today."

Dinah opened her eyes, but gazed at the label rather than at Mark. The bottle was half full. She did not think she had drawn it down that much with a single sip.

"This is your beer." She held it out.

"Keep it," he said, waving it off. "I've had more than enough for one day." His chuckle was self-deprecating. "And you look as though you need it more than I do. At least"—he glanced over his shoulder—"you will if the dishwasher doesn't get the glassware cleaned up before you go into the kitchen."

"Sweet Jesus," Dinah whispered. She tilted the bottle again. "Even by herself she's a regular hurricane. Hurricane Kelly." She downed the remainder of the beer, avoiding his eyes.

"Listen," he offered after a moment, unbuttoning the neck of his white jacket, now stained with a curious combination of colors, many of them tending toward the red and brown end of the spectrum. "I meant it, you know, about being your friend. So about last night—"

Another slam and curse from the kitchen cut them off.

Dinah shoved the empty bottle into Mark's hands and dashed for the door.

IN THE KITCHEN she found Kelly sobbing against the chest of Kevin the dishwasher; confused, he patted her shoulder awkwardly.

"What is it now?"

Kelly lifted her tearstained face from Kevin's chest, her eyes hardened, and she looked beyond Dinah to Mark. "He's here," she gasped out and pointed a shaking finger in the direction of the car park. "Out there. He's done something to the car."

"Perry, call the cops," Dinah said.

Perry held up a cell phone. "Already did."

"Where is he?" Dinah demanded. She pushed past the workstation to shove the back door open. "I'm sick and tired of this—"

"Dinah—"

Mark followed into the back lot, lit eerily by the lights mounted over the kitchen door, and over the apartment. Dinah blinked in the dimness, wishing she had had the foresight to install floodlights. Of course, Rob and Kelly, with their apartment facing on a floodlit yard, would have complained about that, so there was no winning.

Kelly had not been lying. Or hallucinating. The flare of a match as he lit a cigarette pinpointed Rob. He was leaning nonchalantly against Perry's Corolla, gazing on the BMW. As he put away his matchbook, he patted his pocket in a satisfied sort of way.

"Rob," Dinah said sharply, "get off my property."

He turned lazily toward her, taking the cigarette from his lips and blowing a long stream of smoke into the night air.

"I just came for the car," he said.

"We've been through this, Rob." His name tasted vile in her mouth. Dinah's face ached from speaking it. "Kelly's got a security code on it. You can't start it."

"The police are on their way," Perry called from the doorway.

Rob's eyes glittered as he looked venomously at Perry. He put the cigarette back in his mouth and again patted his pocket.

"And now she can't, either." He laughed. An unpleasant sound.

"I told you—I told you! He's done something to the car." Kelly had joined them. "What have you done to the car? It's my car!"

A siren wailed in the distance. Dinah winced.

"Oh, but it's *our* car, isn't it, Kelly?" Rob jeered. "Marital property, and all that."

"What have you done to my car?" Kelly took another step toward Rob; when Mark put out a restraining hand to stop her, she shrugged it off impatiently.

The siren was getting closer.

A slam from the stage door, and Gahan was steaming down on them, full speed ahead. "What the hell is all this ruckus?" His hair stood up on end where he had run his hands through it, tugging as he was doing now. In the weird lighting, casting everything into sharp angles, he looked like a demented avenging Santa Claus. "I've got a rehearsal going on in there, for an opening night just days away, and we can't concentrate with all this noise."

"He's done something to my car!" Kelly stomped her foot on the packed gravel, her hands balled into fists at her sides. Things, apparently, weren't moving speedily enough for her satisfaction.

The siren stopped out front; blue lights strobed near the road.

"Go get the police, Perry," Dinah ordered. He jogged off down the driveway. She turned back to Rob. "Unless you want to be arrested a second time for criminal trespass, you'll leave when I tell you to in front of the cops."

Rob shrugged, smiling wolfishly. "Not a problem. I'll be on my way, then." He flicked the cigarette away, its red ember arcing off into the grass, then pushed away from the Toyota.

"No!" Kelly cried in frustration. "Not until you fix my car."

Again Rob shrugged. "Not until you give me the key code."

"Over my dead body!" Kelly shouted.

"Whoa," Mark murmured.

"Over here!" Perry led the two policemen toward them, gesturing. The same two policemen. Were they the only two in this town? "It's Rob Carvey, officers. The same guy we had to call about the other night?"

Dinah pressed her hands to her cheeks.

"I was just leaving," Rob said genially.

"Not until you fix my car!" Kelly turned her tragic face on the policemen. "He's sabotaged my car, officers. It won't start. Make him fix it."

"Have you done something to her car, Mr. Carvey?" Corporal Teasdale asked.

"It's *our* car," Rob pointed out. "Marital property."

"Let's just have a look, shall we?" The impatient roar was Gahan. "And then you all can get the hell out of here, and I can get on with my rehearsal." Somehow he'd gotten the hood up on the BMW. Teasdale went to the front of the car, beaming his flashlight at the engine, his free hand still at his holster; he never once took his eyes off Rob.

At least they weren't wearing sunglasses tonight.

"There's no distributor cap," Gahan said after a moment.

"I told you." Kelly was triumphant. "He took it. Rob did."

Yet again Rob shrugged. His hand, now motionless, was in his pocket.

"Did you take the distributor cap?" Teasdale asked.

"Why would I do that?" Rob asked, all innocence. "Then the car wouldn't run." He couldn't quite keep the grin from his face.

Teasdale looked up sharply. "Look. The both of you. I think we've had just enough out of you."

"It's not my fault," Kelly cried out in alarm. "I'm the victim here, okay? Make him give the thing back."

"What if I say I haven't got it?" Rob countered.

"What if I tell them I have a temporary restraining order against you?" Kelly demanded.

The two policemen looked especially interested. There was a shift in attention.

"Is this true?" Teasdale asked.

Rob held up his hands. "Hey, don't look at me. I keep telling you guys I'm out of here. You're the ones who keep holding me up. So if you'll just let me go—"

"Don't let him go until he fixes my car!" Kelly shrilled.

"You can't have it both ways." Rob sneered.

"How are we going to resolve this?" Corporal Teasdale's patience was obviously at an end. Probably had been for a while.

"Like this." With a growl that might have been out of a bear in the wild, Gahan grabbed Rob by the shirt collar. "Carvey, you're nothing but a little big man, picking on women because you don't dare pick on men. A bully, that's what you are. Now give over the damn part." Gahan shook him.

"I—"

"In your pocket, is it?" Ganah reached in with his free hand and pulled out the cap. Then he thrust Rob away from him with such force that Rob stumbled and fell to his knees. "Here." Gahan tossed the part to Mark. "One of you lot take care of this. And don't interrupt my rehearsal again!"

He stomped off, still growling.

Dinah recovered first. "Rob Carvey, once and for all, I want you off my property. Do you understand?"

Mark took the cap and looked beneath the hood of the car.

"Did you see that?" Rob demanded. He looked around at each of their faces. "Did you see how he attacked me? I should press charges. Assault and battery, that is. I should press charges!"

"Up to you, of course," Billings said, shaking his flashlight as though not certain it was working. "Don't know what you've got for witnesses. Hard to see out here in the dark." He shook the flashlight again, switched it on and off.

"Wonder when we'll get those body cameras in?" Teasdale asked. "Those might have been a help. But I guess now, Mr. Carvey, would be a good time for you to leave. I'd hate to have to arrest you for criminal trespass yet again this week."

"I told them you're a felon," Kelly hissed at him.

Corporal Teasdale shook his head. "We looked him up. There's no record of a felony, miss. So maybe you'd just better go on home, too."

Snarling, Rob took a few steps down the driveway. "You'll pay for this. All of you. Just you wait."

Thirty-seven

"I CAN'T BELIEVE I missed all of this," Mirelle moaned, sipping away at something that looked like orange juice and probably wasn't; it was obviously a drink chosen to compliment her outfit. She was draped across her lounge chair this morning, wearing the dragon-patterned caftan again; the eyes of the dragons winked in the early sunlight. One pale arm was thrown dramatically over her wild red head. She looked decidedly Pre-Raphaelite. "I was so wrapped up in my part, at rehearsal, you know. We were working on the scenes where I'm trying to kill Charles, so he can join me in death."

Dinah snorted. She'd brought her own coffee mug from home, where coffee makers still existed. "You. In death. Now that's something I'd have a hard time imagining."

"Why, Dinah," Mirelle protested. "That's so unrealistic of you. You know we're all going to have to die sometime."

"And that's so—I don't know—existential of you? Fatalistic? Something like that." Dinah sighed, rubbing her brow. She had a headache. She'd had one all night, nagging her awake repeatedly. Each time she dozed off, she dreamed of blue flashing lights and sirens. It had not been a restful sleep. "How's Gahan going to do you up as a dead woman? Somehow I keep thinking there's no one more alive-looking than you."

"Why, Dinah, darling," Mirelle exclaimed. "If I didn't know you better, I'd think that was a compliment."

"Ah. But you *do* know me better."

The wind had freshened a bit and swung around from the west. The air felt different, as though carrying a note of expectation. In the trees over the porch, a number of birds burst into loud complaint. Grackles? Buzzards? Dinah didn't know.

"This is beginning to grate on my nerves," Mirelle drawled, draining the last of her sunny orange drink and setting the glass on the table beside the chaise. A pile of magazines stood there, but they were all for show; Mirelle did not read magazines. "However am I supposed to concentrate on my role, and my stage debut, with all this crap going down?"

Dinah's nerves were slowly loosening as she leaned her head back in the deck chair and let the morning sun play over her features. It warmed her skin and made her feel lazy. Probably it was burning her cheeks to a brilliant red as she sat. At the very least giving her freckles across the bridge of her nose. Not that she cared. Except for the risk of skin cancer? Her head snapped back.

"You're not listening," Mirelle complained.

"I am, too," Dinah replied lazily. "Sort of. It's comforting to hear your voice. The sound just goes on and on, like muzak. Lets me know everything is normal."

"I don't know if *that* was a compliment or not, either."

"Again, probably not."

The yellow VW screeched into the driveway.

Mirelle sighed. "I won't be getting any compliments from *that* quarter, that's for certain." She looked longing now down at her empty glass, and then back toward the car. "I wish I had another drink."

"Not her again," Dinah moaned. "I was just thinking I might get a nap here this morning. I was looking forward to it, actually."

"It's all this *crap*. I'm telling you."

Alix Mailloux stopped at the foot of the porch steps. Mirelle stirred slightly in her seat, and Alix seemed to think better of coming any closer. The foot she had placed on the bottom stair she now quickly withdrew.

"I've called the police," she announced. Her high voice wavered.

"I offer you congratulations," Mirelle replied. "I assume that's what you're looking for."

"It's been days. I know you've done something to Wallace. And I won't let you get away with it." Alix lifted her round chin; her plump bosom heaved.

Languorously Mirelle straightened, stretching her arms over her head. The dragons on her caftan fluttered gently around her in the slight morning breeze. "Well, when you find him, tell him the bills are due and I'm about to drain the checking account paying them. That ought to get his blood pressure rising."

"This isn't a joke," Alix protested, close to tears.

Did she always sound close to tears, Dinah wondered. Was that what made women like her so attractive to men like Wally, the way they constantly sounded as though they needed the protection of any available white knight? She made a face. How limiting that would be, to be the sort of woman who was always in need of rescue. At least she knew how to knee a man in the face if the occasion warranted.

"No, the joke is that you think I would care enough to do anything to Wallace other than to divorce him at this point. I've already told you that. Remember, my very young and very foolish girl," and Mirelle pointed a long elegant finger at Alix, "that you are my grounds."

Alix stomped her foot, her salmon pink toenails peeking through the intricate straps of her sandals: at that moment she was vividly reminiscent of Kelly.

"It's not a joke, Mirelle," she repeated, a kind of mantra. "You've done something with Wallace. I don't know what. I don't know what you're up to with all those stupid small appliances, either, but whatever it is, I'll find out, and you won't get away with it."

She then whirled, her gauzy skirt twirling about her legs and started back toward the VW.

Mirelle whistled slowly through her teeth. "Hold on a minute."

Alix had to have been too far away to hear the words, but it was the whistle that pulled her up anyway. Like a puppy. Her turn back toward the porch was reluctant.

Dinah glanced between them. More catfight? She hoped they took it down into the driveway, because room was limited up here on the porch, and she didn't know whether she could safely make an escape if things escalated to physical violence. Then again, she decided, appraising the opponents, it would not be a long fight: Alix might be a gym teacher, but the platform shoes she was wearing would prove a handicap; and Mirelle was wiry and quick and angry enough to get in the first jab and be done with it.

Alix's expression was challenging, but wary. Her eyes held the glint of certainty that she had been right about Mirelle's involvement all along.

"Yes?" she asked. "You've got something you want to say?"

Mirelle shifted forward on the chaise, dropping her bare feet to the deck. "Did you just say *appliances?*"

In the driveway, Alix's hands were fisted, ready to fight at the first sign of attack. "You know what I said."

"*Small appliances?*" Mirelle demanded. "Hair dryers? Coffee makers? That sort of thing?"

"Don't play dumb with me." Alix tried to sound threatening, but her little-girl voice couldn't quite carry it off. "You know what I mean. All those small appliances in Wallace's office at school. Hidden under his desk. What were you trying to do? Electrocute him or something? Maybe you didn't know, but you need to plug them in for that to work."

Dinah's jaw dropped. "Wait. First Mirelle's made him disappear, and now she's trying to electrocute him? How can she do both?"

Mirelle's mind was on a more pressing matter. "My hair dryer is under his desk? In his office?"

"Don't try to pretend you don't know," Alix said scathingly.

Mirelle stood. Alix, several feet away, took a step further back, for security.

"He's got my hair dryer? How the hell did he get my hair dryer?" The sun on Mirelle's hair gave her a brilliant corona. "That's *my* hairdryer, damn it! He hasn't got any hair."

"I could use the coffee maker, myself," Dinah added, a bit sadly. Her coffee mug was now empty. "I need more caffeine."

"Ha!" Alix exclaimed in triumph. "So you *do* admit it. Those are your appliances."

"And this proves what?" Dinah asked.

Again Alix Mailloux was off down the driveway on her platform shoes. "I don't know what you're trying to do with those damned appliances, but you won't get away with it. I'm going to the police with your admission." She pointed a hand at Dinah. "And you're a witness. You heard her."

She threw herself into the car and tore out of the driveway with a grinding of gears and a scrape of gravel.

"Well." Dinah sank back in her chair. "She really beats on that car." Mirelle threw her a caustic look. "What exactly did you admit to again?"

Mirelle too sank back onto her chaise, her hands clawing at the air on the way down. "My hair dryer. That bastard stole my hair dryer."

Thirty-eight

THE PHONE RANG inside the house.

"Great," Mirelle groaned. "This is all I need. For that trumped-up tart to start her calling campaign again."

A cloud eased its way across the sun, and the porch was cast into shadow. Dinah shifted on her chair.

"It wouldn't be Alix," she pointed out. "She just left."

"She could be calling from a cell phone," Mirelle pointed out. "She could have started up just as soon as she spun out of my driveway. She could have a Bluetooth connection. 'Siri: harass my lover's wife.'"

"It could just be a telemarketer," Dinah offered comfortingly.

"Another great reason not to answer."

The phone continued its frantic pealing. The cloud overhead was dark and menacing. Was that thunder? "Do you want me to go answer it?"

"Suit yourself." Mirelle plucked up her glass. "I think I'd like to have another drink, because I deserve it. I handled myself remarkably well in that unpleasant situation."

Dinah paused, her hand on the door handle. "What, finding out about the whereabouts of your hairdryer?"

Mirelle tossed her head, brushing past into the kitchen. "Among other things."

The cell phone lay on the counter. "Holstein Dairies," Dinah answered. "Welcome to milk heaven."

"Oh, thank God you've answered. Thank God you're home. Mirelle, it's me. Kelly. I need your help."

"Not Mirelle. Dinah."

There was a moment of silence. Then, "Put Mirelle on."

But Mirelle had disappeared. Her empty glass stood next to the sink. From somewhere deep in the house Dinah heard a muted thump. Did that come from the cellar? No, it had to have been from upstairs.

"She's unavailable at the moment," Dinah said. "You'll have to deal with me, Kelly. So sorry about that."

A sniff. "No need to be so touchy about everything. Anyway, it's an emergency, so you'll have to do."

"Thanks for the vote of confidence." What had Kelly done now? Broken a nail? Cut herself on the glassware she was always smashing? Dinah slapped herself mentally. She had to stop being so catty. Really. "What is it? What do you need?"

"I need you to come bail me out of jail."

Dinah dropped the phone. It skittered away under the table.

Mirelle breezed in, having changed the caftan for a filmy shirt and tank top over pedal pushers and pink espadrilles decorated with fish. She skidded to a stop and stared at the phone. "What's your problem all of a sudden?"

The phone, under the table, squawked incomprehensibly. Dinah had no words. She pointed to the cell.

"Oh, honestly," Mirelle breathed. She swooped down on the telephone and brought it to her ear. "Yes?"

Dinah sank into a kitchen chair, her knees week. The conversation was mostly made up of *yes,* and *mmhmm.* Even with the phone cradled against Mirelle's ear, high-pitched noises still could be heard from it, like those of the unidentified birds in the backyard. Mirelle's eyes lifted ceiling-ward, her brows rising. Dinah sighed and clenched her eyes shut.

"Well, come on, then," Mirelle said at last, ending the call. "Looks like we've got no choice. We're going to have to go down and bail her out."

"Do we have to?"

"Of course we do." But Mirelle's expression was strained, as though her patience was coming to an end. She retrieved the keys from the hook beneath the spice rack. "She's one of us. Isn't she?"

"It depends," Dinah replied darkly, following her outside. She plucked her sunglasses from the neckline of her shirt and slid them on. "On what she's done to get arrested."

"Lock the door, will you? You never know what kinds of weirdos are hanging around." Mirelle led the way to her car. The sky now was definitely moody, with dark clouds scuttling in from the horizon; the wind had picked up, and a few dead leaves skittered across the driveway.

"Assault and battery," Mirelle finally said when they were on Main Street.

"Say *what?*"

"She went after Rob early this morning." Mirelle glared at the El Camino in front of them, doing about twelve miles an hour and looking as though it were on its last legs. Or tires. Probably no way it would go faster, no matter how hard its driver stepped on the gas.

"*She* went after *Rob.*" Dinah searched Mirelle's face for some sign that she was being had. That Mirelle would let her in on the joke soon. "Did I hear that right?"

"Don't be obtuse." Once the El Camino had turned into the lot at the grocery store—the driver flipping them off cheerfully—Mirelle floored the gas pedal. The car leapt forward. "If Rob had gone after her, he'd be the one in jail. I'm not stupid enough to waste my money bailing out that slimeball."

They were approaching the crosswalk in front of the library. An elderly couple, the woman bumping a walker along in front of her, was making their way across the street. At the last minute, Mirelle slammed on the brakes. Dinah held her breath, waiting for the moment of impact. The old man smiled and waved at them. Mirelle's answering smile looked more like a snarl.

"She assaulted Rob," Dinah repeated.

Not that it was difficult to believe, but it didn't quite fit in with the victim image Kelly had been so carefully cultivating over the past several days. Here Dinah's conscience broke in again: after all, Kelly had been struck by Rob that night in the restaurant. Hadn't she? She had certainly claimed she had been. Rob had not been all that vigorous in his denials. Kelly was a victim. Still, Dinah remembered that strange, almost self-satisfied look Kelly had worn at each encounter with her husband since.

"This morning? Where? How?"

Mirelle shook her head. The courthouse loomed on the left. She pulled into a parking spot with a fifteen minute limit. "At the place he was staying at, behind that restaurant. Waldemann's. She broke in, looking for money—"

"She broke into his apartment?"

"Do you have to repeat everything I say? Yes, she broke into his apartment. She says, by the way"—Mirelle narrowed her eyes—"that it's all your fault, because if you'd just paid her under the table like she wanted, she never would have had to go to Rob's for money."

"Oh, screw that." Dinah snorted. She popped the catch on her seat belt, climbed out, and slammed the door on that guilt trip.

Mirelle slipped out as well; the wind whipped her hair back from her face, and ruffled the gauzy shirt about her. "Well, that's what she said, anyway. Apparently she woke up Rob, they got into another fight, and she went after him with a hammer. When he locked himself in the bathroom, she started pounding the door to splinters. He climbed out the window and called the cops on his cell phone."

"Jesus." Dinah looked up at the brick facade of the courthouse; it might have been an asylum. "What a pair of head cases. Both of them. I wish Ross and I had never hired them. I wish we'd never brought them to town."

"Yeah," Mirelle agreed roughly. "And now one of them is living in my house, and I have no way to get rid of her."

"You're the one who's been reminding me that Kelly's a victim. You've been the voice of my conscience."

"I resign, then." Mirelle, too, slammed her door. They crossed the sidewalk to the fall of granite steps to the imposing front door; then those suddenly opened, and Rob appeared.

He smiled his wolfish smile at both of them, and waved a paper. "Look," he said, and laughed unpleasantly. "It's my temporary protection order against my wife." Middle finger erect, he breezed past them.

"See?" Mirelle demanded. "I've suddenly realized that I'm just some weird pawn in a private game those two are playing. And probably have been playing as long as they've been married."

"Grand." Shoulders slumped, Dinah followed Mirelle through the courthouse doors, and out of the wind.

Thirty-nine

"SO WHAT ARE we going to do about her?"

Dinah intentionally kept her voice low. Kelly was upstairs in the guest room, changing out of the clothes she had done time in: her prison garb, as she called it, rolling her eyes; she'd never be able to wear those clothes again. She didn't have much choice in wardrobe left, though, as far as Dinah could figure.

Mirelle was looking around her kitchen, with its splashes of dramatic color, as though she were in a foreign country. She settled onto a bar stool and cupped her face in her hands, pulling the skin tight around her eyes with her fingers. "This would be the one time I'm desperate for a cup of coffee. The irony being that now I know where my coffee maker is, and I can't get to it." She sighed, fine lines appearing between her eyebrows. "We could always break into the school, I suppose. Into Wally's office."

"Thanks. I'd rather buy a new one at Walmart." The prospect of breaking in anywhere, let alone into Wallace Holbein's office, made Dinah feel nauseated. Just what she really wanted out of life—yet another run in with the police. "But what are you going to do about Kelly?"

Mirelle took a deep breath and lifted her gaze to Dinah's face; for a fraction of a moment her eyes glittered—could those be tears? No. It had to be some sort of optical illusion. Gone again immediately. "Me?"

"I—"

Mirelle waved her off. "You told me so, didn't you? Just say it. I know you've been prickly about Kelly, and I've kept after you to show some sisterly spirit, to help me out. I feel like I've been had by her—and now I feel like I've been abandoned. I feel like, because of my dad, and because my own husband was being such a bastard, I thought I understood more about Kelly's situation than you ever could. Now I know that I know absolutely *nothing* about Kelly's situation. She—he—the pair of them—they are nutcases. They're trapped in some weird symbiotic relationship, and I got roped in to play some part I didn't really understand. I'm not sure I understand it *yet*, but I do know for sure that I want out. Just tell me you told me so, okay? Pile it on."

There was an edge to Mirelle's voice, to her words, that Dinah didn't quite understand. "So what will you do? And what do you expect me to do?" A little bottle of nail polish stood on the bar; Dinah picked it up and turned it in her fingers. *Brazilian Sunrise.* Who thought up these names, anyway? She wanted that job. She wondered if it paid well.

A bitter half-smile played around Mirelle's perfectly lipsticked mouth. "Thanks for that."

"I'm sorry," Dinah said grudgingly. Always, it was about Mirelle; always Dinah was called in to clean up the mess. It was exhausting. She kept her eyes on the little bottle of polish, turning it over and over in her fingers.

"Well, this is a cozy scene," Kelly cut in.

Her feet were bare, her footsteps silent as she turned in the middle of the floor. She swept back her hair with a casual hand, her look expectant.

"Is there any coffee?" she asked. "I'm absolutely famished. What's for breakfast?"

"There is no coffee," Mirelle said. "You know the coffee maker has disappeared."

Kelly's sigh was impatient. "Yes, but I thought you would have gone out to get another one by now."

On the counter, Mirelle's hand became a fist.

"Easy, Tiger," Dinah murmured.

"What?" Kelly's eyes swept the counters. Her gaze fell on the glass next to the sink, the remains of Mirelle's mimosa at the bottom. Her small mouth tightened perceptibly. "Did you make anything for breakfast? Aside from drinks?"

Slowly Mirelle flattened her hand again, and with both hands on the counter, she pushed up from her stool. Almost in slow motion, she turned to Kelly.

"No," she said distinctly, "I did not."

Kelly had to be the single most self-absorbed woman in history, not to heed the warning of Mirelle's voice, Mirelle's stance. She tossed her head in obvious disgust, letting out yet another long-suffering sigh.

"Am I supposed to make it for myself, then?" she demanded. "After I've just spent an absolutely harrowing night in the county jail?"

"You know what, Kelly?" Mirelle parked a hand on her jutting hip. "I'd rather you didn't."

Dinah rose slowly from her stool. Everyone else was standing; she felt at a disadvantage. She wondered whether she could imitate Mirelle's challenging stance; probably not, as she didn't really have the hips for jutting. She opted for crossing her arms.

Something seemed to be getting through to Kelly at last. She took a step back. "What's going on?" she demanded, licking her lips. Her eyes flickered between them. "Why are you two suddenly ganging up on me?" When neither answered, she turned beseechingly to Mirelle, widening her eyes. "What's she been saying about me, Mirelle? Don't listen to her. She only wants to turn you against me. Dinah hates me. She's always hated me."

Dinah choked. Kelly turned a look of pure loathing on her.

"Dinah doesn't need to turn me against you, Kelly," Mirelle answered. She frowned slightly, examining a fingernail. "I'm perfectly capable of thinking for myself."

Kelly took another step back. Her hands fluttered helplessly. Her eyes filled with tears. "I can't believe you're saying this to me," she whispered. "I can't believe you're being like this. After all I've been through—"

"Kelly, you attacked your husband with a hammer," Dinah said.

"I had to. He deserved it, you know he deserved it. After what he's done to me—" The tears were rolling down her cheeks. She held her hands out in front of her. "And we all know—I'd never have had to go to him for money if it hadn't been for Dinah. This is all your fault, Dinah, do you hear me? *All* your fault."

"Leave Dinah alone," Mirelle ordered, raising her eyes from her nails. "Take some responsibility for yourself."

Kelly reeled back as though she had been struck. The tears stopped as abruptly as if someone had turned off a faucet. Her lips twisted angrily. "Oh, fine. Let's all rush to poor Dinah's defense. Poor unfortunate Dinah. And let's all gang up on Kelly instead, why don't we?"

"I guess I've heard about enough." Mirelle's face had gone hard, as though carved from stone. "Kelly, I'd like you to find someplace else to stay. I know you don't have any money right now, so you can use the room until your paycheck comes from the restaurant—"

"No." Kelly straightened her shoulders. Two bright spots of color burned high in her cheeks. "I'm not fool enough to stick around where I'm not wanted. I'll get my stuff out now. I'll sleep in the car if I have to, but I won't breathe any more of the precious oxygen in your precious house."

Thrusting Dinah roughly out of her path, Kelly made her way toward the stairs. "This is a madhouse anyway, and you know it. Telephones ringing at all hours of the night, and all those bangings and thumpings—I hope you have a poltergeist, and I hope it trashes the place."

"No," Dinah called after Kelly's retreating back, "that's your job."

"If she trashes my house," Mirelle said in a murderously low voice, "I'll hunt her down and use a sledgehammer. See if I won't."

Dinah didn't doubt it.

Forty

THERE WAS INDEED much banging and thumping as Kelly threw her stuff together and made her final exit. At one point Dinah offered to hold the door for her, but received such a venomous look that she retreated to her stool at the counter. It was probably just safer to stay out of the way.

When the door slammed the last time behind Kelly, Mirelle let out a monumental sigh of relief. She wiped a hand across her brow. "Well, that went off without any bloodshed, anyway. I still feel guilty, somehow. For asking her to leave. What if I'm wrong about her? About them?"

"That's what she wants you to worry about. It's part of the game plan," Dinah observed, listening to the sound of yet another set of tires squealing out of the driveway. "You know, she never once said thanks for your bailing her out. I hope she doesn't skip town."

Mirelle shrugged. "No matter. I put it on Wally's charge card." She looked exhausted. "I wish I had a cup of coffee."

Despite feeling wrung out, Dinah laughed. "Most people at this point would skip the coffee and go straight for the booze."

"Well, we all know I'm not most people."

"You're so contrary. How about tea?" Dinah suggested. She got up to root around in the cabinets. There was remarkably little to be found, not the usual concatenation of empty spice packages and boxes of pasta most kitchen cabinets could be expected to contain. Then again, Mirelle had never been one to cook when a visit to a take-out restaurant would do the trick. There were a few cans, though: several small tins of Vienna sausages, a can of chunk light tuna packed in water, and a can of B & M baked beans: an interesting selection. Dinah could not imagine Mirelle eating any of those things, let alone opening any of those cans; she'd probably break a nail. Shoving the tins aside, Dinah found an ancient box of Red Rose tea bags way in the back. She opened it suspiciously and sniffed. "Do tea bags go bad?"

Mirelle waved a hand, uncaring. She seemed incapable of moving. Throwing Kelly out had sapped her strength. "I don't know. You pour hot water on them, anyway, so they'd be sterilized."

"A cheering thought."

Dinah got two mugs out of another cabinet, then dug a saucepan from the drawer under the oven. She filled this with water and set it on the burner to heat. While she waited, she leaned against the sink, gazing out the window at the sky. What little she could see of it beyond the maples edging the back yard was fully menacing now, ugly bruisy shades of green and gray. It looked as though it should thunder, as though the clouds should open up and deluge them. The branches on the maple trees tossed restlessly in the wind.

"Seriously, though. I understand. I feel sort of guilty about Kelly, too. And angry. Because she's lied and lied and lied and manipulated us all by appealing to our need to believe her. All that effort you expended on her, because we believe women, you and I. What if someone else needed your help, and she was, to coin a phrase, using up all the bandwidth?"

"I know. This is how people get jaded. Because of people like her. The proverbial crier of wolf." Mirelle sighed. She looked unhappy with the outcome of the morning. At a muted pounding, she cocked her head. "Is that thunder?"

Dinah filled the mugs and set them on the counter. She got the milk out of the refrigerator and brought that over, too. "I don't think so. Not yet."

Mirelle uncapped the milk jug, smelled it, then poured a healthy dollop into her tea. She followed that with enough sugar to rot a person's teeth out just by looking at it. "I thought I heard something." She stirred her tea until she had created a little whirlpool in the mug. "Maybe Kelly's right. Maybe the house is haunted."

The knock on the porch door startled them both. Dinah sloshed her tea down her shirt. A policeman was silhouetted at the door, holding his hat with a hand against the wind. "Jesus. Talk about being haunted."

"I'll say." Mirelle set her mug down and stood, adjusting her clothes slightly. That infamous overwhelming charm was slow in coming. "Officer," she said as she held the door open. "And corporal. Please. Come in. To what do I owe the pleasure?"

Teasdale and Billings. Were there no other policemen in the department? Did these two never get the day off?

When Roy Teasdale removed his hat, once inside the house, his hair was not the least bit disarranged. It was as though it were plastic, painted on his scalp. Ken-doll hair.

"Mrs. Holbein, Mrs. Galloway," he said formally, ducking his head slightly. "Mrs. Holbein, the investigation into the whereabouts of your husband has taken on some new developments, and we'd like to take this opportunity to speak to you about them."

Dinah took one last sip of tea before setting her mug down beside Mirelle's. "Should I go?"

Mirelle shook her head, her hair swirling around her shoulders. Corporal Teasdale didn't even blink; he had to be made of stone.

"No, Dinah, stay." Mirelle indicated the door to the living room. "Won't you officers come in and sit down?"

With a glance at the clock over the sink, Dinah followed the three into the living room. Mirelle took her accustomed seat in the white wicker fan chair, while the policemen took up positions on the sofa, which looked far too delicate to support their combined weight. That left Dinah the wing chair, and she shoved the matching ottoman aside, as perhaps putting her feet up was not appropriate to a police interview. If this was a police interview. Officer Billings took a small notebook from his pocket and began writing, his pencil scratching lightly across the top of a new page.

As if to punctuate this situation, there was a sudden crack of thunder overhead.

"Was *that* thunder?" Mirelle asked Dinah, raising a single eyebrow.

"Ma'am, I believe it was," Corporal Teasdale answered.

He set his hat on his knee. His broad face was impassive. Perhaps he truly was made of stone. Perhaps someone had carved that face, and the expression would never change. Dinah tried to imagine, for a moment, Teasdale at home, being just plain Roy. Someone's husband, someone's father. Out of uniform. She couldn't do it.

Mirelle smiled benignly on the two officers, but Dinah noticed her foot, in its gold sandal, tapping repeatedly on the carpet. "Someone was just telling me she thought my house might be haunted." She quirked that eyebrow, teasing. "But I think the only haunting I've had here lately is from you all."

Roy Teasdale's smile did not quite reach his eyes. "Mrs. Holbein, as you know, we've been looking into the whereabouts of your husband. Unofficially, because you, as his wife, have yet to file a missing person report."

Mirelle's smile turned hard and cold, as though someone had flicked a switch. "That's because, Corporal, my husband has been missing from this marriage for quite some time." The tapping of her foot slowed momentarily, but did not stop.

A slight snort issued from the notetaking Billings.

"That's as may be, ma'am." Teasdale's expression did not change, however. "But your husband's boss—the superintendent of schools—has reported that Mr. Holbein has missed a number of very important meetings in the past couple of days, and he's becoming concerned."

"He's called here," Mirelle said. She looked away, out the window, at the wind-tossed trees. "Wrong house."

Teasdale cleared his throat. "As you may have heard, in a recent development—"

He sounded like a newscaster, Dinah thought inanely.

"—his secretary recently found an odd collection of assorted small appliances in his office."

Dinah watched for the reaction; Mirelle, however, gave none. She looked back at the two policemen on her couch and tilted her head, her expression mildly curious.

As if on cue, Billings flipped back a few pages in his notebook and read off a list. "Hair dryer. Toaster. Coffee maker. Waffle iron—"

"Waffle iron?" Dinah repeated.

Two pairs of official eyes flickered in her direction.

"Waffle iron," the officer repeated, as though proving a point.

"I never knew we had a waffle iron," Mirelle murmured.

"In light of these developments, Mrs. Holbein," Officer Teasdale said, pausing dramatically before continuing, "is there anything you would like to say? Anything you can add to our information, to aid us in discovering what's happened to Mr. Holbein?"

Mirelle laughed, just as another clap of thunder, close enough to seem to shake the foundation, broke. She twisted a strand of her hair around a finger. "You make it sound so ominous."

Dinah wasn't so sure about the turn this conversation was taking. Teasdale's expression was unreadable, and Mirelle seemed unwilling to absorb the warning vibes aimed in her direction. Was Mirelle the second most obtuse woman in the universe? Dinah wondered what would happen should she leap up and semaphore to her. She bit her lip instead.

Corporal Teasdale shifted slightly in his seat. "Mrs. Holbein, I think I have to tell you that your lack of interest in in your husband's whereabouts has become a matter of curiosity."

A warning if ever there was one.

Mirelle leaned back in her fan chair, dropping a hand to play absently with the cut-glass ashtray on the side table. "Corporal," she said gently, as though speaking to a recalcitrant child. "In the course of your investigations, you no doubt have found that my husband has left me for another woman. If you've asked enough questions of enough people, you'll have found out that he did this in the most public, most humiliating way he could think of." She turned the full force of her blazing blue eyes on the pair—a gaze that normally could pin men to the wall as though run through with spears. "How on earth, after that, could you be surprised that I'm refusing to allow myself interest in his whereabouts? Would you have me be the wounded, ever-loving, ever-forgiving wife?" She laced her fingers in her lap. "If that's so, you'll be sorely disappointed."

She looked as though she had practiced the speech before her mirror; now she awaited the round of applause that was not forthcoming.

Another rolling of thunder—the sound was drawing even closer. Dinah glanced out the open window, where the sudden breath of wind puffed the draperies outward. They curled in upon themselves, wave-like, before falling back into place. She stood to close the sash. The room was suddenly shadowy and gloomy, so she flicked on the floor lamp before returning to her seat. The lamp cast a lonely circle of light on the patterned carpet at its foot.

"As you know, we have been in contact with a friend of your husband, a Miss Alix Mailloux—"

"Euphemism," Mirelle countered, lifting the ashtray and hefting it as though considering its weight as a weapon.

Billings looked up.

"The other woman," Dinah interjected, before Mirelle could use a stronger term. "Alix Mailloux. A bit more than a friend, I think, as Mirelle has already pointed out."

More scratching of pencil on paper.

"In any case," Teasdale continued smoothly, "Miss Mailloux insists that something has happened to Mr. Holbein. And she further insists that you, Mrs. Holbein, are the cause of whatever that something is. Can you think of any reason why she might allege a thing like that?"

The foot was working again, double time. "Come now, Corporal," Mirelle scoffed. "Surely you could think of a good reason. It's not that hard."

Teasdale did not look as though he appreciated having his intelligence called into question. His lips thinned minutely in his otherwise impassive face. A man of degrees, certainly, and Mirelle had already proven that she did not read nuance well. Dinah gripped the arms of her chair and waited for the crash.

She did not have long. Another roll of thunder echoed through the house; but this time it seemed further away, somehow muffled. Actually, it didn't really sound like thunder at all.

Then came a blinding flash of lightning, and a clap of thunder unmistakably directly overhead. The light went out.

Another sound. From the cellar.

Mirelle's eyes were wide. Dinah thought her own might be, too.

"What the hell was that?" Mirelle gasped.

In the now eerily dim room, the two policemen were on their feet. Corporal Teasdale's hand went to this belt, but when he withdrew it, he held, not a gun, but his long-handled flashlight.

"Mrs. Holbein," he said slowly, "would you mind if we had a look in your basement?"

Wordlessly, Mirelle nodded and rose from the fan chair. With a wave of the hand, she indicated the way back to the kitchen, and through to the pantry, where the cellar door was tucked away under the back stairs. Dinah brought up the rear, following the beam of the flashlight.

When they opened the cellar door, the thumping grew more pronounced. Dinah thought she heard a voice. It was so weak, however, she might have been mistaken.

"The switch—"

Billings passed a hand over it. No response. "No power," he said unnecessarily.

Single file, they followed the steady beam of the flashlight into the cellar. Dinah had never been down here; but then again, she very rarely visited her own cellar if she could help it, or if she could send Perry down there instead. It was the cobwebs; she hated the feeling of them brushing against her hair and skin, like cold and ghostly fingers. The thought made her cringe. She reached out a hand for Mirelle, who shrugged her off.

The thump came again, from the far corner. Weaker, as though its maker were losing strength. Or hope. The beam of light swung around.

"The cold room," Mirelle said.

A door was built into the far wall; solid wood, it sported a shiny lock set. Officer Teasdale played his light over it, picking out the heavy keychain hanging from the single key in the lock.

"Ma'am," Teasdale asked, "when were you last down here?"

"I never come down here," Mirelle answered quickly. "I don't do cellars. I've always left that up to Wallace." She examined the heavy ring of keys hanging from the lock. "And these are his keys. Wallace's."

With a nod of his head, Corporal Teasdale indicated that his partner should try the door. "Where does this go?"

Mirelle sniffed. "The cold room. It was meant for storing vegetables through the winter. Wallace had it fitted out for a wine cellar. He's got the only key."

Even now, however, Billings was turning the only key. At the click, the door was thrust open from the inside.

Wallace Holbein tumbled out at their feet.

Forty-one

DINAH STOOD AT the end of the wind-whipped driveway, watching as the ambulance pulled away with Wallace Holbein as its passenger. The two officers followed in their squad car, after a stern warning to Mirelle to not leave town.

"Do you want me to call Gahan?" Dinah asked. "Tell him you won't make rehearsal today?"

Mirelle laughed mirthlessly. "I may need you to call a lawyer, the way your police pals were eying me in the cellar."

She had a point. In dramatic counterpoint to the discovery of Wally inside the wine cellar, the lights had suddenly flickered and come on again. The bare bulb in the socket behind them, where they stood looking down at Wally's prostrate form, extended their shadows to enormous and grotesque heights. Dinah had stood, blinking, as Roy Teasdale dropped to his knees beside Wally, while the other policeman grabbed his radio mic from his shoulder to call for help. Wally lay supine, breathing labored; his clothes were grimy, one knee of his trousers torn. His face, which did not look quite as round as usual, sported several days' growth of beard.

The wine cellar had smelled like an old outhouse; the floor was littered with empty bottles and opened cans of Vienna sausages.

Perhaps Mirelle was right. Perhaps she was going to need a lawyer.

Dinah wondered what story Wallace Holbein was going to tell, when he *did* get around to telling one. She wondered, too, whether he intended to wait to tell it until the ever-faithful Alix Mailloux arrived to hold his hand and support him through this dark and possibly embarrassing hour. Dinah could almost imagine the bedside scene in the hospital, Wally pale against the sheets, Alix brushing the thinning hair away from his brow, offering him a sip of water when he faltered. Almost. Then her stomach turned most unpleasantly, and her mind's eye veered away to consider something else.

It was difficult. When she closed her eyes, the scene replayed itself over and over. "I don't want her," Wally had gasped, pointing to Mirelle with a shaking hand as the ambulance attendants had loaded him in. "Alix. I want Alix." He'd probably get his wish soon enough.

The rain was growing heavier, soaking through the shoulders of her blouse, each drop making a darker green spot on the lighter green material. The water was running down her cheeks, and she lifted her face into the rain. Her hair hung wet and heavy against her head, and she ran her fingers through it. Around her sandals, now, rivulets of water streamed down the driveway toward the road, where the cars had turned on their ineffectual headlights. Mirelle had retreated to the shelter of the porch.

Lightning flashed. Dinah waited for the roll of thunder off to the west. The storm wasn't even close to finished. If she stood here long enough, it might roll back overhead, and then she could become a human lightning rod. A real one, rather than a metaphorical one.

More cars passed along Main Street, their tires hissing on the wet tar, their headlights reflecting dully off the blackness. Someone honked at her, no doubt looking out for her best interests, whatever they might be. *Stupid woman, doesn't even know enough to come in out of the rain.* She sighed, dragging her fingers through her hair one more time, tugging to make it stand on end. It was no use; she was too waterlogged. She wiped her eyes, then slowly turned back up the driveway toward Mirelle on the porch.

"No." Mirelle held up a hand. She might have been crying, or it might have been the rain smearing her mascara. "Don't. Not now. Come back later, after the restaurant closes. I might be able to talk then."

JULES NAVARRO WAS already at Galloway's when Dinah returned to the restaurant. *Damn.* She had wanted to present a calm and united front to this new addition to the staff when he arrived; it was so important to get off on the right foot, to prevent another chef's mutating into Rob. She sighed, squelching one foot around in her wet sandal. *Not* the impression she wanted to make. Again she ran her hands through her damp hair, trying to neaten it this time; but it was no use. Well, so be it. There was no time to change, no time to metamorphose into something a bit more respectable. This is what she was; and she was the owner. Bedraggled and wet, she took a deep breath, trying to channel Mirelle at her haughtiest, and swept through the double doors into the kitchen.

Several sets of eyes glanced up and away again, barely noting her dramatic entrance. The three of them—Perry, Mark, and Jules—all in their whites, were huddled around the butcher block, where a slab of meat gleamed slick and red. Perry sliced a knife through it expertly, and the other two nodded. Behind them, Lindsey was stirring something in a double boiler.

"I thought," Perry said, "if we butterflied the meat like this, it would be more manageable when it came time to build the dish."

Mark nodded again. "There's less waste that way."

Jules tugged at his dark mustache, frowning. "At the bistro, though, we always did it the way I showed you. Not this way." He took a step away from the block, separating himself slightly from the other two. The protest carried more of a note of uncertainty than the chef intended; he was, she realized, trying to establish his practical credentials. Curious: he'd already cooked for them—his dish had been the salmon paté, which she'd really enjoyed.

"But as you can see," Perry pointed out, "you don't sacrifice anything in quality. You don't sacrifice anything in taste. I really think this is a more efficient way to use what we have."

"And Dinah likes efficiency," she said.

"Oh, hello, dahhhhhhling," Perry crooned, as though seeing her for the first time. "So nice to see you." He came to kiss her cheek.

"Stay away from me with your bloody hands," she warned, slipping away from his reach.

"Not to worry." He wiggled his red fingers at her. "You can always go outside and have another shower." He winked.

Jules Navarro was looking at her askance from beneath his bushy brows. His appearance was dramatic, in a swarthy sort of way; almost the stereotypical southern European chef, if there was such a thing. Perhaps the prototype.

"Mrs. Galloway," he said, assuming a stately tone. His voice was deep. "I had hoped you would be here to greet me." A disapproving note played under his words, as though she had failed to meet his expectations; and these things simply were not done.

Dinah raised her eyebrows, much as Mirelle would. *I am Dinah, Queen of this Jungle.* She thought of Rob, and the idiocy she had put up with under his tenure, her own idiocy in putting up with it at all. *Not again. Not ever again.* Navarro needed to establish his place, she understood; but she also determined to make him understand how things would work around here from the get-go. She smiled, steely, aware of Mark's and Perry's eyes upon her.

"I had intended to be. But *something* intervened." Let them dwell on that *something* for a while and see what they came up with. She skirted the butcher's block to examine the cut of beef, wondering what it was that fascinated them so. It looked like meat to her. That was all. Ross would have known. "I see that Perry and Mark are sorting you out just fine, however."

That Jules was startled at being "sorted out" was obvious. Under his tunic, his chest swelled perceptibly, like that of a peacock just before fanning his tail.

"We were just having a disagreement about a cut of meat for this evening's specials. Of course, how we did it at the bistro—"

"Was how you did it at the bistro," Dinah agreed. She looked from the red meat to the red face of the new chef. "But now you're here."

The chest expanded further. No doubt there was room to pin not just one *cordon bleu*, but several to it. "Mrs. Galloway, as the new executive chef—"

Oh, dear. He really was trying it on from the very start. Well, there was nothing for it but to prick that balloon early and often. She put her hands on her hips. "I didn't hire an executive chef."

"They hire those down at Waldemann's, across town," Perry cut in gleefully.

"Shut up, Perry," Mark said, suppressing a laugh.

Dinah drew herself up to her full height—not appreciable, but there it was. "As you may recall from our interview, I'm trying to create a fully integrated atmosphere here in the kitchen. As such, there are no executives. We are an autonomous collective. All decisions are made by vote of a simple majority."

"And the majority of us," Mark said slyly, "are majorly simple."

"Shut up, Mark," Perry said.

The two burst into laughter.

In the face of this hilarity, Jules's bubble slowly deflated. Even Dinah, in her bedraggled state, felt her lips turn upward. It had to be hard to maintain pomposity amongst such as they: the manic kitchen staff and the drowned rat of an owner. The new chef tugged at his mustache as his eyes darted between the three. He shifted from one foot to the other. But, as Dinah so clearly recalled, he had been very interested in the amount of money she was willing to pay; he was married with seven children. Jules Navarro probably would not be lining up to catch the next train out, no matter how important he felt himself.

For a moment he said nothing. When he did speak, his voice—and his chest—were considerably smaller than before.

"I'll give it a try," Jules conceded. But the look in his dark eyes as he glanced between the three of them was still uncertain.

Forty-two

ONCE THE RESTAURANT had closed up for the evening, Dinah slipped out and drove down to Mirelle's. A single light was on in the kitchen, and when she knocked on the door, she saw, through the window, Mirelle look up, her expression exhausted, drained, and not a little bit annoyed. She stood to unlock the door and let Dinah in.

"I brought a bottle," Dinah said, holding up the Macallan.

Wordlessly Mirelle got out two tumblers.

Dinah poured them both two fingers of single malt and drew up the chair opposite Mirelle's. "So?"

Mirelle just shook her head. There were slight blue circles beneath her eyes that even her makeup couldn't hide.

"You look like you've been through the wringer," Dinah commiserated. "Was it all that bad? Gahan, by the way, sends his love and says to give him a call in the morning. But not too early."

Even Mirelle's smile was weak, as though the battery had run down. "He's all right, that Gahan Godfrey," she said, lifting her drink to her lips. Her lipstick was almost gone, an unheard-of state of affairs. "At least you know where you stand with him. At least he's not sneaking about trying to drive you crazy."

"No. When he wants to drive you crazy, he does it right out there in the open." Dinah grinned ruefully.

She waited for more. Even though Mirelle's demeanor was that of utter exhaustion, the details would come out. Mirelle had never been one to hold onto a story when it made for good theater. Still, she looked worn down now; she looked her age. This was a new and unpleasant idea. They were the same age, with birthdays only weeks apart, but Dinah rarely thought of Mirelle in those terms: Mirelle simply *was*, as a force of nature simply *was*. Yet even in this forgiving light, her skin looked waxy, her hair dull. Her light had indeed been dialed back.

"You remember when I had Perry board up that broken cellar window? It took him a couple of days to get to it, but he finally did" Mirelle turned her glass in circles in its own damp ring on the napkin. "He was so proud of how tightly he'd nailed that thing up. How he swore up and down no one would have an easy time breaking in there."

"I remember."

"That was the window into Wallace's wine cellar. The one he was going to get rid of and never did." Mirelle's expression was wry.

"Okay," Dinah said, setting her glass down and rubbing a hand across her forehead. She was tired, too. There was something here she was supposed to be getting, but she wasn't sure what it was.

"After I had the locks changed on the doors, that's the way Wallace was getting in and out of the house."

Dinah felt her eyes grow wide. "You mean—you don't mean—"

"That's how he was getting in to kidnap my small appliances." Her voice dropped, and she came out with a remarkable imitation of Corporal Teasdale. "Hair dryer. Toaster. Coffee maker. Waffle iron."

"Waffle iron?" Dinah couldn't help herself.

"Waffle iron," Mirelle repeated.

It was still incomprehensible. Dinah closed her eyes, trying to imagine Wallace Holbein skipping over from the school while his wife was at rehearsal, wearing the suits he favored for working, and shimmying in through a cellar window. To steal appliances. "But why? Did he need a coffee maker?" He was balding, so he certainly didn't need a hairdryer. "No, that can't be right. All the stuff was under his desk at school."

Mirelle nodded. "Keep thinking. You're almost there." She drained the last of her Scotch and held out her glass. "Care to pour me another? It'll keep you occupied while you figure this out."

In surprise, Dinah realized that her own glass was empty. Effective stuff. When was the last time she'd actually sat down and finished a drink? She poured out another two fingers for each of them and recorked the bottle.

"I don't get it." Dinah leaned back in her chair, took a sip of Scotch. "Why, then? Don't tell me he was saving them up for presents for Alix. That's hardly romantic. Appliances are bad enough as gifts, but used appliances are totally low class." *Nuthin' says lovin' like a toaster oven.* But Wallace hadn't carted off a toaster oven. Probably Mirelle didn't even own one. Unless Wally had given her one at some point, for a present.

"Sometimes you're such an idiot," Mirelle said, but fondly. She played with the candle on the table, lighting it, then tipping it back and forth in its glass to watch the wax ooze. "It was all part of his nefarious plan. He was trying to drive me crazy."

"By stealing coffee makers?" Dinah frowned. "That's possibly the most bizarre thing I've ever heard of. Even from him."

"I know." Mirelle shook her head in wonder. "All these years of marriage and the man still couldn't figure it out. Stealing my coffee maker isn't going to send me around the bend. Maybe stealing my martini shaker would do it, but not a coffee maker, for God's sake."

Dinah leaned back in her chair and picked absently at her skirt, straightening the seams against her legs. "So. Let me get this straight, will you? When Perry finally got around to boarding up that window for you—Wally was in the house? In the cellar?" The thought gave her the creeps; she felt a shiver go up her back. It was like being spied on. She looked around the kitchen, wondering who might be wandering around in the house while they weren't paying attention. Just as quickly she shook herself sternly: Wally was gone. Kelly was gone. *Don't be so stupid.*

Mirelle took a deep breath. She too looked a bit unnerved, and more than a bit disgusted. "Oh, yeah. I don't know what he'd gone in for that time, though the electric toothbrush was in the wine cellar this morning."

Dinah pressed her fingers against her eyelids. "I hope he brought toothpaste. Then after he ate his Vienna sausages and drank his wine, he could brush his teeth."

Mirelle sipped her Scotch. "No. There's no outlet in there, anyway. For all that, he'd have been just as well off stealing a plain-old manual toothbrush."

"But how on earth did he get locked in?" The candle in its little cut glass holder had gone out. Dinah patted her pockets for matches and found none. Reaching across the table, she snagged Mirelle's lighter.

"Who knows?" Again Mirelle shook her head, her hair swinging. "He'd put something on that door when he first began turning the cold room into his wine cellar, one of those hydraulic things to make it swing shut automatically. I guess in his hurry he didn't take his keys out of the lock, hadn't fully unlocked it—something. The door closed, the lock clicked into place, the window had been boarded up, and there he was."

Dinah snorted. "That's pretty stupid."

Once the candle was relit, Mirelle resumed turning it, letting the melted wax climb up the sides of the holder and solidify. "Why he needed a lock on the damned thing is beyond me, anyway. I mean, we were the only people who ever went into our own cellar."

"He knows your drinking habits," Dinah said darkly. That made her think of her own, so she lifted her glass.

Mirelle flicked a bit of wax at her with a fingernail. "Don't be an idiot. If it's not champagne, you can keep your wine. I'll just drink the hard stuff."

Bored with her game, Mirelle set the candle holder down. They sat silently for a few minutes, considering the flame, which lengthened and shortened, wavering with their breathing. The Scotch was seeping into Dinah's bloodstream, warming her to a slight tingle. She leaned back and sighed. The candle flickered, but remained lit.

"So he's in the hospital," Dinah said.

Mirelle nodded. "Overnight. For observation. He's mildly dehydrated. They gave him an IV." She grimaced. "So there he lies, a tragic victim in his hospital johnny, administered to by the ever-loving Alix Mailloux."

"Better her than you."

"Whatever." Mirelle waved a languid hand.

"All the same," Dinah mused, "it's probably a good thing he's in the hospital right now. It's going to be pretty embarrassing for him, out in the real world, trying to explain his breaking into the house to steal waffle irons."

"He wasn't going to say anything, I don't think. He wasn't even going to try to explain. As soon as Alix showed up—the police called her to let her know Wallace had been found—she started hurling around accusations like a wild woman. I'd locked Wallace up to keep him to myself. To keep him from her loving arms. For revenge."

"As a sex slave?" Dinah suggested.

"Don't be disgusting." Mirelle held up her Scotch and examined the color. "In any case, the thrust of her accusations was that I'd known all along that Wallace was locked in the wine cellar. I'd probably engineered his being there to begin with. How, I'm not sure. Maybe she thinks I drugged him and dragged him down there. I don't know. But she wanted your friend Roy to arrest me right then and there."

"That's when Wally spoke up?"

The sound Mirelle made was not attractive. "Never. He would have kept mum on the whole deal. Remember the embarrassment he'd be saved if the real story didn't come out; and think of the personal satisfaction, on top of that, that he'd feel to have me locked up. No. The police asked about the small appliances under his desk, and he launched into a spiel about how he deserved them, he had a right to them, and it was none of their business why he chose to keep them under his desk at school. By the time he was done carrying on, no one was all that impressed with him save Alix. So I left. What was the point in sticking around?"

That, Dinah decided, was the moral of the story: there was no real point in sticking around. As she'd thought all along, there had to be a divorce. She looked across the candle flame at Mirelle's hooded eyes and felt a sharp stab of pity.

"I'm sorry," she said at last. "I know this must hurt."

Mirelle picked up her Scotch and threw it back in one gulp. She grabbed the bottle and splashed another healthy shot into her glass. "You don't, though."

The words surprised Dinah. She set her own glass down.

"What?

"You don't know how this hurts. You don't know how this feels at all."

Dinah shot a glance to Mirelle's face, which was now hard, bitter. As though the world had caved in. Her voice was sharp, slicing. *She's just lashing out.* Her world had caved in, hadn't it?

Dinah reached out a hand. Another attempt. Mirelle snatched her hand away.

Deep breath. "Look, when Ross died—"

"Stop. Just stop."

Stung, Dinah lapsed into silence. She didn't understand.

"I don't want to hear about Ross. He wasn't all that with a cherry on top, okay?" Mirelle downed her second shot, then stood to carry her tumbler to the sink, tossing her head. "So you can just stop singing his praises to me."

Hold on.

That sound. In her voice. It was angry, almost vicious.

Something wasn't right.

Mirelle had turned her back and was busying herself at the sink, running the water, squirting the dishwashing liquid. Silverware clanked.

"What?" Dinah asked. Her lips suddenly felt numb. "What did you say?"

Mirelle adjusted the stream from the faucet, apparently finding the water too hot. She swished her hands around in the sink, pulled out the sponge, squeezed it between her fingers.

"Nothing," Mirelle answered.

But she did not turn around.

"What did you mean, Ross wasn't *all that?* All what?"

Mirelle didn't answer. She wiped a fork with the sponge, ran it under the faucet, and dropped it into the basket on the strainer. To Dinah it might have been in slow motion, so drawn out was the action.

"Mirelle," she said, her mouth dry.

Another fork. Then a spoon.

Dinah stepped to the sink. She felt danger. Mirelle's cheeks were mottled, her lips a thin line; she stared steadfastly into the sudsy water.

"I've said too much."

"You haven't said damned near enough."

Dinah reached for the sponge, but Mirelle jerked away, as though expecting a slap. "Always it's your precious Ross. Your God-damned precious Ross."

"What—?"

"All the time with you it's been Ross this and Ross that. Ross the freaking saint." Mirelle's chest was heaving. "Well, he wasn't a saint, Dinah, not by a long shot. You should just get over him and go sleep with that Mark. Like I've been trying to get you to all along. You can stop worshipping your precious dead husband because he was just a plain old screwed-up human like the rest of us."

The vehemence forced Dinah to take a step back. "What are you saying?"

"Your wonderful husband was no more wonderful than mine. No more wonderful than Kelly's. He was just a man." Mirelle looked up, her eyes blazing. "A man who couldn't keep it in his pants. Not for Sherry. And not for you."

Everything froze, suspended. Only the words moved, in the air between them.

Dinah's ears were pounding, and she couldn't get a breath. She staggered back as though punched, a hand flailing for a chair, the table, anything to maintain her balance.

"No—"

Mirelle turned back to the sink, threw some more silver into the strainer. She washed and rinsed a dish, but turning, let it slip form her hands. It crashed to the kitchen floor, smashing to pieces.

They both stared at it.

"You—" Dinah finally managed a deep dizzying breath against the realization, leaning on the table for support. "You slept with him. My husband. Ross. You slept with him."

Each moment was a piece of that shattered plate, flying through the air like so much shrapnel. Mirelle urging her to get over Ross, by pushing her toward Mark. Mirelle, hurling the photograph of Ross out onto the porch roof. Mirelle, and Ross.

Seventeen years.

Of what?

And a friendship, from childhood.

Slowly Dinah raised her head.

Her face felt still, her skin cold. She wondered if her heart were beating, if her blood were pumping.

Mirelle's own expression, as she met Dinah's gaze, was defiant, and then slowly—slowly, as though she realized what she had done—melted, crumpled.

She suddenly looked haggard, a woman who had been trying too hard for too long. The angry blaze faded from her eyes, and then the tears came.

"Dinah—" Mirelle held out a dripping hand. "Dinah—"

Dinah's own eyes felt hot and hard in their sockets. Marbles. She could only stare, unblinking.

The kitchen was closing in. Claustrophobic. Dinah pushed away from the table and stumbled toward the door. Out there was the driveway, her car. Out there was away, and she needed to get away.

She dragged the door open and crossed the porch to the stairs, one agonized step after another. Behind her she heard another crash, and Mirelle's voice.

"It was only the once, Dinah. Only once. I meant nothing to him."

Dinah nearly fell into the driver's seat.

"He loved you, Dinah—"

But she locked the door, fumbled the key into the ignition, started the engine.

PART IV

Palate Cleanser

Forty-three

SHE SLOWED AS she approached the restaurant drive. The restaurant that she had dreamed of with Ross, and which was now a lie.

It was difficult to get out of the car.

I've loved this, Dinah thought, staring up at the house looming under scudding clouds and a moon a day or two past full, with its bow windows, its wide porch. A light shown from an upstairs window; a paler light filtered its way through the door from the green-shaded lamp left burning at the hostess's desk. *I've loved this.*

Now she hated it. She knew it was all fake: she'd built a temple to a god who didn't exist. The white porch railings which glowed in the darkness, the swing, the wide pine floors inside—it all mocked her. Everything about Galloway's mocked her, even the name. From a monument built of love for Ross, to a monument to his betrayal: how swiftly it had changed for her. The rain had lessened to a fine mist, but Dinah stood in it still, looking up at the restaurant, knowing she had to go inside, and knowing she wanted nothing more than to strike a match and burn the whole place to the ground.

Why, Ross?

Then *how, Ross?*

A car passed, the sound of its engine rough against the fabric of the night. From the damp grass crickets made their ruckus, as though the world as she knew it hadn't just ended. Dinah sighed. There was no wind; the air on her skin was warm, but the rain had passed.

The porch swing creaked.

Dinah jumped.

A familiar chuckle, and a slight shifting of dark on dark up on the porch. She could see now that the swing was moving slowly back and forth, its lone occupant in shadow.

"Come on up and join me," Mark called. "Take a load off."

She didn't want to, but could think of no reason to refuse. Still, to refuse meant she'd have to go upstairs to the apartment. To her thoughts. To her rage and grief. She picked her way slowly across the driveway and back up the porch steps.

"You're the only one left?" Her voice was strange to her own ears.

He patted the cushion next to him. "I won't bite." In his hand a tumbler glittered in the darkness. "I got you a glass. Come join me."

Dinah took the seat he offered, and the glass, too. He poured something into it; in the darkness she couldn't make out the label. "I've already had a couple tonight," she said bitterly. "I'm fairly certain I don't need any more. I'm probably drunk." She probably shouldn't have driven.

Mark shrugged. She couldn't see his expression. "No matter. It's just more companionable for me." He had his own glass on the side table. "I hope you don't think I'm taking too much advantage, helping myself like this."

"Well, if you're going to do it, make sure you drink the good stuff." She could tell from the smell that it was Scotch. More Scotch. Just what she needed. Or didn't. She took a sip, then held the glass up, trying to see the moonlit world through the liquid.

"Only the best." Mark held his glass out, and clinked it against hers. "Mirelle's all right?"

The name was a stab through the heart. "I don't want to talk about her." Dinah couldn't even bring herself to speak it: the name of the woman whom she'd known since childhood, the woman who had urged her to come back and open the restaurant here, the woman who had betrayed her.

Dinah leaned back and closed her eyes, trying to let the gently swaying swing lull her. Perhaps to sleep. It was no use: the fury still raged. Rather than being dulled as the night wore on and she drank more Scotch, her senses were strung tightly, reacting to every movement of the air, every sound. Her thoughts were like pinballs, crashing off each other and spiraling off again randomly. She drank some more.

Mark might have been studying the bead-board of the porch ceiling, had it not been nighttime and impossible to see that far up.

"Something happened," he said.

Dinah did not rise to the bait.

He rolled his head to the side. "You going to tell me about it?"

"No."

He turned his glass in his hand, studying it. "That bad, eh?"

Dinah refused to look at him. She took another drink. The Scotch was making her reckless. "I don't want to talk about it. Her."

"You're angry."

Now Dinah was sorry she'd said anything. She pressed her lips closed.

Mark poured more whisky into her glass without asking.

"Is it Wallace?"

She shook her head. "Just stop."

Mark held up his hands. "Okay. You can tell me when you're ready. For now, let's talk about something else."

Buzzed, Dinah found even the gentle rocking of the swing disconcerting: the world would not stop moving, would not right itself. Even the stars were moving too quickly.

"Like what?" She lowered her glass, stared at the rim.

"I don't know. Memories. How they tangle up with the present. How they make everything all that much harder."

"Why is that?" Suddenly impatient, Dinah slammed her drink down on the wicker table. She felt, rather than saw, the whisky slosh out over her hand. "Why is that, damn it? Why do we have to carry all this memory garbage around, like some kind of lead weight? Why can't it be that when we're done with something in our lives, we're done with it? Why *do* memories have to ruin everything?"

Mark drained his glass before setting it aside. His laugh was not quite a laugh at all. "You're asking the wrong person, Dinah."

His voice, suddenly, seemed unutterably sad.

"No, I'm not," she countered. "I'm asking you."

When he turned, she leaned forward and pressed her mouth to his. He tasted of Glenfiddich. She ran a hand up into his hair and kissed him harder.

SHE HAD HIS shirt pulled from the waist of his jeans and nearly unbuttoned, her hands running over the fine fur of his chest—reddish-gold, she knew, like his hair, though she couldn't see out here—when the headlights of a passing car flashed over them quickly and were gone. Mark's hand had found its way along her knee, beneath her skirt; he did not remove it as he pulled away slightly, with a low laugh.

"This is probably not the place for us," he murmured.

Another car went by, strobing them briefly with its headlights.

"Pretty soon you're going to have my fly down in the middle of town for everyone to see," he continued against her lips. "And then someone will call the police."

Dinah held his hand right where it was. "If you're so shy about it, then you'd better come upstairs to bed."

"Your bed?" Mark still didn't sound as though he believed in her advance, or in her surrender.

She stood and whirled quickly away from his grasp. "There's no other bed up there."

He leapt after her as though on springs, pausing only to lock the outside door behind them.

"Lock that door, too," she instructed him at the top of the stairs. "Otherwise, we'll have Perry appearing at the least notice." She moved familiarly through her darkened apartment, around the sofa and coffee table, to her bedroom door, where she flicked on the light. She had thrown off her sleeveless blouse before Mark had a chance to get into the room.

"Slow down." He laughed, reaching for her shoulders and pulling her close.

But having made this decision, Dinah found herself in no mood to go slow. Raising her mouth to his once again, she tugged at his belt.

"No," she said.

He looked just as good without clothes on.

PART V

Theater

Forty-four

SHE WAS ON her hands and knees, scouring out the cabinet under the sink, when Mark appeared. He leaned against the kitchen counter, his arms crossed over his chest, clad only in his boxers. The morning sun gleamed in his tousled hair. His chin was stubbled with a day's growth of beard, the scratchiness of which Dinah could still feel on her own skin in places that sent shivers through her when she thought of them. Quickly she turned her attention back to the cabinet, trying hard not to think of those places.

She loathed everything about herself this morning.

"What on earth are you doing?" Mark asked, yawning.

Out of the corner of her eye she saw his stretch, the way his torso tautened, and his boxers settled lower on his hips. She was acutely aware of her jeans and stained tee shirt, and the bandanna she'd wrapped around her hair. Still, hadn't that been the point of these grimy clothes? She shied away from that thought, too.

She leaned into the cabinet, trying to scrub around the drainpipe. The bottles and cans of household cleaners were strewn about her on the tiles. "I'm cleaning under here."

"Surrounded by enough household poisons to kill an elephant," he observed. "Am I supposed to take some message from the symbolism here?"

He was too sharp by half, and Dinah didn't know how to answer. She wasn't certain she knew the answer herself. She paused, sitting back on her haunches. She could not bring herself to look at him, but rather fell to examining the brush in her hand. Some of the bristles were coming out. *Piece of junk.*

She had awakened more than an hour before, and for a while had lain there, examining the contours of Mark's sleeping face. She had almost reached out a finger to trace his cheekbone, but held back. While her skin had still tingled from his touch, from his kisses, at the same time she had felt cold, despite the comforter. Just as she had wanted to wake him, to re-explore his body, at the same time she needed to get as far away from him as possible. This man. Her friend. With whom she had slept. Because she was angry. Because she was hurt. Hurriedly but gently, so as not to wake him, she had slipped out of bed, pulled on some clothes, and gone frantically in search of something to occupy her.

Mark stepped around the counter. He found filters and coffee in the overhead cabinet, and set about filling the coffee maker. Dinah kept her head down, even more aware of his nearness: the scent of him, the sense of him. She thought again in confusion of what she had done with him, of what she had done to him. How she had used him. She clenched her fingers around the brush. More bristles came off in her fingers.

After a bit he held out a mug. Dinah numbly dropped the scrub brush into the bucket of dirty water at her side and took the cup, hot and steaming, from his hand. The coffee scalded her mouth, but she immediately lifted the mug to her lips again. She wanted the hurt. She deserved it.

He settled himself on the floor a few feet away, back against the cabinet doors. A shaft of sunlight cut across the tiles to his legs, his long feet, and knobby ankles. Dinah felt a pang at the sight of those ankles, and quickly took another drink of coffee.

Mark, too, drank his coffee in silence, his eyes following the dust motes dancing in the sunbeam from the front window. At last he set his empty mug down on the floor beside him. Without facing her, he said, "I guess I'm just going to have to ask you this question, Dinah. Because I guess I just have to know the answer."

"What question?" Her voice sounded dry and raspy to her ears.

He cleared his throat. "I need to know who you were making love to last night."

Dinah caught her breath. Thoughts of bad soap operas flashed through her mind. "I don't know what you mean." Her hands shook and she spilled coffee in her lap. She quickly put her mug down on the floor.

Mark looked into her face; his eyes were shadowed. "Were you making love to me? Or to Ross?"

The question stung. Dinah slumped, staring at him, swallowing. *How could he ask that?* she wondered dumbly. She thought of Ross, the way he made her feel, even now, even when she knew what he had done. Had he made Mirelle feel that way, too? She clenched her eyes shut, pressed the heels of her hands into them. How could she possibly say she hadn't been making love *to* anyone, but rather *against* Ross?

Oh, God. How to explain to Mark how she'd used him?

"I guess that's my answer," Mark said, his voice rife with bitterness and disappointment. "I guess I should have known. You woke up this morning and realized that I wasn't him. That I wasn't your dead husband. And you had to get away from me." Abruptly he got to his feet and left the kitchen, as though he couldn't put enough distance between them fast enough.

For a moment she could only stare at the place where he'd been sitting. She heard him in the bedroom, gathering his things.

"Damn it! No, damn it. No, you don't." She clambered to her feet, knocking her cup over, the remains of her coffee puddling on the kitchen floor. She slapped her palms on the breakfast bar. "Mark Burdette, don't you dare put words in my mouth."

"Why?" Re-entering the living room, his face was bleak. "One of us ought to speak the truth." He had his jeans on, his shirt in his hands.

"Then I guess that'll have to be me, since you haven't got a clue what the truth is." But she couldn't tell him the truth, either. She wanted to claw her own eyes out.

"No?"

"No. God *damn* it, Mark! You've got it all wrong." She shook her head, the bandanna fell away, and her hair tangled about her face. She shoved it out of her eyes impatiently. "All wrong."

He crossed his arms. His back was ramrod stiff. The shirt hung from his hand.

"Let's hear it, then," he demanded. "How wrong am I?"

Now she had been granted the floor, she could not find the words. Dinah squeezed her eyes shut again, trying to sort through the mess in her head.

"It wasn't Ross," she whispered at last. "Last night. It wasn't him at all." It was the best she could manage.

"Just words." Mark sank onto the sofa, elbows on knees, hands clasped. His head was bowed.

"No, they're not," Dinah insisted. "It was your name I said, wasn't it? Your name. Not his." But the lie of omission stuck.

Slowly he lifted his head, but his expression was still clouded, his voice full of frustration. "Then what's this?" With a wave of his hand he indicated the cleaning supplies strewn over the tiles. "What's with this cleaning out? What's with your avoiding me?"

"I'm not avoiding you."

He held up a hand. "You said you were going to be the one to tell the truth. So tell the truth, Dinah."

Her throat felt thick, as though she were going to cry. *Don't do it,* she ordered herself sternly. "All right." She threw up her hands. "Listen, Mark, will you? Listen to me. I did something last night I had absolutely no intention of doing. None whatsoever."

"Slept with me?" he asked. The noise he made might have been a laugh. "You came on pretty strong for someone making a mistake, then. And I was totally fooled."

She felt her face grow hot. "Will you stop it?" She wanted to hit something. "You're putting words into my mouth again."

Mark pressed his lips together and waved a hand for her to continue.

Dinah took a deep breath. "I had no intention of getting involved with you, Mark. Because you're partly right. I wasn't over Ross yet." *Wasn't.* The betrayal seared through her again, speaking his name. *Still wasn't. Bastard.* "But last night, things changed for me. Drastically." Her knees felt weak, and her head hurt. *Damned hangover.* She went into the living room, groping for the chaise. Carefully she lowered herself onto it. "People"—she still could not bring herself to speak *that* name—"have been telling me all along that I'm still in love with Ross. But you know what?"

Mark made a derisive sound.

She took another breath; she couldn't seem to fill her lungs. "You yourself said last night that people couldn't help their feelings for each other, since they had so much history together. Well, Ross and I had a history, too. A long one. So it's only fair that you allow me my feelings, too. However mixed up and stupid they are. I can't help them, Mark." Not the feelings she wanted, or expected, but they were still there. What she wanted was another drink. Or to crawl back into bed—alone—and cry herself to sleep. Something other than to feel this way.

"But last night—"

"But last night. Yes." She sighed, her head in her hands. "Last night I made love to a man who wasn't my husband. For the first time since losing my husband. And I enjoyed it. Very much. Do you hear me, Mark? *Very much.* And I shut Ross out of my head. He's been a part of me for half my life, and I shut him out of my head. That scares me, Mark. It scares me a lot. But—I had to do it."

The words fell, leaden, between them. Mark blinked and met her eyes. *How young he looked.* Dinah caught her breath. Maybe it was just how old she felt. She examined his face, and again imagined reaching a finger to trace the curve of his cheekbone. She dug her nails into her palms.

"Something happened last night, before you got home." Mark's gaze was still steady, still probing. "Something you didn't want to talk about. Maybe you'd better say it now."

Dinah couldn't hold his gaze and turned her head. There, atop the piano, was the picture of Ross. Smiling and smiling, the damned villain. She turned back, and Mark was still watching her. Still waiting.

"The worst part about it is that"—she gulped—"I've just discovered that if I'm still in love with Ross, then I'm in love with an absolute shit."

Mark raised his sandy eyebrows.

"Seventeen years. I never so much as looked at another man. Faithful and loyal to the freaking core, that's me."

"And?"

Dinah blinked. "And."

For an interminable moment he stared back, his brown eyes scanning her face. "And. He wasn't."

Dinah did not move.

Another long pause. Through the open window she could hear birds. Traffic from the road. A dog barked somewhere in the distance.

"And it was Mirelle."

The words stabbed between her ribs.

"And I was—revenge."

Forty-five

BY THE TIME she'd cleaned up the coffee, dragged herself through a shower and into some clean clothes, and then downstairs, Perry and Jules were already at it in the kitchen. A song about a girl named Jane played from the speaker on the windowsill.

"It's the Barenaked Ladies," Perry told her happily, carefully measuring spices into a huge silver bowl. "Jules is celebrating my Canadian-ness."

Celebration. Dina had never felt less like one. She couldn't remember the last time she had a hangover.

Jules was doing something unspeakable to a series of Cornish game hens, lined up as though for a firing squad on the butcher block before him. He smiled toothily from under his enormous mustache. "My wife," he said cheerily. "She loves the Barenaked Ladies. And now I have this new job, she loves me, too." He attacked the next game hen.

Dinah turned her pounding head delicately away.

"Where've you been?" Perry selected a wire whisk and turned to his concoction. "Mirelle was here a bit ago, looking for you. She didn't look good at all. But she had to go to final dress."

Thank God for that. Dinah put a hand to her aching forehead. Final dress. She'd forgotten. The theater would open tomorrow evening.

"Are you all right?" Perry asked. He stopped his whisking and wiped his hand on his white jacket. "Dinah? You don't look good, either."

"No." She waved a hand. "Nothing. A headache."

"Ah," Jules said, slapping aside another hen. "I have just the remedy. Let me finish these little ones, and I'll whip that right up for you, Mrs. Galloway."

Easier to just accept it than to argue. "Thanks." Her voice was hoarse, as though she hadn't used it in quite a while. She looked around uncertainly. At the counter on the back wall, Lindsay, who had stepped up to prep cook, was carefully slivering vegetables in festive colors. The dishwasher had not yet appeared; it was early yet for Kevin. Dinah turned back toward the dining room: she could check the bar, the cooler, to make sure that was all stocked. She could do that by rote. It might keep her from being sick. It might keep her from burning the place down.

"Dinah?" Perry interrupted her. She half-turned. "Where's Mark? His car was out back when I came in, but now it's gone."

She looked at Perry sharply. His face, though, was round and innocent. Just curious. Unless—was that sympathy?

She didn't want it.

"He's gone," she said. She tried to keep her voice steady, nonchalant. "He figured, with Jules working out so well, you guys could handle it on your own." She attempted a smile. "He *does* have another job, you know. Probably he wants to get back to it."

Perry made a non-committal noise, and Dinah escaped through the swinging doors. A close one: she had fudged an answer just in time. Now she stumbled blindly through the main dining room, barely noticing the pristine settings arranged by Gillian's waitresses the previous night before they'd gone home. In the west room, she ducked behind the bar and ran her hands over bottles, lifting them and setting them down again, caressing the cool, smooth glass. She wanted nothing more than to drink them all—or to smash them. What was she looking for, again? She had to remind herself. None seemed to be below half-full; most seemed recently opened. Either it had been a light night for drinking in the restaurant, or Dirk had taken care of it all before leaving. She didn't know, and she couldn't bring herself to really care.

Dinah straightened and leaned against the bar, pressing her hands to her hot face. Her head was truly pounding, but this was not just a hangover. At least, not of the conventional kind. The ache had begun as she watched Mark finish dressing, collect the rest of his things. He hadn't even bothered to shower. As he was closing the apartment door behind him, he had suggested she call him— when she was no longer confused.

That could be a long time.

She wondered what it would feel like to cry. Her eyes were dry and gritty, like the desert floor; it hurt to blink. Her throat felt swollen, as though she had a cold. Probably her face was still red, as it had been when she'd checked herself in the mirror after her shower. Perry had said she didn't look good. Surely to cry wouldn't feel worse than this. Maybe it would help, even. Perhaps if she allowed herself a good howl, then it would be all over and done with, and she could set about the business of the rest of today. The rest of her life.

But she was too tired to cry. That was the problem. It seemed like such a difficult thing, to work herself up into a weepy state. Easier just to lean here against the bar and do nothing. Just easier.

She barely registered the slap of the porch door, or the sound of voices from the kitchen. Until they rose precipitously: more arguing. Panicked, Dinah slid down to the floor behind the bar. If they came in here, she wanted no part of it. She wanted no part of any of them. Her head was thumping now; she was dizzy. She groped for the bottle of Tylenol Dirk kept beneath the bar, then realized in despair that she wouldn't be able to shake any out without being discovered.

"I need you back in the theater," Gahan growled, his voice coming closer.

"I need to find Dinah," Mirelle countered. Her voice was higher pitched than usual. Borderline hysterical.

Dinah felt the rage boil up again, and her fingers curled around the plastic bottle, as though around Mirelle's neck. As though around Ross's neck. But Ross was dead; he'd betrayed her, then died.

A lighter tread. Perry's.

"Where's Dinah? Have you seen her?" Mirelle demanded.

"She was here a minute ago. I heard the door. She must have gone outside." Perry's voice was high, too, but with a patent falseness.

Perry. She was surprised to realize that it was his shoulder she wanted to lean against and cry. Perry, who had, as it were, no horse in this race. She leaned back, her head against the bar refrigerator, and closed her eyes. She was dizzy and sick, as though the dining room was a roller coaster on which she was trapped. *Please.* Over and over again, like a mantra. *Please go away.*

"Flowers, maybe?" Perry giggled a little, the way he did when he was uncomfortable. "For the tables? Something like that."

Please go away. She felt the nausea rising.

Mirelle's giant sigh—that long-suffering, put-upon sound. Dinah squeezed the neck of the Tylenol bottle all the more tightly. Footsteps receded; the door slapped in the frame. Still Dinah kept still behind the bar, just to be on the safe side.

A barstool scraped.

"You can come out now," Perry said after a moment. "They're gone."

Dinah dropped the plastic bottle. "How—"

"How did I know? I could see your reflection in the taps, since you ask. Why couldn't Mirelle see it? Oh, because I moved in front of her. I figured you were hiding down there for a reason." Perry leaned across the bar to look down at her where she sat. "Gahan's on a tear, so she probably won't be back in a while. Now might be the time to make your escape, since you apparently don't want to see her. But if you're going upstairs, I'd advise you to lock the door behind you." He reached a hand down awkwardly to her.

Dinah stared at his long fingers for a moment before grabbing hold and struggling to her feet.

"You really look bad." Perry wasn't laughing now. He frowned, leaning closer. "Still just a headache?" He sounded skeptical.

Before Dinah could answer the kitchen doors slapped open. Jules peered around the corner into the west room. "Ah, here you are, Mrs. G." He smiled beatifically as he approached the bar, holding out a steaming mug. "I told you I had just the thing for you, and now I bring it to you." He set it on the bar and waved both hands over it proudly. "Come now, drink it up. I promise it is the good stuff."

Perry leaned forward, gazing into the steaming depths curiously. "What the hell *is* that?" He wrinkled his nose delicately.

Still Jules waved his hand. "I believe it is called 'the hair of the dog,' though I promise you, Mrs. G., that there is neither hair nor dog in it."

Dinah let go Perry's hand and, grimacing, turned her attention to the mug. "This, at least, is good to know." She too looked down into the mixture, trying to see through the steam lifting from the surface of the liquid. That appeared dark, and slightly oily. She swallowed convulsively. The smell roiled her stomach. "What on earth is in it, then?"

Jules threw up his hands, a protective gesture. "Oh, do not ask me to answer that question, Mrs. G. This is a recipe from my mother-in-law, a recipe she brought with her from the old country. It is as much as my life is worth to tell you the secret." He made a fearsome face, drawing a hand, knife-like, across his throat.

"Far be it from me to put you in danger," Dinah assured him weakly. She put out a hesitant hand to the mug, which, oddly, did not feel at all warm to the touch. Again, easier not to argue.

"She can't afford to lose anymore kitchen staff," Perry said. He surveyed Dinah with a speculative, though not unsympathetic, expression in his eyes.

Jules was again indicating the remedy with both hands. "Drink up, Mrs. G. I promise you. It is just what you need." His smile grew wider and more inviting, under the shelter of his great mustache.

She took a sip. The taste was indescribably horrid, far more acrid than she was prepared for; it was all she could do to keep from spitting it across the bar at Jules in his white tunic. As it was, her eyes began to water; her nose began to run. She looked up at Jules's enormous smile through her tears.

"Good, is it not?"

It is not. Dinah's vocal cords seemed to have been burned away. She could only gag. Satisfied, Jules bowed slightly and bustled off, back to the kitchen.

Perry was still eying her in speculation. Once the kitchen doors had swung shut again, Dinah hurriedly set the remainder of Jules's mother-in-law's secret recipe aside. She rested her forehead on the edge of the bar for a moment, her eyes still streaming.

"First week on the job," she gasped out, "and already he's trying to kill me."

"Really. Are you okay?"

Dinah did not lift her head.

"Did you hear me?" Perry leaned over the bar again, a hand on her arm.

"I heard you."

"Are you planning on answering?" Perry fell back into his seat as Dinah straightened. "Listen. I've got to get back to the kitchen, get back to work. But I don't feel right about leaving you here. You really *do* look sick, Dinah. I've never seen you sick."

"I'm fine." Dinah's throat still burned from Jules's secret remedy; her head still pounded, and her stomach still churned. Despite her answer, she really did feel ill now. She looked away. "I don't want to talk about this."

She felt the blood rush into her face, the perspiration breaking out at her hairline, and at the same time her skin suddenly went clammy and cold. *What the hell was in that drink?* She looked at the mug, sitting on the bar, and wondered how it had moved that far away. Was that the phone ringing, or her ears?

"Di—" Perry's voice seemed to come from far away, too. "You look like you're going to be sick." Again he reached out a hand, and his touch was warm. "Should I call someone? A doctor? Do you think you ought to go upstairs and lie down?"

"Maybe," Dinah said weakly, "I should."

Forty-six

DIMLY SHE HEARD movement and voices from the living room; dozing as she was, she could not make out words. At one point the door opened a crack and someone stuck a head in; she kept her eyes closed and lay still, on her back in the center of the bed, the comforter pulled up to her chin. Even had she felt capable of moving, she wouldn't have, for each stirring of the sheets released the lingering scent of Mark. She couldn't think of him.

She had no idea what time it was. Fading in and out of sleep, she noted only vaguely the travels of sunlight across the walls and ceiling. This last time she had awakened, the quality of light had changed entirely: now it was white, rather than yellow, cast upward from the lights in the parking lot beneath the window.

It was the sound of the outer apartment door that had disturbed her this time, she realized groggily. "Still out," she heard a quiet voice say; for a fraction of a second her panicked breath caught in her chest before settling again quickly. Perry's voice.

A bit of shuffling, the creak of the sofa springs. Dinah turned her head for a moment toward the sliver of light between the door and the frame.

"Should we call him?" The deep rumbling was Gahan. What the hell was he doing here? "Find out what's going with them?"

Though Perry's voice grew no louder, it did grow more firm. "I don't think you should."

"Spoilsport."

More murmuring. Dinah strained her ears, staring up through the darkness toward the ceiling and its center rosette.

"Don't touch that phone," Perry ordered. "Put it away." Then, "I don't think she wants to see anybody right now."

A sharp sniff and the groaning of furniture unused to the weight. "You're here."

"I don't count."

Perry. He did count.

"How are we supposed to find out anything, then, if we don't call him?"

"Are you this single-minded in rehearsal?"

"Yes."

"The play ought to be great, then. Perhaps you should go *back* to rehearsal."

"We've struck for the night."

An enormous sigh from Perry.

"So let's call, then." Gahan was not to be diverted. Single-minded indeed. "What's that boy's number? You must have it in your phone. Or perhaps Dinah has it in hers." Creaks. The scrape of a drawer opening.

"Gahan." Perry's tone now brooked no challenge. "No. You have to go. And keep your voice down, for God's sake. I don't want you to wake her."

A long silence. In her bed, no longer drowsy, but paralyzed by lethargy, Dinah felt an anxiety building in her chest. *Don't call. Just go.* She didn't love Gahan right now. Only Perry. She turned over on her side. The bedsprings creaked. There was a moment of silence from the living room.

Perry again, his voice lower: she had to strain her ears to hear. "Why don't you just go on home? Maybe enough damage has been done already. Maybe we don't need to add to it."

"How on earth are we to find out what's going on, then? She won't tell me anything."

Perry sighed. "Did it ever occur to you that she doesn't want us to know? That it's none of our business?"

Dinah could have kissed him, but that act of gratitude would have taken too much effort. *Oh, Perry.* She felt the knot in her throat.

"But she's my friend!"

"Mine, too," Perry replied, his voice softening. "And so I'll leave her alone. Now—I'm planning on staying here on the sofa tonight. I'll make sure she's all right. I want *you* to promise me that when you go home, you absolutely will not call Mark."

"But—"

"I want a promise."

Grudgingly, Gahan gave him one.

Overcome with gratitude, Dinah dozed. In the depths of her sleep, she dreamed of Jules's mother-in-law, a crone in a black dress with a mole on her nose and strangely green skin, stirring away at a cauldron in the restaurant kitchen. Seated at a table transported from the main dining room, complete with gleaming silver and white cloth, Mark and his editor drank from steaming mugs and conversed about Michelin stars. Mark was in his boxer shorts. Mirelle and Ross waited on their table.

Forty-seven

IN THE MORNING, Dinah staggered to the shower and soaked herself, crying weakly at last, and hating every tear. Then she dragged on some clothes. Even the coffee Perry had brewed did not appeal, though she forced herself to drink some to stave off the caffeine-dependent headache that would come later if she abstained. It hardly mattered: her head still pounded.

She supposed she had to check on her investment. The theater. That was hers, in a way the restaurant never had been, and now never would be. Still, she scouted the yard for Mirelle's car: bad enough she'd have to watch Mirelle in the play—her favorite play—without having to talk to her. To see her at all this morning. To see her ever again.

The inside of the theater smelled of paint and carpeting and the upholstery of the fresh new rows of seats. Dinah did not pause in the doorway for long; she hadn't time nor inclination to admire the finishing touches, and the smells aggravated her still-sensitive stomach. Up on the stage, Gahan was making a few last minute adjustments to the set, jollying along his technical crew with cheerful noise and much tugging of his beard. He did not look in the least as though he needed her help—when had he ever? Nor did he look like a man who had been haunting her living room in the early hours.

"Chaos, my darling, sheer chaos!" he crowed, as though this were the only desirable state. He leapt from the stage, ignoring the temporary stairs erected before the proscenium. His kiss on her cheek was warm, long, and prickly. It was all she could do not to withdraw from it. "I love this day, more than any other day." Quickly he shouted an indecipherable set of directions to the two men still onstage, who jumped to his bidding.

Dinah winced. *Too loud. Too much.*

"Aren't you nervous?" she managed to ask, forcing her gaze to travel over the set, the English country sitting room, all heavy draperies and chintz. She wished she lived in that world. Anywhere other than in this one.

"Ah, Dinah." Gahan shook his head. "No. Nerves are for cowards. No pun intended, of course." He waved a hand around, indicating more than just the set, but the lights and all related accoutrements. "You've given me this perfect opportunity. I've assembled a marvelous cast and crew. You know we won't fail you."

Still, Dinah bit her lip. She could picture, in her mind's eye, Mirelle flitting about in her fluttering Elvira dress. Fluttering toward Ross. She definitely did not want to live in that world, then—was *everyplace* to be haunted by Mirelle? She grimaced. "You have everything you need, then?"

"I do," Gahan replied stoutly. He skewed his eyes downward, a quick glance to her pale face. "The question is, do you?" When she looked up, he smiled. "Feeling under the weather last night, I understand. Are you certain you need to be up and about this morning?" His question, now they were face to face, was delicately put; an emotional coward, he never had the nerve to ask straight out about anything having to do with *feelings*. For once, Dinah was grateful for that weakness on his part.

She returned his smile with a tight one of her own, rubbing the pain between her brows as though that might help. "No choice for it. This is the big night, isn't it? Almost as big as the original opening of the restaurant."

Gahan planted another kiss, this one to the top of her head. "Ah, it's going to be bigger, my darling, much, much bigger." He looked as though he wanted to say something further, but one of the stagehands rescued her by calling out a question and pointing into the flies. Gahan lifted a hand and sailed off.

Trying to banish the foreboding his words instilled in her, Dinah left him to his preparations. She wandered out through the stage door into the rear parking lot, where a number of cars, including Perry's Corolla, were lined up. She had seen Perry only for a moment this morning; when she had at last stumbled out of bed, he had a place laid for her at the table, with juice, toast, fruit, and coffee. Her stomach had rebelled at the sight, though she said nothing.

"Are you all right?" he had asked simply.

A blanket lay folded at the end of the sofa, a pillow balanced atop it. People were forever dossing down on her couch. She tried not to think of the last time a man slept there. At least there would be no ensuing difficulties with Perry. When she had nodded, shivering, he had smiled encouragingly.

"Then I'll be running off home, Di. See you in a couple of hours." With that, he was gone.

Now she paused, running a hand over a long scrape, like a scar, in the green paint of Perry's car. The metal was warm from the sun, blazing even in the forenoon. Next to this car was parked an unfamiliar maroon Jetta—had to be Jules's car. Gillian's car was there, too, as well as the road bike favored by Kevin the dishwasher. And Dirk's ancient Saab was now pulling in. She found herself smiling sadly at the vicissitudes of love. *Just couldn't stay away from Gill.* She hoped they'd be good to each other and bet herself they wouldn't. Then she hated herself for taking that bet. She waited for Dirk to park and lock up, then fell in beside him.

"You're here early," she said, ducking under his arm as he held the door for her.

"Got a lunch date," he said cheerfully. "Told Gill I'd pick her up." He grinned, an engaging, lopsided smile that brightened his entire face. "Nervous about tonight?"

"Nerves are for cowards," she said.

In the kitchen, the speaker bellowed out Mawkin at painful levels. Perry and Jules might have been dancing, spinning past each other with a blurry speed. The dishwasher in its corner was already humming. Gillian appeared from the walk-in, her arms fully loaded, and smiled prettily at Dirk. Dinah pressed herself back into the doorway as Lindsay zipped by with a knife.

"How are we doing in here?" she called, trying to sound hearty and supportive, and failing miserably. She could barely hear herself over the kitchen din.

"Under control," Perry called. He threw some butter into a pan, which he lifted from the flames and tipped back and forth with a turn of his wrist. "Waiting on the greengrocer, so we can get on the veg, but that's about it."

Dinah glanced up at the clock. The Dyer's truck was usually here by now. She frowned—and almost immediately heard the rumble of the engine as the panel truck pulled into the back lot.

"Mrs. G," Jules called, pulling a chicken breast out of a thermal box on the butcher block and slapping it down on a large plastic cutting board. "You are better after my mother-in-law's remedy?"

"I am better," she assured him.

Perry grinned over the stove. He tossed her a wink.

"In my mother-in-law's old country, they are as healthy as horses," Jules said proudly, sharpening a knife against a stone. "As healthy as oxen."

"Great." Did horses and oxen suffer from headaches?

Feeling unnecessary and useless, and still less than steady, Dinah eased through the kitchen doors. She found Dirk behind the bar, checking the beer cooler and the levels on the taps. Gillian was on the telephone, nodding as she listened, scratching away at the reservations list. After a moment she rang off and finished her notation. She smiled brightly; she looked chic as always, her hair swept back in a smooth chignon at the base of her neck.

"We're going to have a full house this evening," she said. "All tables reserved for the seven o'clock seating, the last tickets to the 8:20 show snapped up. We'll be turning people away." She sounded pleased as she pressed a button on the phone to reconnect her with the theater ticket office and the summer intern, to compare notes.

It was odd to be so redundant. Dinah supposed she should be pleased at how well her assembled staff took charge and worked together; but in the midst of the anxiety about tonight's opening, she found she had nothing to keep her occupied. She didn't like it; she had to keep busy, or she'd become Kelly and start breaking things. She looked around at the fully set tables—at least, she realized, with something akin to relief, none of them had fresh flowers in their respective bud vases. There was something she could take care of, anyway.

Gillian was off the phone again. "Can you cover the telephone for me while I step out with Dirk for a bit? It's going on noontime, and I'm feeling a bit peckish."

Dinah dug the pair of secateurs from the drawer in the hostess station. "Of course." She was necessary after all, thank God. "I just want to run out for a minute and cut some flowers for the tables. Will that be all right?"

Both Gill and Dirk seemed agreeable. Dinah grabbed a cork-bottomed tray from the waitress station and hurried out. The sun was nearly overhead, its warmth coaxing scents from the burgeoning garden. A number of bees hummed contentedly amongst the deep purple irises. She took a deep breath, trying to calm herself. It wasn't until she was clipping half-opened peonies from the bed surrounding the restaurant sign that she looked down at the secateurs in her hand and felt the shock of realization. They were the same ones she had purchased that afternoon, all those years ago, when she had first met Ross in the garden shop.

Dinah fought the rage until she'd cut enough flowers. Then she turned and hurled the clippers toward the road.

Forty-eight

DINAH HEARD NOTHING from Mirelle all day, and was grateful; but then, she hadn't really expected it, and certainly didn't want it. Every time she imagined Mirelle's manic chain-smoking, hands busy with cigarettes and lighters, she jerked her thoughts away, the scraping of a needle across a broken record. She couldn't bear to think of Mark, either, or the unhappiness she had caused him with her impulse for revenge. Worst, every thought circled back to Ross. *Ross.*

She couldn't allow herself to think.

She dressed carefully, in a fire-engine red dress with a mandarin collar, shot through with gold threads. There would be no mourning black tonight, no mourning black ever again. Rifling her jewelry box, she decided upon a delicate pair of gold earrings in the shape of seahorses. Her stomach was still roiling, her head still pounding, but she still needed to put up a reasonably good show. A debut. For the theater, the company, and for the new, angry Dinah. She turned to look again at the mirror, at her choice of shocking red lipstick, and wiped a bit from the corner of her mouth. She narrowed her eyes. It wasn't as though she was in competition with anyone. The only prize she'd ever valued hadn't really been hers, after all.

The dining room, as Gillian had predicted, filled quickly. Her insides alternately screaming and dulled, Dinah played hostess, meeting and greeting everyone to whom she'd sent special cards of invitation: several members of the town council, the local representative to the House, the president of the bank that held the mortgage, and the president of the Chamber of Commerce. Every dignitary she could think of, quite frankly. At about seven, midway through the seatings, before the show went up, Mark arrived with his editor.

Dinah was shocked at her lack of feeling—any kind of feeling; her smile felt forced, her makeup a mask. To give him credit, Mark didn't look all that much better, though once again he was dressed to the proverbial nines, in a light summer suit over a pale shirt which brought out the depths of his eyes. She realized she was staring at him dully, and, quickly, she turned to his companion.

"You remember Michelle Shore, my editor," Mark said. His tone was formal, and Dinah felt her smile crack. "This is Dinah Galloway, who owns the restaurant."

"And the theater," Michelle Shore added, taking Dinah's proffered hand; she had a firm grip. "How exciting this evening must be for you, after all this planning. And for Mr. Godfrey. Is he around?" Her eyes in her plump face scanned the dining room.

Dinah shook her head, trying to find her voice. "I'm afraid he's lying low until after the show. Over at the theater." She did not, in fact, have any idea where Gahan was; but years of knowledge of him left her certain that he was around somewhere, overseeing some last detail. If the devil was in the details, Gahan Godfrey had been to hell and back more times than she could count. Perhaps he could give her some advice. Or a map.

"A pity." Michelle sighed. "I was hoping to get to speak to him before the curtain went up." She leaned forward, placing a hand conspiratorially on Dinah's arm. "I'm subbing for our theater critic this evening. Jackie's on maternity leave." She threw her hands in the air, rolling her eyes heavenward. "First one of my feature writers, and then another." She winked at Mark. "It's all I can do to hold the *Gazette* together."

"It must be difficult," Dinah said.

I must be trite. She collected a pair of menus and led them toward a table in the center of the main dining room, her back stiff. Better to not give Michelle Shore any reason to remember her previous visit to Galloway's. She shot a quick glance around the dining room as she seated them, even though she knew perfectly well that Mirelle was otherwise engaged, over in the theater, getting dressed and made up. Wally, as far as she knew, was still in the hospital, unless he'd been released to return to the care of the ever-efficient Alix.

A tumbler of Scotch awaited her on the lower shelf of the hostess desk when she returned. *They all wanted her to become blind drunk.* Gillian smiled sympathetically as she whispered past; Dirk waved from behind the bar in the west room when she glanced through the wide doorway. She checked her own vital signs tentatively as she returned her attention to the reservations book: she was still standing. This was promising, at any rate. Even the idea of the Scotch upset her stomach. She gulped down another two Tylenol dry.

For the next hour or so she was only vaguely aware of the comings and goings of the dining crowds, while guiltily aware of the proximity of Mark. She refused to look over at his table, busying herself instead at the desk, shuffling menus when there were no guests to seat, no telephone calls to answer. If he glanced in her direction, she didn't see it; she didn't want to see it. It was with some relief, then, that the time approached for the show; turning the desk over gratefully to Gillian, she slipped out across the parking lot and under the new awning at the theater doors.

HER SEAT WAS near the back in the full theater, below the booth. As the lights lowered and the chatter died down around her, Dinah felt the rise of expectation and dread. *Blithe Spirit* was her favorite play, after all, though thanks to Gahan she still retained a fondness for Shakespeare. That would come later in the season; for now she clutched her program and waited with a churning stomach for the lights to come up.

For the production, Gahan had opted not to use the curtain, since very little needed to be done between acts in terms of set change. The English country cottage sitting room she had seen earlier was now brought to life, its inhabitants completely of it now, rather than working on it, as the stage crew had been. Charles and Ruth Condomine entered and their casual witty banter began; even though it had been years since she had last seen a production, Dinah was surprised at how many of the lines she could still remember by heart. She tried to relax, leaning back in her seat, trying to replace the tension of earlier in the evening with expectation, as the Condomines and their hapless maid Edith readied their home for the arrival of Madame Arcati and her séance.

That's when she noticed them.

Midway down the opposite side, in the two seats directly on the aisle: Wallace Holbein and Alix Mailloux. At first Dinah thought she might be hallucinating, or at least not seeing clearly in the dim lighting. But as the shifting stage lights reflected back on that profile and balding head, she felt her breathing catch. The woman next to him, her head barely reaching his shoulder as she leaned into him possessively: there was no way Dinah could be wrong. Mirelle's husband had brought his mistress to watch his wife's stage debut.

Dinah clutched her stomach. *Oh, God, what else?* The paper rustled as she crushed her program. There was no way to eject the two without a scene. The last thing she wanted at this point was to bring attention to them: Mirelle could not know they were here, or Gahan's show—the Black Orchid Theater's debut—would be ruined.

What in the name of God had they been thinking? Dinah's own thoughts screeched through her pounding head. Why would they show up here, unless their intent was to inflict more humiliation on Mirelle? It was hideous, the shameless and callous way they paraded the affair throughout the small town this was. At least—and surprise tears sprang to her eyes—Mirelle and Ross had hidden theirs. Hadn't she, Dinah, made clear that she wasn't going to be a party to this behavior? That Wally and Alix were not welcome on her premises? Perhaps she should take a page out of the book of the last few days, and call the police—have Roy Teasdale arrest them for criminal trespass. Maybe she should apply for a protection order against them? Except they weren't a danger to anything but her well-being—and that was destroyed already anyway. The whole situation was ludicrous, and Dinah's fury grew. Almost to the point of hysteria. At the same time, her insides screamed for revenge against Mirelle—a revenge that would do the theater and restaurant irreparable damage—so she remained in her seat. Trapped. The program was a ball between her palms.

Elvira's entrance was at the end of Act I. The intermission was at the end of Act II. Could she remain silent and still until then?

Dinah tried to shift her attention back to the play. Charles and Ruth and the Bradmans were in the middle of their séance, and the tension was building. The ache behind Dinah's eyes was growing stronger, more steady.

That's when she noticed them.

What the hell were they doing here? It was all she could do to run down the aisle and grab Rob and Kelly bodily to hurl them out. Perhaps it would be safer to grab fistfuls of her own hair and run screaming from the house? Sitting together. *They were sitting together.* Two rows in front of Wally and Alix. Kelly was on the aisle, Rob next to her, his arm draped around the back of her seat, his hand kneading her shoulder. What the hell were they doing here? What the hell were they doing *together*? As she watched in horror, Rob bent his head and nuzzled Kelly's neck. She pushed him away playfully. What had happened to the restraining orders? Now it was really a case for the police. Roy Teasdale would have to call for backup to get all these people out of here.

Then, of course, down near the front, sat Michelle Shore and Mark Burdette.

Dinah wasn't going to make it through to the end of the second act. She couldn't breathe as it was.

On stage, Madame Arcati swooned. The table around which Charles, Ruth, and the Bradmans were seated was bumping about wildly. After a few moments, it crashed to the floor.

Ruth Condomine cried out. Mrs. Bradman was confused.

Out of nowhere fluted Mirelle's voice. *"Leave it where it is."*

A couple of rows down, Wallace Holbein sat up a little straighter in his seat.

Onstage, Charles became agitated. His wife and guests protested that they had not heard the voice. The couple began to bicker.

After a pause, Mirelle's voice said, *"Good evening, Charles."*

This time, Alix Mailloux shifted in her seat.

Dinah's palms were sweating, dampening the paper in her hands.

Onstage, Madame Arcati was being revived by a frantic Charles. After a drink, she was shown out of the sitting room. The Bradmans and Ruth discussed the medium with a great deal of superior amusement. After a bit of banter, the Bradmans too were shown out of the sitting room. Ruth made a great show of adjusting the fire, then took a cigarette from a box on the mantle and was lighting it when Charles returned. She expressed concern at her husband's nervousness. He offered her a drink, poured himself one from a decanter on the small table stage left. Shivering, he remarked upon the chill air of the room.

Charles carried his drink over toward the fireplace, where Ruth was leaning against the mantle, smoking. When he was midway there, however, the French doors at the rear of the set burst open, sending the white curtains ruffling. Mirelle made her entrance as Elvira.

She was stark naked.

Charles dropped his drink to the floor.

Forty-nine

THE OPENING NIGHT party was not exactly a triumphant occasion; Dinah was grateful when, just after midnight, the crowd—by invitation only, thank God, because there were just some crashers she was sure she'd punch—ebbed away from Galloway's.

Among the first to take her leave was Michelle Shore. "Must go file my review," she said, leaning in and kissing Dinah on both cheeks. "I can safely say I've never seen a production of *Blithe Spirit* done in quite that way. I wonder what Coward would have thought of it. Still, I'd heard that Gahan Godfrey was an unconventional director." She shrugged and smiled.

Mark was nowhere to be seen.

Dinah was showing the *Gazette* editor to the door when they heard the spinning of tires on gravel. Both women turned toward the street, where a BMW pulled out of the lot. It drove erratically, swerving back and forth.

"Was that a man on the hood?" Michelle asked, shaking her tightly curled gray hair. She stared after the taillights. "Or am I imagining things?"

Dinah could only shrug, her smile tight.

Now, the last of the glassware and finger foods cleared away, Dinah bid goodnight to Gillian, Dirk, and everyone else who had stayed on to serve the party. With a last look about the two public rooms, she flicked off the lights and shut and locked the door.

The sound of running water from the kitchen caught her attention as she headed toward the apartment stairs. She turned, hand out to the swinging doors, but paused.

Maybe it was Mark.

Dinah didn't want to see him.

If it was he, she might just hurl herself into his arms and burst into tears against his chest, apologizing, though she knew it was far too late. That friendship was a wash. And it was all her fault.

She didn't want it to be him. She didn't want another breakdown like yesterday's—day before yesterday's, now, she saw, checking the dial of her watch. Just the thought of her collapse caused her to break out in a cold sweat.

She squared her shoulders, lifted her chin, and shoved open the door. Perry, startled at the sink, lost his grip on his glass; he grabbed for it, then juggled it, water splashing all around.

"Phew," he said once he'd regained control. "Almost pulled a Kelly with that one."

"I thought you were—"

"An intruder?" He didn't sound as though he thought that was what she was going to say. He grinned. "Nope. Just little ol' me." He plucked a cloth from the rack over the sink to wipe up the mess he'd made. Then he refilled his glass. "Just thought I'd get myself a drink before I headed home. Care to join me?" He held the tumbler aloft.

Dinah let go of the door, and it slapped closed behind her. "Sure."

It was the first time in a long time someone hadn't immediately assumed the drink she needed was alcoholic. Perry got down a second glass and filled it. Water, apparently the beverage of choice for him. They clinked glasses and drank. Straight up, no ice. The first shock of cold made her aching head pound. *Hair of the dog.* She heard Jules's voice as she drained the glass. There was neither hair nor dog in it. Perry took it to fill again. His expression was mildly amused.

"Come on, Di," he suggested, cocking his head toward the door, his ponytail swinging. "Let's go have a sit-down."

She followed him out the back. He settled onto the stoop, shifting aside to make room for her. "Pull up a stair."

The night was still warm and clear, the air unmoving. The newly installed spotlight bathed the back parking lot whitely, turning everything, including Perry's beater of a Toyota, into sickly shades of gray. Dina looked heavenward, but could see no stars. They must be out there somewhere, just not visible in the light of that brighter star, the spotlight. She sighed, drinking her water. She was surprised to see that her lipstick had not worn entirely off yet this evening; she left a cloudy kiss on the rim of the glass.

Perry was gazing upward as well. He lifted a finger to his lips, then pointed up into the light, where bats flitted after bugs. They were so quick, swooping into the arc of whiteness, and then out again. Dinah strained her ears, listening for the whirring of their wings. An owl hooted somewhere out at the line of trees.

"Nice out here," she said, her voice low. She didn't mean to sound so sad.

Perry chuckled. "Are we reduced to discussing the weather now?" He rocked his shoulder into hers.

Dinah shifted sideways, bumped him back. "How's Jules working out with you?" she asked, rubbing at the smear on the glass with a thumb. That only made it worse.

Perry shrugged. "He's all right, I guess. He knows what he's doing. The act's a little weird, but at least he isn't an ass like Rob." He set his glass down on the step beside his feet; he'd changed into huarache sandals and shorts. The light glinted on the blonde hair on his legs. He looked up again at the soaring bats.

Perry's profile, Dinah discovered, was finely etched, even classical. She couldn't remember the last time she'd looked at him, really *looked*. He was a fixture—like Mirelle's toaster, noticed only when it was missing. She felt ashamed. "Do you think you'll be able to work with him all right? He hasn't gone all pompous on you again like he did the first day, has he?"

"Nah. And if he tries, I'll just remind him that there are no executives here. That we're an autonomous collective." He nudged her again. "All decisions made by a vote of a simple majority."

"And we're all majorly simple." Dinah's voice trailed into a low moan. She turned to press her forehead into Perry's shoulder. "Oh, God, Perry. How could Mirelle have done that? What in the name of God was she thinking?"

There was a long pause. "This isn't just about tonight, is it?"

Dinah stiffened.

Perry drew back slightly, his eyes shadowed, and looked down into her face. Dinah couldn't see his expression.

He seemed to be waiting.

The knowledge burst like fireworks. She blinked. "You knew."

Slowly Perry nodded. Just once.

Dinah slumped. After a moment, Perry slipped his arm around her and pulled her closer. She was too tired to protest, or to pull away.

"Does everyone know?" Her voice was small.

She felt, rather than saw him shake his head.

"No. I wouldn't have, either, but for overhearing them argue, I think right after it happened. They were in the kitchen." He winced. "I was in the walk-in."

Dinah wasn't sure whether he shivered now from the memory or the remembered cold.

"And you didn't tell me," she said. Did she feel betrayed? Could she feel any more betrayed? Again, the tears, prickling behind her eyelids. She looked up into the velvet night again, trying to see the bats.

Perry shrugged uncomfortably. "I didn't. I didn't know what that would accomplish." He too turned to look upward again. "I heard Ross say he was ashamed. That it would kill you to find out."

She took a deep breath. *Not dead yet.* But crushed. The breath hurt her lungs.

"But why?" Dinah's voice, to her own ears, sounded strangled, far away. "Why would he even—do that?" She clenched her eyes shut. "Seventeen years, Perry. Seventeen years."

"I don't know. I heard him tell her how much he loved you—and how much he hated himself." Perry took a deep breath. "And her."

Despite her despair, Dinah could imagine Perry, cowering in the cooler, cradling a pan against his chest, unable to close his ears against the argument, unable to make his presence known.

"And you never said a word," she repeated.

"No. I thought about it." His arm around her shoulders tightened, in case she wanted to push away. "I knew Ross was right, how that would hurt you—I saw how you looked at him, Dinah—"

"I don't want to hear about that."

"—The way I wished Jamie could still look at me. How could I bring that kind of hurt to you?"

"I needed to know. I didn't need to find out—like I did."

He leaned his head against hers, lightly, sympathetic.

"Oh, Di, no one needs to find out that way. Or any way." He sighed. "Believe me. I thought long and hard about what I should tell you."

Dinah felt the misgiving in his pause. "And?"

"And then"—he took a long breath—"Ross died. And I didn't think it mattered anymore." With his free hand, Perry pulled a handkerchief from his pocket and blew his nose. "I thought that was a secret that could—should—die with him." He shoved the handkerchief back into his pocket. "I don't know how you found out. I wish—I wish I could have saved you from that."

Overhead, a plane lazed by, its lights blinking. On its way from Boston, following the flight path of planes to Paris or London or Reykjavic. Dinah wished to be on it, to be away, far far away.

"It's just another kind of death," she murmured.

"Yes."

"She's destroyed my marriage, she's destroyed our friendship, and now she's destroyed my business."

Next to her, Perry sighed. "I don't know as I'd go that far, judging by the audience reaction to the play. I saw some of it—Jules covered for me while I slipped over for a few minutes. Did you talk to her tonight?"

Dinah flinched. "I didn't. I don't want to talk to her again. Ever." She felt the bile in her throat, burning and sour. "We spent tonight avoiding each other. I would have killed her, even in front of the hundred witnesses in the room."

Perry laughed gently, almost sadly. He took her water glass and set it on the step next to his own. A single breath of air blew over them, lifting his hair away from his forehead. His arm tightened slightly again around her shoulders. "She's not a stupid woman, that one. But you have to admit—she caused a sensation."

"She's not my type." Bitterly. *Maybe Ross's, though.* Dinah sucked in a breath. God, how it hurt.

"Mine, either." Perry shrugged. He kissed the side of her head. "I guess not Alix Mailloux's, either, the way she shot right out of her seat."

Straight up, as though someone had pushed an ejection button. Dinah was momentarily distracted by the memory.

"I thought for a minute she was going to rush straight down the aisle and charge the stage. But then she just ran out of the theater." Perry snorted in satisfaction. "If that's the only way Mirelle could think of to get those idiots out of the place, it was brilliant and effective."

In her rage, Dinah had not really thought of Mirelle's performance from this angle. Perry had a point. The Lady Godiva entrance *had* been effective: upon Alix's fleeing up the aisle, Wally, too, had leapt up to run after her. The entire sequence was practically symbolic: if the adulterers were going to wash their dirty laundry in public, Mirelle was going to do away with laundry entirely.

"There must be some law against this, you know," Dinah moaned into Perry's shoulder. "Some public ordinance. We'll probably get closed down. Or fined."

"Or maybe Mirelle will be arrested," Perry replied thoughtfully. She looked up, and he winked. "I understand you've had that experience before."

"Go to hell." She lifted her head and cupped her chin glumly in her hands. "Tell me, Perry, why is it that I'm surrounded by all the assholes and nutcases in the world? Why are they attracted to me?"

"Mirelle, you mean?"

Dinah shifted. "Yes." She still couldn't say the name, or Ross's, either. "Wally. Alix. Kelly and Rob. And Gahan, who, despite not envisioning that particular bit of stage business, seemed to think it was the most wonderful, most original reading of a part ever, the bastard. Jules, who I swear tried to poison me the other night. And—"

"Me?"

He was not who she meant, but Dinah realized then that she couldn't bring herself to speak Mark's name, either. She dug her fingertips into her cheeks, which were, surprisingly, damp, and wished for more Tylenol.

Perry turned to her. "Dinah I can tell you the answer to that. We're all attracted to you because you put up with us, despite our being the idiots we are. You even love some of us."

"No, I don't." She didn't. Not any of them. If she had before, she didn't now, because everyone betrayed her.

Perry shook her gently. "Yes, you do. Of course you do. Somewhere deep down, you know it. I know that you put up with *me* despite the idiot *I* am. And I know that you don't demand that I be anything other than the idiot I am. How can I not be attracted to that?"

She shook her head. "Okay. Maybe you. That doesn't explain why people like Wally and Alix get sucked into my orbit. I don't love them."

"They came with Mirelle. You know that. She's another force field entirely."

"I *don't* want to talk about her." Dinah now ran her fingers into her hair and pulled. Then she threw up her hands. "But that doesn't explain Rob and Kelly, either."

Perry refused to back off. "Dinah. Listen to me. How long did you put up with them? For most of my adult life, I sometimes think. You tried. They just didn't have the sense to see it. Not like Gahan sees it. Or I do. Or even Mirelle."

"I told you. Don't talk to me about her. About *them*."

Perry held up a hand, acquiescing.

His words hung between them, though. Neither of them spoke. Probably Perry gave her far too much credit. She did love Mirelle, and she couldn't deny it; that's what made this betrayal cut so deep. That's what made slicing her best friend out of her life so painful. The friendship seemed ages ago and far away, something she saw through the wrong end of a telescope. Then there was Gahan, glowing with pride as he waved her attention to the stage set birthed of his imagination. And of course Perry, sharing the back steps and glasses of water with her. But Rob and Kelly: a couple whose behavior risked causing empathy fatigue, who didn't care whom they endangered with their manipulative games.

The plane was long gone. Dinah wished she could see the stars. A bat shirred by, quite close. In the grass near the walkway, the crickets set up an enormous racket, made more so by the silence of the night around them. At last Perry reached for his glass.

"Not yours," Dinah said. "Lipstick on it." She held out her hand.

"Who says I don't wear lipstick?" Still, Perry handed it over and picked up the other one. He drained it. "Need some more?"

"Please."

Perry went inside. Then there was a sudden sizzle and pop, and the new spotlight flickered and went out, leaving the back lot in almost total darkness. The only light left fell over her shoulder and into the yard, cast from inside the kitchen. That was blocked out for a moment as Perry pushed his way back outside. He handed her a full glass, water beading on the outside, and resumed his seat.

She could no longer see the bats, and curiously, she missed them. Dinah stared upward. At least now the stars were coming into focus, in a sky so silky it looked like her dress felt as she smoothed it beneath her hand. Was that the North Star overhead? The only constellations she ever recognized were the Big Dipper and Orion, and most of the time not even them, something Ross had always laughed about. *Ross.* She couldn't go there. She sighed, wondering vaguely what time it was.

"Are you going to be all right?" Perry again bumped her with his shoulder.

She took a drink before nodding. "Yeah. I guess so." She looked down into the glass, where the water was flecked with diamonds, the reflections of faraway stars. *Not tonight, though, and not for a while.* After a moment, she said, "Thanks."

"*Moi?*" Perry splayed his fingers against his chest. They were long and pale and thin, pianist's fingers.

"*Toi.* For the other night."

"Darling. Was it as good for you as it was for me?"

Dinah rocked into him, sighing. "I'm serious, you dope. For the other night, and for the morning after. For taking care of me, even though it really wasn't necessary. For letting me be, to quote someone, my idiot self. But mostly for not letting Gahan dial that phone."

Their shadows fell away from the stoop toward the walkway, his a head taller than hers. Perry stuck out a foot and scraped at the gravel before them. "You heard that, then?"

"I was awake." Dinah poked a finger into the side of his extended knee and quickly pulled it away again. "I heard it all."

Perry shifted uncomfortably. "You're welcome, I guess," he managed at last. He shrugged and took a long drink of water. "I just figured you probably didn't need us getting all up in your business about Mark, since whatever happened between you was so obviously double-plus-ungood."

The Orwellian assessment made Dinah smile in the darkness, though it was a wry smile. "What made you think that?"

He tossed her a glance. "Because he left. Because it made you sick."

"Jules's mother-in-law made me sick," she corrected, but knew he didn't believe that. She didn't know how much that mattered, either. She leaned into him again, head on his shoulder. He put his arm around her once more.

"Are you better now?" he asked.

Dinah didn't really know how to answer that question. "Not mentally, I don't think." She sighed. "It's just that my head is so damned screwed up."

Perry laughed. "And your heart?"

"And my life." Dinah took a sip of water. It no longer refreshed. It tasted of loathing. "I hurt him badly, Perry. He was my friend, and I hurt him badly."

Perry squeezed her shoulders and kissed the top of her head. "Never fear, darling Dinah," he said in a kind voice. "We *all* do dumb things. We none of us are perfect, no matter how we want to be. If it makes you feel better, I believe you've got more on the ball than any of us."

Her cheeks were damp. She wiped at them with the back of her hand. He'd said she was accepting, but Perry was the accepting one. Why had she never known this? Why had she never given Perry a second thought? Perceptive, and hiding it all behind a shield of foolishness. No one ever looked at Perry twice; and that, she realized, was his intent. She felt even more ashamed.

"Thanks," she whispered.

"Ross did a very stupid thing." Perry said.

"I don't want to talk about Ross." It galled. Presented with Mirelle, he'd thrown seventeen years down the proverbial drain.

Again, Perry raised his hand. "All right. But I want you to know that you'd be the one I'd choose, if my taste ran to women."

Dinah elbowed him gently. "Knucklehead." She supposed she would be flattered. If his taste ran to women. "Are you a mind reader, too, then?" He'd followed her trail of thought as easily as if it had been that plane, crossing the night sky.

"Why, yes, I am." He waggled his fingers impressively. "I've been practicing. You like?"

"I don't like. You're making me nervous."

"So you probably should just let it all out. Scream, if you want to."

Another blinking light eased its way across the night sky above them, a plane heading southwestward. Where would it be coming from at this hour? What hour was it, anyway? Again Dinah wondered momentarily what it would be like to be on that plane, flying to somewhere far away from here. To a different life.

"This afternoon," Dinah said, watching the plane, "I went to cut flowers for the tables, and I realized that I was using the clippers I bought the day I met him. Ross." She rolled the name around in her mouth, tasting it. Bile.

"And?" Perry's voice was gentle now.

"I threw them." She clenched her eyes shut for a moment. When she opened them again, she tried to find the blinking light of the plane in the sky, which had transformed into a beacon, a symbol of something just beyond her grasp. "I threw them. Right out into the road. Away from me. I just stood there, out in the garden, and watched them fly away. Until they were gone."

"He really did a stupid thing."

"I'm hating him for it." Suddenly the thought of Mark's lovemaking intruded, and how, for the first time in a year, Ross had not spent the night in her mind, in her dreams. "Absolutely hating him. Because—" She had to stop, gulping for air. "Because I love him, that bastard. I love him so much, still. And he did this to me." She'd taken her fury out on Mark. Used him to get back at—a dead man. She wiped her face with the back of her hand again, but the tears kept coming.

"But why shouldn't you?" He was speaking into her hair; his voice sounded odd to her, raw somehow. "Dinah, there's no law that says you have to move on from your feelings, any of them. You had something important with your husband before he screwed it up. Someday you might forgive him, maybe get back there. Or maybe not. But there's no expiration date on love."

It was a tone of voice she'd never heard before from Perry. Dinah sat up, drawing away slightly, so that she could look into his face. In the angled lighting from the kitchen door, his round cheek was pale, washed out; and he wore a faraway expression, full of sadness and longing. He looked many years older than his age.

A pang in her chest. She had never seen Perry look like this, had never heard him sound like this. She felt even more guilty and ashamed, when she realized how little she really knew about him. His car, and where he lived in an apartment over the laundromat downtown, his age. That he had been a former student of Ross's, and Ross had been the one to hire him for the kitchen. And his sexual preference.

"Perry," she whispered, realization hitting her. "I never knew. I never even thought. Forgive me. Please."

Even his smile was sad. "It's all right."

It wasn't. She was appalled by her own lack of perception. She had taken him at face value all the time she had known him, never giving him credit for anything deeper than the youthful foolishness he showed to the world. "Tell me—about him."

Instead of speaking, Perry lifted his water glass and gazed at the stars through the remains. Slowly he turned his wrist and watched the water pour, in a steady stream, to the ground. "Jim. His name. Jamie, sometimes. You would have liked him, Dinah. He would have liked you."

She said nothing. There didn't seem to be anything to say.

"He was older. Fourteen years. We were together from the time I was twenty-two." A sudden spasm moved across Perry's face and was gone. Dinah caught her breath, imagining a much younger Perry, coming out of the closet, a skinny confused kid. Next to her now, he shrugged. "And then—he died. Two years ago."

She didn't ask what Jim had died of. The bleak words were enough. Two years ago. Just a year before she had met Perry, before Ross had hired him to work in the kitchen. Just a bit before Ross had died.

"I'm sorry." She felt tears begin again.

"Yeah." Perry cleared his throat. "Me, too." He looked at her, gave a weak smile. "He was mostly a good man, Dinah. And I loved him. I still do. I'm not in any hurry to stop."

She nodded. "Yes."

"But he screwed up. He got that virus from somewhere—it didn't kill him, but he was weakened, so pneumonia did. For so long I hated him for it. Sometimes I still do. But I love him. So I speak to you as a fellow traveler." Perry blew out a long breath. "Maybe someday I'll feel up to feeling that deeply about somebody else. Someday. But not right now. I don't need to. Even if I were allowed to get on the Ark, I don't feel the need to line up two by two." He held out his hand, looking down into his empty palm. "I'm all right by myself now."

She couldn't speak. The crickets were louder. A light but steady breeze had grown up, and it lifted Dinah's hair from her brow. She was grateful for its cool touch. She was grateful, too, for Perry's arm, still draped around her shoulder as though he had forgotten it there. She reached up to grasp his hand; hesitantly, she placed her other hand in his open palm. Out on the road a truck rumbled by.

"Thanks," she whispered. *For giving me the permission to feel the way I feel.*

Perry kissed her once more on the top of the head, then extricated himself to stand stiffly. "And now, my darling Dinah, it's time for me to hit the road. It's been an exhausting day—and night—all around."

He offered a hand to help her up, but she shook her head. "I think I'll just sit out here a while longer." She smiled tiredly up at him. "I'll be all right. Sometime. Have a good sleep, Perry."

He saluted and turned to his car. In a moment the engine sputtered to life; he waved a hand out the window as he drove off.

Left alone, Dinah looked at the sky. When she stretched out her legs, she kicked one of the empty glasses and sent it rolling down the walkway with a hollow sound. For a moment the crickets fell silent, then burst into song again, louder than before, as though making a concerted effort to drown out any competition. The blinking lights of the jet plane had long since disappeared, but she no longer cared. She could no longer imagine herself on it, flying away: it had only been the whim of a moment. A moment of weakness. A moment of forgetfulness, she told herself briskly, getting to her feet. Her legs felt rubbery beneath her. Because it didn't matter, really, how far she managed to fly away on that or any other plane; Ross would still come along with her.

Fellow travelers.

Dinah liked that. She had to be sure to tell Perry when she saw him tomorrow. And she had to be sure to talk to Mark, someday, too, to explain. Perhaps she should just leave the decision up to him. If there was a decision. At some point, too, she'd probably have to talk to Mirelle, and that would be ugly; but that could wait a while longer.

Dinah collected the water glasses and let herself in through the kitchen door, closing and locking it behind her.

Acknowledgements

Thanks go to Benjamin Bowman (my favorite guy), Sean Giroux, Brooklynn McKay, Hannah Schaller, and Julia Hawkes-Moore, for letting me pick their brains about working back of house. I only ever worked front of house, but that, as they say, was a long time ago, and far, far away; and unlike Gillian, I was terrible at it.

Thanks to Acadia Repertory Theater of Somesville, Maine, for my first ever experience of *Blithe Spirit* all those years ago. Thanks to the wonderful director, Jim Pike, for being my date for that show. Thanks to Noel Coward, too.

Thanks to Oysterband, to Bellowhead, to The Saw Doctors, to Merry Hell, and to Pyewackett, for being my music to write to. Especially, though, thanks to Mawkin, for "My Love Farewell," the theme song to *Cow Palace*.

Thanks to Bay Wrap in Belfast, Maine, for letting me spend hours in the coffee bar, drinking vanilla latté and working on the manuscript at the counter looking out on Main Street. I never knew the joys of working in a coffee house until I met you.

And of course, as always, thanks to Simply Not Done: Brenda Sparks Prescott and Rebecca Bearden Welsh. Where would I be without you two?

Anne Britting Oleson lives with her family and cats in the mountains of Central Maine. She has published three novels, *The Book of the Mandolin Player, Dovecote,*and *Tapiser*; and three poetry chapbooks, *The Church of St. Materiana, The Beauty of It*, and *Alley of Dreams*.

CPSIA information can be obtained
at www.ICGtesting.com
Printed in the USA
LVHW031705030221
678278LV00003B/446